"Splendor o

His angry wife stepped... wadded the cloth into a ball and threw it at him. He barely caught his shout of triumph at the back of his throat and changed it into a grunt as the gown dropped to his feet.

"Now what, you unconscionable brute? Shall we have tea?" Elizabeth demanded.

"Unconscionable brute, is it?" Evan deliberately shook his head as he lifted one hand away from his rigid pose and crooked a finger at her.

"I'll not apologize now, you rotten cur! I won't take back a single word I've said."

"Then we're right back where we started. Only you've taken it a step farther...coming into my room...intending to break my resolve with your woman's wiles. I won't be bound to your whimsy, Elizabeth Murray MacGregor. A husband has rights over his wife."

Dear Reader,

In her third historical for Harlequin, *Man of the Mist*, Elizabeth Mayne tells the heartwarming story of childhood sweethearts who elope, yet, believing they have made a mistake, agree to keep their union a secret. Now, five years later, they must unravel their feelings of hurt and betrayal and learn to accept that their love was meant to be.

Romantic Times had great things to say about this month's delightful new Medieval from award-winning author Margaret Moore. *The Norman's Heart* is "A story brimming with vibrant color and three-dimensional characters. There is emotion and power on every page."

Our other titles include *The Fire Within*, from longtime Harlequin Historical author Lynda Trent, a haunting love story of two people who must choose between the past and the future. And *Birdie*, by Taylor Ryan, the Regency Era story of a young woman who must battle countless odds on her journey to happiness.

Whatever your taste in reading, we hope Harlequin Historicals will keep you coming back for more. Please keep a lookout for all four titles, available wherever books are sold.

Sincerely,

Tracy Farrell
Senior Editor

Please address questions and book requests to:
Harlequin Reader Service
U.S.: 3010 Walden Ave., P.O. Box 1325, Buffalo, NY 14269
Canadian: P.O. Box 609, Fort Erie, Ont. L2A 5X3

Elizabeth Mayne

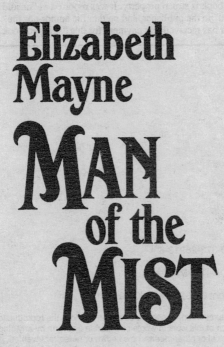

Man of the Mist

Harlequin Books

TORONTO • NEW YORK • LONDON
AMSTERDAM • PARIS • SYDNEY • HAMBURG
STOCKHOLM • ATHENS • TOKYO • MILAN
MADRID • WARSAW • BUDAPEST • AUCKLAND

ISBN 0-373-28913-8

MAN OF THE MIST

ELIZABETH MAYNE

is a native San Antonian who knew by the age of eleven how to spin a good yarn, according to every teacher she ever faced. She's spent the last twenty years making up for all her transgressions on the opposite side of the teacher's desk, and the last five working exclusively with troubled children. She particularly loves an ethnic hero and married one of her own twenty years ago. But it wasn't until their youngest, a daughter, was two years old that life calmed down enough for this writer to fulfill the dream she'd always had of becoming a novelist.

To Alice Maynard Lord
You've kept me sane this past year,
cheered me and helped me remember all those
good people and wonderful times.
God love you.

E.L.M.

Prologue

Edinburgh, Scotland
May 1, 1802 Belltane

"Stars! This bloody wool itches," William Grey muttered, scratching at his bare shanks underneath his borrowed kilt.

Evan MacGregor's laugh echoed down the narrow corridor leading out to the jakes. The inn's lighting was poor, but his vision very sharp as he leaned closer to a scrap of mirror tacked to the wall. He checked the folds of linen and lace spilling over the high collar of his black velvet jacket. Then Evan flattened three fingers and rubbed them upward, inspecting the results of his newly acquired skill of plying a razor blade.

"You'll never pass for a Highlander, Willie, if you keep scratching your arse."

"That's easy for you to say. You've worn a damned kilt all your life. I'm only stuck in this blasted skirt to get inside Bell's Wynd, damn it all."

Evan turned from the mirror. The knife-edge pleats of his red-and-green MacGregor plaid swung easily about his knees. He gave his Cambridge roommate a thorough inspection, then straightened the drape of Willie's *philabeg.* Evan thought it best to cater to the Englishman a wee bit.

"It's a rare man who wears a *philabeg* day in and out in Scotland these days, Willie. A whole generation got in the habit of wearing britches, like my da, and now me. 'Course, that's because you English made wearing a tartan a capital crime. Holding on to it got a man and his whole family deported."

Willie's bulldog jaw twisted in a grimace. "Then why in the bloody hell do we have to get suited up in one tonight?"

"For the same reason we suffer silk stockings and knee britches to get inside Almack's, you dolt—because that's where the prettiest women are!

"Now, mind you..." Evan swung a conspiratorial arm around his English friend's broad back. "Things here in Edinburgh are a bit different than in London. The important thing to remember is, *you can't just dance with any lass.* You've got to be approved to dance with every girl you choose by presenting her to Aunt Nicky first. She rules this assembly with an iron hand. Never mind that she's deaf as a post and a century older than Ben Nevis."

"That's the mountain, right? Ha!" Willie barked. "All right, I've got the rules down pat. You've been over them a hundred times already. Don't ask any girl to dance who's dressed in white...'cause she's a debutante and looking for a husband. Girls with hair hanging down their backs are forbidden, underage and taboo. Widows will let me know they're available by doing something with their fans."

Evan clapped Willie on the back. "You've got the gist of it, mate. Let's go!"

They both halted on the wooden banquette on High Street. Evan self-consciously flicked a speck off his cuff and crossed the street to join the queue lined up outside Bell's Wynd. He'd timed it right. The doors of the renowned assembly hall had just opened, as scheduled, at six o'clock.

Dappled sunlight flickered over the mixed crowd of well-dressed matrons and ladies in radiant shades of evening wear, and men and youths of all ages clothed in an amazing array of colors themselves—clan tartans, dress plaids, cockades and bonnets and exotic fur sporrans.

Evan grinned as the strong and fragrant spring wind played havoc with the ladies' curls, lifted feathers and sent sweet, heady perfumes surging into his nostrils.

At the top of the steps, he had to elbow his way inside the packed vestibule. He felt another surge of anticipation for the evening ahead—his first time out on the town of Edinburgh alone, without a henchman along, keeping close tabs on him. Why shouldn't he be alone, when he'd turn eighteen in another week?

Once inside the vestibule, Evan found that the jostling crowd had crushed a young lass against the wall beside the door. He gallantly stood back, treading on Willie's toes, so that the tall beauty could squeeze ahead of him and regain her place in the line. She murmured a shy thanks and fit in where she could.

Evan noticed two striking things at a glance. The first was her ball gown. The pale blue silk was cut and draped in the latest, up-to-the-minute Empire style, which was only just taking fashionable London by storm. She couldn't have got past him in the crush if she'd worn the hoops that the rest of the Scotch ladies sported. In fact, he noted as he scanned the balance of the ladies caught in the vestibule, she was the only female not wearing hoops.

Which brought him to the second most obvious fact regarding her. Her soft brown curls were pulled back to the crown of her head and fastened with a nosegay of ribbon and heather, revealing her high brow and lovely oval face entirely. But from the crown of her head, down past her waist, her hair fell unbound and unrestrained.

Regrettably, the first beauty who had captured Evan's eye and stirred a warm feeling of lust in his loins was plainly not yet sixteen years of age.

That did not stop him from taking advantage of his height and looking over her shoulder to see what else he could learn about the young lady below her pretty chin.

His covert inspection of two lovely, firm breasts assured him that she was very close indeed to reaching that momentous birthday when she would be allowed to put up her hair and dance with the gentlemen at Bell's Wynd.

But not tonight.

She fumbled for something in her reticule, preoccupied, unaware of Evan's speculative interest in her lovely bosom.

Evan was achingly aware of how sweetly her cheek curved, as well as of the turgid fullness of her breasts, straining against the daring cut of her bodice.

The press of the restless crowd pushed him dangerously close to her, so close that he could detect the sweetness of lavender water drifting up from her hair. But that same waist-length drape of unbound hair intruded on his enjoyment of the arousal she stirred inside him. As a first-year Cambridge man, he felt ages more mature than she, and valiantly tried to direct his attention away from her.

The line at the door bottled up badly. Behind Evan, Willie jostled impatiently. The miss turned a lacy handkerchief and a tortoiseshell comb out of her reticule, but nothing else.

"Oh, dear," she whispered. "I've lost my voucher."

Evan cocked a sharp ear to catch her accents. Her diction was so precise, he was convinced she was English. She lifted her chin, peering straight ahead to the inner door, then looked to the right, scanning the crowded vestibule, searching for a familiar face. Then she excused herself in general to the other people close to them and turned, facing Evan, trying to peer discreetly on tiptoe around and over his wide shoulders.

He was almost completely undone by the pleasing appearance of her face. Her brow tightened lovingly over gentle blue eyes and a slim, perfect nose. Very full lips pressed against each other, indicating that she wasn't, at the moment, happy.

The large man ahead of her shifted abruptly, sending the girl accidentally careering intimately against Evan. At least he was certain that it wasn't intentional on her part that she should graze his semi-erect shaft with her hip.

"Oh, pardon me!" She glanced up at him through thick, curving lashes. Her eyes simply seethed with passion and energy, overloaded by excitement and fright. They were the palest of blues, ringed with a darker circle, and wide and luminous and gently tilted at the outer corners, which imparted to her the soft, innocent appeal of a doe.

They seemed familiar, but then, Evan knew a lot of lassies with blue eyes. He knew many with brown eyes, too. They'd been chasing him relentlessly ever since he went away to school at Eton. She said, "I'm so sorry, but I've lost my voucher. I have to go and see if I dropped it outside, or left it in my father's carriage."

Evan started to reach inside his jacket to give her his own voucher, but he realized he couldn't very well do that and still get inside Bell's Wynd himself. He wanted in Bell's Wynd now more than he had before.

He swung around, finding Willie stuck in the doorway and scowling like a bear. "Willie, can you change places with me? There's a damsel in distress ahead of me. Lost her ticket."

"That's a new approach. Never had that one tried on you before, have you, old man?" Willie leered and poked an elbow in Evan's belly. "You'd think they'd let you get inside the door before some lightskirt offers to drag you out. I don't know how you do it, Mac."

Evan grimaced with embarrassment, mostly because he didn't know what exactly to say to that. He hadn't given a thought to the girl having motives of the kind Willie alluded to, and he wouldn't know what to do if she did. Besides, she was most concerned with her missing voucher.

She hadn't appeared to notice his looks at all. Sooner or later, though, every girl did, much to Evan's chagrin.

"Right you go, then." Willie gave ground a step or two, and Evan squeezed between his friend's large body and the door, then held the crowd back so that the girl could come out, as well.

"You didn't have to give up your place, too," she said as they reached the less crowded wooden banquette.

"Oh, I don't mind." Evan stopped on the edge of the crowd, looking right and left down the line of carriages that had discharged their passengers onto the banquettes but had yet to clear the traffic on High Street. It made him glad he'd taken a room in town for the night. "Do you see your carriage?"

The girl had turned away from him, searching around the boards, looking for her elusive ticket. Then she about-faced and stood on tiptoe, shielding her eyes from the glare of the low sun with her hand. "No."

"You're sure your voucher isn't in your reticule?"

"Quite sure." She moved her hand away from her face and looked directly at him. One look followed another, and then she jerked her head up and down, twice, searching him over from head to toe.

A lot of ladies fussed over Evan's looks, but no one had ever done that to him, and he felt right peculiar because of it. She made him worry that he'd somehow forgotten some vital article of clothing or, worse, got his kilt hiked up over his belt so that he had his arse—or something more personal—exposed. Had he broken out in spots? Forgotten to shave a newly sprouted patch of whiskers off his jaw? "Is something wrong?"

"What's your name?" she demanded.

Well, he almost lied and claimed to be a Campbell, because MacGregors had been doing that for ten generations, just so that their bloody heads remained securely attached to their shoulders. "Who is it that wants to know?"

The pretty girl blinked in obvious surprise at his defensive reply, which certainly didn't answer her question. A little indentation sharpened the lines of her eyebrows, and she pressed her very full lips down. It was a full minute before she said, "Don't you know who I am? I'm Elizabeth...Murray. Aren't you Evan...Evan MacGregor MacGregor?"

Well, Evan didn't say anything, because in all truth, she'd just knocked him speechless.

"You can't be Elizabeth Murray," he said foolishly. "Why, Elizabeth Murray is only fifteen years old—just turned that, in fact."

"And so I did, April the nineteenth. And if you're Evan MacGregor, you recently sent me a watercolor picture of a bluebird you bought from an art student in Paris by the name of James Audubon." She flashed him a smile that revealed beautiful teeth and a deep dimple in her left cheek. "And I might add, Evan MacGregor, you've changed, too! You're taller than Tullie, and ever so much more handsome. I didn't recognize you at all. Oh, Evan, it's been so long!"

There he was, standing on High Street, and Izzy Murray was squealing like any chit of ten and five. Worse, she was throwing lovely, slender arms around his neck and kissing him on the mouth and pressing those sweet, full breasts of hers flush against his chest, afore God and all of Edinburgh!

He thought he was going to die. Blessed Saint Cuthbert, he thought he was going to die. Else be hanged, drawn and quartered right there on High Street by the duke of Atholl's henchmen because here was this tender young lass —not a sennight beyond her fifteenth birthday—throwing herself all over him.

She turned what had only been mild arousal into the hardest bone he'd ever felt in his whole life, kissing him and squealing like a happy piglet, bringing the attention and the ire of half the Highlands down on the good-for-nothing heir apparent of the Gregarach—the Children of the Mist.

Elizabeth Murray was a woman grown, at fifteen years old! He hadn't seen her in ages. In his mind, his Izzy still had plaits, and ankle-high dresses covered by pinafores.

But he'd written her hundreds and hundreds of letters, and she'd answered every one. Not one of which lately had hinted that the changes a lassie goes through to become a woman had already happened to her.

Somehow, Evan got hold of her shoulders and set her back, at the full length of his arms, scowling at that beautiful woman's face that he would never have recognized in a hundred years on his little Izzy.

"I can't believe it. You're Izzy?" He shook his head in denial. "You should have written me that you'd grown up. Why, look at you. I'm shocked. You should have sent me a miniature, or at least given me a hint or two. You could have said, 'Oh, by the way, Evan, did you know I'm five and a half feet tall and I weigh eight stone?'"

"But you've changed, too. I hate to tell you this, but your face is all shaped just like all the MacGregors'. That's what made me ask your name. When you didn't say your name outright, I knew it. You had to be a MacGregor. Anyone else would have said his name right out."

"You didn't need to remind me of that," Evan grumbled, reminded of his not-so-respectable ancestors, who'd got the name MacGregor proscribed on pain of death. "So what are we going to do about this lost voucher of yours?"

"We could just wait out here and talk until Amalia realizes I'm not inside." There was definitely the light of flirtation sparking in her eyes . . . and something else, too. Evan hardly dared to guess what. "She's bound to come looking for me sooner or later. Later, I hope."

More than just mischief was dancing in her bright eyes when she linked arms with him and tilted her pert face upward, smiled and started walking toward Saint Giles's.

"Aye, but you'll still need a voucher to get past the dragon at the door." Evan nervously attempted to disengage himself from her arm.

"I suppose." Elizabeth glanced up and down the crowded street again. "Let's go look for Papa's carriage."

She tightened her hold on Evan's arm, and he had no choice except to escort her up High Street, searching for the duke of Atholl's carriage, which was parked under an overhang at Luckenbooths, next to the cathedral.

The coachman and footman took exception to the duke's youngest daughter showing up arm in arm with a stranger. Izzy's laughing explanation of who Evan was didn't pacify a pair of henchmen old enough to have hunted Rob Roy himself before the proscription act against clan MacGregor was repealed by Parliament in 1774. Both looked inclined to unsheathe their claymores, part his head from his shoulders and then ask, after the fact, why they couldn't get paid the usual bounty.

"We'd best go back and wait on the steps outside Bell's Wynd," Evan said wisely. But Izzy insisted she search the carriage. The henchman and coachman grunted ominously as she did that.

"It's not here," she said with a disappointed shrug of her shoulders that was followed by the brightest smile for Evan. "Well, no matter. Come along, we'll go back and wait at the door. The aunts will miss me soon enough, even if Amalia doesn't."

That said, she threaded her arm through Evan's again, oblivious of the glares of her father's tail.

They returned the way they'd come, under escort this time, and remained under scrutiny the whole time they waited, until one of the Murrays inside Bell's Wynd came out.

As luck would have it, James Murray, who was three years older than Evan and also studying at Cambridge, came to fetch his sister. He recognized Evan at once, and clapped him on the back with a high regard that went a little ways in reducing the glares coming from the duke's henchmen.

As the crowd at the entrance had dwindled, the matter of Elizabeth's missing ticket was easily covered. She wasn't just a daughter of the highest-ranking Scottish noble attending the assembly. Miss Nicky Murray of Mansfield, the patroness of Bell's Wynd, was Elizabeth's great-aunt.

Disaster was thus averted, and Elizabeth reluctantly released her hold upon Evan, to be escorted by James back to her plethora of chaperones.

Cut loose and on his own again, Evan found Willie in the crush and introduced him around. There was no lack of available dance partners for the brisk reels and gay flings. Evan actually enjoyed the ceremony of bringing a pretty young lady forward to Aunt Nicky, who was enthroned on her dais, and securing a polite nod of her head at each of his choices.

During the interludes, he took time to visit with his rediscovered friend in the company of the numerous spinster aunts who acted as chaperones. Lady Elizabeth wasn't enjoying the assembly. What girl would when she wasn't allowed to dance?

Evan's heart went out to the lass over that egregious disappointment. He wasn't so old that he couldn't remember what it was like to sit on the side at a gathering and be unable to enjoy it because of the strict rules of etiquette held by their class.

Worse, he was most confused by his own physical reaction to her. He loved Izzy, in the loyal, altruistic way he loved all his friends and kinsmen.

Their six years of correspondence, following two years in the same schoolroom together, had made him feel closer to her than he did to his own sister. None of his feelings for Elizabeth tonight were at all brotherly. He couldn't help thinking that perhaps they never had been.

He'd always taken on the role of Izzy's protector in the schoolroom. It was so easy to slip back into that comfortable way of thinking of her as somehow weaker than he and needing a champion. But Elizabeth was simply too young to stir in him the feelings of deep lust, desire and passion that alluring older women did. Despite his looks, Evan was painfully shy when it came to making advances to women. He couldn't have borne it if he was rejected, or failed to perform as expected by an older, experienced woman.

Knowing that, and thinking with a head that should have been rational enough to override the heavy ache in his cods, why then did he ask the too-young Elizabeth to dance without Aunt Nicky's permission?

And God only knew why Elizabeth threw caution and decorum to the winds and agreed.

Never, in all of his days, could Evan have predicted that one impetuous dance, one gay and happy highland reel, was to be the beginning of all his heartache and troubles.

Chapter One

London
January 9, 1808

The ink of wintry midnight cloaked the nursery in the Duke of Atholl's London town house. Auld Krissy Buchanan couldn't see a thing. Yet what she heard in the heavy darkness made her eyes widen with alarm. She scrambled out of bed, snatched up her robe and tiptoed to her mistress's adjoining room, taking care not to wake young Robbie as she opened and closed the adjoining door.

The alarming clattering sound came again, louder and stronger in the sleeping lady's bedchamber. "Milady," Krissy whispered. "Wake up! Do you not hear that noise?"

"Noise, Krissy?" From the deep cocoon of her tester bed, Lady Elizabeth Murray mumbled in a husky, caught-in-a-dream voice. "What noise?"

"Lady Elizabeth!" Krissy's harsh whisper rose a shrill notch. "Summat's breaking into yer father's hoose!"

"Krissy? What did you say?" Wide awake now, Elizabeth sat bolt upright, turning to the corner windows, seeking the source of that most peculiar and very distinct noise.

It came again, three—no, four—quick little smacks on the window glass. Krissy gasped, unable to believe that the frightening sounds came from the window glazing. There were no balconies on the third floor, where the duke of Atholl's womenfolk were quartered. How could anyone be out there?

Elizabeth's eyes widened in alarm. "I heard that! What is it, Krissy?"

"A bloody London cutthroat, that's what!" Krissy answered promptly. She snatched her warmest tartan robe closed and stoutly tied the sash before Lady Elizabeth's feet touched the cold floor.

"We'll just see about that!" Elizabeth insisted, rattled, but not panicked. After all, they were hardly alone. Her father wasn't in residence, but the dowager duchess and her entire staff were. Elizabeth glanced at the clock on her nightstand as she lit a lamp. Four o'clock in the morning. Everyone would be sound asleep!

"Summat's outside, banging on the window glass." Krissy armed herself with the iron poker from the hearth. "'Tis your lucky day I'm here to protect you. Miss Nicky gave me fair warning about the tricks and troubles of dealing with the blasted Sassenachs. I kin defend the clan's honor, I kin."

Elizabeth withheld comment as she deftly fastened her robe at her waist. Auld Krissy was clearly frightened, else she would have remembered that little harm could come to any resident of 19 Grosvenor Mews. Without further discussion, Lady Elizabeth hurried to her corner bay windows.

One overlooked the pleasant park fronting Grosvenor Square. The other gave a not-so-charming view of the gables and slate tile roofing of Lord Mansfield's house next door. There was nothing remarkable to be seen on the roof.

Elizabeth opened the drapes and cautiously parted the sheers on the bay window facing the street. London's ever-present deep winter fog enveloped the park and obscured the stately avenue. She could pick out very few landmarks in the thick, heavy mist. "All I can see is a carriage light on a hackney turning at the corner."

Another shower of minuscule pebbles pattered against the glass. Krissy jumped and came within inches of putting the poker through the glass panes. "Blood and fury! Will the demmed bounders scale the walls next?"

"Whisht, Krissy!" Elizabeth warned immediately. "Don't wake Robbie."

"Yes, mum," Krissy said contritely.

Elizabeth did what any sensible young woman safely ensconced on the third floor of her father's abode should do; she disarmed her fractious abigail, urging her to more dignified silence, and raised the window sash. Then both she and Krissy leaned their cap-covered heads out the window to appraise the scene on the street below. After all, Elizabeth thought, twenty-and-a-half isn't so abysmally mature that I can't show a minimum of curiosity.

"Wait, mum." Krissy laid a trembling hand on Elizabeth's sleeve. "Do ya ken who they are?"

At first glance, Elizabeth couldn't rightly say that she did. Thick and heavy fog curled against the walls of the house and lifted up to dampen her chin and cheeks. The mists swirled, stirred by a soft gust of wind, to reveal three men huddled on the doorstep, under the novel haze of a pair of gas-fueled coach lights. The thick fog softened all details of their identity.

"Och, I count three of 'em," Krissy's brogue overlaid the mist. "What kin they want at this hour?"

"Good question," Elizabeth replied suspiciously. Anyone with a shred of decency would have properly rung the bell and summoned Keyes, regardless of the urgency or the hour. That was the way things were done in the duke of Atholl's house. "Suppose I best find out."

Leaning farther over the sill, Elizabeth called out in a chilly voice, to let the intruders know she considered it outrageous form to throw stones at her windows. "Who are you and what do you want?"

The largest of the trio looked up, cupped his hands to his mouth and tilted his face toward the light gleaming on the near side of the entrance door. His voice echoed peculiarly, dampened and magnified by the fog.

"Ha! I'll be bound! So Tullie was right. You are to town. Get up, lass! Come down here and unlock the door. Be quick about it, Izzy!"

"Izzy!" Elizabeth repeated his last word in a harsh whisper, instantly drawing back inside the window. Her heart skipped a beat, then jumped to an escalated cadence. Only one ne'er-do-well in the entire British Isles had ever dared to call her by that dreadful remnant from the nursery in public. *Evan MacGregor!*

"Eh?" Krissy cupped her hand to her ear, leaning her white face closer to Elizabeth's. "What did he say? Who is it?"

Elizabeth ignored the question as she swallowed and sought her courage. She laid trembling hands on the damp windowsill to steady herself, leaning out once more. This time, when she spoke, her voice rang with the cool disdain of the bred-in-the-bone aristocrat. "Tell me one good reason why I should unlock the door of my house for the likes of you, Evan MacGregor!"

"What?" Krissy gasped, and laid her hand over her heart.

"Don't argue with me, Elizabeth Murray! Get down here!" Evan stepped onto the highest step, deliberately placing himself in the circle of lamplight. She caught a glimpse of her brother's red hair as Evan raised his arm in a furious gesture. "Unless you prefer that I heave Tullibardine's bloody body in the bin out back. Make up your mind quick! The marquess has been shot, and he's bleeding like a stuck pig. As bad as he's wounded, he won't last long, left out in this weather."

"Shot?" Elizabeth cried. She backed out of the window so quickly she banged her head on the sash. So did Krissy.

"Shot?" Krissy parroted. "I dinna see Tullibardine."

Elizabeth had. Her brother, John Murray, the marquess of Tullibardine, had become recognizable the moment Evan MacGregor moved away from him. Tullie slumped heavily against the support of the third man.

"What in the name of creation is going on in here? Are you trying to wake every soul in the house?" Amalia Murray demanded as she imperiously swept inside her younger sister's chamber. "Elizabeth, who have you been shouting at on the street? Do you realize what time it is?"

"Hang the time!" Elizabeth exclaimed as she bolted past her sister. "Tullie's been shot! Krissy, make certain Robbie's sleep has not been disturbed, then come downstairs at once to help me."

"What?" Amalia gasped. She stood stock-still, stunned, as Elizabeth ran past her to the staircase.

"What do you mean, Tullie's been shot?" Amalia snatched up her hems, following. "Oh, no! Dear God, no! Elizabeth, come back and tell me it isn't true!"

Elizabeth wasted no time getting down to the entrance foyer. But at the doorway her hands turned inept and clumsy, fumbling with the locks. Amalia caught up to her as Elizabeth swung the door wide open to the three men huddled on the step in the bone-chilling mist.

"What has happened?" Amalia exclaimed.

Elizabeth stood frozen on the doorsill, locked in a horror that went deeper than any life-threatening alarm raised for her brother. Some other portion of her mind recognized the grey breeks and scarlet jacket of a Highland volunteer cloaking Evan's tall body. Her eyes came in full contact with his, and all sense of time and reality ended.

The panic surging into her veins wasn't for the condition of her oldest brother. An unvoiced scream strangled underneath the tight compression of the fingers sealing her lips.

Evan! God help her, Evan sported the well-cut jacket of an officer of Graham's Grey Breeks. He towered over Tullie, her brother. The Highlander's jaw was set, his mouth a grim, dark and austere line that caught the night's deepest shadows. His eyes locked with Elizabeth's. She ceased breathing and thinking, and stood blocking the door.

"God save us!" Amalia whispered a fearful prayer behind Elizabeth. "John, what have you done?"

Elizabeth's nostrils flared as the mist rolled past Evan and washed her burning cheeks. With it came the tang of burnt whiskey mingled with odors off the streets, horses, sweat, blood and dank wool.

"Move, Izzy!" Evan commanded, in a voice grown deeper over long years. It touched her center, glazing her soul like the mists that swept around him and sank quickly to her darkest primordial core. Evan's eyes remained inscrutable, sharp and hard. The mist shrouded him as he came ominously closer, her brother's arm clamped across his wide shoulders. Stupidly, Elizabeth stood rooted to the floor, unable to make any part of her body move under her own volition.

"I said move, lass!" One hand snaked out, touching the silk covering her waist. It flattened and pressed intimately into yielding flesh, urging her backward, out of his way.

"Elizabeth!" Amalia's voice roughened with a fine edge of fright. She caught Elizabeth's arm, yanking her off the threshold, out of the way of the Highlanders bearing her brother John, the marquess of Tullibardine, into his father's house.

Glowing lamps in the foyer illuminated the gap in John's greatcoat. Elizabeth partially roused from the dazzled dream in which she was trapped and dragged her eyes from Evan to stare in mute horror at the wash of scarlet staining the marquess's rumpled linen and cravat. Amalia gasped out loud.

Shaking herself free of the shock of Evan MacGregor's return, Elizabeth gulped. "I'll fetch Dr. Morgan."

MacGregor caught her arm as Elizabeth reached for the cord to summon the servants, commanding, "No doctors, and no servants, Izzy. Corporal Butter can tend to the marquess's injury. There's not a better man in the regiment for bullet wounds. Amalia, fetch hot water, linens, and whatever carbolic you have. Don't wake anyone else in the house. Izzy, lock that door."

"You can't come barging in this house giving orders, Evan MacGregor!" Elizabeth sparked, recovering her wits.

Evan's dark eyes bored deep into hers, sharp and hard, like the eyes of a man sighting the barrel of a pistol on the heart of his enemy.

"Do as you're told," he commanded. He released her arm, but the impression of his strong fingers gripping her wrist remained as he turned to deal with the older Amalia Murray's sputtering protests. She looked on the verge of vapors, the back of her hand pressed against her mouth in horror. Krissy hurried down the stairs and quietly slipped an arm around Lady Amalia to support her, lest she faint.

"Amalia!" Tullibardine rasped. He caught hold of the newel post for support. "Do exactly as MacGregor orders!"

"Well, I never!" Amalia roused herself to the authority she was well versed in wielding with all of her siblings, including her eldest brother, the marquess. "John, I will have some explanation, this very moment!"

"No, you won't!" Evan MacGregor cut Amalia short. "You'll get an explanation once we've got Tullie's bleeding under control."

Amalia started to protest that order, but this time Evan MacGregor shut off her tirade before it could begin. "Woman, the marquess's life is in more danger this minute than his bloody reputation. If you cannot be of good assistance to him, then kindly stay the hell out of our way!''

Without pause, he turned and took Tullie's arm off the newel post and helped him mount the stairs, leaving Amalia's and Krissy's jaws sagging in shock.

Elizabeth blinked, unable to take her eyes from Evan MacGregor's commanding back. Where had he learned to exert such overwhelming authority? Why was he, of all people, here? Her throat squeezed dangerously. Her knees felt as wobbly as ninepins hit solidly by a stone bowling ball.

Krissy had the sense to close the door, barring the cold and the wet from entering the house. She dipped in a deep and reverent curtsy. "So tha's the MacGregor," the servant said under her breath.

"Aye, the very devil himself," Elizabeth whispered between her tightly pressed teeth. She made sure the door was bolted and, leading the awestruck Krissy by the hand, pulled her along in Amalia's wake down to the kitchens.

"Why can we not call a doctor?" Krissy asked.

Elizabeth grabbed the largest tray from Keyes's pantry and slammed it onto the central table. *Shot... Heaven help them all, her brother had been shot! Why? How?*

Amalia had gotten hold of her wits. She tilted her proud chin and stated unequivocally, "'Tis clear enough. John has been involved in a duel.''

"A duel!" Elizabeth protested. Duels were outlawed, and severe penalties were levied on those who engaged in the practice, if the king got wind of it. "What makes you say such a thing? If he had been in a duel, John would have had the sense to have a surgeon present. Think, Amalia. John's never been in a duel in his life. He wouldn't resort to secrecy if he had, not to us."

"And how do you know that?" Amalia countered, obviously flustered. "I can assume he doesn't want Father to know."

Elizabeth muttered, "Oh dear..." She opened a drawer, fetching a stack of clean linens to add to the tray.

"A duel?" Krissy echoed with eyes agog. "Stars! A duel... Over who or what? Mrs. Hamilton's latest memorial, do you ken? Can someone have accused the marquess of cheating at cards, and called him out?"

Elizabeth groaned inwardly. Amalia made hers more audible. They'd only been in town three days, but Krissy Buchanan had already learned the value of knowing the latest *on-dit*.

Dodging a pointed look from her sister, Elizabeth hastily took a cloth from the tray and blotted away a sheen of perspiration from her upper lip. *God save her, Evan MacGregor was in the same house as she and Robbie!* Her heart racketed inside her ribs, and her brain felt paralyzed. Her hands and feet moved with the motility of cold lead.

"Krissy!" Amalia said sternly, fixating on something she could deal with properly. "While you are in the employ of the duke of Atholl, you will not engage in the disgusting habit of repeating gossip belowstairs. Whatever happens in this house does not go one word further."

"Beg pardon, milady." Elizabeth's maid cast a sidelong glance at Amalia, clearly hurt to be the focus of Amalia's formidable ire.

"My dear sister," Elizabeth said, defending her loyal servant, "are you forgetting that you are the one who just suggested Tullie's been in a duel?"

"Well, heavenly days, I don't know that for a fact!" Amalia sputtered. "Don't either of you repeat it!"

"Amalia, please! That's entirely uncalled-for. We both know better." Elizabeth managed an apologetic murmur to Krissy, excusing both her and Amalia's overreactions to their shock.

Amalia curbed her temper, despite the mutiny that sparkled in the Scottish maid's amber eyes. There simply was no one more territorial, proud and possessive than a Scots personal servant. Amalia well knew that Krissy's loyalty was solely to Elizabeth. Moreover, Elizabeth thrived on being original and different. Together, the two of them made an unpredictable, unmanageable pair in the duke of Atholl's household, for which Amalia was responsible.

Evan MacGregor! What next? Amalia thought as she vainly sought her lost composure. She flashed a warning look at Elizabeth. No matter what, she must see that Elizabeth was never alone for one minute with that Highland rakehell! He'd caused enough damage five years ago.

Misinterpreting the reason for Amalia's scowls, Krissy flashed a placating smile of apology, saying, "Forgive me, Lady Amalia. When I gets excited, I forgets myself."

"A proper lady's abigail never gets excited," Amalia said with authority. She was on firm ground here, knowing all the hard-and-fast rules regarding ladylike behavior. "Forgive my sharp words, Krissy. Rare is the day when Elizabeth sets you a good example."

"Well, and I thank you for that vote of confidence," Elizabeth interjected. It had been too much to hope that she'd escape Amalia's eagle-eyed circumspection. God clearly wasn't listening to her frantic prayers that the past be forgotten.

"Humph." Amalia hoisted the tray. "Fetch the water upstairs as soon as the kettle boils, Elizabeth. And before this progresses to disaster, I order you *not* to act like a hoyden." She sailed out the door muttering, "Hanging out the windows like bawds in Covent Garden ..."

Krissy looked crushed at the severity of Amalia's scolding, and she promised Elizabeth, in her sister's absence, "I'll do better."

Elizabeth felt a burst of resentment, coupled with anxiety, surge into her veins. Damn Evan! What had brought him out of the seventh level of hell to which she had consigned him years ago?

"It's not your fault," she told Krissy.

No sooner had she spoken than a more worrisome thought took root. Good God! What was she thinking of? She'd let Amalia go up alone! What sort of interrogation might Amalia put Evan through when they came face-to-face—alone for the first time in almost six years?

Elizabeth slapped her palm against her cheek. She didn't dare let Evan be alone with any member of her family! She prodded the red-hot coals under the kettle with a vengeance, muttering, "Boil, damn you!"

Amalia was the unofficial mother of all the duke of Atholl's unmarried children. She had even delayed her own wedding to Lord Strathallen until next January. Granted, Strathallen had spent the past four years in India, repairing the financial gaps in his inheritance. Amalia had made it plain that her most ardent wish was to have Elizabeth settled before she married herself. In her sister's estimation, time was running out for Elizabeth.

"What got her in such stew?" Krissy asked boldly, once she was certain Amalia was out of hearing range. "'Tis no' like we did summat improper."

Elizabeth stared at the black kettle. A wisp of steam wafted out the spout, swirling like the mist that had swirled up and around Evan MacGregor as he came through the front door. How could she have forgotten the impact of his eyes?

"Milady, did you not hear me?" Krissy asked.

"Oh!" Elizabeth yanked her gaze from the steam and made a futile, belated effort to compose her face. "What was that, Krissy?"

"Och, I knew it! Ya felt it, din't ya?" Krissy executed a fey pirouette between the worktable and the stove, on amazingly nimble feet for one of her years. Her voice sounded so wishful, she could have been reading Elizabeth's mind.

"Did ya ever see such a bonnie mon? Why, what one of me friends at home would believe I saw the bra' Mac-

Gregor himself, striding out of the mists…across our own step…in London! Do ya no' realize, lass, that he's the first of the Gregarach born in ten generations to walk tall and proud, boasting his true name, in London, afore God, king and country? I never thought to see such a sight, ever!''

"You're exaggerating just a trifle, Krissy," Elizabeth commented, without a trilling burr in her speech.

"Faith! I din't!''

"Every MacGregor we know took back their clan name the day the proscription ban was lifted," Elizabeth argued.

"Tha's no' the same thing." Krissy shook her head vehemently. "God strike the bleeding Sassenach all around us, din't the mon walk straight in from the mist, with his head still attached to his shoulders? He did! The old laird, God rest his soul, never set a foot in England in his life. He didna trust the English. There's a new breed of Scotsmen a-coming, and don' tell me I didna just lay eyes upon one who's no' afraid of any mon."

"Krissy, the tribulations of the Children of the Mist aren't important right now," Elizabeth reasoned.

"He's no cadet, lassie. He's the Man of the Mist, the MacGregor!" Krissy insisted, gravely insulted by Elizabeth's apparent lack of respect.

"I've more important things on my mind. Nor is this the time to delve into the tangled history of the clans, Krissy. Save your tall tales for Robbie." Elizabeth folded a hotpad and took a firm grip on the steaming kettle. "The water's boiling."

More important to Elizabeth was to discover how her oldest brother had wound up in the company of the dangerous Evan MacGregor. What mischance had brought Evan from the wars on the Continent at the same time that Elizabeth had to be in town herself?

"Come along, Krissy." Elizabeth hurried through the swinging door to the back stairs.

Krissy harrumphed deeply and followed, muttering under her breath, "Och, ya got no proper upbringing, lassie, ya din't."

Elizabeth was much too troubled to pay heed to what Krissy said. Why hadn't she left Krissy to bring the water up when it was ready? What was she thinking of, leaving Tullie and MacGregor alone? Worse, why had she let Amalia go up without her? What if Evan let slip their secret?

At the landing on the second floor, Elizabeth took a deep breath, stamping an iron resolve on her composure. "I'll take it from here, Krissy. Please go and stay with Robbie. I'll come to bed as soon as I can."

"Och, the wee wean willna turn over once he's to sleep. Are you sure you don' want more help than that?" Krissy asked incredulously.

"I'm sure," Elizabeth answered firmly. "Please make certain Robbie doesn't wake up and go wandering out of his room. We mustn't forget, this is a new house to him. He's never been to London before. I know I'm asking a lot of you, but just keep an eye on him tonight, Krissy. I'm sure we'll have a new nanny for him soon."

"Yes, mum. I'll do me best." Krissy bobbed a curtsy and hurried up the steps to the third floor.

Elizabeth swallowed down the dryness choking her throat as she watched the plump woman retreat up the back stairs. Elizabeth took another moment to remind herself that no one knew the truth about Robbie . . . no one, not even her sister Amalia. She didn't have to feel so frightened . . . just because Evan MacGregor was in the house.

Chapter Two

The marquess's valet opened the door of Tullie's room at Elizabeth's knock. The valet appeared unflappable as ever as he took the steaming kettle from Elizabeth's hands. He had a kind glance for the worry knotting her brow as she asked, "How bad is it this time?"

"Not so bad as it would seem, milady. You may speak with His Grace, if you would like. Perhaps you can help keep his howls to a minimum as Corporal Butter removes the bullet."

Elizabeth didn't hesitate to attend her brother. Murray women were known for their fortitude. She marched across the chamber and found Tullibardine seated on his barber's chair.

Four lamps had been placed on the marble-topped commode at his side. He'd been stripped to the waist, and the lamplight made his fair skin seem unnaturally pale. Elizabeth spared a quick glance at his windburned face before looking for the wound that threatened him.

A small, circular hole steadily seeped blood and fluid just below the upthrusting ridge of his collarbone. The wound mutely testified that a bullet had entered at an acute angle. The freckles glazing John's shoulder were stretched to odd shapes because of internal swelling. Elizabeth thought it was a good thing he'd been hit on the right, being that her brother was irrevocably left-handed.

"Not very pretty, my lord," Elizabeth announced, withholding her questions about the darkening bruises and knots on his face. It was obvious on close inspection that he'd been involved in an exchange of fisticuffs. Funny, she thought, even the battered twenty-nine-year-old John Murray looked more boyish than the grim-jawed Highlander attending him, though Evan was only twenty-three.

Elizabeth's eyes reflexively went past Corporal Butter to seek Evan. He'd shed his coat and was in the process of rolling up the sleeves of an immaculate linen shirt. He turned his back to her and stooped to scrub his large hands in a basin of hot water.

The linen strained at the seams across his shoulders, which had widened considerably since the last time Elizabeth had seen Evan. Her gaze followed the long curve of his back, reluctantly noting that he hadn't gained an ounce of surplus flesh in five years. Maturity had not caused him to let out his belt.

Her mouth tasted drier than ashes, and she tried in vain to moisten it with swallowing. She had as much luck whetting her tongue as she had tamping down the memories that sent her pulse singing and heightened the color staining her cheeks... Evan MacGregor had come home at last.

Elizabeth drew in a shuddering breath and turned to her brother, determined to focus only on him. Amalia grimly handed a glass of amber liquid to Tullie, ordering, "Drink this, my lord."

"How do you feel, John?" Elizabeth asked, in a shaken voice.

"I'll live," Tullie stated matter-of-factly before tossing the contents of the glass down his throat. He coughed deeply, then grimaced. "Get on with it, Butter. Do your worst, before I toss my accounts."

He turned his face away from the injury, stared balefully at Elizabeth and motioned her closer. "Elizabeth, come shield me from Amalia. She'll badger me all the way to Traitor's Gate with her relentless questioning. Come, lass, distract me while MacGregor's henchman fingers the lead inside me."

"My lord!" Amalia sputtered, patting his clenched fist solicitously. "You mistake my concern. How can you make light of such a dread injury?"

Elizabeth wanted to roll her eyes. Amalia and Tullie being civil to one another was as rare as sunshine on Ben Nevis in February. Tullie couldn't stay out of trouble any more than Amalia could mind her own business. Looking him squarely in his now dull eyes, Elizabeth said, "All right. It's time for truth or consequences. What's the woman's name this time?"

Tullie burst into laughter that was quickly squelched by pain. With his good hand, he pinched Elizabeth's cheek, quipping grimly, "Och, dinna ask such a cheeky thing with Amalia listening. God's truth, she'd transport me down under, she would, did I divulge the wrong lady's name."

"That's an idea worth entertaining," Elizabeth bantered. "Imagine the rest our hearts would take if you were out of sight and out of mind for a year or two? You nearly scared my abigail to death, my lord. Throwing rocks at my windows at four in the morning!"

"Och, well..." He grinned sheepishly. "One of my Highlanders suggested we mind the elders and not wake the whole house. Discretion, I believe it's called."

Amalia tutted, shook her head and warned Elizabeth, "Don't encourage any of them."

"And why not?" Tullie argued, a tad drunkenly. "I'd be in a lot worse shape had I not encountered a few fellow Highlanders this night, I'll tell you."

Elizabeth watched as Tullie's approving and grateful glance went to Evan MacGregor. That brought her own gaze into direct visual contact with Evan's penetrating eyes again. Caught, she couldn't have taken her gaze away from his then to save her life.

She felt exposed, like a butterfly in a cold glass case. A thousand dark questions loomed in the depths of Evan's wintry blue eyes, but he said nothing as he raised a lamp aloft, above Corporal Butter's adept hands.

A muscle twitched high on Evan's cheekbone, and then his gaze slid indolently down her exposed throat and lingered on the deeply shadowed crevice between her breasts, crisscrossed by silk. Elizabeth's hands itched to clench the silk wrapper and draw it tightly closed around her body. His look made her shockingly aware of the night rail she wore in his presence.

Only Evan MacGregor's eyes had the ability to send shivers raking over her skin, to draw her nipples taut and contract the smooth flesh of her belly.

The sun creases at the corners of Evan's eyes deepened with pleasure, confirming that he knew the full extent of his effect upon her. An amused twist lifted one corner of his mouth in a wry, mocking smile that made her racing pulse boil, even as she hardened her expression to one of ire and displeasure.

He met her angered glare with his own arrogant challenge, deliberately cocking a brow above his long-lashed, sensual eyes. That look discounted everyone else in the room except her and him. His bold eyes confirmed that only his wants and desires mattered.

"Damnation! Go easy, man!" Tullie swore, jerking his shoulder sharply.

Corporal Butter grated out a curse and lost a pair of long-nosed tweezers. The tool clattered to the floor.

Evan looked back to the serious business at hand. Elizabeth let a whisper of relief escape through her parted lips as Evan bent to retrieve the tool.

"I've got two fingers on the bloody ball. Just a wee bit more, Yer Grace, and I'll have it loose. Give me that." Butter stuck out his hand for the fallen tool.

Elizabeth blurted out unthinkingly, "You must wash that before it is used again!"

Both officer and soldier-surgeon straightened at the same time, staring at her as though she'd lost her wits. Evan's arched brow dropped to a harsh line. His expression now said clearly that she should mind her place.

Elizabeth flushed instantly at the effectiveness of his unspoken rebuke, then let out another sigh of relief as Evan handed the bloody tool to Maxtone. He rinsed it in hot soapy water and put it back in Butter's bloody hand, while Tullie complained in a raw voice, "Balls of fire, Elizabeth! We aren't diapering babies here!"

Elizabeth gulped. More color stole into her cheeks. How she hated to be the focus of everyone's censure! She swallowed again. Amalia nudged her furiously, hissing her concern about Tullie's pain-flecked gray orbs.

"So tell me, my ladies." Tullie bit off each word, matching his speech to the erratic beating of his heart. "How long have you been in London town?"

"Three days. We've just nicely settled in." Elizabeth realized his request for words was a plea for distraction. It didn't matter what she or Amalia said.

"Aunt Charlotte came down first and opened the house. Elizabeth and I accompanied Father to Leinster. He stayed over to ride the foxes with Reverend Baird and Uncle Thomas. They should all arrive promptly at noon tomorrow." Amalia added, for clarity.

"Humph," John grunted. "You needn't have reminded me Colonel Graham is due back on the morrow, thank you." He shot a queer look at MacGregor that Elizabeth couldn't decipher. Corporal Butter grunted, as only a Highlander could. His "humph" could mean anything.

"There's no hope this will be healed by morning, is there, Butter?"

"Not a Chinaman's chance," Butter told him reprovingly.

"Ah, well, that canna be helped." Tullibardine sighed. His pained gaze wandered back to Elizabeth. "And what prompts your rare appearance in London, Elizabeth?"

Elizabeth normally needed little prodding to explain her reasons for avoiding the social life in London to her brother. It was no secret that she preferred living the retired life in Scotland, but with Evan MacGregor able to hear every word she uttered, she preferred to keep her own counsel. Not on her life would she mention that her visit to town had been prompted by a wee imp named Robbie.

Consequently, she failed miserably to come up with any sort of answer to her brother's question. But that didn't keep her concentrated gaze from straying every other moment to Evan.

On the surface, there wasn't any wonder about that. Evan MacGregor was so achingly handsome, most ladies would simply have stared until their eyes were sated. The last time Elizabeth saw him, he'd been the most shockingly beautiful seventeen-year-old she'd ever laid eyes upon.

Now, Evan was a man, nearer to twenty-four than twenty-three. A little taller than she remembered, he'd grown into the whipcord strength that had always served him well. She judged his height to be three good inches over Tullie's six feet. Evan's hair no longer had the wild, untrimmed look of a Highland lad's. Close-cropped waves feathered about his noble head, as black as raven's wings.

Devilishly wicked whiskers, which hadn't been there before, now emphasized the handsome angularity of his jaw. Elizabeth jerked herself out of another fawning display of childish adoration before she made a complete fool of herself.

She wasn't a child anymore. Neither was Evan Mac-Gregor. Try as she might, she couldn't call what had happened between them years ago the actions of impulsive children, either. Grimly Elizabeth forced all memory back into the past. It was best dead and forgotten.

Amalia gasped aloud as a strong spurt of blood shot across Tullibardine's chest. Fortunately, Evan had angled his body so that Elizabeth couldn't see the tools Butter pushed in and out of John's shoulder.

What Elizabeth did see was the amount of color seeping from her brother's normally ruddy face. Beads of sweat now glazed Tullie's brow and neck.

Amalia pressed another tot of brandy into John's left hand. As he gulped that, Elizabeth shot a meaningful look at MacGregor's back, asking, "Pray tell me, brother dear, the rationale behind your taking a murdering cattle thief and his henchman as your seconds tonight?"

The marquess scowled deeply, making Elizabeth wonder if it was pain that caused his expression, or disapproval of her deliberately disparaging words. "Damn me if I didn't have the bad luck to get assaulted on my way to White's, Elizabeth, and felt the need of fellow Highlanders' sure arms. Bullets are terribly debilitating, don't you agree?"

"Assaulted!" Amalia declared. "In Saint James?"

"Regrettably so," Tullie conceded with a gasp. Several moments passed before he forced his voice to continue. "A rather violent group they were, too. The mob did some damage to the club, and other buildings along the way."

"Whatever for?" Elizabeth couldn't prevent shock from showing on her face. "A mob, in Saint James?"

Evan MacGregor cast a considering glance at Amalia, then looked levelly at Elizabeth. "'Twas a pack of rabble whose real target was the Prince of Wales. Carlton House was their intended destination, until they ran afoul of the watch on Saint James. That's where the melee turned into a riot. They overturned several carriages, whose occupants received a sound thrashing. Several shots were fired before the mob finally dispersed. Luckily for His Grace, we Grey Breeks were available to help the Horse Guard put down the riot.''

"There you have it,'' Tullie said sloppily, showing the effects of undiluted liquor. But Elizabeth took exception to his slurred words implying it was normal happenstance.

Incensed, Amalia demanded, "Did they take whoever shot you into custody?''

"Well, now, there's a question I canna answer." John's eyes seemed to glaze over with more pain than he was able to override. "Demmed miserable piece of business, is all I have to say. I'd almost fought my way to White's before the soldiers arrived, but the sight of uniforms and muskets threw another torch under the bloody anarchists.''

"So I am to take it you weren't involved in a duel this night, Tullie?" Amalia asked, deliberately changing the subject.

John Murray quirked his brow, and laced his reply with a rolling brogue. "Och, forgive me, Amalia, for setting the honor of Scotland back another decade, but I found myself without weapons more damaging than my own two fists. You understand that the king takes a dim view of us Scots tramping about his capital city armed to teeth with dirks, claymores and Doune pistols.''

"A crying shame, milord," Elizabeth said impudently. "The king should give you a medal for your forbearance and courage. 'Tis a dangerous city, I fear.''

"Not so much as you may be inclined to believe.''

"Got it!" Butter crowed. He straightened all at once, holding the gruesome lead ball between his bloody fingers before John Murray's astonished eyes.

The coppery stench of fresh blood invaded Elizabeth's nose, making her want to retch from the taste of it, but a

Murray never flinched at the sight, much less the smell, of blood.

"So you have." The marquess exhaled a deep shudder of relief. "Now, which of you ladies can take the neatest stitch?"

That said, the marquess of Tullibardine promptly fainted dead away.

Chapter Three

~~~~~~~~~~

John Murray would have slid to the floor in a boneless heap if Evan MacGregor hadn't caught his elbow and forearm under the man's sinking chest and pressed him firmly back into the upright barber's chair.

Maxtone stepped on the levers, tilting the chair. Between the trio of strong men, they managed to get Tullie firmly secured in his tilted seat.

With his mouth open and his jaw slack, Tullie presented the most ungraceful pose for a grown man that Elizabeth had ever seen in her life. Even so, her pride in her brother's courage went up another notch.

Not one shout against the pain had escaped his lips. He'd chatted through the whole ordeal as if his pain were of no import. Elizabeth knew from her own haunting experiences that the truth was, the human body could only endure so much before one's courage dwindled to nothing in the face of body-racking pain.

She didn't think John's loss of consciousness was taken as a sign of weakness by any person in the room with him.

His muscular arms dangled limp over the sides of his chair. A steady rivulet of blood cascaded out of the deep surgical cut and dripped on the oak floor.

Amalia took advantage of Tullie's loss of consciousness to smooth an errant lock of damp hair from his brow. She bent and placed a sisterly kiss on his cheek. "There, there, my bra' laddie, sleep while you may."

While the surgeon and Tullie's manservant reached for towels to begin mopping up, Evan focused his full attention on Elizabeth. His black brows twisted, and those censorious eyes of his became achingly more intimate. He said pointedly, "Well, then?"

"Well, then, what?" Elizabeth bristled, not liking his peremptory tone, or his blasted appraising look, either! Again he had made her acutely aware that she was barefoot and dressed only in thin gown and wrapper. Hardly suitable attire for a confrontation with a renowned rake.

"Which of you is going to sew Tullie up? That's what." Evan cast a dismissive look at Elizabeth, and settled on Amalia.

"Och, nooo... Not me!" Amalia protested. "My hands are shaking so bad, I can't thread a needle, much less poke it in a man's flesh. I've never done such a thing."

"I'll do it." Elizabeth contradicted all her instincts, which demanded she fade quietly into the woodwork now. Heedless of her revulsion for blood and her deep-seated fear of physical pain, she stepped forward and briskly washed her hands at the basin on John's marble-topped commode. She was one Murray who would die before admitting a weakness to a MacGregor.

Her hands were nowhere near as steady as she wished they could be. The real truth was, she'd never poked a needle into living flesh, either. But she'd go gladly to hell and back before granting that truth to Evan.

Not twenty-four years old, and the man had already made a legend of himself by his valor in battle. Elizabeth had heard her uncle, Colonel Thomas Graham, rattle off chapter and verse throughout the entire Christmas holiday about the adventures of the Grey Breeks, his privately recruited company of Royal Highlanders. The MacGregor had figured largely in nearly every harrowing tale of the ongoing battles with the French on the Peninsula.

But Uncle Thomas had made no mention of having brought his entire company back to England. She'd pose some pointed questions of her own on the morrow, when her father and Thomas Graham arrived from the countryside.

Pretending to a calm she was far from feeling, Elizabeth took needle and thread in hand and lifted the towel draped across her brother's surgical wound.

Butter's stubby fingers pressed the bloody flesh together, showing her where to begin. Elizabeth glanced at Butter's face. His pale blue eyes revealed concern for her brother. Elizabeth vowed to make the neatest stitches she could.

"Had some experience at this, have you, Corporal Butter?" she asked.

"Och, aye, an' then some. Though I daresay I've spent more time sewing up foolish Sassenachs than I have the loyal clansmen that remain. Yer doing fine, lassie. The bullet went in clean. Stuck in the gristle, not the bone. He'll heal quick enough. I've seen worse. Cannonade, now that makes a mess of a man."

"I can well imagine," Elizabeth added dryly. She blinked her eyes to clear them, and concentrated on making small, neat stitches and tying firm knots in the wet boiled thread. An even twenty saw the large incision firmly shut.

Finished, Elizabeth stepped aside so that Butter could apply a liberal washing with carbolic and a clean dressing. She put the needle aside and washed her hands in hot water.

"Good work, Izzy." MacGregor splashed a healthy tot of whiskey in a clean glass and extended the drink to Elizabeth as she folded the towel she'd used to dry her hands.

"My name is Elizabeth, and I never touch whiskey, thank you." Elizabeth had lived long enough to know that whiskey had ruined more good men and their families that she cared to count.

"Drink it. It will do you good," MacGregor insisted.

"Aye, think you so? How much liquor had those men in the mob consumed this afternoon? It doesn't take all that much to make good men forget common sense, Christian duty and the virtue of prudence. You've just come from witnessing the results of unlimited excess, I would say. So I'll pass, thank you."

"Oomph." Evan MacGregor straightened to his full height. Elizabeth feared that his six feet and three inches somehow went much further than it should in intimidating her. "You always did have a tongue that was sharper than a blade honed on a razor strop, Izzy. I see you have added fastidiousness and sanctimoniousness to your store of unpleasant virtues, as well. Suit yourself. Hie yourself back to bed, and see how well you sleep with the smell of blood in your nose. It's no' a pleasant task."

He set the glass down, untouched by her, and moved away. The marquess's bandage was in place. Dismissing the two other men with a wave of his hand, Evan MacGregor slid his arms under John Murray's back and hoisted him out of his chair. He strode across the room, bearing Murray's twelve stone as if it were six, and put the marquess in his bed.

"I believe I can manage from here, milord," Tullie's valet said gratefully.

"I'm certain you can," MacGregor replied. Butter had already taken up their jackets, gloves and hats. "I'll see myself out. Send word immediately if His Grace has any further difficulties. I'll be at my barracks, if he or the duke has need of me."

Silently Elizabeth followed MacGregor and his man to the front door. Evan moved down the staircase with resolute purpose, smashing his diced cap down on his head.

Were his spine forced to be any more erect, it would have shattered into brittle pieces with each determined step.

Not once did Evan MacGregor look back at Lady Elizabeth Murray. Even though he knew she followed him down the stairs, and saw her reflection in the remarkable two-story bank of glass windows that graced the rotunda foyer of the town house. Even though his own batman, Corporal Butter, paused at the door to touch the rim of his cap in a salute, and audibly bid Lady Elizabeth, Godspeed and good-night.

Elizabeth deliberately doused the flow of gas to the experimental lights fronting her father's town house. That action cast their portion of Grosvenor into fog-shrouded darkness. She pressed the door firmly shut and locked it. She remained at the glass-banked door, peering out longingly after Evan until she could no longer see the man striding so purposefully into the night.

There were so many questions she could have asked...so many bits and pieces of news she could have told him...but she'd kept silent. And so had he.

She closed her eyes, feeling the chill of the night seep into her skin where her forehead rested on the windowpane. Mayhap it was better this way...better that nothing be said, that none of the old feelings of the past be stirred up and brought out into the open.

The big house surrounding her seemed to settle at once into its normal late-hour silence. She could hear the sonorous ticking of the grandfather clock and smell the damp that had come in with the fog, mixing with the familiar scents of her father's pipe tobacco and Aunt Nicky's talc.

She took a deep, calming breath and ordered the racketing clatter of her heart to cease. Calm, quiet and peace were all that counted in this world. Decorum and appearances mattered, not desire and impulse. She had to dig very deep inside herself to find the resolve she needed to put this unexpected meeting with Evan MacGregor in its place.

When she found it, she vowed with a vengeance that she wouldn't think about Evan MacGregor.

By sheer force of will, Elizabeth suppressed all curiosity regarding MacGregor's unexplained appearance in London. What Evan MacGregor chose to do with his life was his business.

Elizabeth repeated that fact over and over again. The MacGregor wasn't worthy of a single minute of her thoughts, and she wouldn't give him that. After all, she was a Murray, and every soul in Scotland knew there was no one more determined and strong-willed than a Murray.

Evan MacGregor cursed loudly and fluently as he threw off his jacket and dropped his pistols on the rude table serving as his writing desk in his quarters.

He already hated being assigned duty in London. Blast Colonel Graham's orders to hell and back! The moment his superior returned from his holiday, Evan vowed, he'd demand a transfer back to the Continent. Hell! He'd take six months in Newcastle working with raw conscripts over six months in London recruiting and grooming officers for the king's army.

Damn Elizabeth Murray! Why couldn't she stay home in Dunkeld, where the blasted chit belonged? And if he couldn't have that, why hadn't the divine providence that moved all things turned her into a gross, shapeless, cow-eyed sow?

He'd escaped her siren's wiles five years ago, when she was naught more than a willful, ungrateful, beautiful spoiled brat. What was he to do now that she'd turned into an exceedingly clever and lovely woman of the world?

"Merciful heavens!" Krissy wagged her head and clucked her tongue as Lady Elizabeth quietly shut the door of the adjoining nursery. "There now. Did I not tell you wee Robbie never fluttered a lash through the whole commotion?''

"So you did," Elizabeth said promptly. "But I do like to see that for myself."

"Humph." Krissy grunted in response.

Lady Elizabeth was like that, always putting four-year-old Master Robbie's welfare before her own, as if the sweet little boy were her very own bairn. Not that Krissy could fault her lady for that, especially since Robbie had taken his grandam's death so hard. The poor little mite had spoken nary a word in the three months since auld Abigail Drummond had been put in the ground. Lady Elizabeth had every right to be worried about him.

"Och, what a night of nights this has been. Come, milady, best you get to bed. God save us, we should all drop off to sleep with the ease and peace of a bairn."

Krissy bustled across Lady Elizabeth's boudoir to fluff the pillows on her lady's tester bed, straighten the rumpled coverlet and smooth the sheets. "Do you think Tullie will be able to rest at all, milady? What if the watch should come asking questions? Should I run and tell Mr. Keyes the marquess is indisposed?"

"No. Amalia will see to that. As to Tullie's condition, I'd warrant he's sleeping better than we are at the moment," Elizabeth wisely answered.

"Tut-tut, you just climb up into bed and drink this warm milk I heated for you. It will soothe you right down," Krissy urged. "I canna help noticing you dinna like talking about the MacGregor. Is there summat between the two of you, then?"

"Not that I can think of." Elizabeth evaded a more direct answer to the loyal servant who had been with her for the past three years.

She sat motionless on the side of the bed and stared at the closed door of the nursery—the nursery that everyone in the household probably thought housed a much-loved by-blow of His Grace the duke of Atholl. Nothing could be further from the truth.

Krissy handed her the cup of heated milk, grinning. "I dinna mind admitting the MacGregor's no strain on the eyes, is he, now?"

"If you say so." Elizabeth remained noncommittal, all the while silently praying Krissy would stop. Enough was enough.

"Och, he's verra nice to look upon." Krissy happily voiced that opinion. "He appears to know you well, Lady Elizabeth...I mean everyone. Seems I remember he was often about years ago...at the clan gatherings, weddings and games and such. Am I right?"

"Oh...aye." Elizabeth sighed. She finished the drink and put the cup and saucer on her nightstand, tucked her legs under the covers and said firmly, "Go to bed, Krissy. Get some sleep."

"Aye, well, good night again, Lady Elizabeth. I'll try not to make a nuisance of myself. Pleasant dreams."

Not likely, Elizabeth thought grimly as Krissy bustled to the nursery door.

The servant paused with her hand on the doorknob, remembering something else. "Och! What time must I wake you up?"

"Seven at the latest, if I am to dress, have breakfast and make it to church on time." Elizabeth doused the light beside her bed.

The next suggestion came through the dark. "Milady, I could tell the dowager you're ill...or something...so you could sleep in a wee bit longer."

"Absolutely not," Elizabeth answered firmly. "I'd need gory, bleeding wounds more serious than Tullie's to be excused from attending church with the dowager."

"Well. It was just a thought. Good night, then."

The room became quiet at last. So long as Elizabeth didn't count the steady ticking of her clock, and the ever-audible drip of London's abysmal wet fog, gathering on the upper cornice of the bay windows and plopping noisily onto the stone window sills.

Judging by the soft snores that soon came from the adjoining room, Krissy, who hadn't a serious thought in her head, had dropped off to sleep in the blink of an eye. Not so Elizabeth.

But then, the good and the righteous always slept in peace and tranquillity, while the wicked and the damned were doomed to spend eons atoning for their sins. Elizabeth accepted that as a merciful God's justice.

She didn't deserve to sleep with the ease of an innocent like Krissy. Elizabeth's soul was nowhere near as pure, and her heart was ten times more jaded.

People who lived a lie and kept dark secrets were never blessed with peace in the dead of night. Elizabeth's thoughts drifted far, far away from this bed in her father's London town house . . . to a tiny room in a Scottish border town. A room where the wet had penetrated the thatch time after time, leaving countless stains on sour whitewashed walls.

Time mercifully blotted out much of her memory. Sheer force of will obliterated details and sensations she never wanted to revive. But no matter how strong a discipline she forced on her thoughts, certain things remained fresh, clear and vivid.

The smell of a greasy quilt. The thick taste of a heavy fog that lingered over the village at high noon—flavored with the aroma of haggis and cabbage. The sound of buttons snapping their threads as hasty, too-eager hands tore a sark apart and cast it to the shadows. The heat and texture of Evan's hands spreading across Elizabeth's belly and cupping her breasts.

No, try as she might to force will to overcome and direct all memory, Elizabeth Murray would never, ever forget Gretna Green, and the day she'd eloped and married Evan

MacGregor—May 28, 1802. Only weeks after she'd tossed propriety aside and danced with her childhood sweetheart at Bell's Wynd.

That day had left unalterable, indelible impressions. Never mind the fact that only three living souls knew of that truth—Master Paisley, who had married them, Evan, and herself—the truth was and always would be unforgettable.

Elizabeth blinked dry eyes and glared at the shut door, wondering what in heaven's name she would do now. How would she get through tomorrow? She had asked herself that question every night since May of 1802. All the brash and reckless courage of youth had failed her then, turned her into a sniveling, terrified coward once the deed was done.

Every day of her life since, she'd fought with herself to have the strength and fortitude to go forward, in spite of the dishonor and shame she had brought on herself and Evan, and might have brought on both their families.

In the beginning, that had only been for herself—so that she could continue to hold her head up and look her father and her brothers and sisters in the eye.

Living a lie all the while. Denying the truth. Until it was too late to rectify the wrong that had been done by any honorable means. Until it was no longer possible to hide the ever-evident truth that she was carrying a child inside her.

By then it had been way, way too late to own up to the truth. Evan had gone and done the unthinkable, joined the army and been shipped off to war. Alone, Elizabeth couldn't find the courage to admit what she'd done.

But tonight, the cards in the hand she'd been dealt had turned. Evan had come back. For the first time in almost six years, Elizabeth couldn't guess what suit the next trump was going to be, and she didn't know what her next move should or could be.

God save me, she thought, and closed her dry, aching eyes. Willpower and determination would get her through. It had to. It had failed her only once in her life, that dreadful day—May 28, so long, long ago. *Dear God,* she prayed, *please, don't let Evan discover Robbie. Let me keep my secrets, let me keep my son.*

Chapter Four

Sunday was bitterly cold from start to finish. A little weather never kept the duke of Atholl's hardy ladies housebound on the Sabbath—not when the dowager devoted a Sunday to pursuing the Lord's work.

They began with services at nearby Saint Mark's, which were followed by the annual ladies' guild winter bazaar, a monstrous undertaking that took up the balance of the cold and dreary afternoon. Throughout the whole long, cold afternoon Elizabeth sold rose cuttings to enhance next summer's gardens. The bazaar made a long day longer.

Elizabeth couldn't wait to get home and exchange her somber, very damp walking dress and pelisse for a warm gown of velvet and lace. She spent an hour in the nursery telling stories to Robbie in another effort to elicit whole sentences from her monosyllabic son. Since his nanny's sudden death in October, Robbie had all but quit speaking entirely.

Elizabeth tucked her arm around Robbie's wee shoulders, drawing him close. "How many beans did Jack get from the peddler, Robbie?"

"Dunno." Robbie's shoulders lifted under the light compression of Elizabeth's loving arm. His thick cap of dark curls brushed against her cheek as he turned his face toward the windows overlooking the park.

"You don't know?" Elizabeth asked, cognizant of her inner fear that there might be something wrong with her beautiful, perfect son.

It was bad enough that she was not allowed to claim him as her own, to openly act or be his mother. Her father's acceptance and support of the child came with the stricture that appearances must be kept up.

Elizabeth's father had guessed her incipient condition before Elizabeth, in her youthful ignorance, discerned it herself. Robbie had been born at Port-a-shee, on the Isle of Man, on March 4, 1803, and legally named an orphan and a ward of her father, under his privilege as Lord Strange, lord of the Isle of Man.

For the past four years, Elizabeth had engaged in an ongoing battle to spend as much time with her son as her father would allow. Considering the circumstances of Robbie's birth, she was fortunate to have any contact with Robbie at all, and she knew that. Hence, she had always showered the child with loving attention every chance she got. That wasn't enough for her. She feared her limited concern wasn't enough for the child, either.

Ever restless, Robbie wiggled off the settee to dart across the room to his low shelf of toys and books. He pulled out book after book, discarding one for the next, until he came to a well-worn favorite, a volume of illustrated fairy tales. His cherubic face was as somber as a choirboy's as he leafed through the pages, searching for the story of the giant and the beanstalk.

When he found the picture of Jack trading his mother's cow for three beans, he popped back onto his sturdy feet, ran across the room and laid the open book on Elizabeth's lap. She rumpled his hair and smiled.

"Ah, I see. You brought me the picture. How many beans is that? Do you know?"

Robbie tilted his face up to hers and sighed, deep and long. He held up four fingers, which was wrong, but he said, "Three," which was correct.

"That's right, three beans." Elizabeth smiled as she tucked his first finger under the tight compression of his thumb, making his gesture match his words. "Three beans and one, two, three, four, five fingers. Very good, Robbie."

Unconcerned with numbers, he whirled away and sat in the midst of his toy soldiers and castle blocks. In the blink of an eye, the child was engrossed in his toys and oblivious of Elizabeth's presence.

Fascinated, as always, by everything Robbie did, Elizabeth watched him build a new wall and line a squadron of tin soldiers on its rim, then flop onto his belly to maneuver the pieces.

The door to the nursery opened, and Krissy bustled in, bringing Robbie's supper on a tray. "Well, and himself does love the wee soldiers Colonel Graham gave him, doesn't he? Good eve, milady. I've brought your supper, Master Robert. Come. Up to the table with you."

Elizabeth stood. "Robbie, I'm going to go now. I have to speak to His Grace."

"'Bye," Robbie grunted, engrossed in the toys, oblivious of both Elizabeth and the servant setting up his supper on the nursery table.

Krissy cast an indulgent smile at Elizabeth that, in effect, excused the child's bad manners. Elizabeth made her own allowances for Robbie's not standing when she did. He was so young, a baby still in the nursery. Manners would come in time.

She could no longer put off the necessity of speaking privately with her father, and the sooner the better.

Elizabeth slipped through the door joining her and Robbie's rooms and closed it quietly, but as she checked her appearance, she kept one ear cocked to the activity in the other room. Krissy could talk the ear off a marble statue. Robbie's infrequent mumbled grunts made no difference to her.

Elizabeth ran a brush through her hair and vainly tried to loosen the tightness out of her chestnut curls, tugging on the cluster that draped across her shoulder to stretch it. The moment she let the end of the curl go, it corkscrewed back where it had been.

"Drat!" Elizabeth said. It did no good to brush the wayward curls, or tie them, or do anything but let those curls do what they might. Hence, she rather liked her newly cropped head of hair, adorned in the latest classical style, which was both short around her head like a cap and long and feathery from the curls left dangling at her nape and her ears. She tied a green velvet ribbon that matched her dress around her head and touched a curl here and there, satisfied with her appearance.

Elizabeth lingered at her vanity a moment longer, studying the bluish shadows under her eyes, which hadn't faded, even though she'd spent most of the day outdoors. The intensity of her worries showed. She pinched both cheeks to heighten their color, concluding that that would have to do.

Finished, Elizabeth tiptoed down to the second-floor landing, deliberately pausing to use sound to locate each member of the crowded household.

Keyes exited from the salon, bearing the used tea service on a silver tray. The butler let in and out the happy noise of the aunts, the dowager and Amalia over their rounds of piquet.

Across the foyer, the click of ivory balls accompanied a scolding from Elizabeth's brother James, Lord Glenlyon, to their uncle, Thomas Graham. Tullie was spending the evening in bed, still recovering from the effects of his impromptu surgery the night before. God willing, every soul in the house would remain exactly where they were for the next hour, Elizabeth prayed.

She circled the newel post at the foot of the staircase and crept down the long, carpeted hall dotted with statuary and hothouse greenery until she came to the closed door of her father's study.

Taking a deep breath, Elizabeth dashed the perspiration from her upper lip. There was nothing to be gained from putting off what she had to do. Her soft tap on the closed door just barely qualified as a knock.

Elizabeth had the door open and her head and shoulders well inside the inner sanctum before her knock penetrated as far as the duke of Atholl's desk. "Are you free, Papa? Could I have a word with you?"

John Murray took the time to remove a pince-nez from his nose before lifting his baleful gaze to his daughter. "Ah, Elizabeth, I've been expecting you. Come in, my dear. Do shut that door. Those drafts up that hall are a misery."

Elizabeth stepped across the threshold, grateful that the first and worst hurdle was over—finding her father alone and with time to spare was nearly impossible. She closed the door and took a moment to quell the fluttering of her heart by looking around the study with feigned interest.

Elizabeth was not particularly fond of this study. Though it was her father's room, she had always associated it with her mother. It was to this room that she and Amalia had trustingly come, hand in hand, to be told the sad news of their mother's death sixteen years before. So she had a natural repugnance for this room—though never for the man who occupied it.

Which might have seemed exceedingly odd, because where the rest of the town house might be chilly, the study somehow retained a cozy warmth. Likewise, where the aunts, the dowager and the eight-years-older Amalia might find fault with Elizabeth, her father rarely did.

She wound her way through the maze of sturdy, well-used furniture, chairs and tables that made no pretense to art or style. A cheery fire crackled in the hearth and cast eerie light up to the trophy heads and antler racks. It was a man's room in all ways, tainted by *uisge beatha,* port wine, and tobacco smoke, dark and somber in color, with heavy furnishings that befitted large-boned, heavyset men like her father.

Elizabeth settled in the corner of the wide couch before the fire. "Why is it always warmest in here, Papa?"

John Murray buffed the lenses of his glasses, then tucked them into a coat pocket. "Oh, I would account that to sharing the same chimney stack with the kitchens, I suppose. Didn't plan it that way. But I daresay my father quite enjoyed the added warmth in his later days. So shall I."

"Are you tottering into your dotage?" Elizabeth asked, with a dimpling smile.

"Are you being cheeky, puss?" the duke asked. He poured them both a glass of sherry and handed one to Elizabeth. "What shall we toast?"

Elizabeth took the flute in hand. The corners of her mouth twitched. Her higher principles advised her to hand the glass back and firmly refuse. But to do so would insult her father. Elizabeth could not make such a display. "Well..." she murmured, thinking of her own purposes. "We could ask for a quick and decisive Parliament. All the business of making Britain run smoothly, done in three weeks at the most. Do you think that would be appropriate?"

"Indubitably," the Duke agreed. "Here's to good business, wise leadership and common sense!" He touched the rim of his crystal to Elizabeth's, and tasted the fine wine. The formalities done, he settled on the other end of the couch and gave the flickering flames in the hearth his attention. "You've something on your mind, Elizabeth."

"Yes, Papa, I do." Elizabeth set the full glass on the table at her side. She dropped her hands into her lap and entwined her fingers together to keep them still. "Let's jump straight to the point, shall we? There's no point in my being here in London for the little season. I want to go home, tomorrow at the very latest."

She waited until all the words were out before turning her head to gauge her father's expression. His large head nodded, dipping as he brought his glass to his lips and sipped the sherry. The lamps behind them on his desk made a wealth of white hair glimmer all around his head. The starched points of his collar crackled where they flared up against his smoothly shaved cheeks.

"What? You just arrived here a few days ago, and already you are bored with your friends?"

"My friends, no, Papa. You know very well what I find singularly unappealing. We've discussed this several times, and I can't make my wishes any plainer. I am not in the market for a husband. I don't need one. I won't have one, and I certainly won't look for one, nor display myself on the marriage market here in this filthy city."

"Oh? Can't say I'm surprised to hear that speech again. Elizabeth, you ought to think of something more original."

"Papa!" Elizabeth exclaimed. "It isn't fair to bait me. You know perfectly well what I mean. London is disgusting and dirty. I hate it here. I always have hated coming to London. You should allow me my independence. I do reach my majority in April."

"Hmmm...I'm well aware of your age, Elizabeth," Lord Atholl mused, concerned over his youngest daughter's stated intention of avoiding marriage—no matter the cost. "Amalia hinted this afternoon that you'd have all your reasons to return to Dunkeld in place before you sought an audience with me. Planned a little fait accompli, have you?

What you've offered doesn't sound either urgent or convincing, though."

"Amalia spoke to you?" Elizabeth asked, rattled by that admission. She waited with bated breath for her father's answer. What had Amalia said? Had she mentioned Evan?

"Yes. Amalia and I had a very long and thorough conference earlier this afternoon." The duke sipped his sherry, then put his glass aside and turned to study Elizabeth as he continued. "She tells me that Evan MacGregor put in an appearance last night. What do you make of that?"

"What should I make of it?" Elizabeth ignored the quickening tempo of her pulse. She kept her face impassive, her hands still and her eyes firmly on her father. "He has nothing to do with me, Papa. Why, I haven't seen or heard one word from him since his sister married, five years ago!"

"Is that so?" John Murray inclined his head a bit, to better study his daughter's flawless face. He failed to see a single sign of the heightened interest that he was seeking. Surely his gut feelings weren't wrong?

Of his three daughters, Elizabeth, who had never really known her mother, most favored his late wife. Elizabeth had inherited the wide, intelligent eyes and brows and flawless skin of the Cathcarts.

Unfortunately, her chin and her very full lips proclaimed her a Murray to the core. She had a way of sliding her eyes to the side to study one that reminded him very much of his long-lost Jane Cathcart. She was giving him that look now, just as her mother had been wont to do. Elizabeth was keeping secrets again. There was nothing new about that.

"You are both of a proper age, now," the duke said blandly, probing the still waters skillfully. "You liked each other well enough when you were children. Many a successful marriage has been built on less."

"Marriage!" Elizabeth choked. "All that nonsense about Evan and I was over and done with when he went to Eton. You know that as well as I do, Papa."

"Is that right, puss?" he asked absently, knowing better. They'd corresponded for years, three and four letters a week to one another, right up to the very day Evan's sister married—May 28, 1802. He remembered the date precisely.

"Yes, it most assuredly is. I had every right to admire him years ago. Evan protected me. Mrs. Grasso was a right witch, you know, Papa."

"She was a very good teacher," John Murray said, nonplussed. His daughter flashed an insincere smile. The duke wasn't the least bit fooled. She was throwing smoke and covering her tracks. A bloody ferret couldn't dig the truth out of Elizabeth Murray.

God Almighty knew he'd done everything in his power—everything short of beating a pregnant woman—to get her to tell him the truth at Port-a-shee, when it became glaringly evident that she'd bedded someone.

"And the other thing I've considered thoroughly is Robbie." Elizabeth pounced on another quasi-valid reason. "This doctor you insisted on having examine him will be of no consequence. The only thing troubling Robbie is that he has no one to bond with now that Nanny Drummond has passed. He adored her. He's grieving, that's all. What is best for Robbie is to go back to Port-a-shee, and all that is familiar to him."

"I don't see the significance there. I've fostered the boy no differently than I've fostered any of a dozen other lads over my years."

"Really, Papa? Is that the same thing as having a recognized parent?"

"Don't throw words like those in my face, young lady. You made your choice years ago, and you will live with the consequences of that decision. Count yourself blessed to have the opportunity to know the lad under my patronage.''

"I'm not complaining. I am content with things the way they are.''

"You are? Then what's your point?''

Exasperated, Elizabeth exclaimed, ''My point is, I want to go back to Dunkeld. What's so unreasonable about that? Will you grant me that boon?''

Murray patted his pockets till he found his pipe. He pulled it out and laid the bowl in his palm to scrape out the insides with a flattened pocket nail. It was a handy bit of business to fill the time with, while Elizabeth sat on tenterhooks, waiting. She wasn't going to appreciate his answer. Elizabeth didn't like being told no.

"Amalia thinks this season will be different.''

"Ha!'' Elizabeth choked back a bitter laugh. ''Papa, let's not deceive ourselves, shall we? Not when we both know the truth.''

"Oh? Right, then.'' John tamped two pinches of tobacco into the bowl from his pouch, put the stem of the pipe firmly between his teeth and sat back.

At issue between them was the home truth that mere mortal bairns were not conceived by immaculate conception. Had he even a clue who Robbie's father was, Elizabeth would not be a spinster, she'd be a widow.

The duke had used his powers to make certain no one alive knew what circumstances his youngest child had gotten herself into at a young and tender age. Abigail Drummond had delivered Elizabeth of her infant and raised the child. She'd taken to her grave the identity of Robbie's mother. And no one but Elizabeth knew the identity of the boy's father. And she wasn't talking.

"All right.'' He gave in, handing her the lead she wanted. "Tell me your version of the latest, up-to-the-very-moment truth.''

"War," Elizabeth said succinctly, and stared at him with eyes so pale a blue, they could be valerian plucked off a deserted Greek isle.

Atholl frowned as he put a taper to the candle nearest him and brought that to the bowl of his pipe, puffing and sucking to ignite the tightly packed tobacco.

"War, you say? What's war got to do with you going to Dunkeld? Did I miss the passing of the Cross Truach?"

"War doesn't have anything to do with the passing of a fiery cross, Papa," Elizabeth said exasperated. "It has to do with the fact that there aren't any worthwhile men left in England to court a duke's daughter! They've all gone off to battle here, there and everywhere. Those that haven't enlisted have quit the country seeking fortunes in tea from Ceylon, mahogany in India, cocoa in South America. Have I made my point clear?"

"Oh, aye. England's come a cropper. Can't deny that— what with rising after rising during the last century. But there's plenty of good men in Scotland worth your while, Elizabeth."

"Really?" she said challengingly. "Are you saying my being a duke's daughter there doesn't matter one iota? That one clansman's as good as any other?"

"No," he answered deliberately. "Is there one in particular who's caught your eye then, puss?"

"Papa, you're being deliberately obtuse. You know what I mean. May I go home tomorrow?"

"No, you canna go home tomorrow, or the day thereafter, either. Wouldn't think of sending you back this soon and giving anyone the notion we have something to hide. You'll just have to make do, Elizabeth. And that means you will see to your normal duties during the little season.

"Besides, Amalia vows she'll strangle me if I allow you to waste this season in London, puss. Don't think you should, since MacGregor's come to town."

"Amalia!" Elizabeth cried, her voice choked. "What's she got to do with this? She hates Evan!"

"Hmmm...good point. She definitely dislikes the rogue. I've always wanted to know why. Do you know the answer to that, puss?"

"I believe she's always thought he'd turn out a rakehell, too handsome by half. Most likely she had a *tendre* for him, like every other soul in the whole wide world, and could never get him to bat an eye her way."

"Hmmm... Well, can't say I'm surprised by that. She's five years older than the scamp." Murray laughed and rocked the stem of his pipe from one corner of his mouth to the other. As was his custom, he left it clenched between his teeth, dragging down the right corner of his mouth while he proceeded to talk around it. "My point is, Amalia would like to see you settled and married, Elizabeth. Frankly speaking, so would I. You're not getting any younger, you know."

Smoke wreathed his head while he sat thinking and gazing at the haze.

"You can't ask me to put up with another batty old maid in my house, can you, puss? Nicky and Charlotte are enough for one poor old Scot to manage, aren't they? No, you would be best-off married, Elizabeth. You're not the kind of woman who is cut out to be a spinster. You feel things too deeply, and react to sensations born spinsters are perfectly blind to. No, no. You need a strong, demanding husband, you do. You'll have to trust my judgment on that."

"Oh, no, I won't," Elizabeth declared, with a firmness he found alarming. "Father, I intend to follow in Aunt Nicky's footsteps and take her place as the patroness of Bell's Wynd," Elizabeth argued heatedly. "I can't do that if I'm married."

By the way she switched from endearments to formal address, Lord John knew Elizabeth was beginning to clutch at straws. If their conversation dwindled to the point where she called him *sir*, it would mean Elizabeth's tender feelings were hurt. In that, she had always been easy to read. His older girls had called him *Father* for so many years he rarely thought of them as anything but adults now. But to Elizabeth he had been *Papa* a very, very long and dear time.

"Now, there you're wrong. You are not at all like Aunt Nicky, puss." He took his pipe from his mouth and leveled her a rock-steady gaze. "You need a man."

Bordering on genuine panic, Elizabeth argued. "Surely you're not serious, my lord!"

"You've completely misread the situation between us, Elizabeth. Just because I haven't pushed any of the men forward who have asked for your hand, that doesn't mean that I haven't entertained and declined offers from some of these young pups. There hasn't been a rogue whose character or means I fully approve of yet. I have high standards, you know. Not just any Sassenach will do."

"*Sassenach!*" Elizabeth gasped, shocked. That would never do at all. "What are you really saying? Any old Scot's as good as the next, is he?" Elizabeth was needling him deliberately now. "Papa, you said it was my choice and you would not force me."

"Ah, so I did, in principle. But that was then and this is now." John Murray sighed. "That's why I haven't made any mention of offers before. However, in light of today's reflections, I believe it would do you good to remain in town for the little season. It's only a few weeks—as long as Parliament is in session. Young Robbie will keep safe and sound in the nursery until then...and...we'll see, hmm?"

No matter how nicely he coated the bitter pill, Elizabeth had difficulty swallowing it. "Papa, I want to go home."

"And so you shall, dear. All in good time."

"No, now."

"No, Elizabeth. Don't be tiresome. You're much too old to stage tantrums or resort to hysterical sulks."

"I can't believe you're siding with Amalia."

"I'm on the side of common sense, always, puss."

"Fine!"

Elizabeth stood. She looked down at her father, her mouth compressed, the stubbornness of her chin very telling of her Murray roots.

"Don't expect me to confide in you in the future. I may just go to Scotland without your permission, sir."

"Humph!" The duke grunted.

Elizabeth met his piercing gaze without wavering. He put his smoldering pipe on a porcelain dish on the table and laced his fingers together across his stomach. He was a fit man, in his early fifties. Only a rash fool would have misjudged his vitality and strength by the premature whiteness of his hair. Elizabeth was not often a fool.

"May I remind you of the last time you decided you'd rather be in Scotland than in London with me for a session of Parliament? How far did you get on your little journey home alone during that rising, Elizabeth?"

"That's hardly relevant today. I was an eight-year-old-child then. I wouldn't make the same mistakes."

"Except in your willful thinking, eh?"

John Murray refrained from standing while his youngest faced him with rebellion in her eyes. Long experience had taught him to avoid direct confrontations with Elizabeth. Once she got her blood up, she was the very devil to get to back down.

Should she warrant suppression, Atholl could certainly rise to the occasion and dominate her. But, of his three daughters, he preferred that this one remain on course with her basically easy-to-read and predictable come-ahead stance and attack.

Elizabeth could be very devious if provoked. God knew that was the most strikingly formidable Murray trait that could be inherited. That she had mastered it made Atholl wish his sons were more like their baby sister.

"Well, yes. I suppose I am being willful, sir." She had the grace to blush with that admission.

"Good." He gave her a look whose purpose should have quelled any further rebellious acts. "I want it understood, Elizabeth, that if you do such a foolish thing as to run off without permission anywhere, I *can* and *will* exert the full power of my authority over you . . . whether that is to your liking or not. And if you've come to an age when you think to doubt my will, I suggest you think back to Port-a-shee, and then think again."

That reminder had the effect he sought.

"Papa," she pleaded, "I don't want to defy you, I want to go home. I'm not asking for a trip to Cairo. I see no valid reason why you shouldn't accommodate me. For once in my life, Amalia could make excuses about my absence from town. London won't die without me here to amuse it."

The duke sighed. He propped his elbow on the armrest of the sofa and splayed his fingers across the side of his face. He stared hard at Elizabeth, willing her to accept the decision she'd been given.

She remained as she was, her back to the fire, her hands pressed together in supplication, her face an angelic mixture of entreaty and sweetness. He felt like a cad.

Their discussion would only disintegrate from here. The duke stood, walked around the sofa to his desk and sat in his creaky old leather chair.

Where his youngest daughter was concerned, saying no was easy compared to the monumental effort it took to stand on that decision. It was fair knowledge to one and all that he favored and indulged his youngest more than he had any of his other children.

He silently willed her to leave his study as he returned his attention to the briefs on his desk. She didn't. She stood there by his fire, a living, breathing Christmas angel, praying. Whether her supplications were for him or for herself, he didn't care to ask.

It was some minutes before he spoke, and when he did it was without looking up from the papers he was reading. "Elizabeth, Reverend Baird is kept on retainer for the specific purpose of being available day or night to hear whatever confession you have to offer. Leave my study. Go find someone else to torment. I must read all of these dispatches and proposals before I retire."

"What about Tullie? You haven't said one word about John. He's not going to be available to escort me to all these routs and balls that Amalia says we must attend. I mean, it's a pointless exercise, Papa."

The duke said, "There's nothing wrong with James. He's a good man."

"Papa, he's worse than Tullie!" Elizabeth cried out, from sheer frustration. "James can't be relied upon to get me as far as the door of whatever house I'm going to before he dumps me for the Cyprians across town."

"Now, that's enough slander, Elizabeth! Glenlyon wouldn't dare be so careless with your reputation!"

Last, in final desperation, she threw out her lone remaining trump. "Father, Robbie's not going to get any better just because you've heard of a specialist in London. He's lost the only person that was ever important to him. No Sassenach doctor can change that."

John Murray picked up his pen and dipped it in the inkwell, affixing his signature to a document his secretary had marked as urgent. He dismissed Elizabeth with a stern warning. "Don't start a rising in that direction, miss. Wee Robbie is my ward. I will do what's best for him, as I will do what is best for you. Now, good night, Elizabeth. Let the door hit you where the good Lord split you."

Elizabeth couldn't find words enough to express her disappointment to her father. She stood for quite some time without moving, hating this room, but unable to hate the man who dominated it so thoroughly. She prayed fervently that he would soften and change his mind, because he didn't know what he was doing in forcing her to remain here in London while Evan MacGregor was in town.

It filled her with terrible dread to consider her alternatives. She couldn't imagine what fury her father might give vent to if the worst should happen, and Evan MacGregor came forward and told the duke that he and Elizabeth had run away to Gretna Green and got married when they were fifteen and seventeen years old.

But she knew her father would surely kill Evan.

Elizabeth swallowed what felt like her own heart lodged in her throat. She took a deep breath and tasted defeat. Abruptly she quit the study.

Upstairs, she collapsed on a stool before the fire in her room, watching red-and-blue flames lick their way out from underneath several wedges of split oak. The sight consumed her. She felt like the wood, smoking and burning, aching, ready to burst into flames.

"I'm a coward," she said out loud. "The first and only Murray ever born who was an outright coward, down to the bone. Grandfather George must be spinning in his grave. I've shamed every Murray that fought at Culloden."

It wouldn't do any good to argue with herself that it wasn't true. Elizabeth Murray was a coward. All she wanted to do was run away . . . just as she had from the beginning.

The slightest thought of pain and suffering made her tremble and quake. Thinking back to Tullie's bravado of the night before only made her stomach turn vilely. How had he done it? But that was a man for you!

Woman weren't of that ilk, and little girls were even more vulnerable. Why, her father had only to remind her of one telling incident from her childhood—the one time she'd struck out on her own—and she knuckled under, even today.

She was nearly twenty-one, would be in April—a woman grown, by all rights. But she had no backbone. She didn't

have what it took to stand up to anyone. Oh, she could act
as if she did. Like that time her father had referred to. But
how far had she actually got? Charing Cross, that was how
far.

She wasn't a child now. More importantly, she had a
child of her own, whose best interests were not being served
by her father's insistence that everyone in his household
keep up appearances.

Elizabeth had to do something.

She couldn't go to any member of her family for aid in
any plan that went against her father's will. Elizabeth had
enough common sense to know which of her friends would
help her with no questions asked. Only one had the means
to go against a duke, Elizabeth's long-standing friend, the
writer Monk Lewis. Her only other friend with the gump-
tion to assist her was George, Lord Byron.

Both Monk and Byron adhered to styles that played fast
and loose with society's rigid expectations of correct behavior, though neither had gone beyond the unredeemable
pale. And of the two, Elizabeth was more inclined to put
her faith in Monk Lewis. Monk was twenty years her senior, a confirmed bachelor, and a true gentleman where
ladies were concerned. He'd never failed to give her good
advice in the past.

However, she was closest to Byron. They were of the
same age, and had practically grown up together, so to
speak, being thrown into one another's company at the
same social functions since they'd turned sixteen.

Elizabeth made up her mind to write to Monk. She saw
no good coming of putting off the inevitable.

Chapter Five

Almack's
January 20, 1808

"Well, well, well, here we are again, the lost, the lame and the duckling. Whatever shall we do to entertain the *haut ton*, hmm? See no evil, taste no evil, hear no evil... have no fun?"

"Oh, stop being so nasty, Byron. Just because I can't risk being seen doesn't mean you have to hide behind the potted palms, too." Elizabeth slapped the young baronet's arm smartly with her fan. "Go take your terrible temper out on someone more deserving than Monk and me."

"I wouldn't dream of deserting either of you. Imagine the consequences of MacGregor's temper, should he discover how assiduously you avoid him. Suppose he decided to wreak his vengeance upon skinny little Monk here? He'd make a bloody mess of the poor half-witted sot."

Monk peered through his quizzing glass at Elizabeth. His prominent Adam's apple bobbed between drooping points. "Why would MacGregor want to do that?"

"Never mind, Monk, of course he won't do any such thing!" Elizabeth countered. She bit down on her jaw, hard, glaring at Byron. "I should have never told you a blessed thing. Damn you, Byron, don't make me regret befriending you."

The youth splayed his fingers across the breast of his coat, above his heart, his eyes widening with sincere hurt. He and Elizabeth were the same age, and had known each other forever. True friendship had evolved when each felt the awkwardness inherent in being thrust onto the social scene to sink, swim or flounder. Good or bad, they'd been ardent supporters of one another ever since.

"You misjudge me, Elizabeth. We are both wounded by life's cruelest blow—ill-fated love. I could no more betray your secrets than you would mine," he added apologetically.

Not certain she was mollified, Elizabeth arched a questioning brow. "Then I take it your grumbling originates from some other source. Perhaps you're out of sorts because no one has remarked upon your upcoming birthday? Shall I hire a carousel and hobbyhorses? If you behave yourself tonight, you may just find that you have what you most desire by the end of this evening."

"My dearest Lady Elizabeth, an angel of your stature could not possibly grant me the intercourse I most desire." Byron waggled his thick brown brows suggestively. "Not an angel of the first water, such as you."

Beneath those brows, the most outrageous eyes in all of London simmered with mock heat. Elizabeth pursed her lips and drew back her fan. He blinked, and those clear blue orbs widened in genuine alarm when he perceived her intent to strike him again. "Behave, you pesky little brat," Elizabeth balked. "Don't use those eyes on me. I'm immune."

"Are you? Really?" Byron lifted a brow in a wicked arch, and when Elizabeth's scowl deepened, he laughed with genuine amusement. "You're supposed to melt at my feet and simper, damn it."

"Ladies don't melt," Elizabeth said confidently, but she couldn't keep up the ruse. The corners of her mouth spread in an impish smile. "And gentlemen don't swear."

"I vow, Elizabeth, you sound as pedantic as Lady Jersey. You really should write a poem titled 'Ladies Don't.'"

"It's been done—and overdone, and satirized, as well." Elizabeth sighed. She leaned her chin on her hand, her elbow on the table, to look over Monk Lewis' bent shoulder, watching his pen fly across his sketchpad.

"What would be of greater interest is what ladies *do*." Byron resumed his previous sulk. "I don't want any fuss on my birthday, and well you know it, Elizabeth. Gads! Imagine how hostile I'd feel if people actually jumped at me from all directions, yelling, 'Surprise,' giving me apoplexy and propelling me to an early grave? I'd probably shoot someone, and then have to repent and regret it."

Abruptly he made a fist and slammed it forcefully on the table. "Confound it, Elizabeth! There's not a blessed thing to celebrate about being twenty. All twenty marks is another three hundred and sixty-five days of groveling, begging and explaining myself. I fear I'll never become my own free man...ever. Damn me, do you realize how much I envy MacGregor his age, his luck and his damned bloody daring? He managed to throw off all the traces and escape this bloody coil."

Elizabeth empathized with Byron's straits, but thought better of telling him so. He needed prodding out of his sulks, not comfort that pushed him deeper into his private mire. They were very much alike in that respect. "Byron, you've done it again. I don't want to talk about Evan!"

"It's solving nothing to ignore him."

"You should talk," Elizabeth replied.

"At the rate you're going, you probably won't last another year, old man," Monk quipped.

"Byron, let me put this in perspective for you. We're the same age, correct?" Elizabeth said.

"Almost," he said sulkily. "You'll get to twenty-one before me."

"An accident of birth, Byron, nothing more. Nothing miraculous will happen to me on April 19. Unlike you, I will not inherit any titles, properties or incomes of my own. I will remain exactly as I am, dependent upon my father's good graces."

"Yes, but Atholl treats you decently enough."

"Will you let me make my point?"

"Yes, sorry, go on then." Byron slouched back in the folding chair—sprawled, really—and schooled his face into a patronizing expression.

"You need more practice before you master the art of bored indifference. Go and sit with Brummell if you want to learn that."

Byron took her scolding seriously, and immediately changed his expressive face to show actual interest in what Elizabeth had to say. "Sorry, dear. Go on . . ."

"As I was saying," Elizabeth continued. "I will come of age, and nothing will change. My father is in perfectly good health, robust and active. Heavens, he's still a young man, at only fifty-three. Why, it's conceivable he could live for two score years more. Which, my lord, would put me—if I may take such liberties as to stretch your imagination forty years into the future—at sixty-one, still a chattel of my father. And then my care and upkeep will be passed into Tullie's hands, God forbid the day.

"So, you see, my dear and darling soon-to-be-peer-of-the-realm, I have no sympathy for you at having to face another full, long, agonizing twelve months held on a tight leash. We can all see how tightly bound that strangling cord is. Why, Lord Carlisle draws your leading strings so tight, you're choking right before my eyes."

Byron held up unblemished palms in surrender. "Elizabeth, I beg you, spare me your wrath, your wit, your deadly sarcasm. Leave the artistic license of an unbridled exaggeration to those who would wield that cleaver more gently, leaving less of my blood spilled on the floor at Almack's. My dear, what are you thinking?''

''God's truth, Byron, I am asking myself why I went to the trouble and bother of securing vouchers to get you both in here tonight. You don't deserve it.''

· Monk looked at her with a hurt expression on his face. ''Why, Lady Elizabeth, I'm crushed!''

''Well, you deserve it, Monk,'' Elizabeth relented. He grinned and went back to work, doubled over his sketch pad. Monk always made the best of every moment inside the hallowed walls of Almack's, producing satirical caricatures of the Ton at play to rival those of George Cruikshank. Byron's writings were beginning to gain some notice...but not much. Neither he nor Elizabeth were old enough for much of any respect to come their way. Monk, on the other hand, was well established in his art of writing.

Elizabeth sipped from her cup of spiced punch and leaned forward on her elbow, studying Monk's tablet. ''Why, that's Lady Melbourne. You've caught her perfectly.''

''But look who he's caught dancing with the old crone! Ha! MacGregor! Good job, Monk! Toss the meddlesome old fish back,'' Byron went on cruelly. ''She won't take me in her bed, when every woman her age is panting to have me. Bet she doesn't think twice about accepting Captain MacGregor.''

''You are such a brat!'' Elizabeth exclaimed. ''Why do you talk like that, saying the worst possible things you can think of?''

''Because it shocks you. You react to it. You don't expect me to be a gentleman, Elizabeth. What does it matter? The day will come when all these people here have to respect me for my writing. I'll do it, someday, I vow!''

"Oh, duck! Prepare to be fired upon!" Elizabeth laid her hand on her deep décolletage, as if to contain the wild, ec-static beating of her heart. "He's going to launch another quatrain and slay us where we stand. Grab your hankie, Monk. Be ready for tears at the proper clap of meter and the wrenching twist of a rhyme."

Byron's devilish mouth twitched. "Does your family know you're in such rare, sarcastic form tonight, Eliza-beth? Maybe I should tell Glenlyon you're riding rough-shod over schoolboys again."

"Ah, I made a point without having to draw physical blood." Elizabeth breathed in relief, but Byron's cruel wit stung just the same.

"Ah, here you are, Elizabeth, my pet. What are you do-ing, tucked completely out of sight?" Thomas Graham stepped out of the crush at the refreshment tables and rounded the potted plants—to present himself and his questions to his niece. "And who are these young men?"

"Oh, Uncle Thomas." Elizabeth lurched to her feet, caught out by the last member of her vast family she'd have expected to notice her absence. "Meet my friend, Monk Lewis. He's a novelist, sir, and this is George Gordon, Lord Byron. Gentlemen, my uncle, Thomas Graham."

"Ah, the young poet? Pleased to meet you, Byron." Thomas Graham extended his hand. "Elizabeth has men-tioned your gift many times."

Byron rose to his feet, his young face in a full flush as he extended his hand to the renowned Colonel Graham. He was the man of the hour in London. His testimony before Parliament Tuesday morning, urging all-out war against Napoleon, had made headlines in every paper. The ex-ploits of his courageous Grey Breeks had been touted from one end of the land to the other. "Colonel Graham, my pleasure, sir. I shouldn't think a man of your daring and dignity would be bothered with the drivel I turn out."

Graham cocked a brow, as if to ask whether the young man was being facetious. Of an age with his niece, Byron had the head and shoulders of a good-looking specimen of coming manhood, but clearly no suitability as a possible marriage partner for Elizabeth.

Lewis got even less attention. Graham knew an effete when he saw one. A harmless sort, caught up in his infantile sketches. Graham retained a firm hold upon Elizabeth's hand, speaking in a voice that brooked no argument. "I believe you owe me a dance, Elizabeth."

"If you insist. George, Monk, stay out of trouble." Elizabeth gave her friends a farewell nod, then accompanied her uncle onto the dance floor.

"There's a reel next. You don't appear to pay much attention to form at these gatherings, Elizabeth."

"Why should I? It's all old hat now, Uncle Thomas. This *is* my fourth season. I'm expected not to make a nuisance of myself, and to allow the younger ladies their time."

"Is that so? Since when is the most beautiful woman in the room to be ignored?"

"You're prejudiced."

"Hardly."

Thomas Graham raised Elizabeth's left hand just exactly so as he brought her into a forming cluster. He looked exceedingly handsome in formal dress. It had been quite a while since Elizabeth had seen him in silk stockings and polished dancing shoes, instead of his uniform jacket, gray breeches and Hessian boots. "You're looking rather dashing yourself, tonight. Any particular reason?"

"None that I would compromise by name." His dark brown eyes fairly shone with that deviltry that only a man with a firm commitment for the rest of the evening could emanate.

"Well, you're up to something. I can tell." Elizabeth looked around to see which widow had brazen eyes fastened on *her* favorite uncle. She didn't find any lady making cow eyes from the chairs. In fact, hardly anyone was seated at all.

She paused to see who the three other couples were that made up their set. The more crowded the dance floor became with sets, the harder it would be to remember which couples she started out dancing with. Elizabeth noticed that Uncle Thomas had ousted Glenlyon from the card room and paired him up with a very eligible heiress. Young Emily Percy was fluttering her lashes, securing Glenlyon's undivided attention. A first, indeed!

Amalia nodded regally on the arm of another uncle, Robert Greville. There was no end to the supply of Murray relatives available to escort Amalia about town until her betrothed, Lord Strathallen, returned from India. Another cousin, Caroline Mansfield, looked positively radiant at being captured by the hand of *Evan MacGregor!* Elizabeth abruptly gave Evan her back and faced her uncle. Thomas Graham's patently innocent expression didn't fool her for a minute. He knew exactly who each of their dance partners were!

Elizabeth shot a quick glance her sister's way and found Amalia chatting amiably across Uncle Robert's arm with Evan and Caro. Elizabeth's eyes narrowed at this evidence of a gross family conspiracy.

On the dais, Neil Gow tapped his foot three times, wagging his violin bow above his head to start the band. Music poured forth, filling the hall.

"Mind your step, Elizabeth." Uncle Thomas's graying whiskers twitched above his mouth. "If we stumble out here before one and all, I'll blame your two left feet, not mine."

The old devil! Elizabeth flashed him a sidelong look that contained plenty of heat. "If I had a sword, I'd run you through, sir. Egads! Look at this motley crew! Did you run a charge through the benches on the wall and empty every dowager onto the floor, Uncle Thomas? I see Aunts Nicky and Charlotte among the weaving lines and circles.''

"They like to dance, too." He smiled and made a pass, handing Elizabeth into the hands of his brother-in-law, Robert Greville.

"Good evening, Elizabeth. I had been told you were here this night, but this is the first sight of you I've had."

"Uncle Robert, sorry you've missed me, but yes, I'm here."

"And why are you hiding yourself? Louisa said she hasn't seen you dance once."

"I'm making up for that now. Give Aunt Louisa my love, will you? And the boys."

"*Certes,* but you would be remiss not to give her that yourself, dear."

Four steps, a twirl and another pass brought Elizabeth face-to-face with James. "Glenlyon, how's your luck holding at cards?"

"Rotten. I was run out of the room. I'm not staying one minute past a quarter to eleven, Elizabeth. I've asked Uncle Thomas to see you and Caroline home."

"Why am I not surprised?"

"Cheeky. Off you go. Put her in her place, MacGregor. You're the only one who ever could."

Their fingers touched, and Elizabeth felt cold dread wrap its strangling fist around her heart.

"Izzy." Evan's eyes blazed with heat, implying that he was well aware she'd been deliberately avoiding him. Horrified, she watched the curve of his mouth soften as his gaze dipped to her décolletage. Elizabeth wavered and lost a step. Her neckline hadn't felt nearly so revealing a few moments ago, when she fanned it for Byron's benefit.

"Evan," Elizabeth said through her teeth. She caught up with the steps, turning to have her left arm in sync with his right.

"The pass, now," he said.

"I know what to do," Elizabeth answered, fuming.

"Who's the whelp you're hiding behind the punch bowls?" Evan caught her wrist, twirling her under his raised arm and back again, linked arm over arm for a ronde.

"Lord Byron!" Elizabeth tilted her chin.

"That's the puppy? He's crippled, I hear, not to mention a little too wet behind the ears. I know his guardian, Carlisle. Speaking of which, hasn't the new term begun? What's the *chield* doing in London?"

"Are you trying to be offensive?"

"Are you?"

"What's that supposed to mean, sir?"

"You tell me, Elizabeth. What game are you playing here at Almack's?"

"I don't play any game at all, sir. I consider myself a sponsor of those artists worthy of endorsement and patronage. A noble aspiration, I am told by my elders."

"Is that so? Are you managing a salon, as well, my lady? First reformers and anarchists, now strays and the wretched, too. I am amazed by your generosity to all and sundry, when you lack the slightest compassion for those who should be the closest and dearest to you."

Stung by his heated complaint, Elizabeth said, "Goodbye, Evan. Drop dead."

Elizabeth turned a half circle and was caught in her Uncle Thomas's arms.

"Did I just hear you tell my captain to drop dead, young lady? What sort of ballroom intercourse is that?"

Elizabeth gasped, looking around herself frantically to see if other dancers had noticed her uncle's words. "Uncle Thomas, mind your tongue! We're in Almack's, not Bell's Wynd. You get called a rogue here, you don't get in again."

Uncle Thomas laughed heartily. "You think I care, pet? What's MacGregor done to put such a pleat in your brow? Not very fetching."

"Uncle Thomas, I don't want to be fetching."

"Yes, my dear, but you are, exceedingly so."

"This is pointless," Elizabeth sputtered as they crossed hands and spun in a full circle.

"How so? You look lovely in a temper, dear. Why, I am surprised every eligible man in the room isn't at your feet, offering you the moon."

"You haven't the foggiest idea what it feels like to prance about like a bit of beefsteak dangled before the starving minions, do you? It's demoralizing. I'm only here because Aunt Nicky insisted I come with her and Amalia."

"Tut-tut. Such sacrifice and dedication. Here we go again. Look smart. Robert, she's all primed up and loaded. Watch out."

It was endless, monotonous, predictable, and every fourth pass brought Elizabeth back into Evan's arms. Six times until the last ronde. The music changed tempo, and they remained together through the final march, the full length of the ballroom and back.

Elizabeth felt very much like telling her uncle what she thought of his manipulations, but that would be openly admitting to feeling something she didn't dare admit.

Instead, she and Evan danced as if they were out on icy-bound Larchmont Pond, for all the warmth that emanated between them in that last duet.

They simply came to a stop when the music ended. Elizabeth made a futile effort to remove her hands from his. He retained his hold. His eyes flashed a dangerous warning. "I will escort you to your chaperone, Lady Elizabeth."

Elizabeth responded in kind. "I'm long past the chaperone stage. You of all people should know that." Elizabeth had to tread carefully. "What with coming into my majority soon, and having so very many seasons under my belt, I have a somewhat different status from the run-of-the-mill debutante. So it isn't necessary that you return me to my *chaperone,* Mr. MacGregor."

Elizabeth gave him her back and started to walk away, but the words he growled, in a low and feral voice, stopped her dead in her tracks.

"It is so necessary, *Mrs. MacGregor*."

Chapter Six

"**D**on't call me that!" Elizabeth whirled around to come face-to-face with Evan. His eyes narrowed and blazed at her. She gulped, embarrassed, mortified that she had nearly shouted loud enough to attract the attention of others.

"Go on, Elizabeth," he taunted her softly. "Dare me to raise my voice ... to make a scene ... here. I will, woman."

Catching hold of her temper, she whispered desperately, "Not here in Almack's, Evan, please."

He smiled in terrible triumph, eyes gleaming with the power of the ax he wielded. "You haven't got the gist of this, have you, Izzy? All the trumps are in my hand. You'll damn well do as I say, or I'll expose your dark secret to everyone in this room."

"You wouldn't!" Elizabeth gasped, appalled. Would he?

"Oh, I dare," Evan replied. "It doesn't matter one iota to me what the *ton* thinks of you ... or of me."

Elizabeth couldn't risk testing his resolve. The merest hint of their scandalous runaway marriage would rock the *ton*. If society learned that the marriage had been completed and consummated five years ago, it would ruin Elizabeth for life.

She'd spent the past four seasons masquerading as a debutante, albeit a reserved and unwilling one. That made no difference. In that, time had worked against her. The *ton* would neither forgive nor soon forget the lie she had willfully lived if she were exposed. But she wasn't the only one who would be affected by scandal.

Her sins would ruin Tullibardine's chances to make a good marriage. And Glenlyon's. Scandalbroths didn't just smear the one family member involved in all the brouhaha. They hit every family member, splattering them all with shame, duplicity and disgrace.

A scandal of the magnitude of a duke's daughter eloping and then hiding the fact for almost six years could travel so far via word of mouth that it might very well jeopardize Amalia's long-standing engagement with Lord Strathallen.

Evan knew that. So he smiled like a cat that has just swallowed a mouse whole as he leisurely took Elizabeth's arm and escorted her to a collection of deserted chairs on the other side of the crowded hall.

At a safe distance from any curious listeners, Evan pressed a glass of punch into Elizabeth's hand, urging her to sit by saying, "We can be private here for the moment."

At least as private as any couple could be in a ballroom filled with nearly two hundred people, Elizabeth thought as she sat and took a deep, calming breath.

"All right. Say what's on your mind." She told herself to remain poised and in control, but Evan's very nearness did much to distract her from that purpose.

"I think you know what I have on my mind," he said evenly.

Elizabeth swore not to acknowledge the fire she saw smoldering in his eyes. No man alive should be allowed to give a woman such a longing look with just his eyes. He hadn't been this intimidating at eighteen, had he? But hadn't she become putty in his knowing hands from just such a look? Heated, arousing and sensual.

"You presume much, sir." Elizabeth took the high road, daring to correct him. It was her only defense. "Let us be frank. Until Saturday last, I never thought to set eyes upon you again."

"Did you, then?" He lowered his eyelids, deliberately, giving her a hooded appraisal that set the skin at the nape of her neck tingling.

"I did," Elizabeth said in self-defense.

"May I take that to mean you hoped my military office would ensure you became a young and eligible widow, hmmm?"

"You may take it to mean anything that you like. The point is, sir, we have each made separate lives over the passing time." There, Elizabeth nodded, satisfied that she had spoken bluntly and precisely to the point. "I prefer that we continue to do exactly as we have done."

Evan watched as Elizabeth clenched the cut crystal with taut fingers. He thought the fragile balloon was in danger of shattering, and he would have liked nothing better than to have the opportunity to bring her delicate fingers to his mouth and kiss them, one by one.

When he said nothing in response, she lifted the cup, trying desperately to moisten lips, tongue and conspicuously dry throat, before whispering hoarsely, "Evan, you must see that we can't jump up and announce our transgression to one and all. That would cause the worst damage of all. Too much time has gone by."

"Afraid of scandal, are you, Elizabeth?"

He watched her like a voracious hawk, and she felt as defenseless as a hatchling exposed on the floor of the forest. "I won't lie about it. You know I am."

Evan took a deep breath and turned his face aside for a moment. Her words stung. They had the effect of making him feel less a man...unworthy of her. He needed no reminder that she could marry into blood royal, and most likely had been raised to expect no less. He released the tightness in his chest, couching his words with care. "Then pray, do tell me what solution you offer, Lady Elizabeth?''

"Solution?" Elizabeth blinked. He was asking her for a solution. She couldn't believe her ears. Did she have a solution? Yes, she did, but not in her wildest dreams did she believe he would accept it. "Would it be so terrible to leave things the way they are? Secret? No one knows of it, Evan. No one. Only you and I and the man who married us."

"Paisley." Evan said the lowlander's name, which she couldn't bring herself to utter publicly.

Understanding dawned at the same time he realized what she was really saying. She would refuse to be his wife today, exactly as she had refused to continue to be so, one hour after the marriage was consummated. She had been hysterical then, more child than woman. He had been consumed by the greatest guilt he'd ever known in his life for having hurt her physically, truly hurt and injured her. All because of his clumsy, adolescent eagerness to join their bodies once and for all.

He had made her cry. It had never been in his physical composition to be able to withstand Elizabeth's tears. She shed none now in her aura of icy aloofness, pure and pristine and beyond his mortal touch.

Evan stared at the dancers performing the ages-old and graceful minuet. "I won't belabor the point, Elizabeth. You heard your brother state that I have come into my titles."

Elizabeth lifted a cold shoulder. "Does that signify?"

It was very hard for him not to shout. "You know good and well what it signifies. I am expected to marry, no later than the anniversary of my father's death, June the tenth. There is this minor complication of entitlements under sovereign law, you understand, the need for heirs to ensure the succession. All so that the remaining Gregarach keep the land that rightly belongs to all of them."

She cast her eyes down to the crystal cup in her hands. Robbie's face swam before her eyes. She almost lost control. He had a son, a legal son, unknown, unloved and unrecognized.

Elizabeth felt a new tremor shake her. How would Evan react if he learned of that son? And what damage would her having kept Robbie's existence a secret so long do to whatever regard Evan still held for her? And for what man was one son enough?

No, no, she couldn't risk that. She could not go through that kind of pain again—neither the begetting of another child, nor the delivery thereof. The agony of Robbie's birth remained vivid in her head. More so did the horrible disappointment and physical pain of the begetting.

"I can't, Evan," Elizabeth whispered. "I can't be that wife. You know I can't. Find someone else, do as you please."

Evan wanted to snatch her off her seat and shake her until she rattled. She was already that wife! He threw a checkrein on his surging temper, forcing himself to remain calm and in control, the way he'd learned to be in the army.

His words came out cold, seething with disdain. "Let me see if I understand you correctly, my lady. You suggest I do as I please. Shall I bring my mistresses forward and flaunt them before your very eyes? Are you suggesting I beat the bushes from Orkney to Land's End, searching out any bastards I may have fathered and left lying along the way, in order to elevate them to the Lyon Registry?"

Elizabeth jerked as if she'd been struck. She swallowed. She made herself look at his inscrutable eyes, eyes gone so black as to be opaque and unfathomable. He could be the cruelest, most black-hearted man alive when angered, she knew that from their mutual past. Pushed, she could match him, stroke for stroke, insult for insult, pain for pain. "If that suits you, yes."

"Well, it doesn't suit me!" he snapped.

Elizabeth turned and set the cup on the empty seat beside her, and rose to her feet. "I believe this discussion is finished, sir."

"The hell it is." Evan cast his own cup aside and rose to catch her arm, staying her retreat. "First off, Elizabeth, I have neither mistress nor bastards to claim."

His grip on her elbow tightened, drawing her head closer to his mouth. "Second, there is a legal matter at issue here. This isn't the time or the place to make an announcement, any more than it is the proper place to finish this discussion. We will conclude it in private shortly."

His manner was chillingly correct. She cautiously tucked her fingers into the proffered bend of his elbow. "Be warned, Lady Elizabeth. I loom ever dangerous in your future. There is no going back where we are concerned. I am at that point in my life where I need a wife. I shall have one, whether that suits your pleasure or not."

That he had agreed not to go public this very moment registered true relief within Elizabeth, but she needed more assurance. "Then you agree we may each continue as we have done for the time being? Separate and equal? Each doing as we so please?"

He growled with feral ferocity. "Provided I don't catch you hiding behind the potted plants with a pair of mincing fops again."

"George and Monk are not mincing fops." Elizabeth stared at the hard profile he presented her. "Good heavens, you are jealous!"

"Call it that if it suits you, madame." Evan steered her around the dancers.

No fewer than a dozen Murrays watched their approach with avid curiosity, none more interested than Aunt Nicky.

"Ah, so your captain did find her, Thomas. Good." Aunt Nicky snapped a black lace fan shut against her palm. Her sharp eyes moved from Thomas Graham to Evan and Elizabeth as they came into line. "Good. I'm famished.

Mansfield, are you feeding the lot of us this night, or not? The last minuet is nearly over. We may leave.''

Another infamous Murray relative responded agreeably to Aunt Nicky's questions—Lord Mansfield, Nicky's nephew. He was the same Mansfield who lived next door to the Atholl Murrays on Grosvenor, and he was also Lady Caroline's father.

"Uncle Thomas, you're taking the girls, right?"

"Sorry, I can't, Glenlyon. I've a tête-à-tête of my own. Evan promised me he'd see Elizabeth and Amalia home."

"That's kind of you, Uncle Thomas, but unnecessary," Elizabeth said promptly, turning to her uncle to speak privately with him. "I have other plans, a birthday party following the closing of Almack's. And I do have to wait for Caroline. She's dancing the last set with Edgar Stirling."

"Oh? Is she?" Aunt Nicky raised her quizzing glass and peered around the men's shoulders until she spied Lady Caroline finishing up a competent minuet in the company of the robust Edgar Stirling. "Why, Caroline did not ask me if she should dance with him. I'm not sure I approve."

"Oh, bother, Nicky. This is Almack's, not Bell's Wynd. You've no say here about who's to dance with whom," Aunt Charlotte told her. "They make a nice couple, they do. He's tall and dark, and she's not a mite bigger than an elf. And that red hair. Humph! Very nice."

"I don't approve," Aunt Nicky said authoritatively. "Elizabeth, come here. Let me look at you. Where have you been all evening? You only danced once. I kept count."

"Aunt Nicky, you know somebody has to see to the little things. I had my hands full making introductions for Caroline. Smoothing her way, as always."

Nicky's hand fastened on to Elizabeth's forearm with the tenacity of a peregrine's talons. "You will walk me to the door, Elizabeth. My bones are stiffening."

"You didn't do too much, did you?" Elizabeth asked with concern, genuinely glad to escape Evan's grip.

"Dancing a reel, Aunt Nicky! What's to become of you? Will you need hot packs and water bottles to ease the aches out of your joints tonight?"

Auld Nicky's eyes twinkled as she clung heavily to Elizabeth's arm. "Will you stay up with me changing the water, then? Ha! Not likely. You won't be home before sunrise, I vow."

"If you need me, Aunt Nicky, you know I'll come home with you right now."

"No! No, I've got Constance to take care of me. Keyes will get me up the blasted stairs. He always manages. I'm not going to bed until Mansfield feeds us all, though. He owes us a supper, the old tightwad."

"You're incorrigible, Aunt Nicky," Elizabeth scolded.

"I know." They'd descended to the outer doors. A phalanx of carriages were lined up on the street, one right after the other. Nicky surprised the devil out of her greatniece when she raised her head and called out clearly, "Evan MacGregor, come here to me."

Nicky's power was such that she had only to speak and her wish was granted. Evan MacGregor presented himself before her, bowing formally from the waist, taking hold of her hand and touching it to his lips.

Elizabeth tugged her mouth to one side, trying to remember whether Aunt Nicky was connected by actual blood to the MacGregors. Consanguinity didn't matter. Nicola Murray was Aunt Nicky to three generations of Edinburgh society, and blood had nothing to do with that. No one was more adored or more revered, or held more power in her frail hands.

"Yes, Aunt Nicky. How may I assist you?"

"Ha! You rogue, now you come and offer your kind regards! But where were your noble intentions earlier this evening, when you planned to end your night dancing with my niece? Did you seek my permission then?"

Evan raised his head, showing innocent eyes in a guileless face, seemingly shocked by Nicky's charge. "Aunt Nicky, I fear you are mistaken. I did seek your approval before I took Caroline out for the reel."

"I'm not talking about Caroline, MacGregor. It's Elizabeth you have never asked my permission for."

"I stand guilty as charged." Evan straightened, sharp and handsome in black-and-white evening wear that gave testament to his still mourning his sire's passing. "You have me at your mercy, dear lady."

Nicky's frail fingers tightened on Elizabeth's arm. "Yes, I do, you rogue. Do you think I have forgotten what you did five years ago? Well, I haven't, sir. You owe me an apology."

"For my behavior five years ago, or for my behavior tonight?" Evan asked, with an unrepentant grin.

"Tonight will do. We'll deal with what happened five years ago when you return to Bell's Wynd this season. I shall expect you there, MacGregor, in all your regalia. No excuses. You will apologize to all of Edinburgh for taking Lady Elizabeth Murray onto the dance floor without my permission. Is that clear?"

"Yes, Aunt Nicky." Evan bowed again over her hand. "I offer you my deepest apologies now, if I offended you this evening, my lady. You are correct. I should have spoken to you about dancing with Elizabeth before the reel started. I would have, but I noticed that you had granted Melbourne your hand for the dance. How could I possibly interrupt?"

"No tugging of a forelock from a MacGregor, ever, is it?" Aunt Nicky snorted. "Be that as it may, I shall expect the exact same of you at precisely eight of the clock on the eighth of June at Bell's Wynd in Edinburgh. Be there!"

"By your command." Evan again touched the back of Nicky's hand to his lips, and then he straightened. Nicky audaciously patted his smoothly shaved cheek.

"You always were a charming scamp when you put your mind to playing by the rules, Evan. I like the way you've grown up. Young Thomas has made a man of you."

"Indeed he has, Aunt Nicky."

"Is that Mansfield's arms on that first carriage?"

"Why, yes, it is." Evan stooped so that Nicky wouldn't have to shout. More and more people were surging out the doors to leave, despite the continued strains of Neil Gow's fine music.

"Then get me up in that high contraption of his. I want to have a word with him in private. Elizabeth, I will see you shortly." The old dragon finally released her hold upon Elizabeth's arm.

"As you wish, Aunt Nicky." As Evan bent to gather the frail lady in his arms, he said warningly to Elizabeth, "Stay right where you are."

"She will if she knows what's good for her," Nicky declared imperiously. She dropped one shawl-and-lace-covered arm around Evan's dark evening coat. Elizabeth held her breath, watching as he moved Aunt Nicky inside the tall carriage. Anyone might have thought he was an old hand at assisting the little old lady here and there, though he wasn't.

While Nicky thanked him for his assistance and gave him her wise counsel, Elizabeth slipped back inside the crush departing Almack's and found Caroline had finished her dance with Mr. Sterling.

Elizabeth's thoughts dwelled momentarily on the incident Nicky had brought to mind in her scold. It had been the most wonderful dance of Elizabeth's life . . . a rare moment of delight she kept carefully put away . . . a jeweled memory to last a lifetime. During that long-ago dance in his arms, Elizabeth had first realized she loved Evan MacGregor more than she loved life itself.

Aunt Nicky would never have let them have that stolen moment or make that treasure happen. Because at the time,

Elizabeth had been a mere babe of ten-and-five, and not allowed on the dance floor at Bell's Wynd. She had had to sit with the aunts and her grandmother and learn vicariously all there was to know about dancing and courtship and so on.

Elizabeth cleared her head of the entangling cobwebs of sweet, fond memories. She had friends to gather, and a surprise birthday party to hostess.

She could no more allow Evan MacGregor to interfere with the life she had made for herself in this world than she could allow young Byron to turn twenty in complete anonymity. The trick would be getting from Almack's to the White Lion without Evan learning of her immediate plans.

Tomorrow, after she'd sorted out the tangles in her mind, there would be time enough to deal suitably with Evan's demands.

Elizabeth forced herself to think only of the present. Of course, Byron didn't realize the depth of his charm, but Elizabeth could see his promise. She suspected it would not be long before Byron was the one setting the town on fire. He just needed more time to season properly.

Monk Lewis had gathered up the strays of their crowd and pulled them loosely together. "Caroline and I have to get out of here without being noticed," Elizabeth told him.

"Who are we ducking?"

"Murray relatives too numerous to mention," Elizabeth lied. "You know them all on sight. But for God's sake, if Evan MacGregor asks if you've seen me, tell him you haven't laid eyes on me all night, I beg you."

"Why?" Monk asked, puzzled.

"Because Glenlyon gave him the duty of seeing me safely home. I have no intention of going straight home. We've a party to host."

"Ah, I see," Monk grinned obligingly. "Leave it all to me, *chérie.*"

Elizabeth disappeared behind the hood of a black satin-and-sable cloak. They deliberately jostled their way out in the center of the most awful crush, treading on other people's toes, ducking immediately into the fog to run for carriages parked at the far end of the street.

Elizabeth was out of breath as she collapsed on the cushions and pressed her hand against her racing heart to quiet it. Caroline gasped and threw back her hood, exclaiming, "Elizabeth, are we going to get into trouble for this? I can't displease Father."

"For God's sake, cover your head. Someone might see your hair and recognize you." Elizabeth snatched Caroline's hood back over her telltale red hair, then pulled down the shades.

London's reliable fog was doing its part, obliterating everything but the lampposts from ten feet away. But as she peeked at the mists, Elizabeth wasn't satisfied. Evan knew his way in and around the fog like a panther cat born to prowl in it. She would never be safe.

"Elizabeth, you didn't answer my question," Caroline said in an agitated voice. This was her first season, and she really hadn't gotten the gist of having confidence yet.

Elizabeth sat back and firmly patted her cousin's trembling hand. "No, no. Don't worry. You're perfectly fine, Caro. This will be a respectable party. Don't forget, I've invited John Murray, our kinsman who's the publisher on Little Britain Street, to look over Byron's work. I'm hoping we can interest him. Lady Stanhope is coming, of course. Nothing untoward will happen. I just had to hide because I didn't want Evan MacGregor to escort us to the Lion."

"But won't we get in terrible trouble for dumping him?"

"Not you, dear. Don't worry."

"Elizabeth, you don't think that I would allow you to take the blame for something we both have done?"

"That's what I'm telling you. It won't be a problem. If anyone gets angry, it will be Evan."

"I don't think I would want the MacGregor to be angry with me at all, Elizabeth."

"No, of course not. I'll explain it all to him tomorrow. But tonight I have other plans."

"Elizabeth...the thing is...do we have permission to do this? Several young men asked if they could pay a call tomorrow morning. I wouldn't want to do anything that would ruin my chances. It's early days, and I'm scared to put a foot wrong."

"My! Gentlemen to call tomorrow! That was quick work, dear." Elizabeth hugged Caroline to boost her courage. "See, you're already on your way to being a success. I told you. There's nothing to it."

"Elizabeth, I just don't understand one thing. You do this all so flawlessly."

"Practice, my dear."

"Yes, but...you're beautiful, too. Why hasn't someone asked to marry you?"

"Ha!" Elizabeth laughed. "I was remiss in not introducing you to Lady Jersey. Once you meet that dragon, you'll understand. Will it suffice to say that no one would be caught dead proposing to the *duckling*, Caro? It just isn't done."

"Who's the duckling?"

Again Elizabeth laughed. "Why, I am, dearest."

Caroline's fair brows lifted very high. "How dare anyone call you that! Why, Elizabeth, you are one of the *ton's* most notable ladies. I cannot believe anyone would refer to you by that old fairy tale."

"Now, Jane, it's an old tale. When I first came out, I deliberately made myself as frumpy and ugly as possible. I don't want a husband, you see. It's nothing to get up about. Now, enough nonsense. Monk, are you out there? Who has charge of Byron? We mustn't lose him."

Monk Lewis ducked inside the carriage, whipping off his hat and brandishing his cane. "It worked splendidly, Elizabeth. Murray, the publisher, buttonholed Byron on the steps and asked the poor fool about his writing. The boy melted into his hands like butter left in the sun too long. They just got in his carriage and sped away to the Lion."

Monk rapped his cane onto the roof. "Where to, guvnor?" his coachman called.

"The White Lion in Covent Garden. And I've a guinea for you if you get us there ahead of the crush."

"Hold on to your seat!" Elizabeth warned Caroline.

They were off in a burst of speed. It was a wild, breathless ride for several blocks, before the driver brought the horses down to a steady clip through impeded streets. The crush thickened as they neared Covent Garden.

Excited, Elizabeth ran up the steps to the inn, shaking off her cloak. She had so much to do to see that all was perfect and right. She dipped her finger in the fluted icing of the devil's food cake—what other kind could be given to a rascal like George? It was heavenly. The linens were perfect, the spread of food was enormous, and in minutes the inn was packed elbow to elbow with people who had come to wish the young poet a happy birthday.

Elizabeth left Caroline in the care of Lady Hester Stanhope, a paragon of the first water, and played hostess for the duration, seeing that the party went exactly as it should.

Byron was knocked off his pins. It took him a while to thread his way to Elizabeth. They were the same height, so it was nothing for him to drape his arm around her shoulder and look deeply in her eyes.

"You did it, you little minx. I didn't believe you. That's what I get for thinking, eh, what?" He slapped the heel of his hand against his forehead. "Someday I'll write that poem for you, you know. But every time I try to write about a paragon, every word I know fails me."

"Well, don't you dare write about me. I have no intention of being an ode to your vanity."

"That's a good line. I might borrow it." He laughed and hoisted a magnum of champagne, shouting, "Friends, dear and wonderful friends! You are all here because of one person. Not I, poor ungrateful fool that I am. I propose a toast! To Elizabeth! To the lady of the hour! *La belle dame avec merci!* Elizabeth Murray!"

He tilted the bottle to his lips and drank until the wine foamed into his points and cravat.

Elizabeth caught hold of the dangerously heavy magnum before George broke any of her front teeth trying to pour the blasted wine down her. She did get a lot of it on her dress, but miraculously not one drop in her mouth.

"I forget, you don't imbibe like the rest of us miscreants." Byron kissed her with a heady, wine-flavored mouth.

"Happy birthday, my friend." Elizabeth hugged him. "Now, dearest, before this bacchanal disintegrates, I must get my young and innocent charge out of here and safely back home. Good luck with John Murray. Don't get so tippled you can't talk business, George. Keep Monk around, if you think to start talking about terms. He's familiar with the ropes in publishing from your side of the pen."

"Yes, Mother Murray." George dutifully kissed her cheek, then turned serious long enough to stare sincerely into Elizabeth's pale eyes and smile a genuine heartfelt note of thanks. "You're really a good sort, Elizabeth. You want to make all of us poor sinners over into something better, reform us, polish us up, get us to stop drinking and go to church each Sunday. Maybe you ought to make use of that clandestine marriage. Go back to your husband and have some children of your own. Expend all that mothering instinct on something good and pure, like innocent young children. You'll be a good mother, I vow."

"George, you're drunk. Do you realize what you just said could very well be interpreted as a proposal of marriage?" Elizabeth deliberately turned his words back on him, praying he'd forget the true gist of what he'd said.

"Good heavens, no!" he declared, appalled.

Elizabeth touched his cheek and kissed him on the mouth. "Good night, Georgie. Happy birthday to you. Say your prayers when you go to bed." Elizabeth found Caroline safe in the circle of literary aficionados where she'd left her. Lady Stanhope had promised to take them home in her carriage. They left the party before it could disintegrate into mayhem. Caroline was much relieved, but she still stepped down from Lady Stanhope's carriage with high spots of color enlivening her cheeks. "That was the best party, yet! Thank you so much, Lady Hester."

"Yes, it was nice, Caroline. And a pleasure to make your acquaintance. Elizabeth, good night."

"Good night, Hester, and thank you once again. I am in your debt. Don't hesitate to ask, if you should ever need return of the favor."

"No trouble at all, my dear. I've nothing much to do with myself since my uncle William died. I fear I can't think of anything to keep my spirits up, though these little parties do relieve the ennui for a while. Do stop by whenever you can, dear. I want to discuss my travel plans with you."

"Of course. I will be most happy to do that, but I fear you will find that I am woefully lacking in all the wondrous knowledge of far-off sights the Cathcart ladies possess. I've never been anywhere beyond England and Scotland."

"Nonetheless, I shall like to hear your opinions. You do know all of the most-traveled women of our time. Why, my dear, you're related to every one of them."

Elizabeth pressed the renowned hostess's extended hand with her own gloved fingers. "Thank you, again. Good night, Lady Stanhope."

She turned toward her house, picking the sticky, wine-soaked lace away from her breasts and throat. It was a most uncomfortable feeling, to be sure. She opened her reticule, looking for her key, as the carriage drew away from the walk, then turned back to wave goodbye and thank Lady Stanhope again.

"Hurry, Elizabeth, it's cold!" Caroline was shivering on the top step.

Elizabeth found the key, and it slipped right out of her hand, bouncing onto the cobblestones. She bent in the shadow of Lady Stanhope's departing carriage and grasped the key—but then a black-gloved hand swooped down and pinned her fingers to the cold stones.

Chapter Seven

"Jesus, Mary and Joseph, save us!" Elizabeth yelped with fright, jerked up her chin, and found herself nose-to-nose with Evan MacGregor.

"Not a chance, Lady Elizabeth," Evan said ominously.

Elizabeth straightened as he did, her hand and her key firmly caught in his crushing gloved paw. "You just scared me half to death, Evan MacGregor!"

"Did I? Good. You deserve it. Thank you very much for giving me the most sporting of evenings, Elizabeth. Three hours of absolute terror, wondering where you'd got off to!"

"You're angry." Elizabeth tried to back away, but he wouldn't let go of her hand.

"Right you are. You can count yourself lucky I haven't summoned every runner on Bow Street out to scour this city. Don't you ever do anything like that to me again!"

Elizabeth made the mistake of looking in his eyes. The worry and anger she saw in them almost did her in. She quickly snatched her gaze away, tucked in her chin and apologized. "You're right, of course. I'm sorry. It was very foolish of me to alarm you in such a way. I'm sure I will hear a scolding from Uncle Thomas, as well. I'm sorry to have inconvenienced you, Evan. May I go, now? Caroline's getting cold."

"Wonderful," he said with a sneer, giving no indication of accepting her apology. "Caroline is cold. She's been waiting for you two minutes. I've been shivering on this street for better than an hour. How cold do you think I am? Or do you even care?"

"Yes, of course I care. I didn't mean to put you out, Evan." Elizabeth sought to placate his temper. It didn't do to rile a MacGregor, ever. "I thought you would conclude I'd found my own way home. You did agree that we should both continue with our lives as they are. How was I to know you would stand a vigil waiting for me?"

"Common courtesy should have told you to wait for me to return from settling Aunt Nicky. Add to that the fact that I gave you a direct order to wait for me, which you intentionally and willfully disobeyed. That makes your actions unconscionable."

Elizabeth stood her ground. "You gave your order without consulting with me to discover if I had other plans, sir. Don't think you can stand here and badger me. You haven't the right. Now kindly step aside. It's late, and this is not the time to continue our earlier discussion."

His nostrils flared, and his chin lifted hawkishly. Not one word that she'd said had registered. "You reek of wine."

"Granted, yes, I do. Someone spilled quite a lot of champagne on me. Please, give me back my key, Evan," Elizabeth entreated in a soft voice. "Come back tomorrow. I'll talk to you then."

"Elizabeth, should I ring the bell?" Caroline asked from the top step, reminding them both that they were not alone.

"No!" Elizabeth and Evan said in one voice. They were in agreement upon one thing—secrecy. He shook his head, grimacing, coming to some separate conclusion. "I'm coming in. We're not standing out here on the frozen street to discuss what I've got on my mind."

"You can't come in." Elizabeth's composure had slipped a notch. The manse was dark, save for the lights left burning for those returning in the wee hours. "Everyone's to sleep. It isn't proper. We'll have to finish our discussion at another time."

"She isn't asleep." Evan pointed at Caroline. "You can keep her at your side to protect your virtue...if that's what you are worried about compromising. But we—*you and I*—are going to talk, now, tonight!"

"Evan, you're hurting my hand."

"Only because you won't let go of this damned key." He twisted the piece of brass out of her fingers, caught her elbow and yanked her around, frog-marching her up the steps. "Stop being arbitrary, Izzy. I don't like it, and it's too bloody cold to argue out here."

"Is there a problem?" Caroline asked cautiously.

"No!" Evan told her. He put the key in the lock and opened the door.

Caroline looked nervously from Elizabeth to Evan. She was pale as a ghost; he was brutally furious. Caroline swallowed her fear and spoke up. "Captain, I pray you forgive us making you stand in the cold awaiting our return. I didn't mean to to cause you such a grave inconvenience. I assure you that it was never our intention to put you to such trouble."

"I'm not without resources, Lady Caroline," Evan answered shortly, managing to treat Caroline Mansfield politely, despite his increasing ire. "Not that I don't appreciate your concern . . . belated as it may be."

He closed the door firmly, turned, and removed Elizabeth's cloak from her shoulders, tossing it on the hat stand. "You may go to bed, Caroline. Pleasant dreams."

"But you just said I was to stay and be Elizabeth's chaperone," the younger girl countered innocently.

Evan cast her a forbidding look that expressed how unnecessary Caroline's continued presence was. "Elizabeth is a big girl, not an innocent chit experiencing her first night on the town. She doesn't need a chaperon. Good night, Lady Caroline.''

He spoke with such finality that Caroline knew better than to cross him. But this was most irregular behavior, especially for her older, experienced cousin. Caroline's eyes darted from Elizabeth to Evan and back once more. She held out against the ire she saw on the MacGregor's face only long enough to whisper, ''Elizabeth?''

''You'd best go, Caro. Be very quiet, please.''

''Yes...yes, of course.'' Caroline dropped a hasty curtsy as she gathered her skirts. ''Good night, sir.''

''Please, leave us,'' Evan responded testily.

His gloved fingers tightened on Elizabeth's wine-stained shoulders. Neither of them moved as Caroline retreated up the circular stairs of the rotunda. Elizabeth took a deep breath to calm herself, her ears straining until Caroline's footsteps ceased on the third floor, after the whisper-soft closing of a bedroom door.

No other sound echoed down the open rotunda to the entry foyer. The town house was hushed, save for the sonorous ticking of the clock in the first vestibule.

As she released her breath, dreadful anticipation melted Elizabeth's spine against Evan's chest. His gloves abraded her bare flesh as he removed his hands from her shoulders. He brought them around in front of her, right hand to left, stripping away one glove, slowly, inside out, then the next. Elizabeth's spine tightened. Every muscle from her belly to her throat contracted, hard and tense.

The gloves disappeared, and cold hands cupped her breasts, sending raw shivers cascading along every tautly strung cord in her body. He drew her backward, flush against him, cold, cold, icy hands burning hot against her wet and sticky lace-covered breasts.

''Do you have any idea how many times I have longed to do this?'' His fingers tightened. Evan's head dropped, and warm lips skittered across Elizabeth's bare shoulder. She felt his teeth touch her skin, and ripples of heat shot into her core, shaking the very foundation of her resolve.

"Evan, don't, please!" Elizabeth jerked her head up straight, staring directly ahead into the encompassing foyer. Her voice sounded anguished, even to her own ears. "You said you wanted to talk."

"Talk?" he murmured huskily against the sensitive flesh of her cold ear. "We can talk in bed. You can't claim to be a child any longer, Izzy."

His breath fanned her throat, sweeping inside the dampness at her cleavage. His fingers slipped into the gap of her neckline, cupping her breasts, cold skin to warm flesh.

"Evan." Elizabeth groaned, closing her eyes. "What we did was wrong."

"Perhaps." The seductive timbre of his voice stabbed inside her heart, bringing more aches into play. "A highly correctable wrong at our age today. You're my wife, Elizabeth. I have the right to touch you."

Elizabeth tried desperately to find the willpower to break away, managing only to spin around and confront him face-to-face. Of necessity, her voice had to be low. "No, you don't. It wasn't a real marriage. You have to live together as man and wife. We didn't. It was never valid, really."

"You're wrong, Elizabeth. It was valid. I've made inquiries. Our vows will hold up in court, even so far as the House of Lords."

"But we could have it annulled," Elizabeth pleaded earnestly. "I know that could be done. I've made careful inquiries, too."

"Apparently not the right ones. Annulments only happen when the marriage isn't consummated. We consummated our marriage. It's as valid as the blood you shed, lady."

"Evan, don't be crude."

"Crude?" Evan exhaled in exasperation. "Stop chasing shadows, Izzy. You know the truth. Admit it. And you know what else, Elizabeth? I'll be damned to hell and back before I'll stand idly by watching you put a pair of horns on me with some other man. Boy poet or no.''

"He's a friend," Elizabeth whispered. "You're mad to think there is anything else between Byron and me."

"Am I? A friend who kisses you and pours champagne all over you?" Evan's fingers tightened on her upper arms, dragging her against his hard, unyielding body. "While your husband is left out in the cold—to die hungering for a taste from your lips? No, Elizabeth. You've forgotten one vital flaw of mine. I don't share my toys. Never could as a child. Never will as a man."

He jerked her upward and his lips caught hers, taking what was his and his alone to take. A fine, unchained rage coursed through his veins; he'd been five long and agonizing years without his woman.

A whole lifetime had passed since he'd held her pliant and willing in his arms. He kissed her lips hard, forcing them to open to his demands. If it was war Elizabeth Murray MacGregor wanted, he was the man to give it to her.

Elizabeth pressed desperate fingers against Evan's chin and his smooth, chilled cheeks. His lips were cold where they touched her flesh, but his tongue felt like a heated rod plunging inside her.

Terrified, Elizabeth balled her hands into fists and began to hit him. She wrenched her mouth free. "Stop it! You're hurting me!"

"So what if I am?" Evan caught her arms and pulled her up against him again. "Damn it, Elizabeth, by all that is right and just, I should be able to take you upstairs to any bed in this house and do with you what I may."

"No, you can't." Elizabeth pressed both hands against the pure white folds of his cravat and his impeccable points. Black and white, starkly contrasted, soft and hard. Evan was everything that was opposites to her. "There isn't a vacant room in the house. Caroline and I have to share the same bed. Evan, please, don't shame me this way. I beg you."

"Shame you! Is that it? I'm still not good enough? You're still ashamed of me because I haven't got a string of English titles after my name?"

"No, no. That's not it at all. It's what we did. Please, now isn't the time. Tomorrow, we could meet someplace. Talk this over. Could we do that?"

"Talk?" His brow cocked. "Like we just did at Almack's? That solved a world of my inner questions and doubts. I'll come back here at ten in the morning, and we'll go into your father's study and tell him the truth—"

"No!" Elizabeth's fingers went up to Evan's mouth to silence him.

"Still the little girl, frightened of your father's wrath, Izzy? It's high time you place more value on my good graces than your father's."

"No. We can't do that!" She sought any excuse, desperate to prevent any scandal on her family. "I don't want to hurt anyone, Evan. Think of the talk...the scandal... Not what it would do to us...to others...to Amalia and Tullie... Even James would suffer. Please, I'll meet you...anyplace you say...in private, if you like."

"Clarenden, at whatever room I rent? So long as there's a bed in it? Hell's bells, Izzy, let's save our coins. I've got a perfectly good bed at my barracks, and if you want private, I can clear the whole compound with one shout."

"Evan, don't be so cruel. Don't mock me. Just name your place and time. I'll be there."

He quieted, but the calm that glazed him was a thin veneer indeed. In the pits of his eyes, Elizabeth saw the raging fire of a warrior's anger. He frightened her.

"The east gate at Green Park, noon, tomorrow. We'll ride together. Come accompanied by no more than one groom, and leave Caroline at home. Is that clear enough?"

It was a godsend, if it would get him out of the house now. Elizabeth nodded. "Yes. It's clear. I'll be there at noon."

Evan nodded. He did not loosen his hold, but it was no longer painful. Elizabeth swallowed.

"I want another kiss, Izzy. A proper one. You know the kind I'm talking about, soft and sweet and filled with your heat. I had a cold wait, lady. Warm me."

She knew he was cold. She felt it through the thinness of her dress. He wasn't asking for all that much. "Will you go afterward?" Elizabeth asked. "One kiss, no more?"

His chin nudged the curls clustered on her brow. "Aye, I'll go, Izzy. With an ache in my heart embracing the emptiness that's hung over my soul for five long years. Grant me one moment of relief."

Elizabeth slid her arms around his neck, cradling his head with her hands, drawing his head down to hers, offering all that he asked. Her lips and her mouth as a welcome place for him to enter. To taste in all the ways he'd taught her to taste, all those long years ago.

With the soft compression of his mouth against hers, five years melted away into a single yesterday. She felt the same throbbing heat rise inside her, melting her defenses, turning common sense into blind passion.

Evan cupped her cheeks between icy hands, kissing her hard and passionately, until she couldn't draw a single steady breath. Her legs weakened. Her breasts swelled heavier against the heated hardness of his chest. The slickness that came between a woman's legs when she was deeply aroused seeped from her flesh, torturing her. God help her, had she no will of her own against such blatant wantonness?

She pulled away, only to be caught and pulled back. "One more kiss, Izzy. Then I'll go. One."

"No, go. Evan, we've made too much noise. I know it."

"Damn you, Elizabeth. Come and kiss me again. You can't send me out of here with so little of a taste of you lingering on my mouth. Can't you understand I'm a man who's been starved for five long and lonely years? I need you, Elizabeth. Come to me."

She didn't know what made her so malleable to Evan's command. Why she could not, nor ever had been able to, steel her will against his. Her arms swept around his shoulders, drawn to embrace him like iron fillings pulled to a lodestone. All thought of resisting him fled from her mind.

This time, when he caught her up against his hard body, molding his lips to hers, he twisted her around to pull her into the vestibule that served as a waiting room for visiting servants.

The warm glow from the gaslights on the porch flooded in through the uncurtained windows, turning the small, cozy alcove into a lover's bower.

There, a long cushioned bench stretched the length of the interior wall. Evan tipped Elizabeth down on that bench before she so much as blinked her eyes. He kissed her with blinding passion, obliterating reality with a haze of shared sensuality. Common sense did not return until she felt his cold hand glide over silk and pass the lacy garters holding up her stockings.

His lips silenced her sputtering protests and kept them at bay when he lifted his head to explain. "I'm not going to hurt you, Elizabeth. I just want to touch you. It's all right."

"No, don't. You can't. You mustn't. Evan!"

"Whisht." His lips pressed down on hers, silencing her protest. While she turned pliant again in his arms, Evan's fingers stole upward to her soft, sweet crevice of womanhood. He had to know...now...tonight...if she felt anything for him at all.

He lived the agony and torture of the damned, loving a woman he could never have. Wanting and desiring a woman who would never give her body to him freely. He had to know the truth. Did she want him in any way? Did her body prepare for him? It hadn't, the one time he made her his wife.

She began to shake and tremble and fight him the moment she understood his intent. To touch her there, in that damp and precious spot. How he'd ached to kiss her there, taste her, smell and feel her.

His long fingers made contact with shivering flesh, but her legs pressed tightly against one another and barred his intimate touch. Evan patiently soothed her, waiting for her body to relax. He raked his fingers through her curls and splayed them across the soft curve of her belly. His thumb grazed the cleft between her thighs. He kissed her deeply, toying with her sensitive tongue. He bit her chin and dropped his mouth to the pulse throbbing at the base of her throat.

She shuddered and arched against him. "That's my girl," Evan murmured, tugging her gown off her shoulder and baring her breast to the golden glow of the gaslight cascading in through the windows. She tensed against the hand that lay perfectly still at the juncture of her thighs.

"Izzy, I'm going to kiss your breast and take it in my mouth. I did that before, remember? Open your eyes, sweeting. Look at me. Watch me. Look at me, Izzy. That's it, watch my mouth. I want you to look at me and feel what I am doing to you. I'm not hurting you. You are to tell me the minute I do anything that hurts you."

Evan slowly lowered his head and worshiped her breast with his mouth. He kissed and suckled her; biting her gently to tease and arouse her to the utmost limit, toying with the small, sweet orb deep inside his mouth. She tasted madly of champagne. He didn't let the knowledge that it had been poured upon her by another man distract him from his own purpose. Her breast hardened under his ardent ministrations.

"Do you want me, Izzy? Remember this? You liked for me to kiss you here. Come, darling, give me a little room. Open your legs for me. Elizabeth, I want to touch you here, where my hand is. Open for me. I'm your husband. I have the right to touch you and give you pleasure here. That's it, that's my girl. More. There."

She yielded him enough room to cup her. The answer he sought glazed his fingertips. She was deliciously wet, primed by her own love juices, as ready for him as he was for her. And he was so hard he could have died for the pain of holding back, when he surely must be ready to burst. He wanted to shout his discovery to the world. She would feel no pain when he entered her. She wanted him. Her body wanted his!

A surge of jubilation racketed through his mind, body and soul. He wanted to make love to her so intensely that they woke every soul in the city. All reason and caution left him. He wanted more of her, all of her, everything they had to share with one another now, this very moment. He had his answer now. The only answer that mattered.

"Evan." Elizabeth grabbed hold of his ears, pulling on them so hard she must surely be hurting him. "Evan! Stop! Stop it! You're going too fast! Stop!"

He froze. Aware of himself, and her... and where they were. Evan took a deep, calming breath into his raw and aching chest. She was on the verge of tears, shaking like the last leaf on a winter-blown tree, trembling, frightened... frightened of his desire... his passion. Curse him, he'd done it again!

"Oh, Elizabeth, I'm sorry." He gripped her face between his hands, laying tender, gentle kisses on her eyes, her brows, her cheeks. "Not tonight, not here, my love, but soon."

He staggered to his feet, pulling her up from the bench, holding her, seeing the trembling of her lips and the quivring of her chin. "Poor little Elizabeth, I've frightened ou again, haven't I? God help me, but I'm a fool."

Abruptly his hands dropped from her shoulders. She tared at the buttons of his waistcoat—no higher—and ugged the rumpled, soiled gown onto her narrow shoulders.

Evan's hands clenched and unclenched at his sides. He vanted to touch her, soothe her, end her fear of him forver, but every time he came this close to her, he lost all ense of control.

The clock in the rotunda sounded the hour. Four long nd sonorous bells rang out, and then the house became till and quiet again, save for their erratic breathing.

"Evan, you have to go." Her voice was harsh, shaky, and he wouldn't look him in his eyes.

"I know." He straightened his shoulders, tugging at his vening jacket, running a hand across the wealth of tarched linen at his throat. He couldn't think of anything o say, because everything he might say would further reeal his desperate need for her. And he remembered the nen he'd seen her casually embrace, kiss and touch this night. Doubts and jealousies plagued him. What if she'd een unfaithful in his absence?

He took a deep breath to calm himself. He couldn't lose is control with Elizabeth, ever. It cost him too much. He'd lready risked too much, laying her down across that ench. What if they had got caught? Glenlyon had yet to come home.

"What are you thinking?" Elizabeth asked fearfully. She elt like a bug, caught and fixed on a pin, unable to get way from him.

"I can't talk about it. Not now." He choked out the vords, holding back all accusations, keeping a tight rein on is fears.

If she only knew how she looked to him, with her dazed yes, her swollen lips, and her rigidly erect nipples thrust-

ing at him through the lace of her thin gown. He touched
her hair, which was safe. He wouldn't maul her just because he touched her hair. She'd cut it brutally. It was styled
into a fashionable bob, a fashion he'd seen recently in Paris
but not until now in England.

He laid his fingers on her mouth and stroked it, parting
her lips. "Someone's bound to ask you who you kissed this
night, my lady. What will you tell them?"

"That I ran into a very hard door in the middle of the
night." Elizabeth touched her fingertips to his, drawing her
face away, leaving just their fingers touching. She caught
the scent of herself staining him.

"That's you," he said, reading her mind. "I'll sleep with
you on my fingers tonight. You cannot know how happy
that will make me. Go to bed, Izzy. Take all of your clothes
off, and when you are in bed, touch yourself where I've
touched you. Remember me, Elizabeth. Remember that
I'm your husband, and my wanting of you is as natural as
breathing, eating, sighing and laughing. Go, now, before
forget myself again."

"I can't. I have to lock the door," Elizabeth said.

"I'll lock it when I leave." He cupped her face and pulled
her close, until their breath mingled. He kissed her warm
flushed cheeks and then let her go, standing aside so that
she could leave him. "Go to bed, now. Elizabeth. I'll let
myself out when I'm certain you are in bed."

"But, Evan, my key. I have to have my key. You can't
keep it."

"I am keeping it, Elizabeth. No one has the right to lock
a door between us. I have the right to keep this key. You are
my wife."

Elizabeth thrust her fingers through her hair, tugging it
away from her brow and face. Was he mad, or was she?
"Evan, it isn't fair to the servants to make them stay up a

night, waiting for me to come home and be let in because I haven't my own key."

"How long do you think we'll continue this charade? If you go out another night, Elizabeth, I will be with you to unlock the door with this key."

He was intractable, she could see that. A knot of anger ignited in her chest and smoldered there. "We are going to have to talk this out," Elizabeth said, with a determined, shuddering breath. "Nothing's changed. I don't want to be married."

"But you are," Evan said resolutely. He took hold of her elbow, ushering her out of the alcove, to the bottom step. "Don't press me any further, Izzy. Go to bed."

Elizabeth turned to the staircase. Her knees sagged weakly. Her feet felt so heavy she could barely lift them to the next riser.

Her mind told her to go, to leave him and never look back. Her body ached to return to his arms. Damn, damn, damn! She stopped at each landing, afraid that someone would come bursting out and find her all wanton and ragged, disheveled from Evan's handling, stinking of Byron's wine.

In her bedroom, she went behind the Chinese screen and stripped away her ruined gown, stockings and shift. She wore little underclothing—a sign of the times and the styles. Gone were the petticoats and hoops of her childhood.

Now a stylish woman fit the classical ideal of beauty, lithe and supple; her clothing followed the natural contours of the feminine body. Gone, too, was the protection that hoops and corsets rendered against a man's intimate touch.

The gown she'd worn to Almack's this night was hardly sturdier than the night rail she was about to put on.

With shaking hands, Elizabeth poured cold water into her basin and washed, ridding her body of the perfumes of

the crush, the wine, and Evan's sensuous touch. Shivering
and chilled, she put on her nightgown and crawled into bed.

"That you, Izzy?" Caroline murmured from the other
side of the bed.

"Yes." Elizabeth closed her eyes. She'd forgotten her
cousin was to stay the night. "Caroline, don't . . ."

"Don't what?"

"Don't call me by that awful name. It's hideous."

Caroline pulled the coverlets down from her face and
turned her head to look at Elizabeth. "Did he kiss you?"

"Yes."

"I thought that's what he wanted." Caroline burrowed
into her pillows and was silent.

Elizabeth slid out of bed and crept into Robbie's room.
Her son had thrown his covers off, but his room was warm
from the radiant heat of a well-tended hearth behind a
sturdy safety screen. Elizabeth knelt beside his little bed,
tucking the covers around his sturdy body.

Fast asleep, he was so beautiful her heart ached. She
smoothed a curl off his brow and bent to kiss his soft cheek.
In the flickering firelight, she studied his face, seeking the
truth. Robbie had so much Murray in him, the freckles
glazing his nose and the incredibly dark auburn hair that
fooled everyone into thinking he was her father's by-blow.

It was too soon to tell whose chin he had acquired, but
she did not think that angularity of his cheekbone came
from anywhere except the MacGregor. Robbie's eyes were
Evan's eyes, and his mouth held Evan's wide smile.

Would Evan see past the freckled surface and red hair?
Elizabeth already realized Robbie's hair was turning darker
with each passing year. Hers had darkened to chestnut by
age eight, but Robbie's was turning sooner. Would those
precious curls darken to brown, or turn as black as Evan's?

How much time did she have before the truth was evident to everyone who had eyes?

There were no answers to any of Elizabeth's questions. She brought her hands together, folding them, and bowed her head. "My God," she whispered, "what can I possibly do to make this right?"

Chapter Eight

Evan leaned against the newel post at the base of the
stairway, gazing up at the dome rising above the uppermost floor. Flickering sconces lit the dome against night's
darkness. It was painted sky blue and filled with golden
stars. Heaven was where his angel slept. He ached and
burned. He closed his eyes and laid his cheek on the carved
banister.

The clock sounded the half hour. His eyes played tricks,
and he imagined Elizabeth peering down at him from a
lofty railing high above.

If she asked, he would run upstairs and join her. She did
not ask. She would not ask. Would never ask. If he was to
make a wife of his woman, he would have to start over. Izzy
would never have the courage to admit what they'd done.

He knew that now.

Which meant he must pay court to her, and win the
duke's approval.

The duke. Evan lifted his chin, glaring into the night
darkness of a house that teemed with servants, family, retainers, hangers-on and near relations at all hours of the
day. All were there, ultimately, to serve and please one
man—the duke of Atholl.

For the first time since he'd entered the town house, Evan
felt like an intruder. Had Lord Murray traveled with a sin-

gle one of his hounds, Evan would already have been found out.

His head bent, and he pressed Elizabeth's key between his fingers, as if he could leave its impression permanently on his flesh. He didn't measure up. And Evan knew that, try as he might for all his days, he would never measure up to the standards, the stature or the consequence of His Grace.

He might as well steal away from the great man's house like a thief in the night. He was no better than any common thief. Hell, he was worse. He was an outlawed MacGregor, the first born to the name who had been allowed to publicly use it in two centuries.

What title did he lay claim to? The lowest to be found, a baronetcy, a pitiful half-step above a landed squire in the eyes of the aristocracy. Elizabeth outranked him, and always would. He had no claim to vast wealth or land holdings that would sway the duke's mind in his favor as a fitting husband for the man's youngest daughter.

The duke of Atholl would laugh in Evan's face, did he press his suit, asking for Elizabeth's hand in marriage. He'd never give his consent. They had both known that in the beginning. Nothing had changed that truth in five years.

Elizabeth was as lost to him today as she had been for all these past years.

Angered, Evan turned to the door and put his hand on the brass knob. It turned against his grip and opened. Colonel Graham halted on the threshold, recognizing his adjutant standing rigid before him.

Evan blinked, in shock.

"Captain MacGregor." Colonel Graham's eyes narrowed. His hawklike eyes made a smooth reconnoiter of the empty foyer, noting Evan's disheveled hair, the house key in his upthrusting hand and the shock registering on the young man's face. Telltale color instantly stained his cheeks. "It's rather late, isn't it?"

Evan reacted out of habit, coming to attention immediately. "Yes, sir. I was on my way out, Colonel."

"So I see," Thomas Graham said succinctly, with a glance to the standing clock in the alcove, as he crossed the doorsill and removed his silk scarf and gloves, looking for the butler, Keyes, who should have been there, letting the young man out the door. "Where's Elizabeth?"

"Gone to bed, sir." Evan raked his fingers through his hair, and silently prayed his greatcoat concealed the no-longer-polished manner of his appearance. The caustic sweep of Graham's eyes told him that nothing had escaped the Colonel's inspection. "She forgot her key. Would you give it to her in the morning, Colonel?"

Graham took the brass key in hand and studied it a moment longer than necessary. "That's a little peculiar, wouldn't you say, MacGregor? I've never known Elizabeth to surrender her house key."

"It was in my coat pocket, sir. I'll be off now. Good night, sir." Evan bolted over the doorsill, aware that he was rushing out the door, leaving unanswered questions in his wake. Halfway down the steps, he saw a hackney stopping at the curb. Glenlyon had returned.

They passed one another on the sidewalk. James Murray hailed the cabby, telling the man to wait, astutely realizing Evan was on his way back to his barracks. He grinned sloppily as he clapped Evan on the shoulder.

"What luck! You won't have a long, cold walk tonight, MacGregor. Leave the door open, Uncle Thomas, I'll lock up directly." James's breath frosted in the cold air, laced with liquor. "How was Byron's birthday party? What did you think of his fast crowd? Can't say I much care for Elizabeth running with that hellfire-bound cub, but they've been friends since they came out of the nursery. There's always the chance Byron might come up to snuff."

"Didn't make the party, Glenlyon. I mustn't keep the cab waiting. Dreadful cold night. What say we save the chat for another day?"

Evan deliberately stepped around Elizabeth's brother and strode resolutely to the waiting cab. He didn't need Glenlyon's glib conversation tonight. Evan was well familiar with Byron. They'd all grown up together. That didn't mean he wanted his young wife associating with the young rake. As he climbed into the cab, he paused to look back and saw Colonel Graham still at the door. Evan snapped a crisp salute to his commander and disappeared into the cab, fuming.

So that's why Elizabeth reeked of wine, he thought darkly.

"Where to, sir?" the cabbie asked.

"Battersea Barracks," Evan answered. As the wheels began to turn, he added, "As far from Grosvenor as you can get me."

Chapter Nine

"Am I late?" Elizabeth gasped as she ran into the dining room, red faced and breathless from a dead run down three flights of stairs.

Lord Atholl did not lift his gaze from the face of his pocket watch until she reached her empty place at the table and came to what could only be called parade rest. He closed his watch with an audible snap and tucked it into his pocket as Elizabeth mumbled apologies to the remainder of the family. "Elizabeth."

"Yes, Papa?" She peered around Tullibardine's shoulder and Aunt Charlotte's expansive chest to make brief eye contact with her father, then did her best to allay the worry that knotted Robbie's brow by giving the boy a soothing look.

"Three minutes is excessive. Five inexcusable. Seven grossly exceeds the bonds of common courtesy, but eleven marks a record. This family has never stood waiting at their places eleven whole minutes before morning prayers in the near fifty years that I have been coming to the table. I will not entertain any excuses. You may ply the dowager and the aunts with your exaggerations at their leisure after this meal has ended. I trust they will see you suitably chastised. This will not happen again."

"Yes, Papa. You're correct. It won't happen again," Elizabeth said, with another apologetic sweep around the crowded table. James raised his hand and slid a finger across his cravat in a cutting motion, leering at her wickedly.

Oblivious of Glenlyon's gesture, the duke said, "See that it doesn't. Reverend Baird, you may proceed."

"Will everyone bow their heads, please . . . ?"

They all did. Elizabeth kept her folded hands very close to her chin and mouth to keep all responses she might have made to Glenlyon firmly at bay. Next to her, Tullie blew out of the side of his mouth . . . at her. No, at her décolletage! She hit him hard and hissed, "Stop that!"

He grabbed his wounded shoulder, whispering, "Thank you, Jesus."

Elizabeth closed her eyes in embarrassment.

Reverend Baird closed his rambling blessing with an amen. A dozen Murrays chorused, "Amen."

At the foot of the table, the dowager commanded, "Sit down and eat!"

In the chaos that followed, Uncle Thomas picked up the slack when Tullie's teasing stopped. "So, pet, what's your excuse?"

"Yes, I want to hear this." Tullie leaned forward. "Might work for me someday, though I can say with reasonable authority that being late for breakfast isn't my long suit."

"I haven't got an excuse," Elizabeth answered as she unfolded her napkin and spread it on her lap, silently damning Evan MacGregor to an eternity in hell.

"No excuse?" Thomas Graham barked, just loud enough to set Elizabeth on pins and needles. "That sort of reasoning would never hold up in the army, my dear. Can't you think up an interesting lie, such as 'I just got in'?"

"No, Uncle Thomas, I was home numerous hours ago. I overslept. That's all the excuse I can claim."

"Gads! I'm destroyed. Well, don't keep us waiting to-morrow for no reason at all. I hate to see good food get cold. You have no idea what it's like to eat on the march, Elizabeth. Makes one appreciate the comforts of home." Uncle Thomas nodded to the footman offering him gravy to put on his biscuits. He took his fork and knife in hand, then put down the fork and dug in his waistcoat pocket. "I believe this is yours, Elizabeth."

Elizabeth's eyes locked on to the shiny brass key in her uncle's hand. It could have been a scorpion, for the horror that showed on her face. She choked on her own tongue, and jerked up one hand to snatch the key from him. She quickly hid it below the drape of the tablecloth.

"Where did you get it?" Elizabeth asked.

Thomas Graham thought his niece's reaction was a touch on the strange side. Her face flooded with color, and her eyes darted one way and then the other, practically bouncing, as though she'd had a load of grapeshot dumped inside her head.

"Evan handed it to me on his way out the door this morning. He requested I put it back into your hands."

"Oh." Elizabeth took a quiet breath to calm her racing heart. "Thank you."

"You look shocked."

"Oh, well, yes. I thought I'd misplaced it."

"In Evan's pocket?" Uncle Thomas smiled knowingly. "Understandable. MacGregor does have the most interesting pockets."

"Really? How deep would you say they are, Elizabeth?" Tullie drawled suggestively, waggling his thick brows at Uncle Thomas over her head.

"Oh, yes, very." Elizabeth nodded her head and kept nodding, oblivious of Tullie's innuendo and the footmen stopping at her left side with platters of hot food.

Thomas Graham cleared his throat. "I do admit it caused me to wonder how you got inside the house, if your key was lost in Evan's pocket."

"How did I get in the house?" Elizabeth swallowed, but her head kept bobbing. "I was already in the house. He left. Yes, that's right. He left."

"I see." Thomas flashed a scowl at Tullibardine before he turned his attention to his food. "What time was that?" he asked idly.

"Two...three...no...four— No, three. That's all."

"That's nice." Thomas looked back at Elizabeth's profile. Her attention was now focused on the smallest person at the table, Robbie. The duke had been asking the boy questions, which he stoutly refused to answer with more than a shrug of his wee shoulders.

Elizabeth's high color receded. She was now as pale and wan as the fish on her plate. Thomas deliberately cleared his throat again. "Elizabeth, are you actually going to eat all of that?"

Tullie burst out laughing.

Elizabeth looked down to find her plate overflowing with prawns, kippers, ham and fried eggs. Appalled, she turned to Tullie.

"Don't give me that look, puss. You asked for it all." He sliced the ham on his own plate with somewhat impaired proficiency. "You just kept nodding and nodding to every footman who came by. You can't blame the servants when you don't know your own mind. Though I would like to know what MacGregor's secret is. There's a few ladies I wouldn't mind seeing as dazed as you are this morning."

"Your Grace," Elizabeth said with heat.

"Yes, puss?"

"Shut up!" Elizabeth picked up the plate and turned around, beckoning Mr. Keyes with her eyes.

"A problem, ma'am?" Keyes took the plate in his white-gloved hand. A kipper flopped onto Elizabeth's trailing hem. She snatched it up and jammed it in Tullie's coat pocket.

"There! We're even. Now act your age. You start this foolishness, but the disgrace of it always lands in my lap. Uncle Thomas, will you ask the marquess to show me a modicum of respect, please?"

"Of course, Elizabeth." Thomas Graham looked over his niece's head at his nephew.

"Oh, for God's sake, Elizabeth, get that grim scowl off your face. So you were late to table! The world did not end when His Grace closed his pocket watch." Tullie dangled the fish by its tail, tilted his head and let it drop into his open mouth. He chewed with noisy relish and winked at Graham, totally unrepentant about tormenting his sister.

"Elizabeth, the marquess does have a point." Uncle Thomas resumed eating. These petty squabbles had gone on for years, and would continue until time ended for those two. Graham saw no point in interfering, knowing the bantering actually spoke of a great deal of affection between brother and sister.

Keyes returned though the swinging door, bringing Elizabeth a clean plate with scrambled eggs and toast on it. As he placed it before her, Elizabeth felt that every pointed look from around the table she received was deserved.

At any moment the vultures would start picking her apart. Why did she have gray circles under her eyes? Why were her lips so swollen, and the delicate skin around them raw and sensitive? She pressed her lips together and tried to concentrate on the food, only the food. Her throat constricted. She couldn't swallow anything.

Elizabeth put her fork down and waited until Uncle Thomas finished his conversation with the hawk-eyed Amalia and the dowager.

"Did you have a question, Elizabeth?" Uncle Thomas asked.

She took a deep breath, leaned close and asked softly, "Did Evan say anything when he gave you my key?"

"Such as?" Thomas Graham sat back in his chair, pretending to look completely baffled. At the crestfallen look in his niece's eyes, he made a better effort to probe deeper into her benign question. "Oh, perhaps about when he might see you again? Is that what you mean, pet?"

"Yes...that is, I...ah...we're to ride in Green Park at noon, today...Evan and I."

"Ah, I see." Thomas considered his next words most carefully, allowing for what he knew Elizabeth's daily routine would be. "He said nothing to me about having an engagement this noon. I must tell you, he is scheduled to be the duty officer in my absence at the field today. Sorry, pet. You know how it is in the army—duty first."

"Oh." Elizabeth touched her napkin to her mouth and worried again if it was as apparent to everyone else as it was to her that she'd been kissed well last night.

"I tell you what. As soon as I am able to return to the field, I will inform MacGregor to make an accounting. It's the least I can do, Elizabeth." Thomas said. "But I wouldn't expect to see Evan before evening, at the earliest. A bit late for a ride in the park."

"Don't go to any trouble, Uncle Thomas. I'll see Evan by and by. It wasn't at all important."

Thomas Graham knew a bald-faced lie when he heard one. Elizabeth was like a skiff hitting a flat calm. All the wind dropped out of her sails. Her shoulders drooped and seemed to shrink. A little frown pleated her brow as she returned her attention to her food. But she didn't eat enough to keep a bird alive. She just picked.

Thomas scowled at that. Now that he thought about it, Evan had acted peculiar, as well, this morning, not normal for him. MacGregor had seemed to leave the duke's house in the foulest, most cockeyed, most unexplainable mood Thomas Graham had ever witnessed in his adjutant.

There was definitely something more to this!

Elizabeth on the other hand, was like soft clay this morning...impressionable and malleable. Each time she put down her fork, Thomas told her to eat something else, this or that, whatever was left on her plate or could be added to her plate from the sideboard. Elizabeth really needed someone to manage her, take charge and give her life some order. She reminded him very much of his late wife, Mary.

"If you'd like, I'll ride with you in Green Park after breakfast," he offered. "I have some time before your father and I must report to the floor of the House of Lords."

"Oh, no, that wouldn't be right. I know Father has things he wants to discuss with you before today's bout of testimony. I'll be fine, Uncle Thomas. I'll sit with Aunt Nicky. She'll be very fussy, today. Too much excitement last night. And I always read to Robbie before he takes his nap."

"I'd say you need one, too," he said knowingly.

"Perhaps," Elizabeth agreed.

Breakfast ended with another Murray ritual, the dispensing of the daily post. When her father called her name, Elizabeth excused herself and hurried to the head of the table to receive her letters. She was happy to be done with the morning's interrogation.

The ladies held forth in the morning room, where they always gathered after breakfast. Elizabeth sat at her usual place, next to the windows facing the park. Robbie was settled on the floor at her feet, playing with an array of farm animals while the ladies visited.

Elizabeth smiled at the healthy stack of letters before her. As a child, she'd learned to anticipate news from faraway friends and relatives, and she'd taken to writing letters at an early age. It was the only thing that had sustained her in those long and lonely times that followed Evan's going off to Eton. Where they had been fast and ardent playmates, they became copious and frequent correspondents.

Elizabeth was, at twenty, a creature of long-standing habits. She sorted her letters into three categories, personal, social and business, ranking each according to importance, from the least to the greatest. The best were always saved for last, to savor, enjoy and anticipate as much as to linger unhurriedly over.

She habitually scanned all her mail for the one signature she most dreaded and, ultimately, most longed to see.

Evan's crisp monogram had not graced an envelope addressed to Elizabeth Murray since that tragic spring day in 1802, which had ruined both their lives. She saw shortly that today's mail was no different from the day before in that regard.

The elder aunts received the most letters and invitations. So much that sorting them required the assistance of each lady present. They grouped together at the table where the aunts played piquet later in the day, and the girls filled in as secretaries, jotting notes, marking on the dowager's large calendar what must be attended, when a gift should be sent, and so on.

At ten, callers began to arrive. Caroline's beaux lined up like handsome marionettes and marched in, stiff and proper, to be introduced. Elizabeth returned to her chair near the window while this was going on, her personal letters as yet unopened, because she read and answered those in private.

She watched Caroline greet her callers in the way Amalia had for Elizabeth for the past four seasons—rising to be introduced, smiling, helping the conversation along if it lagged, or if Caroline was caught unawares by some remark or lost track of a name. Elizabeth made note of details to tell Caroline when they could speak privately.

Mostly Elizabeth kept in the background, keeping Robbie amused and quiet. She felt most peculiar when some of

Caroline's young men somehow dismissed her completely. The maiden aunt—the family spinster—there and accepted, but no longer of any social consequence.

Not that she wanted to steal any of young Caroline's thunder or felt any jealousy toward the lovely young girl, fresh from the country and so very new on the London scene. No, Elizabeth saw this as another affirmation of the choices she'd made in her life.

She passively listened as Aunt Nicky roundly scolded Edgar Stirling, with renewed respect and understanding for his boldness in dancing the last dance with Caroline the night before.

It wasn't so terrible to be a paragon, Elizabeth thought. Nicky was. Given time, Elizabeth hoped to step into her great-aunt's shoes. Perhaps not here in London, but definitely in Edinburgh, where society was smaller and closer-knit.

That was the only direction her life could take. Marriage to someone of her station was completely out of the question, and had been since the day she'd eloped to Gretna Green. Elizabeth's index finger impatiently tapped a staccato on her personal letters. What to do about Evan?

There could not be a repeat of last night. No, that sort of thing must be nipped in the bud, stopped before it plunged the both of them over a precipice, into the most sordid sort of disfavor. Oh, how she wished she had someone she could truly confide her troubles to, someone to help her sort out the best course to take.

She was close to her father, but she could not tell him of her relationship to Evan. Aunt Nicky was wise in so many ways, a treasure of information and lore about all the people she had known in her long life, how they had lived and loved, survived monumental scandals, but Elizabeth could not share the burden of her troubles with Nicky, either. Nicola Murray had never stooped to loving unwisely or foolishly or below her station. She was a paragon, unblemished, pure and correct.

The only person she could ever talk to of this was Evan himself.

Perhaps the next time they came face-to-face with one another, she could explain how important it was to her that they behave in a manner that was above reproach. They both had their reputations to consider.

They had to come to some informal agreement—as soon as Evan was available. Elizabeth wondered how to arrange a private meeting. That could be tricky. They certainly could not talk freely in her father's house. Judging by the fireworks that had risen in their two meetings last night, the conversation would be spirited, to say the least, with both of them so certain of their opinions.

Elizabeth sighed, unhappy because there would be no resolution to her worries by this afternoon.

Morning calls did not take long. They were over and done with almost as quickly as they had begun. The rules of the *ton* required that the gentlemen pay their respects and depart. Fifteen minutes was the longest any dared to stay.

At precisely eleven, Keyes served tea, and when that was done and Elizabeth excused, she had time to herself until supper at seven o'clock. Tonight they were dining at home, *en famille,* which meant one dressed formally, but no guests outside of the family and their retainers would be at the table.

As she exited the morning room with Robbie's small hand firmly clasped in hers, Elizabeth's tense shoulders relaxed with the advent of free time. The first she had been granted since rising at seven.

Only she hadn't risen at seven this morning. She couldn't. She had lain in bed, staring at the ceiling dry-eyed, in abject terror, until half past six, trying to solve her impossible dilemma. Sometime before seven, she had dropped off to sleep.

As she hurried upstairs, she realized she had nothing to do. No ride with Evan. No talk. No solutions. No relief from the great burden of fear his presence in London caused her.

Distracted, Elizabeth absently said goodbye to Robbie at the door of the schoolroom, leaving him in the capable hands of his tutor, Mr. Griggs, for the hour and a half that remained of the morning, before lunch was served at one.

In her own room, she put her unopened mail on her writing desk and picked up her ledger to check her finances. Byron's party had severely dented her account. Shopping was out of the question for the balance of this quarter. The most she could afford would be to go to Lane's Bookstore on Little Britain Street and use her subscription at the circulating library.

That, she decided, would be better than brooding. So, after making arrangements, Elizabeth set out walking uptown, with Caroline Mansfield, and a footman accompanying them.

A number of acquaintances were scattered about the aisles of Lane's Bookstore when Elizabeth and Caroline arrived. Elizabeth had a short conversation with her good friend Monk Lewis, who was on his way out the door. After he left, she'd no sooner turned around to look over the shelves than she heard Lady Sarah Jersey's outspoken drawl greeting Caroline.

Lady Jersey's dark tresses were pinned elegantly on the crown of her head, emphasizing the swanlike length of her throat. Caroline's butternut-and-cream walking dress clashed horribly with Sarah's exquisite magenta ensemble. In comparison, Elizabeth's russet velvet seemed as out of place as last year's withered leaves.

"Well, well, well, Lady Elizabeth, so you've come out of your cocoon at last, and joined the land of the living," Lady Jersey said by way of greeting. "I haven't forgiven you for not attending my ball, you naughty girl. Don't think I shall extend another invitation, when you go to such lengths to avoid me."

"I'm sure I did nothing of the kind," Elizabeth responded, trying to place in her mind what affair she'd been invited to and missed, since she deliberately missed so many. "Did we fail to send a regret in time to alter the seating at your table?"

Lady Jersey turned around, drawing up beside Elizabeth. She reached out a black-gloved hand and patted Elizabeth's wrist. "Not to worry, dear. As always, Amalia made acceptable excuses for you. Though why a little snow kept you home, I'll never know. How have you been? You do look pale. Are you sure you should be out in this weather?"

"I'm fine," Elizabeth said, wondering why that seemed to be the most frequent answer she made to everyone. She hadn't been ill, but everyone seemed to think she had. That was most peculiar. "You are looking splendid as always, Lady Jersey. I'd kill to know the name of your modiste."

"Would you?" Lady Jersey laughed in delight. "Ah, but I'd never tell. I keep the lady locked in the attic, and I don't share her with anyone."

"That's probably true." Elizabeth quirked a smile. As wealthy as Sarah Westmorland had come into her marriage, she might have a whole army of modistes tucked in her attic. Elizabeth found it hard to believe she and Sarah were the same age, the differences between them were so vast, making Lady Jersey seem ever so much older and mature.

"Your little cousin seems to be doing quite well during the *petite saison*. I've just told Amalia that it would be a shame to rob Caroline of the fun of the grand season, and I have volunteered to sponsor her, myself."

"You did?" Elizabeth said, taken aback.

"Don't looked so shocked, darling," Lady Jersey responded candidly. "I'm not an ogre . . . well, I'm not when I like someone. Our Miss Mansfield is a true original, full of bounce and spontaneity. She reminds me of myself at that age—no, at sixteen. By the time I was her age, I was a well-married, over-the-anvil matron. Which reminds me, Elizabeth, what do you make of that *on-dit* in last week's paper? Have you any idea which duke's daughter ran off and eloped in 1802?"

"What?" Elizabeth lurched sideways, tripping over her own ankle as she turned around to stare at Sarah.

Lady Jersey stared right back with an outrageous black feather dipping across her pretty brow. "Oh, don't give me that scandalized look. I won't buy it, not when I made my bones with the *ton* doing just exactly that—eloping. That's the third time this year that rumor's been put into print, and I want to know who it is. Did you know that the betting at White's has reached proportional limits? And that your sister, the prim and ever-correct Amalia Murray is the out-and-out favorite in all the betting, ten to one?"

"Amalia?" Elizabeth gasped.

Lady Jersey leaned close to whisper, "Yes. I wouldn't lie to you about that. Jersey tells me everything that goes on at White's. So far I haven't convinced the cad to let me dress up as a page and accompany him there. The man can be a dreadful bore when he puts his mind to it. That's the trouble with you nobles. You've no sense of fun."

"That's ridiculous." Elizabeth stuck to the point, repudiating the rumor, at least as far as her sister was concerned. "Anyone with half a grain of sense ought to know better. Amalia was born levelheaded. She'd never do any such thing. Besides, she's engaged, has been for ages."

"Ah, but that's the rub. Strathallen's been in India forever and a day, hasn't he? Why, we wouldn't know him from Adam. Naturally, I wouldn't know him at all. I've never met the man. But those who give credence to this rumor point out that it is most peculiar that the duke of Atholl permits his second-eldest daughter to wait six years to marry. Why, he married Charlotte off to Menzies before you left the nursery. Everyone knows Charlotte wasn't widowed a year before he passed her on to Drummond. You know how people talk, dear.''

"Well, they shouldn't," Elizabeth snapped. "They should do something useful with their energies, like nurse the infirm or open a school for the children of their tenants. All this gossip is what I hate most about London."

"Oh, please." Lady Jersey laughed in amusement. "Don't be naive, Elizabeth. This is 1808. The constant flow of the *on-dit* is what keeps the town alive. Otherwise, we should all be bored to tears, year after year, of seeing the same old faces and doing the same old things."

"Well, quite frankly, Lady Jersey, I expect we shall be returning to Scotland shortly, and I wouldn't care if I never came back to London."

"While I, on the other hand, have no intention of ever rusticating so thoroughly. I even hate going to the countryside for the dog days of summer. It's a dreadful bore, and the only thing that makes it tolerable is the truth that London in high summer stinks worse than a piggery."

"I guess it's a good thing the Lord made us all different, then," Elizabeth concluded with a dry throat. She turned down another aisle and began to seriously concentrate on the books she intended to select.

"Oh, Elizabeth, have you looked outdoors since we came in?" Caroline wanted to know. "The weather looks most inclement. I just heard several gentlemen say they are certain it's going to snow."

"Whatever is the problem?" Lady Jersey put a book back on a shelf. "Don't tell me you've taken a constitutional in this dreadful weather, Lady Elizabeth."

Elizabeth knew exactly where this conversation was going. Caroline was inveigling a ride home in Lady Jersey's carriage. "You've pegged me right, Sarah. I thought a brisk walk would do us good."

"You'd both freeze if you tried to walk back home. Caroline, stay close, dear, I'll see you safely home. Elizabeth, what do you think of York? Does he have a daughter old enough to have eloped six years ago?"

"Heavens no!" Elizabeth gasped.

"I'm merely repeating what has been in the papers." Lady Jersey insisted.

Yes, and who would have done such a thing? Elizabeth wondered. Who had the nerve to leak such a rumor to the newspapers? It sounded like something juvenile that Byron might do when he was in his cups. But she didn't really think he'd stoop to something that low.... He'd know it would only hurt her. Byron might be callous at times, but he rarely was deliberately hurtful.

For that matter, Elizabeth didn't care one bit for the calculating manner in which Lady Jersey was staring at her. At least with Tullibardine housebound for a spell, she didn't have to worry about his getting wind of the bets at White's. There was no telling how that hothead would react.

Amalia, for God's sake! Who was at the root of such a spiteful thing? And then it hit her.

Evan MacGregor!

Chapter Ten

Evan's horse pranced restively as he opened his pocket watch for the third time since arriving at the east gate of Green Park. It was twenty past the hour of noon. He'd arrived early, wanting the extra moments to compose his thoughts.

This meeting was crucial, and it would be up to him to convince Elizabeth that, no matter what the consequences were of revealing the truth of their marriage to her father, it must be done. It should have been done that very day, and he had no excuses to offer for why it hadn't been owned up to at the time. In truth, he knew his own behavior had been less than honorable. The only offer he could make in his own defense was that it had been Elizabeth's wish to keep their marriage secret.

He self-consciously reached inside his heavy coat and touched the brittle parchment that was all the proof he had to show the validity of their marriage. Elizabeth would have burned the document if he let her retain possession of it back in 1802.

He had to convince her they could weather the storm of scandal, together.

But Elizabeth was nowhere in sight. He snapped his watch closed a fourth time and tucked it inside the pocket of his weskit, took the reins firmly in hand and turned his horse around, urging the beast to a brisk canter.

Mentally he forced aside the irritation Elizabeth's cowardice caused him. He knew full well how terrified she was of crossing her father. Hell, he wasn't looking forward to confronting Atholl with the truth, either.

Evan had only to reflect upon the past eight hours of self-imposed mental anguish to know what a formidable foe he was pitting himself against, but the confrontation had to come. His honor demanded that he set the record right.

Whatever the consequences, real or imagined, when all was said—when the blood had spilled between Evan and John Murray—they would face each other man to man.

Five and a half tough years as a soldier had taught Evan that even the most powerful men alive were only human; living, breathing beings whose blood flowed just as easily as his own. A man's will and honor were everything. Nothing else mattered.

Where Elizabeth Murray was concerned, Evan MacGregor's honor decreed that his will must reign supreme—over her father's will, over society's rigid decrees regarding class, and over Elizabeth's determination to go on as they had done.

At Grosvenor Park, he drew in the reins, slowing his horse to a stately trot. The wind blew harsh against his ears, raising the tiers of his greatcoat.

The sky looked ominously threatening, bitter and cold. He could taste the ice as it formed off his breath. Come evening, it would surely be snowing. Were he looking for threatening omens to put him off and discourage him, he'd certainly have found them in the winter-bound atmosphere.

He moved forward, undaunted, knowing his purpose was right and true, certain of what must be done to set his and Elizabeth's world to rights.

As he approached the corner house at Grosvenor Mews, Evan opted against tying his mount to the hitching post while he presented himself at the front door, seeking formal admittance to call upon Lady Elizabeth. He knew the value of the element of surprise.

What better tactical advantage could he use against Elizabeth than to arrive discreetly, in the guise of a returning foster son, entering the house through the back. He could think of none better as he surrendered Breacan to a capable groom and hurried to the house.

Keyes answered his knock upon the rear door in his shirtsleeves, wearing the black apron he habitually donned when polishing sliver.

"Why, by my soul," Keyes exclaimed. "It's Evan MacGregor. I'd know you anywhere, sir. Come in, come in. Look, Mrs. Pierson, it's young Evan MacGregor, come to pay a visit. And hasn't he turned out well! Let me have your coat and gloves, sir."

Evan smiled wryly, wishing his arrival would put a genuine smile of welcome on some other faces in this house, not just the butler's. The redoubtable Mrs. Pierson curtsied to him and chatted briefly about how handsome and strong he'd grown up to be. Evan replied in kind, praising her for being the kindest woman he'd ever laid eyes on south of the Tweed.

Keyes led him across the first floor to a cozy parlor whose adjoining sunroom Evan remembered overlooked the park.

"I've come to see Elizabeth." Evan stated his purpose as Keyes opened the door to the parlor.

"I'm sure she's about the house somewhere, sir. Ah, Your Grace, look who has come to visit. Captain MacGregor."

Seated near the fire, Tullibardine let the day's newspaper fold into his lap as he looked up. "Evan, old man! I was wondering when I'd see you again. Come in, come in. Join me. We're about to have lunch shortly. You'll stay, of course. Keyes, see to another setting at the table, will you?''

"Certainly, my lord," Keyes bowed out.

"You're moving your arm fairly well, Your Grace," Evan said as he formally stopped at the marquess's chair and offered Tullie his hand in greeting. "I assume you're recovering well?"

"A little stiff at the moment, but getting better by the day," Tullie admitted as he rose from his chair, clasped Evan's hand and shook it warmly. "Good to see you again so soon, MacGregor. To what do I owe the pleasure?"

"Frankly, my lord, I've come to see Elizabeth. We were to meet for a ride in Green Park, but I assume the weather put her off."

"It would put anybody off. I've been holed up here by the fire most of the morning. It's getting worse out there by the hour. Wait here, I'll check her whereabouts."

Tullie stepped over to the sunroom and opened a French door, calling out to someone out there. "Eh, wee Robbie, where's Elizabeth? Do you know where she's got off to? No? Well, run upstairs and see if you can find her, then. Ah, that's a good lad."

Tullie stepped aside, allowing a small boy to dart around him before he shut the door. The child ran full tilt across the room, nimbly leaping the footstool set before Tullie's chair, and scooted into the hallway; a blur of dark auburn hair, black shortcoat and checkered pants propelled by shoeless feet.

"Care for some coffee?" Tullie asked, turning to a table laid out with scones and biscuits and a polished samovar.

"Love some." Evan gladly accepted the offer of a hot drink. Tullie fixed him right up and encouraged him to help himself to the scones, and then they both settled companionably in opposite chairs, conversing easily, catching up with the past.

Tullie's warm welcome went a long way toward putting Evan at ease as the minutes ticked away and Elizabeth did not present herself.

Evan was just about to ask what room she was might be in when the boy came back. He sidled up to the marquess's elbow, interrupting him midsentence. "Gone."

"Gone where?" Tullie took the interruption in stride. "Come on, wee Robbie, spit out the rest."

"Out," the boy said cryptically.

"Well? Out where?"

"Lane."

"Lane? What lane?" Tullie exclaimed.

"Books."

"Oh, Lane's Bookstore. Well, why didn't you say that to begin with? No sense pulling teeth about it!" Tullie grumbled. "What's she gone there for? And how come you didn't find out when she left? It's bloody cold out."

"Walk," said the boy. Then he turned around, heading for the sunroom, where he'd obviously been playing when Evan came in. The marquess reached out with his big left hand, collaring the boy, hauling him back to him.

"Hold it, scamp. When did she leave?"

"Dunno." The boy wiggled, trying to escape. He turned and flashed a look at Evan, who was smiling broadly at Tullibardine's unusual mode of communication with one small boy. The lad flashed a smile back at Evan, exposing a mouthful of sound milk teeth, which confirmed for Evan that he wasn't but five or six at the most. If he was five, he was tall for his age. "Whuzzat?" the boy asked.

"Oh, so you noticed we've got company, did you? If you'll show some manners, I'll introduce you."

The boy's eyes wandered over the epaulets, braid, beribboned medals and brass buttons on Evan's red uniform jacket. He was clearly intrigued. He pulled his shoulders back and straightened, then touched his brow with his fingers, saluting. *"So'diers!"*

"The scamp's an egalitarian, Evan. Doesn't give a fig about rank. You'll have to make allowances. This is Robbie Murray of Port-a-shee, and this, my good young man, is the MacGregor, captain of His Majesty's Grey Breeks, nicely home from Portugal."

"Sir." Robbie folded his arm across his stomach and bowed from the waist.

Manners, indeed. Evan smiled. "Nicely done, sir." The introductions over, Evan sat on the edge of his seat to be on the same level as the child. "I'm very pleased to meet you, Rob Roy. I've got a grandfather who proudly bore that name."

Robbie blinked twice, looking taken aback for a moment. He deliberately leaned closer to Evan, squinting his long-lashed eyes at the man in front of him. He brought up one pudgy hand and put a finger to the polished button at the top of Evan's scarlet jacket.

"Are ye from Scotland?" Robbie asked.

"I'll be damned!" Tullie shouted. "Four words! A whole damn sentence! MacGregor, you've broken the dam! Answer him!"

"I will if you'll give me a chance. Aye, Rob Roy, I'm a Scot, a Highlander from Balqehidder, between Loch Katrine and Loch Lomond. Do ya ken where that is?"

"Och, no. Is it near Dunkeld? I ken where that is." The boy spoke in a soft island brogue that wasn't so hard on the letter *r*.

"I'll be double-damned." Tullie sat with a heavy thump onto his seat, his face flushing with outright astonishment. "Wee Robbie, I didn't know you had it in you."

The boy cast a dismissive look at the marquess and returned his attention to Evan's medal-covered jacket. His fingers strayed to the ribbons and medallions, touching the brightest, a campaign pin Evan had received from the king of Portugal. "You're in the cavalry," he deduced correctly.

"Aye. Would you like to see my horse after lunch?"

Robbie tipped his head to the side, lifting the focus of his eyes upward, to study Evan's face, instead of his military decorations. The concentrated squint left his expression, and he reverted to a one-word answer. "Now."

"Sorry." Evan gave him back a single-word refusal. "Impolite." That said, Evan looked over the boy's dark head to Tullie and arched his brow in an unspoken question.

Tullie let his big hands steer Robbie toward the sunroom. "You can go back to your toys, Robbie. Mayhap, after luncheon, you can see the MacGregor's charger, if you are wearing yer boots. Go on, now. Play a while, and let us menfolk talk."

Robbie obviously needed no encouragement to return to his toys. He was out of sight in the blink of an eye.

"What was that all about?" Evan asked, when the French door shut behind the boy.

Tullie gulped his coffee, then shook his head. "Wee Robbie doesn't like to talk. The laddie gives new meaning to the word *parsimonious,* only he's stingy with words. Doles them out one at a time. I vow, he hasn't said more than one word at a time in my presence since he came over from Port-a-shee. Elizabeth is the only one who can coax more words out of him, and those are few and far between, when the scamp can make one do. Pleasant child, though. I'm rather fond of him."

"Seems a likable little chap," Evan concurred. "What happened to his parents?"

"Damned if I know!" Tullie exclaimed. "All I know is that he's another one of father's vast army of wards and foster sons. Got no papers with this one, no pedigree to speak of, or none that His Grace is mentioning."

"How old is he? Six?"

"Good heavens, no. You missed that by a league. He's four—won't be five for several months."

"Really?" Evan sat back in his seat, stunned. He said, "Wee Robbie's verra tall."

"Aye, Robbie's got promise there. Wait till Elizabeth hears you got him talking sentences the minute he laid eyes on you. The way she dotes on the lad, she'll be right furious."

"Speaking of right furious, I'm about to get that way, if she doesn't show up. What's this about Lane's Bookstore? How'd you deduct that from the few words the child said?"

"Habit. Elizabeth borrows books from Lane's whenever she's flat broke. She'll be back shortly. One o'clock at the latest," Tullie said, with a glance to the clock on the mantel.

Evan didn't need an explanation for that. The duke of Atholl's household ran by the clock. At one, luncheon was served. It was ten minutes shy of that mark now. So Evan settled back with his hot cup of coffee and waited.

Soon enough, there came the sound of a carriage on the street. The French door crashed open as Robbie burst into the room, shouting, "Jersey!" He shot across the parlor in a dead run for the front door.

"Curses. Pray the witch doesn't come in." Tullibardine put aside his coffee and hastily reached up to straighten his collar and cravat. "The very last thing I want to do today is be polite to Lady Jersey over lunch."

Evan stood to glance out the window that faced the street. Sure enough, Lady Jersey's carriage had stopped at the curbstone. Elizabeth and her cousin Caroline were descending from it with packages.

He felt his blood quicken. The moment of confrontation was at hand. And now they had something more important to discuss . . . a small wean named Robbie. Evan's jaw tightened as he renewed his pledge to end this farce, today.

"What time do you expect Colonel Graham and the duke to return?" he asked Tullie in a bland voice.

"Ah." The marquess finished knotting his cravat. "I'd say no later than four, given the past days' schedule."

That propitious bit of news caused Evan to rub his palms together with deliberate anticipation. He'd have two full hours following lunch to get some straight answers from Elizabeth.

Chapter Eleven

As Lady Jersey's carriage moved away from the curbstones, Caroline regarded the cold sky, which was laden with dark, bruised clouds. "Do you think it will snow, Elizabeth?"

Elizabeth sorted through the packages in her arms and handed two of them over to her cousin. She shot a quick look at the threatening sky. "Looking at this sky, it certainly ought to."

"Good," Caroline said around a carefully moderated yawn. "I, for one, won't mind a night at home. I need to catch up on my sleep. Are you coming home with me?"

"No," Elizabeth said as she handed over Caroline's purchases. "It's almost time for lunch, but thank you anyway. If you get bored with staying in because the weather's bad, you can always come next door and join us. I'm sure there will be a card game of some sort going on while the weather blows."

"That's why I bought so many books," Caroline added conspiratorially. "I love to sit in bed and read. Bye, now. And thanks for taking me to the party last eve."

Elizabeth watched her cousin run up the steps of her father's house next door. She rang the bell and was almost instantly welcomed inside the house. Elizabeth turned to her own front door, ready to get out of the cold.

Privately she welcomed snow, because it allowed a convenient escape from all but the most compelling of social duties. Being housebound for a week or more would be a godsend, in her estimation. She could only hope the weather would do the same to Evan MacGregor—keep him far, far away from her.

"Has Papa returned from Parliament?" Elizabeth asked Keyes as she surrendered her outer garments in the foyer.

"Not yet, milady." Keyes shook the ice off Elizabeth's cloak and folded it neatly across his arm. "We expect His Grace to arrive promptly at four."

"Good," Elizabeth murmured, tucking her small package of books under her arm.

"Lady Amalia wishes to speak with you, before luncheon, she said," Keyes drawled.

"Me?" Elizabeth's eyes rounded. "What did I do wrong?"

"I'm certain nothing, milady," Keyes said soothingly. "She's waiting for you in the green salon."

"Oh?" Elizabeth handed him her hat and gloves, then turned and walked down the hall to the small and intimate green salon at the rear of the mansion.

She found Amalia working diligently over a dried floral arrangement, which definitely needed enlivening. "You wanted to speak to me, Amalia."

Amalia turned around and motioned to Elizabeth to shut the door and then come closer. "Yes, I do, but privately."

Elizabeth secured the door and crossed the large room to the table where Amalia had a good supply of dried flowers spread out, waiting for her use.

"I want to get one thing understood." Amalia said, turning back to the arrangement.

"And what is that?" Elizabeth asked blandly.

"Forgive me, sister, but I must speak my mind. I don't intend to tolerate a repeat of five years ago, Elizabeth."

"I beg your pardon," Elizabeth said, caught unawares by the unexpected attack.

"You may beg my pardon all you like, but I haven't forgotten that your behavior with Evan MacGregor shamefully humiliated all of us the last time the two of you came together, during his sister Marie's wedding celebration."

"What?" Elizabeth's color rose, and so did her voice.

"No, no," Amalia said calmly, as sure of herself as she could be. "From what I've seen thus far this little season... we're going to be treated to more of the same."

"I haven't the foggiest idea what you are talking about," Elizabeth countered in self-defense. Although what specific charge she was defending herself from, she truly didn't know. Amalia knew nothing.

"I'm talking about the fact that you deliberately avoided taking the escort home last night that James had provided you through Uncle Thomas."

"I explained to James and Uncle Thomas that I had a previous commitment. Hester Stanhope saw to it that Caroline and I arrived safely home after Byron's party."

"Byron, is it?" Amalia's eyes narrowed. "Elizabeth, do you even listen to what is said about him? He's... disgusting!" Amalia shivered, as if she were speaking of some slug or vile insect slithering across the priceless carpet at her feet, instead of a human being. "If you think for one minute that Father would approve of a match between you and Byron, you'd best think again."

"I don't think any such thing."

"Well, you'd better not entertain such an outlandish idea. I heard Father and Uncle Thomas speaking to that point this morning after breakfast. Byron's completely amoral."

"How would you know? You've never spent one moment talking to him."

"Elizabeth," Amalia argued, "I've had considerably more experience with society's rakes than you. You must trust my judgment on such things. This habit you have of questioning everything I say or suggest is distressing.''

"Stop right there, sister. You've strayed far and wide from the point. Let's go back to your original complaint. What is it you think happened years ago that causes you so much shame and anguish today? What's Evan MacGregor ever done to you to cause such worry on my behalf?"

Amalia was capable of using leveling looks herself. She stared hard at Elizabeth, her expression one of well-placed motherly concern.

"I am referring to Bell's Wynd. Don't tell me you don't remember how offended Aunt Nicky was by your actions the night you danced with MacGregor before all of Edinburgh, with your hair down and your skirts flying like some..." Amalia's tirade ran out of steam, for lack of a disparaging enough word.

Elizabeth supplied. "Trollop, maybe? For heaven's sake, Amalia, I was fifteen ... a child. And that incident is long since forgotten, by everyone except you and Aunt Nicky."

"The point I am trying to make, Elizabeth, is that you act out of character around Evan MacGregor."

"I most assuredly do not."

"Yes, you do. You always have, from the time both of you were thrown together as children in the same schoolroom. If you weren't telling off poor Mrs. Grasso and making her life difficult, then you were flouting all the rules and customs of polite behavior at Edinburgh assemblies. Now you're a lady grown, and I expect you comport yourself within the bounds of behavior you've been taught. I'm asking for decorum and moderation. Is that so difficult?''

"What's your point, Amalia?" Elizabeth asked testily.

"The point is, MacGregor has been invited to lunch with us *en famille,* and I'm certain Tullie's extended the same invitation for this evening.''

"Fine." Elizabeth snapped, shaken by that announcement. "I have a headache. Make my excuses to the marquess. I'll remain in my room."

Amalia set her teeth on edge. "Blast it, Elizabeth, that's precisely my point! Such behavior couldn't be more obvious or more telling."

"Telling of what?"

"You will not hide out for the duration in your room, reading romances and drivel. It's high time you faced reality. Evan MacGregor cares nothing for you. He never will, and all your petty games and pranks won't change that fact. If you think giving him the cut direct in your own home will do anything to alter how he feels about you, then you are sadly mistaken, young lady. It is high time you put aside your childish infatuations and face the world the way it truly is."

Seething with frustration, Elizabeth asked, "What is it you really want, Amalia?"

"Frankly, sister, I want you married. The sooner the better. You're getting more stubborn and set in your hoyden ways with each day that passes." She faced Elizabeth squarely, reaching out with a warm hand to stroke a wayward curl from her sister's face, changing tactics with the gesture of affection. "I know he hurt you, Elizabeth. The exact how or why of it escaped me. You are very good at keeping secrets."

Amalia paused to sigh, deeply. Elizabeth stood rigid, her face turned to the side, her chin set and resolute. Amalia slipped an arm around Elizabeth's waist, drawing her close to comfort her.

"I'm not blind, Elizabeth. I never have been. Why, I don't think I'll ever forget the expression of pain on your face at his sister Marie's wedding. Your heart was crushed, because Evan ignored you completely and wouldn't so much as dance a reel with you in good fun. I tried to explain he was older then, and young men haven't much time for girls of fifteen. I mean, just because the two of you had flouted custom for one dance at Bell's Wynd, that didn't mean he would be exclusively yours for the rest of your life. You always were possessive where Evan was concerned, Elizabeth. Right from the day he came to live with us.

"What I'm trying to say, darling, is perhaps now the time has come for the two of you to—"

"No, it hasn't!" Elizabeth interrupted vehemently.

"I was going to say *make peace with one another,*" Amalia countered, just as forcefully.

Grim-jawed, Elizabeth said, "I want nothing to do with him."

"Then I suggest you strive to treat him with the same courtesy any other of Uncle Thomas's aides-de-camp would be treated in our home. Be polite and gracious. You were entirely uncivil last Sunday night, when Evan brought Tullie home."

"How would you know? You were swooning for most of his visit."

"I certainly wasn't," Amalia countered, but her cheeks were flushing with color anyway. "Father would take a dim view of any lack of hospitality."

"What exactly is this? Why am I being ordered to be nice to the man? What's your purpose?"

Amalia blinked twice. "Elizabeth, please use your head. Father is helping Lord Mansfield find a suitable partner for Caroline. We will no doubt be entertaining a number of young men on her behalf over the coming days. While I agree entirely that Evan MacGregor would make a poor in-law for any of us, he could be suitable for Caroline, who is just an earl's daughter."

"Caroline?" Elizabeth drew away from Amalia, staring at her with horror inching into her eyes. For a long moment, she was too flustered to rally a response, and when one came it was scathingly discordant. "You think Caroline would benefit from a match to a vagabond soldier of fortune? Good God, Amalia, have you lost your wits? MacGregors have been reiving Mansfield cattle for centuries!''

"Nonsense." Amalia brushed that objection aside with a wave of her diamond-and-emerald engagement ring. "No one takes reiving seriously in this day and age, Elizabeth. We both know that. Nonetheless, I expect—no, I *demand* that you comport yourself in as civil a manner as befits the daughter of a duke. Now, go and change your dress to something appropriate for an afternoon at home."

On her way out of the green salon, Elizabeth thought mutinously, *I'd as soon slit my own throat. Egads, rumors of elopements, gossip and matchmaking from Lady Jersey! What next? Evan matched to Caroline Mansfield? Impossible!* Elizabeth wished herself to only one place on earth—Dunkeld, far, far away from the terrible strain and upheaval of London!

"Snow! Snow!" Robbie shouted as he darted around Elizabeth in a race to the front door.

"Come back here, wee Robbie!" Krissy hollered from the third floor. "Yer no' going outside till ye put on yer boots!"

"I'll get him," Elizabeth told Krissy. Robbie was too quick for Krissy to catch.

"Out!"

"Not now, Robbie, we're going to have lunch first," Elizabeth told him. She took hold of his hand to direct him away from the front door. In just a few minutes, the whirling flakes of white had begun to coat the windowpanes and ledges, and adhere to the street. Robbie jumped up and down, shoeless and sockless, overly excited by the splendor outdoors. "You want to wait till there's enough snow to make a snowman, don't you?"

"Out!" he demanded. "Play!"

"No, Robbie. It's time to eat. How many times must I tell you to put on your shoes? It's winter." Elizabeth was determined to be firm. "You'll get sick, running about with bare feet."

"Play, now!" Robbie shouted, and reached for the doorknob just as Elizabeth's hand closed over his. She bent down, laid a hand on his soft curls and whispered in his ear.

"I promise I will take you out after lunch . . . if you keep on shoes and socks."

He flashed her a mutinous look of his own concoction. "Not hungry."

"Very well." Elizabeth straightened and called upstairs to Krissy. "Krissy, you'll have to come down and get Robbie. He may take his nap, now."

"No!" Robbie evaded Elizabeth's attempt to contain him and bolted down the hallway at a dead run. He slammed into Tullie and Evan MacGregor as they exited from the parlor behind the billiards room. The boy lurched around Tullie, but was captured by Evan and lifted high into the air. Elizabeth ceased running immediately.

"Here, now, where's the fire?" Evan laughed.

"Lemmego!" Robbie demanded.

"Please don't!" Elizabeth pleaded, catching up to the little boy, Evan and Tullie. "That is, let him go."

Krissy clattered down the stairs, screeching for Robbie to stop and behave himself while she put on his shoes.

"Praise the Lord," she gasped as she rounded the newel post and found Robbie still captive and in the house. "I thought for sure I'd be chasing him from one end of the park to the other, milady. Likes snow, he does."

Tullie grumbled an aside to Evan. "Hates shoes, he does."

Elizabeth could hardly make herself look at Evan, holding the child so easily in his arms. Was she the only one who saw the striking resemblance in their faces?

Robbie wiggled valiantly, kicking his bare feet, pushing at Evan's shoulders with surprisingly strong and sturdy arms in an effort to be released.

"Thank you for stopping him," Elizabeth said. "We go through this practically every day. I'll take him."

"You do and you'll be taking a handful," Evan said crisply. "Settle down, Rob Roy. That snow isn't going anywhere."

"Out!" Robbie demanded, but not with as much vigor as before. He touched a tentative finger to the golden fringe dangling from the epaulet on Evan's shoulder.

"Aye, well, I heard you the first time, laddie." Evan gestured to Krissy to give him Robbie's shoes and socks. "But I can tell you for a fact, wee Robbie, that no soldier worth his salt goes out in the snow without his boots on."

There were several chairs in the hallway. Evan sat on the nearest and put Robbie on his knee. "I haven't put on a pair of shoes with laces in years and years, old man. Let me see if I remember how it's done."

"Don't like shoes." Robbie asked. "Sidiers wear buits, not shoes."

"Is that a fact?" Evan said. "That depends on what the uniform of the day is, my good man."

"I want buits like yers." Robbie jabbed his thumb into his chest. "Tall buits, cavalry buits. I don't want to wear shoes."

Elizabeth's jaw dropped. Tullie grinned and hit her lightly on the shoulder, then pointed at Evan and whispered, "The two of them have been doing that all morning. Robbie's talking a blue streak to MacGregor, like the two of them were old cronies from way back when. Damned near knocked my socks off when I heard it the first time."

Shocked, Elizabeth sat down in the chair beside Evan, listening to the two of them talk. Evan deliberately tried to cram the wrong shoe on a foot, and Robbie cried out, "No, yer doing it wrong! The other foot! Put it on my other foot!''

Evan turned the shoes over and looked at the soles. There wasn't much difference, except in the way the shoes had been worn down over time by the little feet that went in them. "Pick one.''

"That one,'' Robbie chirped. "On this foot.''

"Right you go, then.''

Evan made a great show of grunting and tussling with an uncooperative shoe. Robbie laughed in delight as the laces proved to be as stubborn and contrary as the shoe. He completely forgot about the snow falling outdoors.

"Phew! What a job that was!'' Evan put Robbie back on his own two feet, then rubbed his own stomach, saying, "That worked up my appetite. I could eat a horse. Where do I go to get some food around here?''

"I know where t' get summat t' eat.'' Robbie grinned and took hold of Evan's hand, pulling him onto his feet and said, "Come on. I'll show you.''

Tullie laughed and slapped Elizabeth on the back. "The wee bantling's been having us all on, Elizabeth.''

"I never!'' Krissy swore.

Dumbfounded, Elizabeth let herself be pulled along to the dining room by her brother.

The rest of the family was already there. It had gone a few minutes past one, but luncheon was not on such a rigid schedule as breakfast, especially when the duke was absent.

Robbie insisted Evan sit right beside him, which put them both across the table at the opposite corner from Elizabeth. With all the chattering that went on during the meal, she wasn't able to listen to Robbie's animated chatter. She *had* heard one upsetting piece of conversation: Evan had promised to show Robbie his horse after lunch.

Chapter Twelve

Elizabeth had never seen Robbie more excited than when Evan had set him high atop Breacan's withers and slowly walked the charger through the stable. By the time Robbie's excursion was over, he was tired and ready to nap.

"Take me to your room," Evan commanded Elizabeth the moment they'd handed Robbie over to Krissy in the nursery.

Startled, Elizabeth looked at Evan's eyes and found them as dark as deepest midnight in the Highlands. Try as she might, she couldn't seem to draw back from the spellbinding pull they exerted upon her.

She knew what was uppermost in his mind. It wasn't proper. Good Lord, his request—no, his *demand*—was scandalously improper for a maiden to give in to. But then, she was no maiden...and he was the husband to whom she must defer.

Evan tightened his fingers upon her arm, drawing Izzy closer. The scent of rosewater, warmed by her skin, emanated from her clothing and the soft curls rioting around her head. It beckoned to all of his senses, awakening in him the need to touch, taste and revel in her true essence—woman.

The uncertainty in her eyes unbalanced him, made him reckless and moody. She looked quickly away, tucking in her chin, nodding, silent and acquiescent, and led him down the hall.

The hall in that wing of the house was shorter, narrower, lacking the ornate tables laden with dried floral arrangements and footmen's chairs that graced the dowager's stately wing. Four raised-paneled doors faced each other with the precision and regularity of posted sentinels. An oriel window dramatically lighted the end of the hall. There, a fainting couch and tea stand offered any lady a place to rest while she looked over Grosvenor Park.

Elizabeth moved on silent feet to the last door on the right. She paused to listen for sounds elsewhere before taking the knob in her hand and twisting it.

Evan laid his hand on the upper panel and pushed the door wide open. Her bedroom was dark, save for the glow of a banked fire in the inglenook. Elizabeth escaped his negligent grasp as she crossed the threshold, turned toward the wall and raised her hand to a round knob jutting out from the plastered and wallpapered wall.

Almost immediately, pulsing yellowish flames bloomed from four brass sconces set high along the papered interior walls, flooding one side of the dark chamber with light.

"Good Lord!" Evan whispered, shocked by the instantaneous brightness. "Gaslights. You've got gaslights indoors."

"Aye," Elizabeth whispered, her fingers still on the controlling knob. She raised her other hand to her mouth, touching the soft indentation above her lips, as if uncertain of what she wanted at that moment, darkness or light. Evan could give her either in the blink of an eye. "I don't like them—too garish and bright. Papa had the works installed in the cellar this summer past, but there are critics who say he dabbles in dangerous arts."

"Huh." Evan nodded in frank amazement, impressed, but uncertain as to how well he might like the constant brilliance himself. That explained how he could see the cupola of the dome from the foyer on the first floor in the dark of night. "Common folk will surely cant against them."

"Aye." Elizabeth nodded, turning the knob until a small glow burned steadily from the brass bases. It plunged her room back into semidarkness and wintry shadow.

"Lord Mansfield says if we survive this winter without blowing ourselves sky-high, he'll consent to try Papa's scientific experiment in his own house. Papa talks constantly about flooding all of London with gaslights to ward off the night. He claims they would be a deterrent to criminals and mischief-makers. His engineers testify that lighting the city is feasible, and most of the constables agree proper lights could do away with most burglaries in one fell swoop."

Slowly, taking great care that his boots not make noise on the floor below, Evan crossed the room to the bay windows he'd chucked stones at. He peeled back the curtains and parted the sheers, then stood gazing at the falling snow, lost in deep thought. He turned back, surveying Elizabeth from across the darkened room.

"In spite of the great lights, nothing else has been changed. The house is the same as when I lived here, too, remember?"

"Yes," Elizabeth nodded, reminded once again of their years in the schoolroom, prior to his going on to Eton. The duke of Atholl lived an ordered, regimented life. If it was January, he was in residence in London. April and May found him and his household at Blair House in Atholl. June, in Edinburgh. August, he resided at Port-a-shee on the Isle of Man.

Any other time of the year, he ensconced himself at the old castle of Dunkeld, deep in the Highlands, above Gormach and Rattray. The duke was a landed gypsy, tied to much, locked down to little.

Two sessions of Parliament and Amalia's first season had passed during Evan's two years in the duke's vagabond household. Evan's presence had made Elizabeth's lonely and isolated existence more bearable.

"For the most part, Papa doesn't care for any sort of radical change. Even when the curtains or the linens wear out and have to be replaced, he insists that the same tapestries replace the old. That way, he has continuity from year to year and visit to visit. It's the same at Dunkeld and Blair House and Port-a-shee. He took me to Port-a-shee, to the Isle of Man, once . . . that summer."

"Which summer?" Evan asked, knowing exactly which summer she meant, but needing to hear her say it.

"The summer after—" Elizabeth swallowed "—we eloped."

"Did he? Took you to traipse in the coves and the woods and go fish and hunt like one of the boys, he did?"

"Not exactly, but we did that, too, in the end," Elizabeth said. "We can't stay up here, Evan. One of the servants might come up . . . or Amalia."

"She still rules the roost, doesn't she? And you still let her?"

"This time next year, she'll be married, in her own house then. Come, Evan, you've seen nothing's changed. Can we go now, please?"

His head turned, his eyes fixed upon her tester bed, piled high with eiderdowns and pillows, soft goosedown mattresses, warm, snug and inviting, wide enough for the two of them to sleep and love the rest of the cold, lonely winter away together. "Why is Caroline bunking with you?"

"That was just for last night . . . because we were coming in so late," Elizabeth explained. "But we're crowded here this year. Tullie had to move back home. So James, Uncle Thomas, Reverend Baird and Papa have all the available rooms on the second floor. The dowager, Aunts Nicky and Charlotte and Amalia have the suites. That leaves me to share this room when necessary."

"That still leaves a room on each floor vacant." He knew the duke's town house as well as she.

"For guests, company. You know the Murray motto... always prepared."

"Damned inconvenient," he swore as he strode purposefully back across the Turkish carpet to her. He raised both hands, flattening them on the flocked wallpaper at her back, trapping her.

Elizabeth groaned at the temptation his nearness offered. Why had she let impulse direct her to lower the full brilliance of the gaslights? Shadows, and the winter-afternoon darkness, added too much mystery to the Man of the Mist's presence.

"Scared, Izzy?" he drawled deliberately.

"Not at all," Elizabeth lied. She stared purposefully at the elegant fold of his cravat, doubting if even Tullie's expert valet, Maxtone, could copy Evan's style. For a man who had been gone from society for better than five years, Evan had a decidedly elegant air to his grooming and his dressing that spoke of the Continent.

She was trying to figure how to phrase a question in that direction when his head dipped and his mouth came into her line of sight, obliterating his cravat from view. "I want a kiss, Elizabeth. I want more than that. God help me, but I want to take you down on that bed, hike your skirts up to your waist and bury myself inside you. How long do you intend we play this bloody game?"

Elizabeth's chin jerked up haughtily. "I'll beg you to remember I am a lady. I'll not stand for such swearing in front of me."

"Ha!" He caught her proud chin between strong, tight fingers, lifting it higher. "I remember a time when every word you said was preceded by bloody this and bloody that."

"And you delighted in corrupting me, as I recall, teaching me every swear word you knew in Gaelic and English.

May I remind you I'm no longer a mere child and eager to shock every soul I meet? I'll thank you to remember that.''

"Aye, I see you've become the prim and proper lady of the manor," he drawled, completely unrepentant.

His head bent, and his lips caught hers. Then his hand dropped to Elizabeth's breast, making Elizabeth's protest mute. She lost the battle before it had truly commenced when he pressed into her, deepening the kiss till he took her breath away.

"You, Elizabeth Murray," Evan whispered huskily, "are quite some piece of work...with this skewed logic and twisted reasoning of yours." An irresistible grin spread across his mouth, reminding her that a man like him, thought very differently from the way she did.

Elizabeth's pulse thrummed in her veins. She caught her breath, holding back the impulse to surrender to him completely. Their combined past had taught her never to act on rash impulses...not with Evan.

His mouth hovered over hers. "Suppose I apologize for the crudity, my lady? Do I amend the error of my ways, will you reward me another kiss?"

Her hands flattened against the rock-hard pressure of his chest, keeping him at bay. "You forget, sir, I know to what your kisses lead."

"Aye, do you, then?" His smile widened. "Mayhap I shall just take what I want at my leisure."

"I'll scream." Elizabeth's heart pounded against her ribs, so loud and so strong he must surely hear it.

"Be my guest," he invited, undaunted by her threat.

Her eyes darted to the door just two—no, three feet away from where she stood pinned to the interior wall by the closeness of his body.

"Evan, stop. You can't continue to do this. It isn't proper." She shook her head, refusing to let her mouth come any closer to his. "You can't be caught in here with

me when I'm not supposed to be...when we're not... Don't
you realize what my father would think, or say—?''

His lips glided across her mouth, putting an end to her
prattling. ''That's what makes it all that much more necessary.''

His kiss drugged her, blinded her to proprieties and the
strict dicta of the day, which decreed a woman of virtue *did
not* entertain a gentleman in her boudoir.

Where Evan MacGregor was concerned, Elizabeth Murray maintained no sense of decorum. She melted into his
arms, caught by the spell of his lips as they worked their
magic on hers.

Whatever protest she might have made was lost in the
pleasure of his warm, soft lips gliding warmly over hers.

Elizabeth closed her eyes. What purpose was served by
token resistance? None. His fingers tightened on her jaw,
preventing any retreat. Her arms wound around his neck,
and her body softened, welcoming the hard compression of
his. She opened her lips beneath the pressure of his, to accept him inside her.

They might have continued thus indefinitely, but for the
sharp clatter of a door opening, which yanked them both
out of the mindless haze of passion and need washing over
them.

Evan jumped back, releasing Elizabeth, and she whirled
around to see who it was that had barged into her room.

At the door to the nursery, Krissy threw both hands up
to her cheeks. Around her wide skirts, Robbie poked his
little head into the room, lisping, ''Wuzzat?''

''A thousand pardons, milady! Sir!'' Krissy gasped at the
fierce, forbidding expression on Evan's face. ''Och, I didn't
mean to intrude. Wee Robbie wants his storybook.''

''It's all right.'' Elizabeth ran across the room to the
basket beside her stuffed chair, lifting the book she knew
Robbie would most want. High color stained her cheeks;

even her neck burned inside the prim collar of her winter gown.

Robbie snatched up the book and strutted back to his nursery. Krissy bobbed two curtsies, quickly, and ducked behind the closing door, but not before Elizabeth saw her smile broaden appreciably.

"Now you've done it, MacGregor!" Elizabeth muttered crossly as she stamped into the hallway.

Evan hurried after her, catching up on the stairs, chuckling. "Why, Izzy, if I didn't know better, I'd say you are embarrassed!"

"Will you stop taunting me?" she hissed under her breath. "Have you forgotten how much servants gossip belowstairs?"

"Think you I care what they do?" he argued heatedly. He caught hold of her arm, deliberately slowing her descent to the first floor. "You are not going to make me ashamed of my passions, Elizabeth. No, if it takes me till the end of eternity, I'm going to teach you to accept your own, as well as mine. That's a promise you can count on."

Elizabeth gasped. "Whisht!"

The foyer door opened. Keyes stepped inside, folding an umbrella, and looked up the circling stairs at Elizabeth and Evan.

"Good afternoon, Captain, milady." Keyes's steely brows lifted, as always, in an inquiry after their needs. "Will you be going outside, sir? I've just salted the steps."

"Ah, ever thoughtful and prepared you are, Keyes," Evan said easily. His fingers tightened on Elizabeth's arm. "I think a brisk walk after that heavy lunch is in order."

"Yes, Captain MacGregor, and a lovely sight snow is in London, though treacherous to the unwary." Keyes slid the umbrella inside the blue-and-white Chinese vase next to the carved hat rack.

"Then by all means fetch Lady Elizabeth's warmest cloak, and my greatcoat. We'd both enjoy a walkabout in newly fallen snow. A rare treat for London. By my recollection, it will be gray mush on the morrow."

"Regrettably, that it will, sir," Keyes replied from long experience. He turned to the chore given. Elizabeth kept silent, though she didn't want to walk out with Evan. They'd been gone from the company of her family long enough, under the guise of showing Evan's charger to Robbie. Amalia would be asking questions. Especially now that she'd got it in her head that Evan and Elizabeth should make a pact of friendship.

Elizabeth knew when to keep her opinions to herself.

Keyes came with their outerwear, as well as sturdy, fur-lined galoshes for Elizabeth. She donned gloves and a woolen scarf to protect her ears and throat and suffered having her cloak secured at her throat by Evan's adept hands.

Even with gloves on, he competently managed silk frogs and eyelets. Keyes held the door open for them, advising them not to stay out overlong, adding that he'd have hot cocoa ready when they returned.

"This is ridiculous," Elizabeth fussed as soon as the door shut at her back. "We were out for half of an hour with Robbie gloating over your prized horse. It's freezing out here."

"Elizabeth, stop being so contrary," Evan fussed right back. "Look around you. It's beautiful."

On the sidewalk, she grudgingly tilted her head, studying the heavily clouded sky, which was nearly obscured by the downward swirl of huge flakes of snow. Evan was right. It was beautiful.

With her gaze turned skyward, it seemed as if hundreds and thousands of snowflakes were falling directly into her eyes. Falling snow had always seemed so wondrous, magical and profoundly beautiful. Rare in London, expected at Dunkeld, Port-a-shee and Blair House.

Evan slipped his arm around her waist, guiding her across the icy street to the deserted park.

"It is beautiful, isn't it?" His voice came out deep and frosty in the winter air, pure, the only sound for miles, save for the steady thrumming of Elizabeth's escalating pulse.

"Incredible," Elizabeth agreed, trying to get her physical reactions to his closeness under control. "Look at the elms. Why, their limbs are coated already. If it keeps snowing, there will be enough for a snowman."

"We tried that once," Evan recalled with a familiar laugh. "Made the dirtiest snow fort ever, and got ourselves blackened with coal dust, to boot, in the snowball fight that followed. Old Grasso had a fit and boxed my ears. We both had to have baths in tubs down in the kitchen before we were allowed back inside the manse. I expect the servants wound up burning our clothes."

"I don't suppose the snow is any cleaner today." Elizabeth reached up to the nearest elm to scrape off enough of the white stuff to make a single handful of snow. "There will be no forts or snowball fights from this lot. It's hardly enough to make one snowball."

She packed what she held neatly into a ball between her gloved palms, then lifted one kidskin glove and examined the palm. Sure enough, the telltale smudge of London's dirty winter air was there on the fingers of her glove.

"As I reminded Keyes, it will be gray sludge by morning. Pity," Evan said.

Elizabeth dropped the snowball and dusted off her dampened gloves. "You're right. By morning, most of it will probably have melted. What makes the air so dirty here?"

"Coal fires and soot." Evan shrugged his broad shoulders under the many-layered drape of his greatcoat. Elizabeth paused, regarding the elegant cut of his coat, then swept him with an appraising look from head to toe.

"Who's your tailor? It isn't Weston."

"No, it isn't. Haven't time to be a London dandy, nor the inclination. What I had made on the Continent will have to do. I won't be here that long, anyway."

"You won't? Why? Where are you going now? When are you leaving?" she asked.

"Why, Madame MacGregor, I'm touched. I had no idea you cared."

"I didn't say I did, and please don't call me that!" Elizabeth's response bordered on being testy, but then, Evan could drive her mad within the blink of an eye. "Would you please answer my questions?"

"The answers to your questions depend on Parliament, and whether or not they decide to back Wellington's forces in Portugal."

"You're going back, then, when Uncle Thomas returns to the fighting?" she asked.

"That," he replied, "depends upon my orders, as always. The way things stand at the moment, he and I will return to Portugal as soon as the new recruits are trained and ready. We're sorely needed."

Elizabeth shrugged and turned away, glad to know that his time in London was limited. The other side of that particular coin made her fear the grave dangers he craved. Life would always be unsettled and dangerous, were she really married to the warrior.

She sloshed determinedly through the snow-coated grass lawn of the park. "My uncle Archie Cathcart writes that Napoleon can be beaten now that England has got the naval advantage. He says the navy still grieves the loss of Lord Nelson."

"That is true," Evan said. "Colonel Thomas speaks of your Uncle Cathcart with great admiration."

"I expect so. They're friends, as well as brothers-in-law. Do you think we'll be like that in our middle years, still friends with so many people, admirers of their deeds?"

"If we live that long," Evan allowed.

"Oh, don't say that." Elizabeth turned to face him, carefully studying his solemn features. So handsome, so reckless and brave. So utterly impossible to resist. Had he followed his father's wishes, he'd have made a fine doctor. Instead, he'd gone his own way, taking up the dangerous duties of a soldier of the Crown. He could be wounded or killed in the next engagement he faced. She might never see him again. Elizabeth swallowed hollowly, unable to fathom her own mind.

"Who's to say which of us will live to see thirty-five or forty, or advance to Aunt Nicky's august years? Napoleon must be stopped, and it will take a great many men to do it."

"Do you like the fighting? The constant killing?"

"Like it? No, of course not. No man in his right mind would, but it has to be done... by someone. We can't stop now... not until that Corsican is put in his place. I'm not going to waste my breath trying to explain it to you, Izzy. Your father or Thomas Graham can do a better job explaining the reasons for war than I can."

"Nobody has to explain it to me. I understand the morality behind England's participation. What I don't understand is why you ran off to join the army. Your father was dead set against it."

"So he was, but that didn't stop me," Evan said firmly. He turned away from her, scuffling through the frozen grass, crushing minuscule drifts under the soles of his polished boots. "I was quite stripped of all my other choices at the time, as I recall. Your words when we parted were most effective. You said you never wanted to see me again as long as you lived."

Elizabeth straightened, facing him squarely. "We both said cruel things when we parted. We were children, and both of us were very upset by what we'd so recklessly done."

"Is that how you see it? Infants, then?" He turned his back to her, preventing her from seeing his expression. "Sorry, I don't see it that way at all. Never have."

She took a deep breath of the sharp, cold air. "Evan, we've got to find some way to put that behind us. I didn't mean half the words I said that day. I was upset, and frightened, too. Whether you like it or not, see it my way or not, I really was just a child, in over my head."

He turned to face her, his strong, handsome face full of anguish. "I wasn't frightened, Izzy. Not until you repudiated me. That stripped me of all defense for my actions, and left me utterly terrified of what would happen when the almighty duke of Atholl got his hands on me.

"Have you any idea what kind of a life you condemned me to? What it was like to go back to Cambridge and wait for the summons to come? To dread each rising of the sun, knowing that at any moment a hundred Murray Highlanders could descend upon my simple Cambridge abode, drag me out of my bed and haul me back to Dunkeld for judgment?

"God save me! I couldn't live with that. No man, deserted by the woman he honorably loved and desired, could. We may have been too young, but I had not ruined your virtue or taken your virginity lightly or carelessly. I married you, Elizabeth. Granted, it was the only way I could at that time, but I had acted honorably, and would have stayed by your side through all the troubles to come.

"By forcing me away, by your repudiation of our love, you cast me into hell on earth. You made me a despoiler of innocents. That's what your cowardice did."

"You needn't have feared retaliation," Elizabeth said, but at his harsh glare, she dropped her chin to her breastbone, unable to answer the pain she saw in his eyes. She whispered, "I've never told Papa."

"Aye, to this day, I've assumed that much."

"No one in my family knows. I never confided in any of them, not even Amalia. There's really just you and me and Mr. Paisley," Elizabeth said carefully, knowing she was playing loose with the truth. Byron knew. Monk Lewis knew. So did Elizabeth's solicitor.

"And his wife as witness."

"She passed." Elizabeth began to shake her head. "Sarah Westmorland...Lady Jersey...said Mrs. Paisley passed away the night Sarah wedded. She and Lord Jersey eloped the year after we did."

"We heard about that scandal in Ireland. Colonel Graham said if he was Westmorland, he'd have taken a bull-whip to Jersey, peer of the realm or no. His reason, that the wealthy cit's daughter was a tender ten and six. Jersey's title meant nothing to Colonel Graham. My blood ran cold imagining what he'd do to me."

"You haven't told Uncle Thomas?" Elizabeth asked curiously, not all that certain some confidence hadn't been exchanged between the two men. After all, they were comrades-in-arms, friends.

"God save me, no!" Evan shook his head emphatically. "I'd sooner be hauled up before him on a charge of treason than tell him I took his favorite niece to Gretna Green and eloped with her...then deserted her. He'd have had my cods served up to the whole bloody regiment, and me a eunuch for eternity. That man's straighter than an Edinburgh presbyter."

Of her own accord, Elizabeth fell into step beside Evan, cocking her ear to the sounds their boots made on the squishy snow. "We've got ourselves in a royal pickle, worse than the one Prinny made with his Catholic marriage to Mrs. Fitzherbert."

"Aye," Evan agreed. "But as I said at Almack's, it can be rectified. We're of age now, both you and I."

Elizabeth moistened her lips, preparing to say the worst. "That's assuming both of us want to be married. I haven't any liking for the married state, Evan."

He caught her elbow, yanking her about to face him. "Well, that's just too bad, Elizabeth. You should have decided that before you lifted your skirt the first time."

"Oh!" Elizabeth gasped, insulted to the bone by his base and unnecessary words. She raised her hand and slapped him as hard as she could. "How dare you! That's just like a man, to throw all the blame at me! You cad, you bastard! At fifteen I hadn't the foggiest idea where all your kisses and touches were leading me! You did, you unconscionable scoundrel!"

Chapter Thirteen

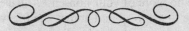

"The hell you say!" Evan caught her hand before she could strike him again. "You knew exactly where we were headed, you lying little baggage. You drove me wild with your flirting and teasing, tormenting me night and day, writing me letters full of wishes and desires. I've kept every one of them, so don't you go trying to put a different spin to the penny now, Izzy Murray. It takes two to tangle between the sheets."

"You are the crudest man alive, to speak of such awful things to me!" Elizabeth railed back at him, furious, tugging on her wrist to free it from his restraining grasp.

"Damn you, Elizabeth!" Evan got the better of her, turning both her hands aside so that she couldn't batter and strike him. "Cease this childish tantrum at once, else I'll end it for you."

"Oh!" Elizabeth stomped at his feet with her heavy weather boots. "Don't try that sanctimonious, autocratic tirade on me, Evan MacGregor. Do you dare to raise your hand to me, I'll have you locked up in the darkest cell in Newgate for assaulting my person."

He yanked her up against his chest, her arms caught and trapped at the small of her back. "There isn't a law in this land that will put a husband in Newgate for anything he does to his lawful wife. I said, stop this, Elizabeth!"

As she struggled vainly against him, the lush fur collar of her cloak tickled his chin, but he was in no mood to be amused by her threats or her actions.

"You devil, let me go!"

He tightened his grip around her body, deliberately making it difficult for her to breathe.

"Lady, you made your bargain with this devil years past. I will tolerate no more of your nonsense. I have given you adequate time to grow up and accept the fate we both selected five years ago. We are legally married, Elizabeth, husband and wife. From here out, you're going to live up to your vows. On that you can make book."

"What did you say?" Elizabeth ceased her struggling, deliberately lowering her voice, lest someone in the houses adjacent to the park overhear their argument. "What exactly is it you demand, MacGregor?"

"A wife, lady. I couldn't make it any plainer. Can you get that through your thick skull?"

"Damn you!" Elizabeth struggled to strike him again. "I won't! I'm not! Let me go! Don't you dare threaten me!"

Evan dropped his hold upon her, furious, incensed by all the words they'd spoken, which had gone so far wide of the mark he'd intended that it was impossible to rectify. He backed up two paces, breathing heavily, struggling, yet determined to make order out of chaos.

"Listen to me, Izzy Murray. You're a woman now. I like the way you've turned out at twenty as well as I liked you at fifteen. You're pretty, and you know it. I expect you've had your head well turned by a sea of compliments from all your London swains. I got a stomachful of them at Almack's on Wednesday. Know you this—I'm through playing childish games."

"If you think this is a game, you've lost your mind," she sputtered.

"You've got that right. This is real. I'll give you till Sunday to explain the way of it to your father—not one day more. That's as long as I'm holding back from claiming what's mine. Have your bags packed and ready, because I'm coming for you at noon, Sunday, after church. You're going home to Balqehidder as my wife, and that's that. Cross me if you dare."

"Cross you if I dare?" Elizabeth shouted. "You've got your nerve, Evan MacGregor! I'll cross you! By God, I'll most likely shoot you, you arrogant, insufferable, pig-headed man!"

"Think you so?"

"I know so. The nerve of you, MacGregor! Do you think that I'm going to march into Papa's study and say, 'Oh, by the way, Papa, did you know I eloped five and a half years ago? So sorry, it just slipped my mind to tell you.' If you do, you, sir, have got another think coming!"

"I don't care how you tell him, Elizabeth. You've had years to find the words." He caught hold of Elizabeth's cloak, where the black silk frogs held it closed over her heaving chest.

"Let go of me!" she demanded.

He deliberately used the trapped fabric to draw her up on her toes, nose-to-nose with him. "Lady," he warned, "you forget to whom you are speaking...your husband. I'm the one empowered here. Seven hundred years of English common law backs up my claim to be your lord and master from the day you vowed to love, honor and obey me until death do we part. I've had enough of this nonsense, do you hear? The game is over. From now on, Elizabeth, you will do as you are told."

He saw that she wasn't cowed in the least. Defiance sparked out of her eyes. She'd have bitten a nail in two, if she'd had one between her clamped teeth.

"The day will never come that a MacGregor tells a Murray what to do," she responded haughtily, freeing her cloak with a determined yank.

Five years of military discipline kept Evan's formidable temper in check. He wasn't going to lower himself to striking a woman, no matter how much Elizabeth goaded him. He nodded. "So this is the way you want it, is it? A test of wills between us? So be it."

"Call it whatever you like!" Elizabeth said cockily, straightening her cloak.

"You think to back me down? We'll see what your father has to say about it then." Evan spun on his heel, stomping through the slush toward the stately mansion at the corner of the block.

Elizabeth's eyes rounded with horror. He wasn't supposed to call her bluff. He was supposed to let her have her way, damn him! She caught up her hems and ran after him.

"Evan! Come back here! Don't you dare! Stop! Don't you dare!" He was mad, beyond thinking rationally. So angry he'd march right into the house and confess all! He'd be killed! "Evan! Evan, for God's sake, stop! Listen to me!"

Evan was not beyond reason completely, though it would not hurt if Elizabeth thought he was. He was angry, but it was a rational anger, born of the certainty that Elizabeth Murray would be more reasonable if she had something akin to the fear of God hanging over her head. Her father's wrath would be just the ticket.

"Evan, damn you, don't make me do this!"

Elizabeth packed snow into a hard, firm ball in her gloved hands, and let a missile fly with deadly accuracy. She had good aim, having been taught by Evan how to throw objects such as snowballs in winter and rocks in summer with a boy's precision.

The cold, wet ball struck the mark she'd intended. The back of Evan's head. Before he had so much as a chance to react, she readied another.

"What do you think you're doing?"

The second snowball caught him in the jaw, taking him totally unawares as he turned. Elizabeth laughed at the astonishment registering on his face.

"Elizabeth! Stop it, damn you!"

"Damn *you!* No, I won't stop!"

She had another ready as he wiped off his jaw. She had to stop him, by any means possible, even if that meant assaulting his dignity. "You're the one who needs to stop, Evan. You're acting like a sanctimonious pig. How dare you threaten me! How dare you show up in London after five long years and start making demands on me! You haven't any rights whatsoever. I won't be forced to do anything."

His black-gloved hand finished wiping snow from his collar, then dropped to his side in a clenched fist. Elizabeth kept her next missile ready, packing it harder and firmer.

"If you want to discuss our situation with me, say so. I'll give you my reasons and answers, but don't you come roaring like a bloody king, acting like you have every right in the world to take over my life, sir. There is no commitment between us. What happened five years ago, was a single act of passion, which we both regretted the very moment the deed was done. I am no more your wife today than I was five years ago at Gretna Green."

His breath frosted the air before him. The bitter cold made Elizabeth shiver, but she held her resolve, waiting for his answer. He dusted damp snow off his gloves. "What is it you are demanding, Elizabeth?"

"That you admit it wasn't only me who repudiated the marriage. You did so, too, sir. We both agreed we'd made a dreadful mistake, that we had acted with the impetuousness of the youths we were at the time. We made no commitment to ride out the storm of scandal, sir. It was agreed we would never broach the subject again.''

"No." Evan shook his head. "Your memory is faulty, Elizabeth. 'Twas you who backed out of the vow and wanted no part of the consequence."

"It wasn't me who ran away and joined the king's army, sir. You did that."

"I bought my commission three months after we'd married, Elizabeth. Before I did that, I waited for you to come to your senses, and realize that what we'd done had to be owned up to. I lived in dread of the post, each and every day of that summer, hoping for word from you. One word and I'd have gone to your father, faced him then and there, as a man should have done.

"You, Elizabeth, stripped me of what little honor we could have gotten from our deed."

His boots crushed the snow as he returned to where she stood armed and ready to pummel him with more snowy abuse.

"You're the one who forced us into a limbo of shame, cowardice and dishonor. All because of a little blood and a few disappointing moments of pain. That was your choice, Elizabeth. Not mine."

"And it's still my choice today, sir," she said, as intractable as ever. "I'll say it once again. A union between us serves no more purpose today than it did five years ago. We are unsuited to one another. I would never be the wife you envision. I have no liking for the duties of the marriage bed. I have sworn to never debase myself in such an awful manner ever again. We have each of us made lives for ourselves, with goals and plans that continue into the future.... A solution for our transgression of the past is available, would you but use your head to reason this out."

"Solution, Elizabeth? Short of widowhood, what solution is there?" Evan sneered.

"Annulment, sir. If not that, divorce."

"Divorce?" he shouted. "You think I will stand aside silent so you can marry another man? Not while I live and breathe, you won't."

"It could be quietly done, avoiding a scandal brought to the floor of Parliament. You need only go to one of the colonies—say, the Windward Isles—and reside there a year. I have made inquiries as to how to go about such a thing."

"I need go?" he growled in a feral voice, one that reminded Elizabeth that, as a Highlander, he could easily revert to becoming a dangerous predator. It was that underlying ferocity that made all true warriors such as he fearsome in battle.

"If divorce has no appeal to you, we have two other options, including annulment," Elizabeth reasoned.

"No." Evan stoutly refused that idea, as well. "I will not lower myself with more lies. I've already told you, the blood was shed, the marriage consummated. Like it or no, I will not go before a judge and unman myself publicly, Elizabeth Murray."

"Then secrecy is our last alternative. As five years have passed without public knowledge ever coming of our rash foolishness, we should go on as we have done."

"You fail to get the point, lady," he said chillingly. "As of this day, I find myself in need of a wife."

"Then get you one." Elizabeth held her ground. She would not back down.

Evan said nothing as he studied her strong jaw, the selfsame jaw that her father and her brothers had inherited. Intractable. It was her most telling Murray trait. For a man, that could be an admirable quality; in Elizabeth, it spelled disaster.

He could be just as stubborn and resolute. That was what had them caught in this situation. One of them must back down. She wouldn't, because it would mean she must face the consequences of their actions, and submit her will to his.

She'd been a strong and willful girl at fifteen. Today she was appallingly single-minded and set in her views.

He wanted more than anything to convince her how right it could be for the two of them, married, sharing the same house, the same bed, caring for one other. God, even if they had to settle for a thatched croft on the high side of Loch Lomond, it would be a wonderful life.

The cold air swirled around Evan, bringing winter's cold mists up to stroke his cheeks and glaze his brow. He saw that he had gone about this all wrong. Elizabeth wasn't going to budge from her obdurate stance. By his show of authority, he had only made her more determined to stand her ground. In a test of pure will, she was determined not to bend one inch.

"Let me see if I have you straight, my lady," he said coldly. "Pray, outline your solution to my stated need. Where do you propose I get the necessary vessel in which to breed the heirs to Balqehidder?"

Elizabeth released the tight breath held in her throat. "Why, simply, sir, I am telling you to select any woman you like. Marry her, for I will make no mention of my prior claim. The legalities can be ignored."

"Legalities ignored?" he shouted. "By God, Elizabeth, they cannot!"

"Yes, they can!" she argued. "They have been from the start. By our very secrecy, employed from the moment the deed was done, we have ignored the legalities of it. And so can we continue to do. You, sir, are considered a free agent by all within our circle. I will not stand in the way of your seeing to the baronetcy's issue."

"And you? What of your own future? Do not think I will stand silent, should you move to take a husband other than I!"

"I have told you numerous times. Please hear me this time! I will never marry! Nor will Father press me. We, he and I, have agreed. The choice of a husband is totally mine to make and I have no intention of ever taking one. I don't want interference in my life. I have things to keep me occupied long into the future years.

"You may not think it much, but correspondence occupies the major portion of my days. It's a worthy objective for anyone's life. Regarding what is required of me socially, I have groomed myself to take Aunt Nicky's place at Bell's Wynd. That will keep me occupied and busy down the years. There you have it—my plans for my life. It will in no way interfere with yours."

She had neatly tied up all the loose ends of their lives, as if they were packages to be stored in the attic and forgotten forever. Evan saw that. He wanted to shake the very daylights out of her, but the sting of her words, of the plans and goals that eliminated him from her life, kept his hands rigid at his side.

She blithely ignored the passion that raged between them, as if borne on the mist.

Did he but put his hands on her this very moment, she'd respond. Her body drew him. Her beauty, her scent, her mystic woman's allure. He realized, too late, that the only way he would bring Elizabeth willingly into their marriage was by seduction.

He stopped himself from mentioning that, cognizant that she had abhorred the physical union of his shaft plunging into her body. Up to that point, all that passed between him and Elizabeth Murray had been beautiful and perfect.

She was the woman God had made for him. To force her would be to rape her . . . to take her against her will. Evan would not do that.

So he had no choice except to bring her willingly to him by other means. Hence, he must take charge of both their circumstances, and control all future contact between them.

He could not let her go. His heart would not allow him to relinquish all claim upon her. The only hope he found embedded in her words was that there was no other man who had taken paramount interest in her affections.

Yes, he could force her hand, by appealing to her father or by making public their vows. But would not that also be forcing her, just as unwilling, into his bed?

It would; in his mind, it would. He wanted her to come to him freely, of her own volition, to realize all that he realized, that the union between them would be beautiful, passionate and fulfilling for both of them.

Nothing less would ever suit him than her complete trust that he would never hurt her again.

He gathered his thoughts, thinking this through, devising a plan that would accomplish his objective in as timely a manner as possible. Evan cocked his head to his right shoulder, his eyes intently studying the strong, square face wrapped in wool and furs before him.

Odd... She was a woman, and yet had made no mention of love in any of her testimony. Why not? Women were silly things, romantic and pleading for love in the most unlikely places.

"I find it most peculiar you have made no mention of love in this, Elizabeth. Are you telling me that you no longer believe you loved me with all your heart and soul in 1802?" he asked bluntly.

"No, of course not." Elizabeth blinked, stunned by his question. "I have always loved you, Evan. It is because of my love for you that I give you the freedom to seek another to fulfill the duties of a wife. I am aware of my limitations and weaknesses. Regardless of that, I will always love you."

"You have a most unnatural way of showing it."

At those harsh words, Elizabeth looked away, turning her gaze to the snow on the ground. "I'm sorry that I have failed you. I do regret it, and wish that I could be a woman fulfilled, as other ladies are, but I have long since learned to content myself with my cold practices. It cannot be helped. This is the way God made me.''

It could be helped, Evan knew. He should bed her again. He was no longer a callow, inexperienced youth. He could pleasure her in ways she never dreamed. Again he cursed the impulses of youth that had brought them to this course.

''Your altruism is laudable,'' he answered. ''Divorce is out of the question, whether in some far-flung colony or a court of law here.''

Elizabeth exhaled deeply, relieved to hear him agree to that. There would be no way to avoid a scandal, were he to take her to court in England or Scotland. Monk Lewis's suggestion of doing so in the colonies was only just slightly more acceptable, because of the great distance of the Windwards from London.

Society as a whole shunned divorced women, but Elizabeth saw it as bearing little more stigma than did spinsterhood, in reality. A spinster, even one as revered as Aunt Nicky, was still regarded by all and sundry as an unnatural creature...a failure as a woman. To Elizabeth's great shame, she was just that...a failure. She prayed that Evan would not make her admit that final indignity to him. She hurt badly enough as it was.

''Nor will I be party to some farcical appeal for an annulment. You will not drag my manhood through a court of appeals like that, Elizabeth.''

''That leaves us with one choice, Evan. Secrecy.''

''Quite so,'' he said ominously.

Elizabeth let fall the packed snow from her hands and brushed off her gloves. She thought fast and hard, taking quick measure of this small victory. She found no recourse in Evan's hard face. His opaque, night black eyes had not softened one bit.

''Will you give me your word of honor as a gentleman, swear that you will never tell a living soul about our past?

Even if...even if you feel yourself provoked...will you keep your silence?''

"You ask too much, Elizabeth. I canna give that."

Elizabeth blinked a snowflake from her lashes. "Then how are we to go from here?"

"We can't, Elizabeth. It's wrong. It's dishonorable. It's beneath the both of us. I want your permission to speak to your father, but I am warning you, even without your agreement, I will press my suit to him. It's as simple as that. I can do it either of two ways, Elizabeth. Tell him what was done in the past, or else speak to him of marrying you by special license shortly in the future. The choice of how I approach him is yours."

"You haven't listened to a single word I've said," she whispered, shocked.

"Aye, I've heard every one—more than a stomachful of such nonsense. The one who isn't listening is you. I've told you, I've made up my mind to do the right thing. That's the way it is going to be."

Elizabeth shook her head. "Evan, my father will kill you if you tell him of the past."

He won't, said his eyes.

He will, because of Robbie, thrummed her heart. God, please tell me how can I protect him? Elizabeth thought.

The temptation to throw her arms around his neck and hold him to her as a last, desperate measure was so strong, she almost surrendered to that impulse. But she couldn't, under any circumstances, let him know that by his very stubbornness he was now forcing her hand.

Her only choice left was to flee...to take Robbie and leave England...to get as far from this tangled coil as the two of them could go. She took a deep, cleansing breath of the cold air and smiled tremulously.

"Of course, you must do as your honor sees fit," she admitted, adding privately, *And I must do what I must to protect you, you foolish, foolish man.*

She tucked both her damp gloves around his arm at his elbow, fingers tightening as she spoke blithely. "I am so glad that we had this talk, Evan. I would like us to be friends again. You have no idea how important that is to me. There has never been anyone whose friendship I ever treasured more than yours.

"It's been very hard, these past weeks, to know that we were at cross purposes. But all that's behind us now, isn't it?"

"Friends, hmmm?" He fell into step beside her, walking through the winterland of the snowy park, unbalanced by her odd shift in mood. "Soul mates, Grasso used to call us."

"Ah, yes, so she did," Elizabeth concurred. "Black soul mates, and wicked little demons, as I recall. We did torment the old biddy, didn't we?"

"Aye, we did."

Evan could see the usefulness of allowing her to think that they could just be friends. Friends could easily become lovers. That might be the very best way to bring her to heel.

He would do that, he vowed privately. He would bring Elizabeth Murray to him. She would beg him to make love to her, to give her the fulfillment she so foolishly thought she did not need. He put his mind to it then and there. She would submit, come hell or high water. She would submit to him in all things.

Elizabeth Murray would learn that he, a MacGregor, would and could tell her what to do.

She prattled on while they walked the snowy park, as Evan became accustomed to this new role he was forcing himself to play.

Elizabeth's tight fingers on his arm told him subtle things about her...things he had always known, yet somehow had lost sight of since that night, when Tullibardine had got shot. Elizabeth Murray was possessive—of friends in particular—protective, too. Since he was jealous of her associations with eligible men, he wondered if she would feel jealousy, too.

They walked in companionable silence. A smattering of snow dotted his shoulders, and Elizabeth reached up to brush the flakes off the top layer of his greatcoat.

"Tell me about Port-a-shee," he commanded when their eyes met.

The question came out of the blue, rocking Elizabeth to her foundations. Then she remembered having mentioned her father's house on the Isle of Man earlier.

"No." Elizabeth turned her face to the wind, disengaging from the seductive draw of his eyes. Had he any idea how hard she had to work to resist him? She glared at the frozen trees, which were coated now with nearly an inch of snow on every horizontal branch.

"Tell me what you thought of it," Evan commanded. "I find it most peculiar the duke took you there, when historically he would only take his sons to Man."

"He took you," Elizabeth countered.

"Yes, but I met his requirement, being male. He never offered to let Amalia or you accompany us. I know he forbade it both years when you demanded to come along, too. What made him change his mind?"

Elizabeth's shoulders lifted negligently under the warm protection of her heavy cloak. She regretted having mentioned Port-a-shee at all. "It was a test of wills. The duke's against mine."

"Ah, I see. So he relented, then. You wore him down, did you?"

"Yes, I must have." Elizabeth moved onto the frozen lawn, both hands out to catch drifting snowflakes. They were huge and fluffy, whirling in the wind like goosedown floating from a ruptured pillow.

"I suppose you don't know it, but in the summer of 1802, Blair House was under siege. Amalia and I were in a constant state of war. Papa announced he'd had enough by mid-August. He said a trip to Port-a-shee would put an end to my rising. I think I told him I wouldn't go to the Isle of Man if it was the last place on earth with bread and water. Which," she added as an aside, "was the state of my diet after a month of fruitless revolution."

"Amalia again, hmmm?" Evan said, to encourage her to continue.

"Ah, yes, she's the bane of my existence—besides you," Elizabeth said teasingly. "She made the two years that followed our, uh... Oh, this is silly. I hate having to guard my tongue every hour of the day and night. I've learned well how to do it, mind you, but at least between us, I can be frank when no one is listening. I'm just reluctant to make that a habit, Evan."

"May I suggest you euphemistically call it our *adventure,* then?"

"There, that does it splendidly. Thank you." Elizabeth grinned again. She was achingly beautiful when she smiled. He actually hurt, because he could not draw her into his arms and share that smile over a kiss. "Anyway, after our *adventure,* Amalia was as suspicious as a cat is curious. She can't leave well enough alone, you see."

"Tell me about Port-a-shee, not Amalia. Didn't you think it the wildest, fiercest, most beautiful place on earth?"

Elizabeth dissembled. "I found it hot, ugly, cold and wet. And, yes, it is the most splendid place on earth. The very rocks sing with the wind, night or day. I'd never been any place like it in my life.

"When I got there and found out how thoroughly you men had hoarded it my whole life, I wanted to shoot Papa, not grouse. But that's another story. Tell me about Ireland. What were your duties there?"

"Humph," Evan grunted, unsatisfied by her answers. "Can't say I remember all that much about my first year in the army. I drank lots back then, got myself into stupid fights and spent way too many hours on scut duty, or else in the brig. Graham got me straightened out, eventually. Will it suffice to say I was flogged enough to gain some sense in my thick head?"

Elizabeth frowned. "You're stretching the truth, aren't you?"

"Would that I were. No, Elizabeth. In the beginning I was not a model soldier. It was a difficult adjustment from spoiled son and rowdy student to disciplined man."

"I'm sorry," she said honestly. "That was my fault, wasn't it?"

"I can't blame my bad habits on you, Elizabeth. I tipped each bottle with my own hand. Graham made me face that."

Hindsight told him now that he hadn't needed to run away. He could have stayed and paid the piper, but then, what did a boy know about being a man? Little, damned little; he knew that now.

"The mist is thicker there," Elizabeth said, returning to her walk and the topic of Port-a-shee. Since he had opened up and let her glimpse his torment after their elopement, she felt it important to reveal some of her own. Some, not all.

As he fell into step beside her, Evan said, "Aye, I though so, too."

"Fairy's song—Port-a-shee—sounds mystical in Gaelic. No one understands it anymore. Like Latin, a whole beautiful language is lost." Elizabeth sighed. "Papa has built a new house on the Isle of Man and renamed it Castle Mona, so that his English guests will understand what he means, but it loses the beauty and mystery of the old tongue in its translation. Sometimes I hate England, Evan. What she's done to us."

"What we've done to ourselves, Elizabeth."

In Evan's years of being fostered, the duke of Atholl had become his father in loco parentis. Evan had learned more than the mystery and the intricacy of the English tongue; he'd been taught manners, decorum, the vagaries of court behavior, politics and how to survive as a Scotsman in a world ruled by English law, power and money.

"What was that?" Evan turned to look at Elizabeth, having lost whatever words she'd said in his reverie.

"I said I stayed at Port-a-shee a full year."

"Ah, I did not know that." Evan stopped dead in his tracks, brought to a halt by her words and the sudden thought they caused to explode in his mind. A year...a full long year...when it only took nine moons to bring a child into this world. Was wee Robbie his son? He closed his eyes to hold back the hurt. But when he opened them again, he saw Elizabeth in a whole different light.

Had she gone it alone? Confiding in no one? Until her father had noted her physical changes and used his prerogatives to remove her for a little while from society's view? He felt his blood thrum in his ears, thinking, *Tell me the truth, Elizabeth, tell me.* But all he could manage to say was "Why?"

She reached for a low-lying branch of the nearest elm, tugged on it forcefully, then released it abruptly, just to watch a shower of snow fall to the covered earth. She turned back to look at Evan with a face that hinted at the sullenness rampant during a thwarted teenage year. "If you must know, I reigned triumphant as an enfant terrible. The dowager and the aunts declared me unfit for gentle company."

"How so?" He wanted to comfort her, and didn't know how to go about it. *Tell me, Elizabeth, tell me all of it.*

"Will it suffice to say I was moody, rebellious, ornery, headstrong, spoiled rotten and probably demented?"

"No."

She met his gaze levelly, holding her head up proudly, then shrugged a pretty shoulder. "Too bad. I'm not saying any more. Everything is best forgotten."

She looked so vulnerable then, Evan wanted to cradle her against his heart. He wasn't the only one who had come away from Gretna Green terribly wounded. Never in his worst nightmares had he given a thought to what she might have faced as a result of their one tryst. Was Robbie his son? She came to him and tucked her fingers into the crook of his arm. "I'm cold now. Will you take me in?"

"Will you still talk freely to me if I do?"

"Yes." Her eyes met his, conveying something very private. They knew most of each other's darkest secrets. She asked for more than understanding in her silent appeal, she asked for his trust, and willingly gave hers to him.

Evan patted her gloved finger and calmly walked her down the long paved walk crossing the park. "We can work this out, Elizabeth," he said reasonably.

"Can we?" She deliberately changed the subject. "I wonder how late it is?"

"Since we haven't heard any bells chiming, I would hazard it's a little shy of six."

"Good," Elizabeth answered. "After dinner, I intend to get a good night's sleep. I've plans for tomorrow. Hester Stanhope is hostessing an afternoon salon. I'm hoping Byron will be allowed a chance to speak."

That one again, Evan thought. "I doubt he will. I saw Carlisle at Green Park this morn. He's hot on Byron's tail, furious at the expenses the wastrel's run up on his latest holiday away from academia."

"He admires you, you know."

"Byron?" Evan asked in surprise. "Whatever for?"

"Don't you know? All the young bloods at Cambridge still talk about your legendary throwing off of the traces. How you escaped your father's men and evaded capture. Very brave, milord."

"Ha!" He laughed. "Did I, then? Actually, what I did was purchase a commission, ironclad, from the duke of York's mistress. The army had me by the short hairs. Neither your father nor Lord Lovat could get me released from the Crown's clutches. It wasn't all bad, though. I did have the excellent good fortune of coming under the wing of the best fighting man I've ever had the chance to know, Thomas Graham."

"He took you in? Actually?"

"Aye, though to tell the truth, he probably should not have bothered. The Irish seemed to know I had a death wish."

Elizabeth murmured. "You were always bold, Evan."

"Totally lacking in foresight, is what my father claimed," Evan admitted wryly.

"Have you gotten over it? This recklessness?"

"Somewhat. I control it now."

Elizabeth paused at the curb of the street that separated the private park from the houses it served, and sighed. "I missed your letters the most."

She gazed at the bank of glass fronting her father's house. Evan neither heard nor saw any indication that she wished to hear him echo the same loss, the same regret.

Her lips parted, and her tongue touched them, bringing moisture to the luscious surface. He was captivated by that gesture, wanting to kiss her, desperate to taste once more her sweetness and her fire.

"That's what started all the trouble," she said.

Evan started, frowning down at her. "Surely—"

"No, no..." She interrupted him, to clarify what she'd said. "The post is sacrosanct to Papa. He would not countenance a violation of the privacy of the post. It was Amalia, asking me questions after our weekly flow of letters stopped. She is worse than a terrier with a rabbit locked between its jaws. She always wants to know the why and what of things. Why we were no longer friends after so many, many years of faithful correspondence. What had you done that made me not write to you? What had I done that had caused you to sever all contact completely?

"In midsummer, Amalia visited your sister and her new husband in Edinburgh, and came home raving about what had become of you—a runaway with a contraband commission. She and I were at daggers drawn all the time then. I was tired of her bossy ways."

"I see."

"Girls are supposed to be meek and mannerly, biddable. Amalia told Papa I was intractable."

Evan threw back his head, laughing. "Indeed?"

"Oh, yes. Papa says I'm more devious a Murray than Grandfather George, who laid siege to his own home, Blair House, in '45, and then led half the clan to slaughter at Culloden. I suppose it's true. Amalia still hasn't a clue of the truth." *And never will,* Elizabeth added silently.

"Devious or no, I would be content with you as my wife," Evan said.

"No. I prefer things the way they are. In that I am like Papa. I'm glad you've pulled in your horns, MacGregor." She followed that bald statement with another. "I suppose you want to know the sordid details."

"Only if you want to tell me. But know you this, Izzy, Amalia is Amalia. Neither you nor I can change her, nor should we want to."

"I think she is the strongest of us."

"You mean of Tullie, Glenlyon and you?"

"Yes. Charlotte doesn't count. She's been married and in her own home for ages and ages."

"Agreed. Amalia is a strong and sure woman, certain of her purposes and what's right and wrong." Evan granted that.

"So am I," Elizabeth insisted. "I don't have to be the one to rule the roost, though. I have learned to exist peaceably alongside her and Papa's authority. When the troubles began, I thought I had to fight for every scrap of freedom that I wanted. Like that dance when I was fifteen.

"It was such a little thing, one Scottish reel—but, oh, the turmoil it caused. You would have thought one scold afterward would have been enough, but no, it went on and on for days, for weeks, even. If it wasn't Amalia nagging at me over how wicked I had been, it was Aunt Nicky, Aunt Charlotte, Grandmother, and my sister Charlotte, too."

Izzy smiled impishly, her grin so totally endearing that Evan was tempted to lay her down in the snow and make love to her then and there. He shoved his restless hands inside the deep pockets of his greatcoat.

"Why, a week after that dance, you'd have sworn I'd kissed the devil's own toe. And, of course, by then there was another assembly... and, woe is me, I was a fallen woman who hadn't yet had a chance to get up on the pedestal to fall off it first!" Elizabeth laughed. "Such a big to-do about nothing."

"Naturally." His eyes twinkled with the same shared mischief. He stopped suddenly on the deserted street and swept his arm across his belly in a familiar gesture of their times. "Miss Murray, may I have this dance?"

"Why, Mr. MacGregor!" Elizabeth gently tapped his arm in a mock scold. "I cannot possibly dance with you."

"Oh, but you can, lass," he taunted, pulling her into his arms. "To hell with the wags and scolds. Let's dance!"

He caught her close and spun her across the frozen ground, whistling a familiar strathspey. Elizabeth laughed boldly, twirling and spinning with him, as breathless and light as the wind in his arms, as sure on her feet now as she had been at fifteen.

They came to a happy stop on the edge of a patch of ice that glazed the cobblestones. Elizabeth panted, one hand pressed against her wool-and-fur-wrapped throat, the other fast behind his neck.

"Do you have any idea how it pained Aunt Nicky to have to blackball her own niece?" she asked impishly, with eyes that fairly sparkled beneath a fringe of dampened elf-locks.

"Did she?" Evan said, reminding her he knew Nicola Murray, too.

"No." Elizabeth had to admit the truth. "But she did have half of Edinburgh laying for you. Only you cleverly thwarted her again. You didn't attend the next assembly." Izzy wagged a scolding finger under his nose.

Evan caught hold of it and drew her closer to him, close enough that he could bite that gloved finger, just a tad fiercely, enough to make her yelp. Elizabeth shivered deliciously and leaned into him, a smile softening her lips.

Evan said most solemnly, "I fear, sweet Elizabeth, that I was in no condition to ride ten leagues and back a mere two days later. The penalty for young Scotsmen who step beyond the bounds of Edinburgh society's expectations is not a diet of unending scolds."

Izzy's eyes widened in surprise. "You don't mean...your father skelped you? Why, Evan, he was auld...and you were a man grown, even then."

"Aye." Evan grumbled at the uncomfortable memory. "Not quite sixty, but I assure you, my lady, my da had the arm of a man half his age to the day he died."

Elizabeth was genuinely shocked by his admission. "You never even hinted at that in your letters after Bell's Wynd, or mentioned it before we traveled to Lanrick Castle for Marie's wedding."

"Surely you don't think a proud lad would own up to getting his arse whipped for dancing with the girl he loved, do you? If I had, I'd have been the first swain that ever did."

"Then why..." Elizabeth's voice trailed off into silence.

"Why did I continue to write you letters? Why did I deliberately seek you out when you came to Lanrick for Marie's wedding?" Evan's arm tightened across her back.

"Well, yes, why?" she said, puzzled.

"Because you were forbidden to me. Da made that clear, with no ifs, ands or buts. His Grace the duke of Atholl could look much higher than to poor Lanrick, Loch Lomond and Balquhidder for a match for his most treasured daughter."

"But... when we came to the gathering, no one said a word to me—especially not you. And it was just like before, when we were children. You and I were together all the time... until..."

She turned her face away for a moment, then looked right at Evan. "Why'd you do it, Evan? Suggest we run away and marry at Gretna Green?"

"Because I fair burned to have you, Elizabeth Murray, and it was the only way. Remember, you're a lady, and ladies don't."

She leaned lightly against his embrace, her hands on his shoulders, echoing the position of their momentary fling... the position he most wanted her to be in... embraced in the circle of his arms... And she laughed her delicate, musical lady's laugh, amused.

"That's what Byron says—ladies don't." She seemed to become aware of the intimacy of their position all at once, and she lifted her gloved hands from his shoulder and upper arm.

"I fear I've heard so much talk about romance that the whole idea of it is highly overrated in my mind now." Elizabeth shuddered as she made clear a home truth. "I can't see or imagine wanting to do *that* again—ever! Once, in my case, was most certainly enough."

Elizabeth relaxed at last. She'd said it, made her position clear. Surely now he understood that he would always have had to look elsewhere for gratification of his base needs . . . not to her.

Evan watched the movement her mouth made as she dismissed lovemaking with repugnance, but at the same time she came intimately closer—her mouth dangerously near to his. How was it that she could speak and think one thing, while her body declared another? Which one was the truth?

Her moist, parted lips tempted him to close the distance between them once and for all. He bent to catch those lips, to taste her anew. Driven by the eternal demon inside him, wanting her, only her, and no one else. He could no more resist the lure than he could stop the next beat of his own heart.

She would not yield him her mouth, but resisted, her fingers kneading against his greatcoat. He nipped at her lips, catching them, pleading his own case with the only means he had to woo her—his desire, his lips, his body.

"Evan." She turned her cheek against his, whispering huskily. Her hands trembled against his chest, holding him at bay. He caught her lips and kissed her, deeply, lovingly, with all his heart and soul. And she melted in his arms, all the woman he could ever want to hold, to love forever.

Their lips parted, and she whispered his name. "Evan . . ."

"Oh, God, yes, Elizabeth. What? Tell me what you want. Tell me how to touch you, what will please you, anything, everything. Whatever you want, whatever you need, I'll give it to you, I swear on my father's grave . . . I'll get it for you. Tell me."

"Stop this. Don't do this to me anymore."

Chapter Fourteen

Evan pulled away so sharply, he nearly slipped on the
mirror-bright ice at their feet. He looked as though she'd
burned him with searing coals, instead of mere words.

Elizabeth swallowed as he came rigidly to attention before her. She'd touched the right nerve—the rawest one—
and for a split second, she felt as guilty as sin itself.

Oh, the anger that seethed and blazed from his eyes cut
her deeply... to the bone... but she knew she mustn't waver or yield him an inch. He had to be made to understand. Now, before this awful coil unraveled any further.

He caught the cuffs of his sleeves, yanking them down
below his wrists. The tendons in his throat knotted more
ferociously than the muscles in his jaw. Elizabeth didn't
doubt for a moment that, had she been a man, he'd have
beaten her to a raw and bloody pulp right there on the
street.

She shifted uneasily. Instinct commanded she prepare to
defend herself, if need be. The door to her father's house
stood two hundred yards away. She could run to safety,
even on glaring ice, she hoped.

He lifted his right hand. She expected to hear him shout,
curse, bring down the Horse Guard. She wasn't at all ready
for the low, feral growl that issued from the back of his

throat. "You callous, coldhearted bitch! You'll use anything, won't you, to have your way?"

Elizabeth blinked, backing up, mindful of the direction she needed to go. His extended hands clenched impotently before her, then turned into hard fists that dropped to his sides.

"Damn you, Elizabeth Murray."

"Damn me? Damn you, Evan MacGregor! One of us has got to put a stop to this pointless kissing."

"Pointless!" His voice roared out over the cold street and reverberated back at Elizabeth from the buildings surrounding them. "By God, woman, you enjoy kissing just as much as I do."

"No." Elizabeth backed up farther. "I don't. I didn't. I mean . . . you always take it to mean more than it does."

"You like it! You respond, damn you!"

"Yes. Yes. Yes! So what? So what if I do? That's the point. It ruins everything . . . turns you into a bloody madman! Oh, damn you, go away. Why did you have to come back? Just to torment and torture me? What more can I say? How can I tell you I don't want you? Not like that! Damn *you*, Evan MacGregor." She turned and fled.

Evan caught her at the steps of her father's house, yanking her back to him. Her cloak swirled around both of them, tangling in their limbs. His fingers dug ruthlessly into her upper arms. His breath came harsh and hard on the cold air between them. Elizabeth trembled at the furious set of his jaw. "Do you realize what you have just done?"

Elizabeth bravely lifted her chin. "I've begged you to cease badgering me at every turn. I've stopped you, the only way I know how."

"No." He shook his head vehemently. "You took advantage of the one weakness I have inside me, my love for you. That has sustained me, lo these many years, Elizabeth. It's kept me going when I would rather have laid down my sword and died. Well, you've killed it now, girl.

Stabbed me in the heart. We're finished. You want cold-hearted and calculating, lady? I'll give you that.''

Again his fingers tightened, and he shook her once more. "We're finished, you hear me? I will wipe you from my mind, my heart and my soul. From here on, you are out of my life forever. You have what you want, Lady Elizabeth Murray. I'm done with you completely.

"I pray to God the day will come that you'll come to me on your knees, begging me to help you. I won't. I'll turn my back on you and walk away. Never again will I lay myself vulnerable at your feet, to be crushed under your cruel whims and heartless vanities. That's what you can take to your grave.''

He thrust her around, pushing her ruthlessly up the steps, and hammered on the door with his fist.

Keyes's gray brows hiked in a gentle inquiry when he opened the door and found them on the steps. Music flooded the foyer. Elizabeth recognized Amalia's accomplished bow stroking her violin in accompaniment to Glenlyon's adept fingering of the Broadwood pianoforte.

"I'll have your cocoa ready in a thrice," Keyes promised by way of welcome.

"*Uisge beatha* would suit me better," Evan said in clipped tones.

"Very good, sir," Keyes responded. "Whiskey it is."

"I'll take my cocoa upstairs, Keyes." Elizabeth managed to speak in modulated tones as she surrendered cloak and gloves. She sat on a cushioned bench and shed her warm boots, then stood and dared to risk a look at Evan's face as he shook off his greatcoat.

His cheeks were ruddy from the cold. His mouth was a severe slash below the proud protrusion of his straight and noble Roman nose.

The warm lights of the foyer showed his eyes to be midnight blue, all the heat and fire inside them banked. He stared at her as if she didn't exist anymore; he was as dispassionate as an emperor regarding a slave.

Elizabeth swallowed against the resistance of a dry throat and pulled her pride up from the trampling he'd just given her. She hadn't courted his hatred, but it was obvious that that was all he bore her now. She deliberately refrained from physically soothing the throbbing hurt that remained in her arms from the force of his grip.

"Thank you for the pleasant walk in the snow, Captain MacGregor," Elizabeth said for the sake of appearances. "Good night, sir."

"Good night, Lady Elizabeth." Evan bowed stiffly, correctly, but that was also a formality, nothing more. He turned on his heel, stalked into the billiard room and never looked back.

And something very precious and private died inside Elizabeth's heart. Quickly, before Keyes could make note of the tears filling her eyes and spilling down her cheek, Elizabeth hitched up her skirt and ran up stairs.

She made use of the hour remaining before dinner was served to compose herself. She would not allow a single crack or weakness in her mental armor to show before her family.

During dinner, Elizabeth managed not to reveal any trace of the hurt she felt inside. Evan's presence made her air of calm difficult, but not impossible to retain. His mood was black and silent. He ate little, drank much and contributed nothing to the flow of conversation, making Elizabeth doubly glad that her grandmother, the dowager and the aunts declared they would prefer having an early evening. Released, Elizabeth fled to the dubious sanctuary of her room.

Evan would have needed a butcher knife to cut the air inside the duke of Atholl's billiard room as the hour of midnight approached. Colonel Graham's rum-soaked

Havana crook, and the duke's specially blended pipe tobacco, generated enough atmosphere to smoke German sausage. In comparison, the mild Virginia cheroot in Evan's hand seemed redundant, neither adding to nor detracting from the heavy, fragrant fog cloying the air.

It was a first; he'd never smoked with the duke before. In his youth, he'd shared a contraband cheroot or two with Glenlyon and Tullibardine...behind the stables, of course. Never in the house. He'd smoked with Colonel Graham many times since becoming an officer. Smoking was an army tradition, a man's tradition, and deeply tied to a young man's coming of age and being accepted in powerful circles. Evan participated, but had no true fondness for the habit.

He sprawled in the heavy chair, his boots stretched to the roaring fire, a warm balloon of excellent brandy in one hand, the cigar in the other. In the leather armchair opposite, Lord Murray effortlessly chugged out concentric smoke rings, one inside the other.

Across the room Glenlyon and Colonel Graham competed ruthlessly with one another, blasting the ivory balls to kingdom come with each breaking of the rack. One, then the other, ran the table, while Tullibardine sat on a padded stool, chiding them over their skill, or lack of it, with a pool cue.

The ladies had retired upstairs, and all the servants except Keyes had been dismissed. Evan bode his time, awaiting Colonel Graham's convenience, anxious to return to their post.

John Murray broke their agreeable and mutual silence by the fire. "You look a little more the thing now, MacGregor. The brandy has mellowed you somewhat. Have you warmed up, then?"

"Aye." Evan grunted the response that was necessary. In truth, the brandy, preceded by numerous applications of fine Scotch whiskey, kept Evan from feeling his feet. They could be burning to charred stubs inside his boots; he didn't know, and he didn't care.

"Damned fine brandy," Atholl continued. "The best smuggled ashore in at least a decade. Believe your father had a nip or two from this same batch the last time I saw him alive."

"Did he?" Evan inquired.

"Came to me, you know, as the court of last resort, to have you yanked out of His Majesty's services." The duke stirred in his armchair to reach for the bottle and refill his glass. Evan watched, bleary-eyed, as the duke poured another inch of the potent liquor into Evan's crystal balloon.

"Don't know how you managed it, seeing that you weren't but a boy at the time, but there wasn't anything I could do to have your commission revoked—even though the bloody thing was a forgery."

Evan lifted the fragile crystal to his mouth and tasted the brandy anew, savoring it as much for the taste as for the smooth way it slid down his throat without a single trace of burn. He thought it a good thing he was stretched out, nearly flat on his back. Otherwise, the wicked French brew would have knocked him off his pins.

"I expect this brandy softened him up then, had him leaving in better humor than when he came. Wicked brute when he was crossed." Evan's brain was functioning, more or less, albeit primitively. The red haze of rage that clouded his afternoon had diminished somewhat.

"Never met a MacGregor that wasn't, when his back was up. You've learned a modicum of control in that direction, I see," the duke said.

Had he? Not judging by the hard words that had crossed his lips this day. Evan closed his eyes. They burned. He was tired—exhausted, really. Sleep might come, but never rest. He opened his red eyes a minute later, to the same cheerfully burning pyre roasting the soles of his boots.

The room was warm, too warm. He'd shed his jacket and weskit a long time ago. His cravat dangled down his chest, his stiffened collar had been removed and his studs disposed of in his pocket.

"I suppose we should come to some amicable decision about Elizabeth," Atholl said.

"In what regard?" Evan asked coldly. The mention of Elizabeth tightened his jaw, his fingers, his scrotum, blinded him anew with purple rage. He mustn't forget to whom he was speaking . . . the ninth Lord Strange, lord of the Isle of Man, duke of Atholl, current owner of the last fortress within the British Isles to undergo a siege, Blair House.

"It's obvious, isn't it?" John Murray said.

Evan swallowed hard, willing the fuzz coating his tongue and his brain to evaporate. It wouldn't. He mumbled stupidly, "No, sir."

"Good God man, is the brandy that good? Have you forgotten you came indoors with bloody murder on your mind? Ha!" A deep laugh rumbled from the duke's expansive chest. "I've seen that look on your face a time or two. Elizabeth has a tendency to get under a man's skin, she does. Thought for years it was only me she goaded to the point of bloody murder."

"No, sorry, sir. I don't follow you at all."

"Do you not get my drift, sir?" Atholl said testily.

Evan crushed out the burning coal in his cigar and turned his head to meet Atholl's stare. The man glared right back at him. Evan knew he must look as disreputable as hell, but still, he'd never seen His Grace look so.

For a fleeting moment, Evan imagined that the duke knew all and saw all. But surely that had to be the brandy and smoke befuddling Evan's eyes. Evan blinked and tried to focus his eyes on the elder, but the duke's features swam before his eyes in multiple forms.

The duke dropped his pipe onto a bowl on the table at his elbow, tossed the dregs of his third glass of brandy into his throat and shambled to his feet, pulling out his pocket watch to gaze at its face. He shook his head, muttering, "Well, that can't be helped, then, MacGregor. No, no, no. This will never do. Great Caesar's ghost, it's gone half past midnight. See here, Thomas, I'm completely off my schedule."

He marched across the room to the windows and threw open the shutters, allowing a snow flurry to blast into the billiard room.

Evan coughed as he stood up. He didn't dare polish off what was left in his glass.

"Thomas, have you looked outside? It's coming down like a righteous Orkney blizzard. The street's buried under two feet of snow. No, no. This won't do. No sense in your traveling halfway across England in this. MacGregor, I'll have Keyes fetch you up a room."

Evan felt the trap closing. He watched with impotent horror as his commanding officer strode to the window to evaluate the deepening storm.

"Humph!" Graham gripped his cigar between his teeth. "You were right, MacGregor. It's only gotten worse, just as you predicted. We should have left before dinner was served. We'd have made it across town then. That tears it. Atholl, my adjutant and I are staying the night."

Inside, Evan screamed, *No!* A thousand excuses came to mind, all engineered to get him out of this bloody house, away, far, far, far away, from Elizabeth Murray.

Ever efficient, Mr. Keyes instantly answered the duke's summons on the bellpull. He patiently assured the duke he'd anticipated just such problems—impassable roads and a storm that wouldn't let up. London would shut down for the duration. Keyes had everything in hand—beds warmed, food on hand, all the accoutrements needed to outlast a winter storm.

"We'll have to do this again, my boy." Atholl turned, addressing Evan, as he picked up the day's paper and fanned the thick smoke toward the open window.

"Certainly, sir." Evan fumbled with his collar button, raked his fingers through his hair and caught his discarded coat and vest in one hand.

"It's settled, then," the duke said cryptically as he dropped the paper on a desk.

Evan wanted to ask, *What's settled?* But he didn't dare. The duke dismissed him, wagging his hand in the direction of the door. "Go on, then. Keyes will lead you to a room. It's all settled. We'll do this again in the future. Most enjoyable."

Evan retained enough sense to head for the door and escape into the lighter atmosphere of the hallway. He caught his hand on the lion topping the newel post and stiffened his back to military precision prior to marching stiffly up the stairs. At the landing, he caught himself, made a brain-whirling right-face and proceeded to weave his way down the hall, rigidly avoiding pilasters and columns, topped by busts of Roman emperors—save the one of Julius Caesar. During the tussle to keep Julius from shattering, Evan's marriage license fluttered to the floor. One corner of the document stuck under the closed door of the duke of Atholl's suite.

Oblivious to his loss, Evan blinked owlishly when Keyes opened a door for him. A sense of déjà vu swamped Evan's weary brain. It was the same chamber he'd occupied as a boy, complete with the high single bed and mahogany wardrobe, and the desk and chair facing the bank of two windows overlooking the park. Nothing appeared to have been changed, from the chipped china bowl and pitcher at the washstand to the thick quilts folded at the foot of the bed.

Evan stumbled—no, staggered drunkenly—toward the neatly turned down bed.

"Will there be anything else you need, sir?" Keyes steered Evan's lurching form onto the bed, rolling him to the center, on his back.

"Breakfast is at seven sharrrrp," Evan said, dropping his hand flat on his chest, scratching through the linen to his skin. "Wake me in time, will you, Keyes?"

"Certainly, sir. At six it is."

Chapter Fifteen

Two feet of snow covered London the next morning, stalling all services and hindering all deliveries. No post had arrived for the duke to sort and dispense at the end of the morning meal.

A trifle disappointed by the lack of mail, Elizabeth made to excuse herself from the table and go to the morning room with the rest of the ladies the instant it was possible to do so.

"Elizabeth, I want a word with you in private," her father said as she got to her feet.

Elizabeth shot a glance in his direction, alarmed by the tone of voice in which he'd addressed her; it had been much too formal. "Right now, Papa?"

"Yes," he replied. "In my study. I'll meet you there."

"I'll get Robbie settled with Krissy, then be right down," Elizabeth promised. She flashed a second look across the room, this one directed at Evan MacGregor. His face was perfectly bland, and when his eyes met hers, they stared right through her, as though she didn't exist.

Elizabeth was more than a little rattled by that as she took Robbie's hand and escorted him up to the nursery. "Can I no' play wit the so'dier?" Robbie asked for the third time.

"Oh," Elizabeth said in surprise. "I don't think so, Robbie. I imagine he's going back to his post shortly, sweeting. That's what soldiers do."

Robbie's small brow puckered. "Come back?"

Elizabeth did not know what to say to that. Obviously, Robbie thought he'd found a friend in Evan MacGregor. She sighed, because the truth was the best answer to give. "No, Robbie. I don't think the MacGregor will ever come back."

"Dead?" the boy asked cryptically.

"No. No, of course not. He just has his duties to see to." When she saw his crestfallen expression, Elizabeth added, "I'm sorry, Robbie."

His face became perfectly bland. Robbie stared right through Elizabeth, as though she were as transparent as glass. The exact same way Evan had done, just moments ago.

Regardless, Elizabeth gave the boy a hug and kiss when she left him with Krissy. Then she hurried downstairs to her father's study.

Well, she thought, *there might be a thousand things Papa wants to discuss when we're snowbound.* But as to what they could possibly be, she hadn't a clue.

There was a roaring fire in the study, stoked with splits of oak. Keyes was just opening the drapes on the dim morning light, and had set a tray with coffee on a sideboard for their use.

"Have a seat by the fire, Elizabeth," her father said. invitingly. "I'll join you shortly. Let me get some things from my desk. Oh, yes, Keyes, please advise Reverend Baird I would like to speak privately to him when I finish my business with Elizabeth."

"As you wish, Your Grace." Keyes backed out, drawing the door firmly closed.

Elizabeth settled in her favorite corner of the chester-field, stretched her boot-covered toes toward the fire and folded her hands in her lap.

"Do you want some coffee?" her father asked as he rummaged through his desk, rattling papers. "Now, what did I do with that?"

"I'm content as I am," Elizabeth said briskly, bringing her speculations closer to home in her own mind. It was very likely her father had found a suitable replacement for Mrs. Drummond and wanted to discuss that with her. She hoped to have some say in who was hired to care for Robbie.

"Ah, I've got it!" John Murray crowed.

Elizabeth glanced behind her and saw him coming to the fireplace with a paper and his favorite pipe in his hand. He stopped at the silver service to pour coffee, add cream and sugar, and stir the hot liquid till it was mixed.

Elizabeth waited politely until he'd set his cup and saucer on a side table beside a chair. The leather creaked as he settled into the seat. He sipped his coffee somewhat noisily, since it was steaming-hot and fresh brewed. Elizabeth kept her fingers from twiddling and stopped herself from asking, "What's this all about?"

As he took a second sip, her father's eyes fastened on Elizabeth's face, but she could tell nothing from his patent expression.

"Elizabeth, before we begin—" he put aside the cup and saucer "—is there anything you'd like to tell me?"

"Such as?" she asked uneasily. "No, Papa, I can't think of anything. Well, perhaps there is. Robbie got into your study the other day, and he might have broken one of your umbrellas. Keyes assured me it wasn't so far gone it couldn't be repaired. Is that what you're asking about?"

"Not exactly." He sat back in his chair, comfortable now, in control, civilized. But his left hand held a folded page of parchment that he repeatedly tapped against the padded armrest of his big chair. He stopped his left hand and extended it toward his daughter. "Elizabeth, I want you to look at this and then explain it to me."

"Explain it to you?" Elizabeth couldn't imagine what he was talking about. She frowned as she leaned forward and took the paper from between his fingers; then she sat back again and carefully opened it along its worn creases.

That was when her heart dropped down to her toes. Her hands shook. The document crackled.

"I'm waiting," said the duke. "Explain."

Elizabeth shook her head. No explanation came to her. She cleared her throat. She shook her head once more. "I can't," she managed to say in a choked voice.

"You're going to have to do better than that, lass," said her father, in the sternest tone she'd ever heard from him.

"Where did you get this?" she asked.

"I'm asking the questions here, Elizabeth. Tell me exactly what that document is."

"Why, that's quite obvious, Papa. It's a marriage license," Elizabeth answered, too quickly, conscious of the purple flush stealing into her cheeks.

"And?"

"Well, surely you don't think it's real. You couldn't possibly think that."

"Can't I?" he said ominously. "Are you claiming it's a forgery? Signed by Master Paisley himself."

Elizabeth gulped. She was damned if she did, damned if she didn't. "Ah, truly, Papa, I don't know what to say. Won't you be kind enough to tell me how you came to be in possession of it?"

"Gladly. It fell out of the MacGregor's coat pocket when he stumbled upstairs to bed last night. Why didn't you tell me the truth, Elizabeth? That you and he had run off and married years ago?"

Trapped, Elizabeth really didn't know what to say. She still shook her head, as if by doing that she could somehow deny the evidence she held in her shaking hands. "I can't explain. I couldn't explain."

"Do you know what you've done? Are you a complete coward? Do you realize—" his voice rose in pitch and volume "—that you've bastardized the man's firstborn son and legal heir? Elizabeth, the man will kill you when he learns the truth, and I won't be able to do a damn thing to prevent it!"

Shaken, she made the only answer that she could. "Well, he doesn't know about Robbie. Surely he doesn't ever have to know."

"The devil you say!" her father thundered. He came out of his seat, close to violence, snatching the document out of Elizabeth's hands. "God save me, I could strangle you with my own two hands! When I think of the hell you've put me through…the lies you've told me…time and again. God help me!"

Lord Atholl strode across his study, grievously agitated, working valiantly at controlling his mighty temper. At the edge of his desk, he turned around, glaring at Elizabeth's stricken face. He raised his right hand and pointed a condemning finger at his youngest daughter.

"You will make this right. You created this scandal, and you alone will repair it. You have twenty-four hours to bring the MacGregor to me to discuss a marriage contract. Do you fail to do that by this time tomorrow, Elizabeth, you and your son will be disowned and put out of my house and left to starve in the street.

"Go! Leave my study. I will have nothing more to do with you. Do you value the hide on your back, do nothing to make me raise my hand against you. Go!"

Chapter Sixteen

~~~~~~~~~~

Elizabeth's head hurt dreadfully, and it wasn't the laughter at the card table that caused the ache. It was Evan MacGregor. Three times this morning, after leaving her father's study, she'd approached Evan and made an overture to speak privately with him. Three times she'd been curtly and rudely refused.

Damn him to hell and back, she wouldn't ask again!

Since their bitter parting last evening, Evan had staunchly refused to acknowledge Elizabeth's existence in any way, shape or form. If not for her father's demand making it of utmost importance that she speak civilly with Evan this very day, she wouldn't have tried at all.

Elizabeth exhaled deeply as she crossed the cozy parlor to the sun porch where Robbie was playing with his toy soldiers. Today, the boy had warm knit socks on his feet, but his small shoes had been cast off and he sprawled on his belly, at eye level with his toys. He was concentrating fiercely, moving tiny horses and little men hither and yon on a rag rug that was his make-believe battlefield.

A coal stove had been lighted to warm the sunroom, yet frost still glazed all the windowpanes. Outdoors, it continued to snow, a veritable blizzard that pelted the house, covered Grosvenor Park and obliterated the street.

Elizabeth sat on a wicker chaise in the sunroom, closed her eyes and rubbed her brow. What to do? How to say what she must? And who, pray God, would protect her from MacGregor's righteous anger when she told him Robbie was his son?

Inside her skirt's pocket, the parchment license crackled, reminding Elizabeth of her furious father's ultimatum. As if she could explain Robbie MacGregor to Evan with a few simpering words.

Behind her in the parlor, conversation rose and fell with lively volume as the men vocalized their regrets at not being out hunting in this fine weather. They were all Scots to the last. A little snow rarely stopped things in the Highlands. Life in London was a tad different.

"Wha's wrong?" Robbie asked, looking up from his toys.

Elizabeth dropped her hand from her brow and said, "I'm fine, Robbie. I've just got a little headache because the house is all stuffy."

"Oh." His rosebud mouth formed a perfect circle. He got up from the floor and climbed onto the arm of Elizabeth's chaise and put his soft hand against her brow. "Sorry."

"Me, too, precious." Elizabeth brought his small hand down and put a kiss in his palm. "It's all better now."

He stretched his little arms around her neck and squeezed her tight, giving her a bear hug and a kiss on the cheek.

"What a touching scene," said a voice from the open doorway. "Why, if I didn't know better, I'd think you actually liked children, Lady Elizabeth."

"Och, the MacGregor!" Robbie chirped. He bounded off the arm of Elizabeth's chaise and ran pell-mell across the room, charging Evan's legs. "Come see my sidier dhu."

"The Black Watch, eh?" Evan laughed.

To Elizabeth's great surprise, Evan allowed the small boy to give a mighty yank on his hand, pulling him over the threshold into the sunroom. The two of them promptly folded their legs onto the oval rag rug and commenced to discuss the merits of Robbie's battle plan.

For several minutes, Elizabeth sat perfectly motionless, her lips parted in complete surprise as she listened to Robbie rattle off one question after another and answer in complete sentences any question that Evan posed him.

"What are these, Rob Roy?" Evan pointed to a handful of stout round twigs whose frayed ends proved they'd been broken by the force of a child's clumsy hand.

"Tha's me cannons." On his knees, Robbie scooted closer to Evan, touching the twigs. "Mickle big guns to blow the bloody Sassenachs to kingdom come, God take 'em."

Evan leaned back his head and laughed. "Och, you're a bloodthirsty bantling, laddie!"

Elizabeth frowned at Robbie's unnecessary language, but refrained from scolding him. Instead, she got up and closed the French doors and came back to her seat.

By then, Evan had produced his *sgian dhu* and began to whittle the splinters off Robbie's frayed cannons. Elizabeth reached into her pocket and pulled out the marriage license. Her father's daughter in all things, she tapped the folded document several times on its creases before concluding exactly how to phrase her next words.

She hesitated a long time before speaking. Evan sat crosslegged on the rug, with his back deliberately to her. The more he whittled, the closer Robbie came to him, wiggling like an eager puppy that had been ignored too long.

It cut Elizabeth to the bone to see Robbie's small, pudgy hand resting on Evan's broad shoulder.

In her dreams and her faraway secret wishes, she had imagined such a scene—father and son together, sharing a rare bond. It hurt to know that the next words she spoke might ruin the tenuous friendship between boy and man. So she chose her words with utmost care.

"Robbie, love, would you give Captain MacGregor this paper? I'm told he dropped it on his way to bed last night."

Evan deliberately ignored her and kept his back and head from turning at the sound of Elizabeth's voice. Robbie, on the other hand, looked up from the whittling and spied the creased parchment in Elizabeth's hand. It was no trouble to him to come off his knees and take the document from Elizabeth's fingers. He thrust it under Evan's nose, saying, "Tha's yers, MacGregor."

Elizabeth saw the jolt of recognition whip down Evan's rigid spine. His right hand came up and slapped the front of his red coat, then thrust inside and felt the empty pocket in the lining over his heart.

Elizabeth wet her lips, then said, very cautiously, "Papa knows. It was that document he wished to speak with me about this morning."

An agonizingly long, cold moment passed before Evan took the paper from Robbie's hand and placed it back in his pocket. Then he resumed whittling, saying, "In your own words, lady, that changes nothing. We're finished. I have said all I intend to say on the subject."

Fear brought Elizabeth to the edge of her seat. "You cannot mean that, Evan. I mean, it's gone beyond the two of us, now. Nor was it my fault that document was mislaid. On top of which, there are certain things you must know... about Robbie."

At the mention of Robbie's name, Evan swiveled around, hissing, "Whisht! Woman! Keep a civil tongue behind your teeth! I'm no' a blind fool. The bantling's hair may be Murray red, but he's a MacGregor to the bone. Now, get out. Leave me and my son be. We've no use for you anymore. Dare you broach any subject with me again, you'll be feeling the power of my hand."

Elizabeth gasped. He meant it. He meant every harsh and cruel word he'd said the day before! She came to her feet, shaken, and then, without another word, turned and fled to her room upstairs.

Robbie sat back on his heels, his head turned from one angry adult to the other, knowing something of import had happened. He didn't quite understand the spate of words the MacGregor and Lady Elizabeth had exchanged, but he knew where his loyalties lay. Lady Elizabeth was his friend, and he had never doubted for a moment that she loved him.

He started to get up and follow her, but the MacGregor chose that moment to hand him a neatly notched and whittled cannon that came very close to imitating the real thing. Amazed, Robbie settled back on his haunches.

"Do you like it, then?" Evan asked the boy.

"Oh, aye, 'tis the best cannon ever. Ta. Can you make another?"

"Whisht." Evan accompanied his words with a conspiratorial smile. "In the blink of an eye, I can."

Robbie's loyalties weren't so easily swayed. He moved back, peering through the open French doors, watching Lady Elizabeth's determined departure out the sitting room door. Evan watched the boy shake his head, confused. "Why?"

"Why, what?" Evan asked, his hands already busy forming another fat, frayed twig into a blunted toy cannon.

"Jamakermad?"

"Say it again, please?"

"Why did ya make Lady 'Lizbeth mad?"

"Oh, that?" Evan shrugged his massive shoulders. "It's called strategy, my boy. You ever been fishing, Robbie?"

"Uh-huh." Robbie nodded. "Caught a mickle big fish. The duke said so."

"And pray tell me, my boy, what did you use for bait?"

"Inchworms," Robbie said gravely.

"Well, sparring with Lady Elizabeth is like using an inchworm to bait my fishing hook. Do you follow me, laddie?"

"Oh, aye! Yer gonna catch her? Like when we play boggle-about-the-bush an' I catch her."

"That's it, exactly. Can you keep a secret, Robbie? Never, ever tell it to anyone, until I say it's all right for everyone to know it?"

"Oooh," Robbie said gravely. No one had ever entrusted him with a grave and serious secret. "I know I can."

Evan wrapped a conspiratorial arm around the boy's shoulder, drawing him close enough to whisper in his ear. "I'm your daddy. Honest and true."

"Ya are?" Robbie's eyes got huge.

"Aye," Evan told him. "And I want to make Lady Elizabeth your mama. Would you like that?"

"Ye can do that?" Robbie asked, amazed. "How?"

"By marrying her, come the twenty-eighth of May. Officially, in the muckle big kirk across the way."

"Saint Mark's?" Robbie's eyes got bigger than before. "God's truth, ye are?"

"Aye, Rob Roy MacGregor, by hook or by crook I will. Now, don't you go telling my secret to anyone, cross your heart and hope to die."

Elizabeth spent the afternoon wearing out the rug in her bedchamber, pacing back and forth.

"I vow," Krissy fussed as she put away a stack of clean linens in the wardrobe, "I've never seen you in such a state, milady. What troubles ye so?"

"Men," Elizabeth answered darkly.

"*Och.*" Krissy clucked her tongue, bustling across the room to put down the open window and seal out the draft. "There be nothin' ta handling them!" She shut the window with banging force. "Bide awhile and take yer time, milady. Ignore the lout that's got you wringing yer hands. He'll come around, I vow.''

Krissy's advice couldn't have been farther off the mark, in Elizabeth's opinion. Ignoring Evan MacGregor was what had gotten her into this predicament. Ignoring her father's edict would be tantamount to suicide. At this point, she could no longer afford just to think of herself. Robbie's needs and concerns had to come first.

Elizabeth strode to the window that Krissy had just closed, parted the drapes and gazed out through the frosty panes at the park and the sky. The storm was beginning to let up, but it might be days before the streets were passable to traffic.

"Mayhap I should fix you a powder from the chemist," Krissy offered in a concerned voice.

"Krissy," Elizabeth said, "I'm fine, thank you. I am trying to think things through."

"Well, you don't look fine to me," Krissy chided. "Tha's all we need, is for someone to take sick. Couldn't get a doctor here today if our lives depended upon it. Eat your biscuits and drink your tea, Lady Elizabeth. 'Tis a sin to let good food go to waste."

"Krissy, you're a worse scold than Amalia," Elizabeth complained, but she sat to her small table anyway, and tried the fresh tea. Her hands gave away the truth by clumsily handling her spoon and clattering against the china cup filled with steaming liquid.

Her throat felt raw, her voice thick. She wanted to think it was a consequence of too much shouting and arguing in the cold yesterday, and loss of sleep.

While she finished her tea and crumbled a scone apart, Elizabeth sternly told herself she was not going to be sick. She drank two cups of tea. By then, her stomach was in full revolt, siding with her headache.

Elizabeth bolted for the garderobe. That small chamber, at the rear of the third floor, was bitterly cold. The water in the standing pitcher was glazed with ice, but cold water accomplished what tea and scones hadn't, taking the flush off Elizabeth's cheeks.

Once she'd repaired herself, Elizabeth went downstairs to the kitchen in the basement and begged a piece of plain toast from Cook. The kitchen was warm and cozy, and Elizabeth settled there for a while, testing the toast's ability to calm her stomach.

It was nerves that had her upset, she realized. Nerves because the problem of Evan MacGregor wouldn't go away. She didn't want Evan to think badly of her... to hate her. That was somehow absolutely unbearable.

With a sad and regretful sigh, she contented herself with a small truth. His hatred was probably for the best, in the long view of things. She would get used to his hatred. Hadn't she'd got used to his absence?

Come evening, Robbie's active day ended with supper in the nursery. He was content to bed down early, because he'd missed his afternoon nap completely when Evan took him outside to build a snowman. Elizabeth felt slightly better when she joined the whole family in the dining room for an earlier-than-usual supper.

Numerous activities had been planned to pass the evening, since there would be no callers to entertain. Glenlyon shuffled a deck of cards at a table populated by Amalia, Aunt Nicky and the dowager. Evan and Uncle Thomas observed the progression of a game of chess between Tullie and the duke. Aunt Charlotte's knitting needles clicked steadily from her chair, nearest the cozy fire.

Elizabeth elected to join Aunt Charlotte near the fire, and as she took a seat in the empty armchair. "You're looking peaked, dear," her aunt said.

Elizabeth took up some mending from a basket at their feet and threaded a needle. "I'm fine, Aunt Charlotte."

"No, you're much paler than usual."

"It's winter, Aunt Charlotte. Everyone is a little pale in winter." Elizabeth slid the needle into the small tear in the knee of a new pair of Robbie's woolen trews and began to sew on a reinforcing patch, muttering, "That child spends his whole life on his knees."

"Little boys do that, my dear," said Aunt Charlotte.

"Of course they do," Elizabeth agreed. "Except Robbie is excessive when it comes to wearing out the knees of his trews."

"Humph!" Aunt Charlotte snorted. "Put him in a *philabeg*. He won't wear out any knees save the two God gave him."

"And how much luck do you think I would have sticking him in a kilt, Aunt Charlotte? When every man he lays eyes on in England is wearing trousers?"

"You're the one fussing over the mending, dear."

"So I am," Elizabeth answered. "But it's also a labor of love to fuss over a wee bantling."

"You've a kind heart, Elizabeth." Aunt Charlotte turned to gossip. "We won't be going to Lady Stanhope's salon, will we? Did you read what it said in the paper about Lord Byron? Am I correct in concluding he will be doing a reading here next week, for your Thursday literary society, Elizabeth?"

"Ah, yes, the reading." Elizabeth blinked her dry eyes. In all, she felt so dull, so sluggish, she couldn't fathom how anything managed to stick in her befuddled brain. She really needed a good night's sleep, desperately.

Her literary salon... That was important...a chance for the scamp to read some of his work to a select and appreciative London audience. Important... Elizabeth clung to that thought, but Evan's cold dismissals of last night and this afternoon kept intruding. Had he meant those terrible, harsh words? Then she remembered her father's ultimatum and almost burst out laughing in hysterics. She was fussing and worrying about a blasted literary salon next week, when she ought to be figuring out where she and Robbie were going to go tomorrow.

Elizabeth inhaled deeply. It hurt to lose a friend like Evan. She couldn't help but think she'd handled it all very badly. She would have to find some way to apologize for having taken such base advantage of his earnest vow on his father's grave.

That had been callous of her, to use his pledge to her own purpose. And Evan was right—what she'd done was unforgivable. It was what she wanted; she'd accomplished what she wanted to accomplish. She should feel relieved and satisfied, even happy that the end had justified the means.

But she didn't feel any of those things. She felt very badly.

"Today's weather won't affect what's scheduled for next week, Aunt Charlotte." Elizabeth said firmly, trying hard to sound like her usual, brisk self. Then she covered her mouth with her palm to hide a very deep yawn. "I'm going upstairs to bed, early for a change."

"You do look peaked, my dear. But I've already said that, now haven't I? Such beastly weather. And I was so planning to enjoy going to Lady Jersey's."

Of course—tonight was the rout at Lady Jersey's. Amalia had already sent their regrets. Elizabeth actually regretted not going. She'd have done anything to get out of the same house where Evan MacGregor was. But all she could do was excuse herself and go to bed early.

Evan MacGregor was no happier about having to remain a guest in the duke of Atholl's house another night. Yes, that gave him every opportunity to observe Elizabeth, which was agony of the worst sort.

When he coupled the unrelieved misery Elizabeth's closeness caused him with the frequently hard glares he received from the duke, Evan decided he would have been much happier back at his barracks.

"Would you play a game of piquet, MacGregor?" Tullibardine asked.

"Piquet?" Evan inquired as he brought the scattered deck back to hand and shuffled it with long, supple hands. "As you wish, Your Grace."

"Stuff it, Balquhidder," Tullie grumbled as he took the vacant seat at the table, flexing his wounded shoulder as he made himself comfortable. "Don't stand on formalities. We've known each other too long for that."

Evan smiled, liking Tullie the more for his dismissal of unnecessary protocol. Tullie was the least socially conscious Murray Evan had ever known. The duke's heir was brash, bold and earthy, and likable to the core.

"I bid seven. Your eyes tell me your hangover's worn off," Tullibardine told him. "Which probably means I won't be able to fleece you for a Scotch pound."

Nothing could be further from the truth, Evan thought as he picked up his hand and scanned the cards he'd been dealt. "I've had better days, sir. I'll bid ten."

Tullie stuck an unlighted cigar between his teeth and scowled at his own hand. "Damn. Point. I'll bid— No, it's yours. Take it."

"So be it." Evan smiled and laid out his first trump, the king of spades.

"Where's Elizabeth? Gone to bed already?"

"Are you asking me? How should I know?" Evan put down the queen of spades and waited for Tullie to give him the trey in suit. He added, in a flat, toneless voice, "Let's pray that means she won't wake up as contrary and irritable as ever."

Tullie's eyes widened with feigned innocence as he threw out a two of hearts, thereby taking the lead. "Why, Elizabeth is the most even-tempered Murray I know, sir. She never has fluctuating moods, like most ladies. I can't help but notice that she has had some great difficulty sleeping as of late, however."

"Is that so?" Evan inquired dryly. He set aside, untouched, the glass of claret Tullie insisted on pouring him. He couldn't bear the taste of more of the duke's wicked blends or brews . . . not with the headache the smuggled brandy had given him. "Why ever should Lady Elizabeth have trouble sleeping?"

"Ladies often do, when they have a man on their minds," Tullie added ruthlessly, watching the MacGregor's face for any reaction he could elicit. He'd ground his jaw so many times in Elizabeth's presence today, it was a wonder MacGregor had any back teeth left at all.

Evan allowed himself an inner groan over Tullibardine's aimless chatter. He forcefully put a rein on the impulse to bolt upstairs that rose at the image put in his mind . . . Elizabeth sleeping . . . in bed . . . Was she naked? Were her lips parted? Did she dream of him?

Damn! Why couldn't he blot the blasted woman out of his mind? Elizabeth did not need him. He wouldn't go to her until she begged him to come. Hell, he wouldn't go then, either!

Tullibardine cleared his throat at the same time he cleared the board. "Thank God for bad weather. I was supposed to escort Amalia and Elizabeth to a rout at Lady Jersey's tonight. Worst duty a grown man can have is a flock of spinster sisters underfoot. Amalia sent our regrets. Did you know that Elizabeth told me this morning she wanted to ask you to come with us to the rout? Only she's too shy to ask that of you."

That, Evan knew was a bald-faced lie. He looked at Tullie's bland face and threw down his remaining trump. "What do you want? Me to turn my pockets inside out? Your lead, Tullie."

Tullie leaned across the table as he pulled in his trick and whispered another confidence with the dramatics of one telling state secrets. "Elizabeth has a *tendre* for you, old man. Always has. Always will."

"Does she, then?" Evan managed to say through his teeth.

"Had a tiff, have you?" Tullie concluded at the same time he tossed aside all pretense at innuendo.

"To coin a phrase, that's putting it mildly." Evan granted that admission just to see how far Tullibardine would run with it.

"Hmm, she's a maddening woman." Tullie scratched his jaw with the cards in his hand. MacGregor was still angry. Last night at this time he'd been bloody furious, close to committing *mille mhurders*. Tullie wasn't surprised. Elizabeth could be quite insulting when she put her mind to it. Being of a curious and playful nature, Tullie had ventured out to join them yesterday. Only he hadn't found Elizabeth and Evan in the park playing. No, they'd been arguing heatedly.

Tullibardine had overhead some of the words exchanged between the two of them before he had quietly retreated inside. He hadn't been surprised. He had noticed a very strong undercurrent between them the night he was shot.

Evan and Elizabeth fought and argued a lot. That happened occasionally to couples who were madly attracted to one another and wouldn't admit the attraction.

The proof of MacGregor's temper showed in the tensing of his jaw above the impeccable folds of his cravat.

Tullie decided to play the devil's advocate. "Elizabeth told me she was very sorry for having angered you last night. It's difficult being a proud Murray, you know. Why, I'm certain she wants to apologize, only she hasn't found the acceptable words to say, yet. When one is proud by nature, the right words and the right moment can be difficult to find."

"Indeed?" Evan added unsympathetically. "To quote Mungo Maxtone, 'From the wind of the Murrays, God save me.'" Hadn't the marquess any other topic of discussion besides his sister? "I believe most mere mortals would wait till the last judgment before hearing any Murray apologize."

"Do you really think so?" Tullie frowned. "Are we all that bad?" He studied the remaining cards in his hand, oblivious of what play should be next.

Captain MacGregor was supposed to have immediately jumped to Elizabeth's defense, claiming their argument was more his fault than Elizabeth's. Tullie had only stretched the truth a little bit to play on Evan's sympathies. He cared, Tullie assured himself. Evan *had* to care. What were a few angry words between two lovers?

Brightening with another idea, Tullie held his tongue until the MacGregor had beaten him so soundly he could not refuse to play a second game to win back his lost coins. Over the next game, Tullie played just as poorly, more interested in the conversation than in the cards.

"Did you know, Captain MacGregor, Elizabeth has one of the finest collections of romantic poetry? We're to have the pleasure of a reading next Thursday afternoon, here at Grosvenor Mews."

"I believe I heard mention of it at breakfast, Your Grace. It will most certainly be a most important event."

"I'm certain it will be," Tullie declared facetiously. "There is so much to be learned from the literati. I may cast my accounts in anticipation."

That broke the ice. Evan threw back his head and laughed. "Why, Your Grace, I'm scandalized. What has happened to your patronage of the arts? What of *noblesse oblige?*"

Tullie rolled the cigar around to the other side of his mouth without touching it with his hand, and grinned wide enough to show the neat rows of his upper molars. "Frankly, Balquhidder, I can't stand mincing fops."

And so the evening went. At a quarter past one, they called it a night. Evan and Tullie retreated up the front stairs together, the last to retire. They wished each other a pleasant good-night, parting company in the hallway. Evan opened the door of his guest room and entered, shutting the door softly at his back.

Chapter Seventeen

One small lamp on the desk and a fire in the hearth hardly did anything to illuminate Evan's chamber. Holding her breath, Elizabeth pressed herself back into a shadowy corner as Evan crossed to the desk under the window embrasure. He stood for a moment gazing out the window at the snow while he shrugged his coat and weskit off his shoulders.

He gave the uniform jacket a shake and checked its many pockets, then draped both garments over the ladder-back chair. His attention remained fixed on whatever it was he was looking at out the window while his lean fingers deftly popped the studs from his shirt, one at a time. His high buckramed collar made an audible snap against his throat when it was released.

Then, with the points of his cravat dangling past his waist, he spun around on one highly polished Hessian and glared straight into the shadowed corner where Elizabeth waited.

"What are you doing in here?"

Elizabeth raised her chin in a frank challenge. "I've come to beard the lion in his den."

"Get out!"

"No." Elizabeth deliberately stepped forward, putting the cheerfully burning hearth at her back, knowing full well the sheer silk of her night rail would turn to gossamer.

Evan halted his forceful march forward, stopping several feet away from her, his brow and his eyes gone black with anger. A small, delicious shudder swept up and down Elizabeth's spine as she looked him over, from the top of his glossy head, down to the polished lasts on his boots. There was something oddly appealing about Evan in shirt-sleeves and trews. She'd always liked him best when the mystifying outer layers were peeled away to reveal the lean, tall man underneath.

"You're wearing braces," she remarked casually, allowing her gaze to linger deliberately before returning to his eyes. "I thought all the king's men kept their breeks up with a stout belt."

His eyes never wavered from hers, but his right brow rose in a calculating arch. "I don't believe I care one bit for the game you're trying to play, lady."

"No game." Elizabeth shrugged. The untied ribbon on her night rail gave a little more. The silk dropped negligently off one shoulder. This time, Evan's eyes strayed, following the cloth, noting the fullness of the breast that had been partly uncovered.

"That's it!" A low and feral growl preceded all movement. He spun around on his heel and stamped to the door, yanking it wide open. "I'm putting you out, ya dammed wicked witch!"

Elizabeth was prepared for exactly that. "No, Evan. I'm not going. You're going to let me stay. You're going to teach me not to fear your passions."

"No! I'm no trained monkey, willing to dance attendance upon your leisure. Once, I would have taken you *tocherless*, but I'll be damned if I will today. Now, get out!"

That stung enough to make Elizabeth wince. "What are you saying? I'm no good to you without a massive dowry, Evan MacGregor?"

"I refuse to stand here in the middle of the night, arguing with you. Are you going to leave or not?"

His previous remark hadn't stopped stinging. Elizabeth clenched her arms before her, angry now, pressed very close to the edge of her temper herself. This was not going at all the way she'd planned it. Again her chin lifted in that manner that spoke clearly of her Murray roots. Just to be arbitrary, she said, "No! I'm not!"

"So be it!" Evan shut the door. He turned around, propped his shoulders on the raised panels and folded his arms across his chest. "Remove the night rail."

"Oh? Is that the way we're going to play this? You're going to attempt to shame and humiliate me? It won't work, Evan."

That nasty, arrogant brow of his rose once more, making Elizabeth want to slap him. *He could be so bloody infuriating!* It was one thing to confront him wearing only her night rail, but it would be something else indeed to face him without a stitch of clothing on, and he knew it.

"Fine!" Elizabeth said in angry capitulation. She yanked on the gown's neckline, and the whole garment tumbled past her knees.

Splendor of God, Evan groaned quietly. His angry wife stepped gracefully out of her night rail, wadded the cloth into a ball and threw it at him. He barely caught his shout of triumph at the back of his throat and changed it into a grunt as the gown dropped to his feet.

"Now what, ye unconscionable brute? Shall we have tea?" Elizabeth demanded.

"Unconscionable brute, is it?" Evan drawled. Oh, but she was outrageously beautiful when she was angry. He felt tempted to kiss her, beginning at her bare toes and working his way agonizingly up to the top of her tempestuous brow.

Evan deliberately shook his head as he lifted one hand away from his rigid pose and crooked a finger at her. Her eyes darted from his face to his hand and back again with lightning speed. She came toward him with long, angry strides, shaking her head, her fists clenched.

She didn't say a word until she was a scant foot from his chest. "I'll no' apologize now, ye rotten cur! I won't take back a single word I've said."

For a long moment, Evan managed to control his hands, preventing them from touching her. But the angry rise and fall of her heaving breasts undid his resolve. He caught her upper arms, yanking her up against his chest, able to feel the exquisite torture of her breasts grazing his chest through the thin linen of his sark.

"Then we're right back where we started, wench. Only you've taken it a step further... coming in my room... intending to break my resolve with your manipulating little woman's wiles. I won't be bound to your whimsy, Elizabeth Murray MacGregor. A husband has rights o'er his wife."

They were nose-to-nose, eyeball-to-eyeball, certainly close enough to kiss, but Evan tightened his grip upon her shoulders, preventing that kind of connection. He spun her around at the same time he yanked open the door and physically propelled her out into the cold, empty hall with a resounding slap on her bottom.

"Guid nicht, ma gey lassie."

Before Elizabeth had the chance to catch herself and turn around and slap him, he'd closed the door and turned the key in the lock.

"Oh!" she fumed, outraged, furious, and utterly beside herself. "You ... you ..."

Evan leaned against the locked door, listening to the choking and sputtering as words failed Elizabeth completely. The door jolted on its hinges when she kicked it, once, then a second time. By then she must have realized she was naked as the day she was born in an open hallway.

He put his hand over his mouth to stifle a wicked grin that surfaced from deep within him, least it come surging out in a shout of triumph. He held that shout until he distinctly heard the sound of Elizabeth's bare feet on the floor overhead. She was too angry to consider proprieties as she slammed her bedroom door with all her might.

She could raise the roof off the entire house now, as far as he was concerned. He bent and picked her night rail up from off his boot, and flipped the silk around his shoulders. Her fragrance wafted into his nose. It made a poor substitute for the warm-bodied, living, breathing woman he'd forced away. But there was more than one moment of sweet, heady pleasure at stake here. There were all the pleasant and wonderful nights of the rest of their lives ahead of them.

His cods refused to recognize that fact. Evan sat on his chair to remove his boots, but didn't. It wasn't likely he would get any sleep tonight, as aroused as he was.

He sat awhile with Elizabeth's gown still circling his neck, and thought back to Tullie's odd prattling that evening. Something about boy poets and romance.

Romance, Evan snorted. When had Elizabeth given a fig for romance?

"God and Saint Columba save me." He stood up and threw Elizabeth's gown onto the eiderdown and pillows at the head of the bed.

He would have to have a drink, something potent, to stave away the demons of the night. The only place to find that was downstairs, at the bar in the billiard room, or else the duke's study.

He chose the billiard room, and Tullibardine's whiskey. He stood drinking at the window overlooking the corner of the street, and the park.

The sky had cleared to the northwest, and a huge, white full moon hung low over the wintry landscape. The elms raised ice-coated branches into the air. Drifts blanketed the earth, obliterating paths, curbs and ruts.

As he tasted the thick whiskey a second time, he recognized its origin by the sharp burnt flavor. It was Irish malt, distilled, from Bushmills. Heaven knew he'd drunk enough of the stuff to imprint the flavor permanently on his brain during his year in Ulster. Evan laughed coldly at his own stupidity. Both for drinking and for loving. What foolishness had made a randy boy think he knew how to love a woman?

Why hadn't he been just a little more normal? Off chasing every skirt, like his mates at Cambridge? But no, he'd had to be different.

Too many women had called him pretty as he came into those early randy years. Women older than his mother had tried to lure him into their beds. He'd been too reserved, too shy, to take it for what it was, a necessary physical release.

It had never been his intention to go into marriage a virgin himself, ignorant, inexperienced, and lacking control. It had just happened. Because he couldn't bring himself to pay for a whore or put his rod in someone else's wife. He'd been hoping to change his status when he went to Edinburgh with Willie Gray.

And then Evan had met Elizabeth Murray anew.

He'd been raised to respect and honor women of all ages. To love them all—even those who had made him blatant offers he had to refuse. And the girl he loved more than life itself, he'd hurt, because of his own inexperience.

And continued to hurt with his cruel thoughts and unreasonable demands. Elizabeth didn't deserve his spleen. For God's sake, he loved her. Only her. There had never been another woman in his life, ever. Just Elizabeth.

He rubbed cool fingers over his dry, burning eyes. What to do? What to do? What was wrong with them? Had he ruined the love they had by forcing it upon Elizabeth when she was too young and innocent to be ready for marriage? Shades of Hades, he hadn't been ready for marriage, either!

It was all his fault. His lack of control had ruined everything in the past. His lack of control threatened to ruin what could be made of their future.

Always, always, he lost his control. Bloody stupid. When was he going to learn to control his temper...his emotions...his pride...his rod?

Evan tossed the last of the whiskey down his throat. It did no good whatsoever to brood. He'd best try to get to sleep. The moment he returned to his room, he heard footsteps on the floor above. Elizabeth's room was above his.

He tipped his head, listening to her pace, back and forth on the polished floor. So she couldn't sleep any better than he. He wasn't surprised.

What a bloody rotten coil. They were two reasonable people. Why couldn't they solve this dilemma? The urge to crawl into bed and bury his head under the pillows, thereby blocking the sounds from Elizabeth's room, almost did him in. He should have taken Elizabeth into his bed, not sent her away! Why was he such a stupid, bloody fool? Such a bloody awful fool!

Evan didn't go to bed. Instead, he calmly walked out his door and turned to the back stairs, treading cautiously as he passed Colonel Graham's and Glenlyon's rooms.

Chapter Eighteen

"Why do we haf ta go?" Robbie mumbled sleepily as Elizabeth buttoned his warmest coat.

"Whisht," Elizabeth whispered. "Keep your voice down. We mustn't wake anyone."

"Why?"

"Because they need their sleep." Elizabeth sighed as she straightened. She drew her cloak around her shoulders and fastened the frogs. Then she cautiously opened the back door, took the boy's hand in one hand and a heavy valise in the other.

Outside, the stars had come out, and a full moon hung in the northwestern sky, radiating ample light onto the snow-covered ground. Elizabeth set the valise down and closed the back door, making certain it was secure.

She stood for a long, long moment staring at that shut door, acutely aware of the momentous decision she was making. It frightened her to think of never seeing her father, her brothers and sisters, her aunts and grandmother ever again. She knew she would miss them much more than they would ever miss her.

A tear ran down her cheek and she let go of Robbie's hand to quickly wipe it away. Resolved, certain of her love for the child, she bent and lifted her son with one arm, holding his small body close.

She cast one more look around her, looking to see that no servants were up and about to remark upon her departure. "All right, Robbie, we'll go quietly now. We can talk again when we get past the park."

Robbie had round eyes for the snow-covered park. The sidewalks on Grosvenor had been shovelled. On Bond Street the drifts became impossibly deep, much too deep for Robbie's short legs to manage. In order to make any sort of progress, Elizabeth had to carry him all the way to Charring Cross. She let out a relieved sigh when she spied a crew already at work in the wee hours, clearing the sidewalks along that road.

Robbie dozed against her shoulder as Elizabeth stood in the pre-dawn darkness reading the livery's schedule posted on the billboard outside the gates. She had nearly an hour to go before the billeting agent opened up shop.

An hour, Elizabeth realized, could be a very long time for a tired, sleepy and curious little boy.

She had very limited funds, but she chose to use some of her ready coins on the side of prudence. There were both coffee shops and inns across the street from Charring Cross livery. Elizabeth chose the inn.

It was warm and quiet in the public room. The sleepy proprietor promised a hearty breakfast as soon as his help came down to prepare it. Elizabeth ordered porridge in the meantime and paid for it with one of her coins.

"Where be ye bound, mistress?" the proprietor asked when he set the bowl before her on a well scrubbed oak table.

"Southampton. We're bound for Virginia," Elizabeth lied. Should anyone trace her or Robbie's tracks, she wanted them to be misled from this point on.

"Well, I don' envy you traveling this time of year. Best time to travel to America is in the spring, I hear."

"Well, it can't be helped." Elizabeth answered.

"The coaches won't be running on schedule, mistress, 'cause o' the storm. Might take a day or two before they be moving agin. I've a room upstairs ye can let."

"Thank you, but I won't need it," Elizabeth said.

The innkeeper settled back behind his counter, dozing on and off, as easily as Robbie did. Elizabeth kept a close watch out the window and an ear cocked for the sound of bells ringing promptly at 6:00 a.m.

At a quarter after the hour, a black coach stopped at the corner at the same time a hackney stopped outside the livery. The livery agent disembarked from the hackney. The private coach remained where it was.

Elizabeth waited a few minutes more, rousing Robbie and deliberately spooning all the oatmeal into him that she possibly could, for the nourishment it provided. Then she gathered up her valise and reticule, and settled her sleepy son on her shoulder. Thanking the innkeeper for his hospitality, Elizabeth stepped outside, into the cold, brisk morning.

She crossed the quiet street and purchased a ticket on the next coach to travel to Southampton, which she was assured by the agent would be leaving no later than noon.

Elizabeth thanked him and said she would be waiting at the inn across the street, and would verify the departure time a little later in the morning.

Her business completed at the livery, she walked up the opposite side of the street from the inn. She didn't hurry and she didn't dawdle. Her step was merely purposeful, bringing her to the waiting black carriage.

"Jesu, Elizabeth!" Monk Lewis exclaimed as he bounded out of the carriage. "I've been coming here religiously for the last four days at promptly 6:15, just as your letter asked. I never once dreamed you'd actually do it."

His coachman also bounded down to the street, relieving Elizabeth of her one piece of luggage, which he hurriedly stored out of sight in the boot of the carriage.

"We'd best do this quickly," Elizabeth said as Monk took Robbie from her arms and gave her a boost into his carriage. "I'm pretty certain I've covered my tracks, but one never knows."

Monk handed Robbie up to her, then climbed into the carriage himself. "Do what you can to get us to Gravesend, John," he told his coachman. "You don't have to break any records for speed. Just get us there safe and sound."

"Right you go, guv," the coachman said, and closed the door. The carriage rocked as he climbed onto the box; then, with a shout and a crack of his whip, they lurched into motion.

"Devil take it, Elizabeth," Monk exclaimed as he spread lap robes over Elizabeth and Robbie. "Will you do me the courtesy to explain what this is really all about? And, pray tell, whose child that is in your arms."

Elizabeth looked Monk Lewis straight in his eyes and considered how much and how little she wanted to tell him. Since it was his ship and his good graces that were allowing her to travel without cost to his plantation in the Windward Isles, she felt she owed him some sort of explanation. But just how much to divulge was the question.

"You know my reason for going to the islands," she calmly explained. "I must get a divorce, as quietly as possible."

"Aye, that much I did know," Monk snapped. He was clearly troubled by her decision to flee England. "But why are you taking that child with you?"

Elizabeth sighed. She hoped she wasn't putting her trust in the wrong person. Monk had a kind heart, and he was her dearest friend. "This is my son, Robert Evan MacGregor, and I do not ever intend to surrender custody of him to his father."

"Sure as the king's a George, you've got to be joking!" Monk reacted as though she'd kicked him solidly in the stomach. "My dear Lady Elizabeth, you do not mean to tell me that Evan MacGregor is this long-lost missing husband of yours?"

"Precisely," Elizabeth said grimly.

Monk swore very fluidly, and at the end of his speech, he raised his cane and banged on the carriage wall to contact his driver. "Stop the carriage at once."

"Eh, what, sir?" the coachman inquired.

"For God's sake, Monk, you can't let me down at this stage of the game. I've no one else to turn to."

"Circle Westminster," Monk commanded his driver.

"Monk, you mustn't leave me stranded, just because you know my husband's identity now!" Elizabeth began to feel a terrible sense of panic.

Monk waved her protests aside. He turned his graying head to stare out the isinglass at the sluggishly flowing Thames. A good long time passed before he elected to speak again. "Lady Elizabeth, with all due respect, I believe you are making a dreadful mistake. One that will surely come back and haunt you in the months and the years to come."

"Monk, please." Elizabeth held out an imploring hand. "I have not come to this decision lightly. Nor would I have done so if there was any chance or hope of an actual reconciliation. The MacGregor has no further interest in me as a wife, or as a woman. It is over between us. In truth, sir, it was never even begun. So I beg you, do not make this any more difficult than it is."

Monk vehemently shook his head. "My lady, I cannot be silent. A year in the Windwards is not a jaunt to Bath. The man you just named as your legal husband is the largest landholder on the island of Dominica. My own plantation is minuscule by comparison."

"Surely you jest," Elizabeth gasped.

"No, I do not," Monk answered her flatly. "Lady Elizabeth, you have no concept of what you would be facing.

The tropics can be unbearable to those who are not used to it. Nor can I offer you cooperation from the governor, when a new appointee has yet to be chosen and does not take office until March the first. These things have to be presented properly, and certain proprieties are required, even in the colonies.''

''What difference that?'' Elizabeth failed to see his point.

Monk sighed. ''To begin with, you will have to apply for divorce once he takes office, and then be under his scrutiny for the year of residency that follows before your case may actually be heard in his court. Some of these colonial officers can be extremely pedantic, and they are often influenced by personages with extremely high connections. Without grounds or proof, the governor may refuse to hear your case. Then what will you do?''

''Then I'll go to a different island.''

Monk sat back against the squabs, his narrow aesthete's shoulders swaying with the movement of the coach, his pale, questioning gaze on Elizabeth. ''My dear, there are many islands, but only one governor.''

Elizabeth lifted an unconcerned shoulder. ''Then I shall convince the man, by whatever means it takes.''

The duke of Atholl was not a habitué of White's, as a rule. He belonged, but as his life was filled with activity day in, day out and he had no wife he wished to avoid, he rarely made more than token appearances at the club.

However, during the week following Elizabeth's latest, well-planned rising, His Grace had been taken to task more times that he cared to admit. His mother and her opinionated sisters could be somewhat trying—especially when it came to their views on what should be done about Elizabeth. The three harridans stood foursquare against him, condemning him for his ultimatum, which had led to Elizabeth's flight out of the country. He, they all reminded him, had severely overplayed his hand.

Elizabeth traditionally did not do well when given ultimatums. Hence, the soon-to-be-common-knowledge scandal, was all his fault, in the eyes of his esteemed mother and her sisters.

Such skewed logic would drive any man to his club. Atholl was no exception.

His sons were cut from different cloth than he, especially Glenlyon. Under the guise of investigating Glenlyon's vices, the duke entered White's late in the evening on Sunday, February the fourteenth—Valentine's Day.

James would be in the card room on the third floor, where the serious gambling took place. In that, James was as predictable as he was degenerate. Thus far, all that redeemed James in his father's eyes was the truth that he stayed out of dun territory. Rather than losing, as Tullie did, Glenlyon had the incredible knack of beating all odds. He won consistently.

So long as he kept winning, Atholl knew, he would never break James's prurient fascination with games of chance. Tullie had been much easier to cure of this vice.

However rare his appearances were at White's, Lord Atholl wasn't expecting stunned shock on the faces of so many casual acquaintances as he handed his scarf, coat and cane to Peterkins in the lobby.

Then, there was another peculiarity of the hallowed club—the book. That stood on its own stand, closed as always, but filled with the essence of many a man's heart and soul, and in some cases his pocketbook. Its purposes were manifold; it served as a bulletin board for members who wished to contact another, a log of time spent inside White's hallowed walls, and a records book.

And nowadays, Atholl understood, the young bloods used the book to place wagers, both outlandish and modest.

Which was why, when Peterkins hailed him by his title and twenty heads in the expansive lobby lurched about, mouths gawking and eyes fixed straight on the book, Atholl's suspicions were raised as high as the rafters topping the fourth floor.

He made no bones about his business, asking Peterkins to send upstairs to Glenlyon, informing him that he wished to speak with the young man immediately downstairs, in the colonial bar.

Then he strode to the book. He opened to the back with the length of purple ribbon that marked the last entry and began scanning. What he read amounted to men's gossip, really.

When he'd read enough of the drivel to satisfy his curiosity and then some, the duke flipped to the last page, took his gold pen from his pocket and uncapped it, dipped it in the inkwell and added his own remarks, dated them, and signed his initials to the last recorded bet. His wager: five hundred thousand pounds sterling that Lady Amalia M. was not the eloped miss of 1802 recently mentioned in the London *Post*.

Once the words were written, he paused to stare deeply into space. Thus far, the rumormongers had not focused on his favorite, Elizabeth. But in time, her absence would be noted and give rise to speculation. Something must be done. As he was putting away his pen in his coat pocket, Glenlyon bounded down the steps from the upper floors. "Father! What brings you here, sir?"

"The need for a quiet word or two," the duke said, gesturing to the doors of the colonial room, where smoking was permitted. He removed his pipe from another pocket as they stepped into the well-appointed chamber, whose standing trophies included some of the most incredibly ferocious and fantastically striped Bengalese tigers.

At the long bar, several young men were engaged in a heated discussion about hunting in Africa. Down the length of polished oak and spotless brass, Atholl spied his quarry.

Evan MacGregor nursed a drink alone.

MacGregor glanced over his glass, into the mirror facing him, and damn near dropped the heavy-bottomed glass from of his hand. He straightened from his crouch over the bar, and spun in an about-face. "Your Grace, what brings you to White's at this time of night?" he inquired, with laudable, but thoroughly false, nonchalance.

"Damned peculiar that everyone keeps asking me that." Atholl cut the captain a cold glare, not much different from the one he turned on his son next. "Why the hell didn't one of you scotch that bloody bet when it was first made, two weeks ago?"

"What bet?" Glenlyon asked, with a puzzled expression on his face. Evan MacGregor stared back at the duke with the darkest black-eyed look Atholl had perceived in at least a decade. If Atholl hadn't wanted cooperation from the scamp, he'd have had his cods for his bloody effrontery.

"The one about your sister, you idiot," Atholl replied. "Or did you put it there in the first place?"

"Elizabeth?" Again James Murray sputtered, completely ignorant of what bet his father referred to. Gambling was James's vice, though he rarely paid a moment's notice to the wagers in the hallowed book, or the drivel that they generated.

"James did not make the original wager, Your Grace," Evan said easily. "George Gordon, young Lord Byron, did. I gather it is his idea of a joke. His parting shot at the ungrateful, unappreciative *ton*, on his summary dismissal back to Cambridge. I wouldn't be a bit surprised if he's the one who placed the carefully worded rumors in the *Post*, as well."

"Well, it's a lot of bloody nonsense. I've put paid to it myself," Atholl declared.

"I'll have to have a look at this." Glenlyon spun on his heel, calling to a waiter, "Joseph, give my father a brandy and see that Captain MacGregor is replenished before I come back. And put it on my account.''

The duke joined Evan at the bar, propping one foot on the brass rail footing the standing bar. The bartender brought his brandy, and Scotch whiskeys for both Glenlyon and MacGregor. There was no point in mincing words. "I'm going to be blunt, sir," Atholl began. "We both know exactly what Elizabeth is up to. Are you man enough to take charge of this debacle and put it right?''

"Beg pardon, Your Grace?" Evan judiciously deferred to the elder, watching warily as Atholl scraped the bowl of his pipe and repacked it with tobacco. "I believe I explained myself thoroughly earlier this week, Your Grace. My hands have been tied in this matter from the first.''

"Damn young bloods. Haven't got the brains God gave monkeys, the lot of them." Atholl grumbled at the noisy group at the end of the bar. "So, you're saying you haven't the balls to put Elizabeth in her place, sir?''

"No, I've never said that, Atholl." Evan met the duke's heated glare without flinching so much as a muscle over the insult hurled at him. Man to man, they were equals. "Elizabeth believes she remains under your protection, sir.''

"MacGregor, do you know where she is?''

"Yes, Your Grace, I do," Evan replied with cool certainty.

"Then, sir, I'd say the time has come for you to assert your own authority.''

That was precisely the answer Evan had never dared to dream he would hear. His shoulders relaxed imperceptibly and he took his glass from the bar and sipped his whiskey, savoring the taste of victory.

Atholl clamped his pipe between his teeth, and took a taper from a stand on the bar. "That being the case, sir, I'll state my position clearly. I don't interfere in my daughter's lawful unions. Deal with her fairly, MacGregor. Granted, she's been my favorite since the day she was born, but a more headstrong and stubborn woman has never walked this earth. In some ways, I envy you the opportunity of bringing such a worthy woman to heel.''

As he lit his pipe, he puffed deeply to draw smoke through the tight wad he habitually packed. It wouldn't burn worth a damn, which was half the challenge of smoking a pipe, in Atholl's mind. It kept him busy, tending it, and it kept others at bay, while affording him the luxury of valuable time lost in deep thought.

MacGregor was one of the most patient watchers he'd ever come to know, drinking his whiskey slowly, not at all intimidated by the duke's propensity for enjoying his smoking habits. He had all of James's generous brandy quaffed when he pulled out his pocket watch and idly checked the time. It was a quarter past eleven. Murray shut the case with a snap and inserted the watch in his weskit pocket, then dropped a coin on the bar as a tip for the waiter.

As he turned to leave, he said to MacGregor, ''We'll be leaving for Scotland on Saturday. You may drop by at your leisure to discuss settlements.''

''Thank you, sir,'' Evan said as he thrust out his hand to the duke. The elder gripped his hand fast, and Evan blurted out, ''I'll be seeing you before you go, then.''

''See that you do.'' Lord Murray responded with a firm pump before releasing him. ''I'm a fair man, MacGregor, once my tempers have cooled. I would have rather had the two of you confront me with the truth at the time, but that's rain washed to the sea. You're both adults now. Elizabeth will have to learn to defer to you. I'll be expecting you to come and discuss settlements. She doesn't leave my house *tocherless*, no matter the harsh words I gave her, son.''

''Yes, sir.'' Evan's shoulders squared beneath the heavy wool of his red coat and the wealth of braid swinging from his buckramed epaulets. "Tomorrow evening? Say, seven?"

"That will be fine." The duke turned and walked out of the colonial saloon.

In the lobby, Glenlyon stopped him. "I thought you wanted to speak to me, Your Grace?"

"And so I have done, Glenlyon. I'll see you at the table in the morning."

Chapter Nineteen

April 6, 1808
Edenchip Plantation
Dominica, Windward Isles

Elizabeth tied the ribbons of her wide-brimmed straw bonnet in a sassy bow beneath her chin, then stepped onto the sunlight-flooded veranda. Shirtless and brown as a berry, Robbie played in a sandbox with four of the island children. A mulatto by the likeable name of Mother Grace, along with three devoted collies, watched over the children playing beneath the shade of a monumental oak.

To Elizabeth's eye, a more idyllic scene could not be found anywhere else on this wide green earth. She stood for a moment on the steps of the house, looking over the land, the mountains and the big, beautiful blue sky. To the east a rising bank of thunderclouds crept over the sea. There was nothing new about that. It rained on Dominica almost as much as it did in Scotland.

Mother Grace's eldest son, Samuel, smiled broadly as he gave Elizabeth a hand up onto the driver's seat of the sleek phaeton. "You look ah-pretty-pretty, Lady Mac, like hibiscus flowers gone full bloom. That new guvnor gonna melt like boiling sugar at your feet, betcha one."

"Why, thank you, Samuel. I do appreciate your compliments." Elizabeth returned his smile as she took the reins in her capable gloved hands. "I should be back shortly after noon. Do serve luncheon at the usual time. Don't make the children wait on account of me."

"Yes ma'am." Samuel bowed. "It ain' right, Lady Mac. Him English sending for you to come to Government House. Should-ah be him coming here t' call on you, he should-ah."

"It really doesn't make any difference to me. I just want to get the process started and over with," Elizabeth answered. She clicked her tongue to the horses and slapped the reins. As she rolled down the curving drive, she waved good-bye to Robbie and his playmates.

After the bitter cold of England, Dominica Island was paradise. Monk Lewis had been so concerned that she was doing the wrong thing, going to the wrong place, but everything could not have been more perfect. Even the fact that Evan owned a plantation on the island had worked to her benefit. Instead of having to rely upon Monk's charity, Elizabeth and Robbie had a place to stay that rightfully was their own to take. Nor did she have to fear that her limited monies would not cover all the necessities, like food and clothing. The plantation was bountiful, and in comparison, the food one small boy ate, and Elizabeth's own meals, took nothing from Evan's wealth.

The estate had been aptly named Edenchip by the first MacGregor settler. It most assuredly was a little bit of Eden here on earth.

Though it was limited in acres of level arable land, the steep, mountainous hillsides Evan owned sprouted incredibly valuable and abundant native crops: vanilla beans, coconuts, oranges and limes, and cocoa—which produced that most craved and therefore priceless commodity in England, chocolate.

With those crops to depend upon, it didn't matter that Dominica's limited lowlands yielded only what could be used on the island—sugarcane, wheat and cotton.

Unimaginable birds of every color of the rainbow, every shape and size, nested in the groves above the white sand beaches and up the heavily forested mountainsides.

In the nearly two full months that she had resided on the island, Elizabeth had yet to find time to climb the top of Morne Diablotin. Each exploratory walk she took had brought her to some enchanting waterfall, spring-fed thermal pool or lush green-filled glen. The temperature was perfect, neither hot nor cold, year-round.

When the rains came, as they frequently did, it was certainly not the bitterly cold rains of Scotland. If that didn't make Dominica a heaven on earth, Elizabeth didn't know what more it would take. At the same time that such a perfectly temperate climate gladdened her, it made her very sad that she would never be able to return home to Scotland.

For Robbie's sake, she tried her best not to dwell upon sad thoughts and precious memories of the Highlands. She lived in the present, enjoying each splendid day God gave her with her son. She didn't think about her own bleak future as a social pariah, an outcast, a divorcée.

She couldn't have come to the island at a more auspicious time. The MacGregor's factor had just been newly buried in the Christian cemetery at Roseau, and no letters had, as of February the tenth, gone out to England informing Evan that his factor needed replacement.

With a snap of her finger, Elizabeth had stepped into the void and taken charge of all of Edinchip's ledgers, accounts and correspondence.

It served her purpose to leave off informing anyone in England of the factor's death.

She had trained all her life to manage an estate of Edinchip's size, but she had never had the chance to manage anything, because of her sister Amalia.

Monk Lewis had briefed her on nearly everything she could expect in Dominica, which had helped her assimilate and exact her plan as soon as she and Robbie had come ashore. As Mrs. Evan MacGregor, the limited island world was open to her.

Autonomy felt exceedingly good.

Of course, all that would change once her petition for divorce was finalized. Elizabeth was also just a little bit resentful of the fact that Evan had never once mentioned the full extent of his holdings. All she had really ever known was that he was heir to Lanrick Castle, which overlooked Loch Katrine. But then she would be the first to admit that she had never spent any time discussing Evan's wealth, or questioning him about where he derived his income. That simply wasn't done.

However, now that she was, in reality, acting as his factor, managing the plantation and keeping its ledgers, as well as sending the quarterly statements and transferring monies to his bank in London, she had to admit she had more than a passing curiosity about his true income.

He wasn't a penniless officer in the king's army, as she had assumed him to be. The wealth from Edenchip alone could make Evan a force to be reckoned with in society back home, did he choose to make use of it.

The township of Roseau nestled above the island's deepwater harbor, protected from all but the strongest winds out of the west. The sea was the most beautiful crystal-clear blue that Elizabeth had ever seen in her life. Each time she came into town, the natural beauty of the harbor and the neat-as-a-pin settlement charmed her.

While her hands were occupied with the driving, Elizabeth tried to organize her thoughts before meeting with the governor. A solicitor she had consulted with some time back in England had prepared for her a writ of divorce, which she had brought with her to Dominica. Once the new governor arrived, only just last week, Elizabeth had sent

Samuel into town to present her petition on her behalf.
Regrettably, there wasn't a solicitor on any of the islands,
so it was definitely a good thing that she had come to
Dominica prepared.

After Samuel delivered the document, it was simply a
matter of biding her time, waiting for the summons to be
heard before the bar. It was what she was going to say to the
governor that had her full attention now. She tried to pose
every sort of question in order to be prepared to testify
succinctly. The fact that there were no solicitors on the island to assist her could be a drawback if she needed further assistance. She also hoped the new governor had little
understanding of the law, as many of his predecessors had.

At the whitewashed Government House, behind the
bustling market square, Elizabeth turned her phaeton and
horses over to an island lad, promising him several pennies
if he kept a good eye on her horses. She paused a moment
under the shade of a magnolia in full bloom to shake the
dust off her dress, loosen the strings of her bonnet and fin-
ger-comb her hair. Then, with hat and reticule in hand, she
walked to the colonnaded veranda of the governor's residence.

Elizabeth found the red-coated sentries as reassuring as
the long, quadrangular barracks complex behind the mansion. She was glad to know there was a strong British army
and naval force in the colony. There was trouble in not-so-
far-away Hispaniola, strife and constant turmoil since
the assassination of Dessalines—the self-styled emperor
Jacques I. Add to that the ongoing sea troubles with England's former colony, America, and Elizabeth had good
reason to be thankful that a sufficient number of good
English soldiers were on hand.

The adjutant, Captain Carson greeted her with a smiling welcome. "Good morning, Lady Elizabeth. How good
of you to be so prompt. The governor prefers to keep a

tight schedule. I trust my request hasn't inconvenienced you."

"Not at all." Elizabeth looked around the cool anteroom, blinking owlishly as her eyes adjusted from bright sun to shady darkness. "I did not expect such a speedy audience. The new governor only just arrived."

"Four days ago," Captain Carson agreed. "And an eventful four days it has been. Come with me. I'll get you settled in his office and then let him know you're here."

"Thank you," Elizabeth said demurely.

The governor's private office was nearly as austere and spare of decoration as the public anterooms. Along the south veranda, all the shutters were wide open, allowing the prevailing breeze and warm sunlight entry.

There were only four actual pieces of furniture in the well-proportioned room. The first was a large standing chest of some sort, filled with narrow, flat drawers and rectangular doors. A gleaming native-mahogany desk, devoid of any clutter save two inkwells and a pen stand, was flanked by two chairs. One, with a tall back, was for the governor to sit on, and a smaller one was set just off to the side for his guest to occupy.

Captain Carson drew up the second chair and bade Elizabeth be seated. "Major General Mack will be with you shortly," he said. Then he bowed and went off to find the governor.

While she was alone for a moment, Elizabeth checked her gloves for spots and smoothed the neckline of her summer-weight walking dress. She'd had to order a whole new wardrobe for both her and Robbie after they arrived. Their winter wools were completely out of place in this sunny clime. She really liked the lightweight cottons made on the islands, and had discovered that the market was abundantly full of all the necessities of life—sandals, lace, straw hats, parasols and cotton gloves. Her sister Amalia would be shocked by Elizabeth's bare arms and exposed throat so early in the year, but on Dominica, Elizabeth's mode of dress was considered very modest.

Elizabeth sat with her back straight, her hands folded properly and her gaze serenely fixed on the portrait of King George, and waited . . . and waited . . . and waited.

Although the name was common, she didn't know of any Major General Mack. He didn't come, and she began to get restless. Somewhere soldiers practiced maneuvers. She could hear the cadence of their tramping feet carried on the wind.

Elizabeth took a deep breath. She twiddled her thumbs and stopped that activity the minute she realized it was happening. She shifted in her chair, looking to the back wall, where a wardrobe chest stood, occupying the whole rear wall.

In one of its cubicles, a mantel clock ticked steadily. It was past ten. Her appointment had been for precisely nine, and she had arrived promptly, with minutes to spare. Elizabeth let out an exasperated breath, then resumed her previous position, face forward, eyes on King George.

Several more minutes passed before she discerned the tramp of Hessians on the meticulously polished tile floors, accompanied by the clank of a cavalryman's saber. Those familiar sounds reassured her that at least the adjutant was returning. Her ears strained to detect the voices speaking just beyond the closed door. Captain Carson to his commanding officer, she hoped. To her great relief, the doorknob rattled and the door itself began to open.

Elizabeth thought it highly unlikely that the new governor outranked her in the peerage, so she didn't have to stand to meet him, and she certainly would not curtsy to someone of lower rank. However, in view of her petition and the favor she sought from the newly appointed official, she thought it might be to her benefit to grant him the courtesy of standing to meet him.

So, as the door opened, she rose from her chair and turned to meet the new governor. The pleasant smile formed by her lips instantly froze.

"Lady Elizabeth." Captain Carson bowed and said, most correctly, "May I present to you the governor of the Windward Isles, Major General Evan MacGregor."

Elizabeth's heart felt as if it dropped all the way down to her toes.

Evan clicked his heels ever so correctly, not precisely bowing to her, merely inclining his head and shoulders somewhat. He lifted his brows almost imperceptibly, as if to mockingly ask if she was going to swoon. She didn't.

"Thank you, Carson. My wife and I need no further introductions. That will be all." Evan closed the door.

Elizabeth sank to the seat of the chair, stunned, speechless, unable to catch her breath. The airy room suddenly felt stifling and hot. Maybe she *should* faint.

She stared at his impeccable uniform, at the stars gracing his collar and the braid crossing his chest. He looked incredibly handsome and fit. *What, dear God, was he doing on Dominica? How had he found her? And when had he been given such a massive promotion?*

Evan strode to the rear of the room, opened a cupboard door and filled two cut-crystal glasses with sherry. Elizabeth flinched with every step he took crossing to his desk. He negligently tossed a linen napkin onto the corner of his desk and handed her a glass, saying, "Don't offend me by refusing the sherry, Elizabeth. You're going to need it."

He got no argument on that score. Elizabeth took the glass in hand and immediately availed herself of a healthy sip. The wine singed the back of her throat and seared a burning hole in her stomach moments after she ingested it. By the time she actually caught her breath after the shock of Evan's entering this room, a small furnace had been ignited and spread like wildfire throughout her body.

Evan adjusted his chair to a more appropriate angle, then sat and put his glass of sherry on the polished surface. From a pocket, he produced a key that he used to unlock the desk. But before he pulled back the drawer, he said, "I'm going to begin by telling you, I applaud your mettle. You have proven to me that you have an incredible capacity for duplicity, in taking my estate on this very island as your hideaway.

"It would have been far better for all concerned had you taken Monk Lewis's advice and returned to Grosvenor Mews the moment you learned I was a property holder on these islands. I understand that you learned that particular fact within two hours of your leaving your father's London residence, on the morning of February the twelfth. I want you to keep those facts in mind for a later conversation. We will get back to that another time.

"You have forced me to go to a great deal of trouble gaining this office and obtaining the rank necessary to hold it. Because of you, I have called in favors that I would not have impinged upon for years into the future. That has cost me much in the long run. More's the pity for you.

"Truly, Elizabeth, your courage is outshone only by your unmitigated gall and rank stupidity. Need I say more? Court is now in session."

Overwhelmed, Elizabeth wordlessly shook her head. This was not the Evan MacGregor that she knew how to deal with. All she seemed capable of doing was staring at him while her brain grappled with the reality that he was here— a flesh-and-blood reality, right before her very eyes.

Elizabeth numbly watched his lean muscular hands open a drawer and bring out a felt-topped leather desk pad, a rolled tube of papers that she recognized, a candle, sealing wax and a flint box.

In two blinks of her eyes, he'd struck a viable spark to the candle's frayed wick and coaxed a flame to rise, then set the silver candle holder aside. While the candle burned and smoked in the soft morning breeze, he sat back in his chair, took his glass in hand and sipped his sherry.

The sultry air fairly crackled with tension and brewing storms to come. Elizabeth felt he must surely sense and be aware of the sluggish pounding of her pulse in her veins. Time seemed utterly frozen.

She took a second sip of the sherry, swallowed carefully and set the glass on the napkin he'd left lying on the corner of his desk.

He sat in the governor's chair and said absolutely nothing, simply stared at her with grim-jawed anger.

Neither of them said another word. When he'd consumed half the sherry in his glass, he turned his attention to the documents, carefully removing the ribbon, though Elizabeth saw that her seal had already been broken.

She wanted to get up and run back to Edenchip, hide, crawl in a hole, do anything that would get her out of this room. All she could do was sit there, frozen, more frightened than she'd ever been in her life, listening to the slow *thud, thud,* of her heart as he read her petition for divorce out loud, with deliberate and meticulous care.

When he turned to the fourth and last page, Elizabeth felt the last scrap of steel in her spine disintegrate. "Evan, maybe this would be a good time for me to explain that."

"Court, Lady Elizabeth, is in session! Be silent until you are given leave to speak!" he commanded, speaking with all the authority of his office. Elizabeth subsided in her chair and snapped her mouth closed.

Finally he completed reading the last page and let it fall on the top of his desk and curl in over on itself. He leaned back in his chair, steepled his fingers and stared at her with eyes that were as cold as ice. Elizabeth tamped down the urge to squirm in her seat. She had never, in her whole life, felt so completely ill at ease as she did at this very moment. Evan opened his mouth, as though to speak, but another terrible minute dragged by before he gave voice to any of his thoughts.

"Where did you have this document prepared?"

She found she'd been holding her breath. "The law firm of Eggersby, Winslow and Peters, in London, prepared it for me. I commissioned it in January."

"Which of those esteemed members of the bar drafted it?"

"Silas Peters, the elder."

"How many copies did you commission?"

"Only one. I was told the court would authorize copies when and if it was accepted for adjudication."

"There are no other copies?" Evan demanded.

Elizabeth shook her head. "No. Only one."

He continued to stare right through her, cold and heartless, as cunning and exacting as the highest judge of the empire. Abruptly he reached across the desk for his stylus and dipped it inside the first bottle of ink. He turned the last sheet of parchment over and put his pen to the paper.

"Your petition for a divorce on the grounds of nonsupport and desertion has been considered by this court at length, Lady Elizabeth. In this court's eyes, the charges you have made against your lawfully wedded husband have no basis in fact and cannot been verified. Nor do I find your irresponsible charge of mental cruelty to be proved beyond a reasonable doubt.

"As an officer of the English court, I am outraged by the amount of the Crown's time you have spent waging a frivolous and infantile battle. Had you spent anywhere near as much time or energy learning the skills of a good wife, you would not be sitting in this courtroom, taking up my valuable time with nonsense. I suggest, Lady Elizabeth, that you return to Edenchip and begin actively working at making your marriage succeed. Petition denied."

Evan signed his name with a flourish and blotted the ink. He touched a stick of wax to the flame and put the indentation of his signet on the blob of red wax.

He rose to his feet and handed her back the last page, which contained only the date adjudicated and the findings of his court.

The petition itself, he kept.

"Good day, Lady Elizabeth." He bowed, ever so correctly. "I believe Captain Carson will provide you a satisfactory escort home."

"That's all you're going to say?" Elizabeth yanked the rolled paper out of his hand. She watched in horror as Evan's expression hardened, despite the fact that his voice remained incredibly civil and polite.

"I believe I've spent sufficient government time on a frivolous lawsuit that has no foundation in fact, my lady. However, should you care to instruct me further, then by all means, bring your personal grievances to me after duty hours. I will be most happy to discuss them with you at my leisure."

That said, he gestured eloquently to the door. Elizabeth caught up her bonnet and thrust her arm through the strings of her reticule. She gave him a polite view of her rigid back. "Good day, sir."

As she put her hand on the doorknob, he said, "Lady Elizabeth."

She paused to look back over her shoulder. "What is it?"

"I'll be home every night from here on out. See that my supper is ready. You may expect me at sundown."

Evan expected her to scream like a shrew, or else slam her way out the door. Again Elizabeth Murray surprised him. She left as quietly as she'd come.

Chapter Twenty

❧

"*Madame, donnez-moi la hachette. C'est moi qui tue les poulets.*"

"No, no, no!" Elizabeth laughed wickedly, refusing to surrender the hatchet to Mother Grace. "I'm going to kill that chicken! *Mais d'abord,* I'm going to catch it. I'm going to chop its ugly little head off, and then I'm going to pull off every little feather and throw it in a boiling pot!"

Robbie fell over in the grass, squealing with glee. "Stop laughing, you little heathen!" Elizabeth scolded and wagged the toy hatchet above her head. "Robbie, get up! Marie, Timothy, everybody, form a circle! Don't let that chicken get away."

Elizabeth hiked up her skirt and ran after the squawking bird, wagging the toy hatchet wildly about her head. The children screamed with laughter each time the bird got away from one of them or dodged Elizabeth or ran between Mother Grace's skinny legs.

Elizabeth lunged for its tail feathers. The plucky chicken put forth a mighty effort to fly, and soared high enough to bobble over Robbie's head and waving arms. It escaped into a copse of trees beyond the wooden fence circling the lawn.

Elizabeth landed on her belly, the head of her hatchet buried in a tussock of grass and dirt. Five children pounced on top of her, giggling and laughing and out of breath.

"Yer not a good chicken killer, *Maman,*" Robbie said.

"I'm not, am I?" Elizabeth tickled him, and then tickled every one of the other children in turn.

She feigned a dramatic sorrow when she slapped her own cheeks and wailed, "Then we will not have a *fricassée de poulet. Pauvre petites,* we shall all go to bed without ze supper, *ces soir.*"

Elizabeth improvised her patois on the spot, the same way the natives appeared to do, drawing from common words in French, English and Spanish to make their meaning clear.

Robbie wrinkled his nose, "Ugh! What's a fricasay sour?"

"Roasted chicken, I think." Elizabeth sat up, hugging the boy sprawled across her legs. She tapped the end of his sunburnt nose and said, "Robbie, I have something important to tell you."

"What's that?" he asked as he put both hands on Elizabeth's cheeks and patted them lovingly.

Elizabeth took a deep breath as she shot a meaningful look at Mother Grace, who wisely shooed the other children away with the promise of a sugar cookie fresh from the kitchens, granting Elizabeth and Robbie a moment of genuine privacy. "Your papa is coming home tonight."

Robbie's precious mouth compressed the way Elizabeth's often did. "Here?" Robbie asked, mystified. "The MacGregor's here, in Dominica?"

"Yes, in Dominica," Elizabeth repeated.

She was so very proud of Robbie for the wonderful way he'd adapted to island life. When she thought about all the upheaval she'd caused in his once well-ordered life, she was amazed at how he took each new day on the island in stride, as though he'd been born to be an adventurer.

She had been brutally honest with the child on the voyage to Dominica, telling him she was his real mother and who his father really was. She'd answered every question he asked, as truthfully as she possibly could.

"How did he find us?"

"Well," she said, as she rubbed her chin against the top of his head, "I think my good friend Mr. Monk Lewis told the MacGregor where we are."

"He didn't keep our secret?"

"Well, I don't know exactly. Monk might have. Your father is a very smart man, Robbie. He could have found out some other way. But the point is, he is here on the island, and this is his house, and we're his family. So, tonight, I guess we're going to have to welcome him home and start learning how to get along together as best we can, all three of us."

"But..." Robbie obviously was troubled by something. He asked, "Did the governor give you a divorce?"

Elizabeth rocked her son back and forth in her arms as she stared at the distant top of the green, forested mountain.

"No, Robbie. The governor didn't give me a divorce. He said I didn't have enough grounds, or any proof." Beyond that, Elizabeth hit a snag. Should she tell Robbie his father *was* the governor? That might just confuse him. "No, the governor declined to hear my case."

Robbie tilted his face up to hers. "I'm glad."

"You are? Why?" Elizabeth asked. Robbie shrugged his shoulders and mumbled, "Dunno. Jus' glad."

"Oh, no." Elizabeth tweaked his nose. "Don't you go clamming up on me, little man. Don't go holding out on me, when you're all I've got in this whole world. I love you, Robbie MacGregor."

Robbie tucked his face down to his chest, not meeting Elizabeth's eyes. She didn't expect a declaration of love from him. Maybe, in time, he'd come to love her. But nothing would ever make up for the years of his life when they'd been apart. And right this moment, Elizabeth was very frightened about the immediate future. Evan could take the child from her. As if to prevent that, Elizabeth tightened her arms around the boy's narrow shoulders.

"Are ye mad at the governor?" Robbie asked. "Is that why you wanted to kill a chicken?"

Elizabeth smiled for the boy's sake. "I think I was letting off a little steam. I didn't really want to kill the chicken. To tell the truth, Robbie, love, I don't know how to go about it."

Robbie twisted around to scan the yard from the curved drive to the rocky bluff that dropped down to their own private beach. He counted each of the red-coated soldiers he could see and then looked back at Elizabeth. "Want me t' go tell Mother Grace we need ten chickens t' feed all the Sassenachs, and Papa, too?"

"You do that." Elizabeth let him get up. "But stay out of Willie's way when he uses the hatchet, Robbie."

She watched her son's sturdy legs pumping as he ran barefoot across the lush green lawn, unrestricted by unnecessary clothes, free and natural. And she envied him his ever-buoyant good spirits and his simplistic view of life. Evan's armed guard, which had escorted her home, were just men to be fed supper, in Robbie's innocent eyes.

Elizabeth took a deep breath, glad she'd gotten over the first hurdle of telling Robbie about the coming change in their lives. She got to her feet, dusting off leaves and some dirt from her gown, and stood for a little while, studying the sky.

Dark angry clouds rose behind Morne Diablotin. Jagged streaks of lightning highlighted their underbelly. It was going to be a stormy night. A shiver ran across Elizabeth's back, and she hugged her arms against her body as she faced the rising wind. The Man of the Mist was coming home. God help anyone who dared to cross him tonight.

Elizabeth went indoors. The children of the plantation could run and play, heedless of the importance of this day, but the rest of the residents of Edenchip didn't dare rest for one moment.

She called Samuel, and they went through the entire house, room by room, making certain there wasn't a single thing out of place, that every surface was dusted and polished and gleaming to the eye.

Upstairs, Lottie Seguin had finished putting clean linens on every bed. Even Robbie's playroom was as neat as a pin. Satisfied, Elizabeth sat out on the veranda overlooking the sea. Soon she needed to take a bath and decide what she was going to wear to dinner.

Her one valise had not contained anything London-smart, or gorgeous enough to turn the head of an angry man. The simple gowns she'd had made for everyday wear were too plain. But Elizabeth was wise enough to know that if she didn't do something to enhance her appearance, the coming confrontation with Evan MacGregor could prove disastrous.

Ever thoughtful, Samuel brought her a cool lemonade to drink while she sat staring over the western sea and sky. "Whatcha we do about *tout les soldats,* Lady Mac? They be hungry-hungry soon."

Elizabeth looked down at the lawn. Sentries stood at various strategic locations around the property. She didn't need to be told the reason for their presence here, any more than she'd ever needed to be told the reasoning behind the existence of her father's ever-present tail. Evan was making doubly certain she'd be here in the house come sundown.

The question was, since they were on a rather small island, where did he think she could possibly go?

Her answer to that was nowhere. It wasn't possible to run away anymore. Elizabeth Murray MacGregor had run out of choices. Here, at Edenchip, she had to make her stand.

To answer Samuel's question, she said, "Tell Cook we have to feed them. So long as they're billeted here, we have to provide food."

"I tell her ya-ya, *vite-vite*. Make big gumbo and bouillabaisse."

"And chocolate pies," Elizabeth suggested. "Captain... excuse me, Major-General MacGregor has a sweet tooth, if I remember correctly."

Samuel's dark eyes brightened. "Such a mouthful, Mayjar-henerrr-all. All English mon important, ya-ya? Make big sir's soldiers special rum punch."

"Do that." Elizabeth sipped at her lemonade and turned to enter her bedroom through the open French doors. "I'll be down directly."

It didn't take her very long to decide which dress to wear. Her best was a pale yellow frock sprinkled with embroidered flowers, ribbons and lace. The cut of it was stylish, Empire-waisted, with a low bodice. Elizabeth took the gown out and hung it in her dressing room. She refused to worry about the cost of her and Robbie's island wardrobes, and the insignificant dent she had made in the plantation's first quarter profit. Evan wasn't mean-spirited enough to accuse her of deliberately stealing from his estate to provide for Robbie's needs. What he'd think of her expenditures for herself remained to be seen.

While she soaked in her tub, Elizabeth went over some of the questions that had come to mind since her morning encounter with Evan. It still stunned her to think of him as now having a higher rank than her uncle, Thomas Graham. She also wanted to know how he'd managed to get appointed to the governorship of the Windward Islands. Had he bought the commission? Been given it as a reward for duty and valor? Was it because he owned property here? And, last of all, how had he learned where she was? Had Monk Lewis betrayed her?

It was so silly, her thinking. Hadn't she just gotten past her guilt and self-recriminations over running away? Yes, and she'd happily put aside all her fears about being found by her father. Freedom. That was what she'd found. Freedom to be herself. Freedom to be Robbie's mother. Now all she could do was think about the pain she'd caused her family. All the damage she'd done to Evan's good name.

Her father was right. Evan would never forgive her for hiding Robbie, for making his son a bastard. He would never love or trust her as he had so many years ago. That was the price of Elizabeth's ignorance. She could never make it up to Evan . . . or to Robbie. And she truly feared the day when her son would despise her as deeply as her husband did.

Elizabeth reached for a towel and climbed out of the tub, taking care to step on the braided rug and not drip any unnecessary water on the polished wood floor. There was a great surplus of servants about Edenchip, but Elizabeth preferred the privacy of having the master bedroom all to herself. Only the quiet and efficient Lottie Seguin came in to clean, sweep and dust once each day.

As she rubbed her hair dry, Elizabeth gazed out the open windows. The sun of the afternoon was gone, hidden behind a bank of ominous thunderclouds. Already the tree-covered crest of Morne Diablotin was wreathed in mist and dense fog as the sun slowly sank into the sea.

A shiver swept across her shoulders and skittered down her spine as Elizabeth wound the long length of cotton around her torso. Half of her feared the evening and night to come. The other half merely wanted to get past it all, past the accusations, the questions, the anger.

That part of her wanted peace, and recognized that on Dominica she had achieved the contentment that had always eluded her in England or Scotland. Yes, that half of her needed to nurture others, in order to continue to feel as though she were a necessary part in the scheme of things.

Here at Edenchip, she was necessary. She made a difference.

She picked up a brush to take the tangles out of her hair and stepped out from behind the bentwood screen. Then she stopped.

Standing in the wide-open French doors of the upper veranda was His Grace, the governor. Elizabeth immediately tightened her hold upon the cotton swaddling her very damp body. The other arm she left dangling, with brush in hand. She raised a brow and said, "Good evening, Evan. I didn't hear you come in."

"That's because I haven't . . . come in, yet." Evan's right hand rested on the hilt of his sabre. His left hand was in motion, raising to remove his gleaming Cavalry helmet from his head as he stepped across the threshold into the room.

The setting sun touched his hair and glazed his bronzed cheeks with ruby highlights. In the span of a heartbeat, Elizabeth saw confirmation of Robbie's fiery auburn curls in the sable wreathing Evan's head. He tossed his helmet to the cushions of a big rattan armchair and came to parade rest in the center of the room, looking the furnishings over with a caustic eye.

The way he inspected every inch and quadrant confirmed what Samuel and Mother Grace had told Elizabeth when she arrived at the plantation. Evan MacGregor had never before set foot on the island of Dominica.

Eventually his critical inspection turned to Elizabeth. He took in her artless pose, and the damp drape of the toweling around her body. Elizabeth tried to blot out the memory of the last time she'd stood before him nearly just so, and vulnerable. But she couldn't suppress the humiliation she'd felt, and because of that memory some heat stole up her throat to color her cheeks.

Had she offered him a sincere apology then, would he have acted differently? And now...what now? It wasn't any easier to think of the right words, or to form them, today. He didn't look as if he were interested in hearing anything she had to say, apologies or otherwise.

She did manage to gird herself with an impermeable coat of pride as defense against his forthcoming insults. She watched him strip off a pair of immaculate white gloves, which he folded and slipped into a pocket of his lightweight coat. After a moment or two of frank appraisal, he said, "You look exceedingly robust, Elizabeth. I take it island life agrees with you."

The blandly spoken, candid compliment shattered her defense, by the very virtue of its forthright honesty.

"Yes, I believe it does, and thank you for the compliment. You also look to be in the best of health."

"What, pray tell, informs you of my health? You have not asked after it, nor given any indication my well-being, or lack thereof, matters one iota to you, madame."

Her eyes told her quite a lot about the well-being of the man underneath the regalia of a pristine uniform. She hoped he'd look in on Robbie, so that the boy could see and ask questions about the many medals and ribbons that decorated the left side of Evan's jacket.

"What? Is my garrulous wife at a loss for words? How very odd." He unhooked the buckle of his saber and removed it, casting both belt and scabbard onto the same cushioned seat as his helmet.

"What would you like me to say?" Elizabeth asked.

For a fraction of a moment, Evan's mask of indifference slipped, revealing his disgust, his anger and his outrage. Then he blinked his eyes, and all emotion disappeared from his face. She could liken it only to his having closed the shutters of his soul.

"Not a damned thing!" His jacket was the next article of clothing removed. He strode across the room and threw open the hallway door, hollering across the stairwell for Corporal Butter to come upstairs at once.

Coward that she was, Elizabeth took that opportunity to escape into her dressing room.

Dinner was served promptly at eight. Evan took his seat at the head of the table, and Elizabeth took hers at the foot. No guests had been invited to join them. Elizabeth did not know if any of the dozen or so soldiers who had escorted her home that morning remained at Edenchip, now that Evan was in residence.

The food was excellent, well seasoned and cooked to perfection. Evan ate well and heartily. Clearly, little daunted his appetite. Elizabeth had trouble swallowing each mouthful.

After the last remove, Evan took a bottle of wine from Samuel's hand and waved him out.

Elizabeth straightened in her chair as Evan's chair scraped ominously against the floor. She touched her napkin to her mouth. Evan stood with wine bottle in hand and ambled down to the foot of the table. His bonny Gregarach *philabeg* swung about his knees.

For his first evening at home, he had made only two concessions to the temperate climate. The first was a collarless island-cotton sark that was open at his throat and unbuttoned to expose his chest. The second was that there was no tartan draped across his shoulder.

Were they on friendlier terms, Elizabeth would have told him straight out how bonny he looked. But his aura of menace kept her silent. She wouldn't risk speaking before she was spoken to.

He stopped at the edge of Elizabeth's chair and filled her wineglass nearly to the rim. Then he drew out the empty chair on her left, sat, and filled his own goblet.

"I propose a toast, Lady Elizabeth."

"What would that be?" Elizabeth asked cautiously. No MacGregor dressed in Highland garb was ever to be trusted out of hand.

Evan rested his elbow on the armrest of his seat and turned the goblet toward the light, contemplating his next words. When they came, he shocked Elizabeth down to her very wary toes.

"I propose a toast to new beginnings, clean slates, and starting over."

Shaken, Elizabeth took her glass in hand. "All right, I will drink to that."

"Excellent. An amenable wife. How lucky can a mon get?" Evan lifted his glass and repeated his toast, then touched the rim of his crystal to hers and drank. "Now it's your turn. You make a toast."

Elizabeth considered his challenge. She raised her glass and said, "To incredible coincidences, friendly betrayals and inexplicable promotions within the ranks. Cheers."

She touched her glass to his and then drank. He didn't. "Are ye accusing me of betrayal, lass?"

"I'm accusing someone . . . elsewise you wouldn't be here."

"Well, then, I think you'd best look in a mirror. You betrayed yourself. I followed you from your father's house to Charing Cross."

"No, you didn't!" Elizabeth gasped. "No one followed me!"

"Are ye saying I'm a liar?" Evan drawled, in a very menacing tone.

God, but his eyes glittered like hot coals. Elizabeth swallowed. She wanted to run. Instead, she lifted her chin and said, "Don't be putting words in my mouth, Mac-Gregor. I looked, and I didn't see anyone following me. If you'd been on my trail, I'd know it."

"I was there, lass, and ye didn't know it. I waited awhile in the cold, while you piddled away an hour in the White Horse Inn's public room. Then ye came out with wee Robbie and bought a coach ticket. After that, ye walked up the street and got in Monk Lewis's black carriage. He drove around Whitehall two or three times before you convinced him to take you and Robbie to Gravesend."

Elizabeth didn't know whether to believe him or not. "Monk could have told you that."

"Aye, he could have. You woke up wee Robbie to force feed him a bowl of runny porridge. I don't think he cared for it."

At that observation, Elizabeth's mouth dropped open. "You really were following me!"

"Aye, I said I was."

"I don't understand. If you were following me, why didn't you try to stop me?"

"Ah, that brings me to my next toast. Raise yer glass, Elizabeth," he commanded.

Completely baffled, Elizabeth did as she was told. Evan leaned across her to tip the bottle and fill her glass to the rim. He hoisted his glass to the flickering candles on the centerpiece, considering the deep red color of the wine. "To sons a mon never knows exist! Born and raised fer bastards, every one."

That stung. Elizabeth pulled her glass back where he couldn't touch it. "It wasn't like that."

"Oh, aye? Then what was it like? I've been handed the wean's birth certificate, and told by yer own father to do with it as I see fit."

There was a world of anger in his words, anger against which Elizabeth had no defense. She didn't waver an inch in meeting the harsh glare in his eyes head-on as she raised her glass and audibly clicked glass against glass. "To wee Robbie—victim of his mother's ignorance."

"Why did ye no' tell me, Elizabeth?" Evan demanded. "Before it all went so wrong? I'd have come to Dunkeld and faced yer father. Ye know I would have."

She brought her glass to her lips and drank. Then she held the glass in her lap and sat looking at the wine that remained. "I didn't know enough to tell you."

Evan used one finger to pick up her chin and make her look at him. His eyes declared he didn't believe her.

"God's truth, Evan, I didn't know." Elizabeth jerked her chin away from his hand.

Deep-seated anger flashed across her face and set like stone in her stubborn Murray jaw. Her lips compressed, then relaxed once more, and she stared off into empty space, as though she were actually looking back in time.

"Amalia and I fought day and night. The aunts complained that I was moody. Grandmother told Papa I was ill-mannered. Then Papa decided to take me to Port-a-shee. We were out to sea, crossing to Man, when he told me he knew I was carrying a child. My father told me, Evan! Think how stupid I was, to not even know what was happening in my own body.

"Papa told me I had to name the father...so that he could take steps to have the man who had dared to touch his daughter hanged, drawn and quartered. His threats only made me more determined to say nothing, and to deny the truth.

"Even when he'd explained exactly how babies were conceived, I didn't believe Papa. How could he have known what was happening to me? It was my body. I wasn't telling anyone anything. Then one day, I really felt the baby move inside me. Not some fluttering jiggle, but a good strong lusty kick. I put my hand, just so, and pushed back on this big stomach in front of me, and the baby responded.

"Oh, Evan, it was almost Christmas by then. You were in Ireland, and I didn't want Papa to kill you. I couldn't write to you and tell you, for fear that the letter might somehow fall into the wrong person's hands."

"You should have told yer father the truth, Elizabeth." Evan said. "That would have been better than going it alone, all by yerself. He'd have sent for me and married us up proper in the kirk before the babe was born. I don't care one bit for the idea of you bein' martyred and punished, nor for any mon raisin' his hand against ye."

"Papa didn't strike me," Elizabeth said in defense of her father. "It is beneath his consequence to strike a woman bearing a child." Elizabeth raised her glass, and proposed another toast. "Here's to foolish brides who run home to Papa!"

"So ye did." Evan lifted his glass to hers. The crystal rang as they banged the rims together.

Elizabeth's glass was empty when she set it down. Evan immediately filled it.

"Are you trying to get me inebriated, sir?"

"What do you think?" Evan tilted the bottle to his own glass, splashing wine against the cut crystal. Then he sat staring at Elizabeth.

"I think you're being extremely evasive. Why didn't you answer my question? If you followed me when I left London, why didn't you try to stop me?"

"Perhaps I wanted to see what choices you'd make."

"You were testing me?"

"No, I wouldn't call it that, not when ye've got the knack of makin' me blood boil the first week at my new post. That petition for a divorce damn near gave me apoplexy. I came close to beatin' ye for that one, Elizabeth Murray Mac-Gregor. Mark my words, woman, I would have, if it had been seen by any officer's eyes but mine own."

"MacGregor, the last time I laid eyes on you, you made it clear you had no use for me, whatsoever! That's grounds for divorce. You threw me out of your bedroom!"

"Aye, because there's an apology due, still owin'."

"Well! Here's to apologies neither one of us will ever hear!" Elizabeth angrily picked up her glass. "Or say!"

"I'm not here to play games!" Evan slapped his hand down on the table. The nearly empty bottle jumped. So did Elizabeth.

More judiciously, Elizabeth proposed a different toast, "Fine, then, here's to the headache I'll have tomorrow."

Evan let his brogue roll, full of innuendo. "I promise ye the pain you'll be feeling t'morrow will be a great deal lower than yer head, lass."

He touched her glass in a salute, and they both drank.

Elizabeth set her empty glass down on the table and pushed it far away. That didn't stop Evan from pouring the last of the wine into her crystal, saying, "We're not done yet."

Elizabeth drummed her nails on the tablecloth. Evan leaned to the side of his chair, raising his next toast. "Ta lust, an' doin' it wit yer boots on, ta beget a son."

"It didn't work that way the last time. You must have done something wrong, being barefoot. Or maybe that's the reason I can't keep boots on Robbie."

Elizabeth grudgingly touched his glass and barely sipped her wine. She held her glass up and stared hard at Evan as she said, "To forgiveness, compassion and love, and husbands who haven't the slightest clue of what any of those virtues are about."

"Ha!" he shouted. "I'll damn well drink to that." And they both did.

"My turn," he said. He tilted his head back and stared at the glittering chandelier suspended from a plastered medallion on the ceiling. "I think it's time for a wee bit of Robbie Burns," he said, and closed his eyes. "Let me see if I can remember the rhyme."

Evan picked up her glass and put it in her right hand, then took his glass in his left and slid his fingers gently down her wrist to take her hand in his.

"'Had we never loved sae kindly, had we never loved sae blindly, never met—or never parted—we had ne'er been broken-hearted,'" he recited. "Ta Robbie Burns, poet extraordinaire!"

Elizabeth brought her glass to his, tapping it gently, then saluted him and drank. A tentative smile touched her lips. "I know of a poem that suits us. Would you drink to it?"

"Aye." Evan's eyes crinkled. His fingers compressed gently on her hand. "But only if it was written by a Scotsman."

Elizabeth's smile widened, and a small giggle escaped her throat. "It was."

"Well, then, let's hear it."

"Roseberry to his lady says, 'My hinnie and my succour, O shall we do the thing you ken, Or shall we take our supper?' Wi' modest face, sae fu' o' grace, replied the bonnie lady; 'My noble lord do as you please, but supper is na ready.'"

"Where did you get that one?" Evan demanded. The tiniest hint of a smile twitched about his mouth. "Or did you spend the afternoon planning your revenge?"

Elizabeth stoutly defended her choice. "Robert Burns."

Evan's smile cracked open. "If that's Robbie Burns, he stole it from Anonymous. I thought you were going to quote some god-awful rhyme of Byron's."

Elizabeth held up her glass and demanded, "Drink, sir."

"Verra well, I'll drink to my hinnie lady."

They made the crystal ring again and drained their glasses, then set them down. Evan swung around in his seat, looking to the swinging door of the butler's pantry. "Ho, my good man. Elizabeth, what's the butler's name?"

"Thomas... No, Samuel." Elizabeth clapped a hand over her mouth, stifling a giggle that came out of nowhere.

"You don't know how to hold your liquor." Evan wagged a finger at her while shouting, "Ho, Samuel!"

Immediately the swinging door opened and Samuel entered, carrying another bottle of claret that he was still wiping clean of the dust from the cellar. "Ah, now here's a man I can rely upon,'' Evan said. ''That's exactly what I was going to ask for, another bottle of wine.''

Samuel adroitly removed the cork and placed two clean glasses on the linen and poured a sampling of the decanted bottle for Evan. Then Samuel awaited Evan's approval before filling his glass and serving Elizabeth.

''Ah, you're a jewel, Samuel. Leave us the bottle. I can manage from here.''

Elizabeth waited until the servant had departed before asking, ''Can you? What makes you so certain? I'll bet if you stand on one foot and try to touch your nose, you'll go toppling over.''

''Not on this milksop.'' Evan grinned. ''I was weaned on *uisgue beatha* with a kick to it. The only thing French that comes close to Balquhidder mash is Benedictine brandy. That's 'cause it's been aged for a century.''

''Humph.'' Elizabeth wasn't convinced. The claret affected her. She leaned back in her chair and stared at the ceiling, watching an exotically colored moth batter the chandelier. ''I've run out of rhice . . . I mean, rhymes. Oh, oh, my head's spinning.''

''None of that, milady,'' Evan scolded. ''There'll be no escaping the reckoning on account of tippling.''

''What reckoning?'' Elizabeth asked baldly.

''Ours,'' Evan answered. He matched the lifting of her proud chin with a raised brow and a set expression that said he wasn't going to back down.

''I'm no' afraid of you.'' Elizabeth called his bluff.

''Aye, I know that.'' Evan raised his glass to his mouth and had a healthy drink. ''But the night's young. You'll likely change your mind by morning.''

''Ha!''

Chapter Twenty-One

Elizabeth was on her feet and out of her chair before Evan set his glass down. "What's this?" he drawled. "I don't advise you to run for the wood. I've left a few sure traps to stop you."

"I'm not running." Elizabeth put the table and numerous empty chairs between them before she stopped. "I'm taking necessary precautions for self-preservation. Don't forget, MacGregor, I know your diabolical mind. I'm perfectly aware that you've got a sentry posted every ten feet around the perimeter. So why should I run?" She lifted a pretty shoulder. "I said, I'm no' afraid of you."

"Truly?" Evan slowly rose from his chair. By the time he stood straight and tall, Elizabeth had backed up the width of two more chairs. Evan smiled.

"Stop leering! You're doing that purposely to frighten the wits out of me," Elizabeth said haughtily. "Save your black scowls for the soldiers under you. I'm immune."

If she was so immune, then why was she so restless, guarded, and unable to settle to any fixed point? Evan raised his right hand and crooked his finger, beckoning her to him. She backed up another step and stoutly shook her head no, refusing.

"So be it." Evan gave her a verbal warning just before he flattened his hand on the table and bounded over it—centerpiece, candlesticks, chairs and all.

Elizabeth yelped and took off running, thinking, *All right, so I am afraid of you!* She caught hold of the doorknob, spun to the right and slammed the door shut in Evan's face.

While he had to deal with that, she snatched up her hem and ran up the stairs. The dining room door burst open, and Evan made the breakneck right turn to the stairway without a hitch in his stride. Five steps ahead of him, just inches out of reach of his long arms, Elizabeth ran for all she was worth.

His long legs gobbled up the steps two at a time. One more step and she'd reach the straightaway of the upper gallery, a tall, cavernous hall that let the prevailing winds filter from end to end and cool the house on even the hottest days.

His fingers scratched at her elbow, so Elizabeth spun around to face him on the landing. She dodged under the wrap of his arm and laughed, then ran the whole length of the hall and out onto the veranda.

The southwest side of the veranda was cluttered with furniture, chaises and settles, a hammock, a daybed and whatnot tables to make sitting out enjoying the cool breeze comfortable.

But the mist had come down from the mountains, blanketing the house and veranda with a sheen of moisture and gentle, obscuring fog. Elizabeth escaped into the furniture grouping and hid behind a settle.

Few lights were burning on the upper floor of the house, so she couldn't actually see Evan when he skidded to a halt outside the door. She could hear him. The upper veranda did not completely encircle the manse. Elizabeth knew she was trapped if he came her way.

Evan cocked his ears to the night, listening for movement, for any hint of a sound that might give away Elizabeth's hiding place. The night had come down wet and heavy. Thunder rumbled out of a distant bank of clouds. The mountain was obscured by mist.

Slowly, taking care with each step he took, he followed his instincts, tracing the lingering fragrance of Elizabeth's perfume. He turned toward the master bedroom, passing across a band of soft light spilling out one set of French doors then rounding a corner, and another. The whisper-soft scuffling of a slipper against wood spun him around in time to see Elizabeth bolting out from behind a rattan settle.

It took him two heartbeats to run to her and bring her crashing down on a cushion-strewn daybed. She fought like an unbroken mare, twisting and bucking, trying to unseat him. Evan captured her hands, pressing both into the cushions beside her head. She panted heavily to catch her breath. He had no need to exert such labor.

"Now, lass, you were bragging, afore you so judiciously bolted," Evan drawled. "Would ye care to amend that pretty lie about not fearing me?"

Elizabeth bravely lifted her chin. "I don't see any reason why I should."

"Humph," Evan grunted. "You've a quick tongue, *ma dow.*"

"I'm not your sweet dove!" Elizabeth declared contentiously.

Evan shifted his weight, trapping both her hands together under one of his, and reached down to grasp her knee and remove that barrier to intimacy.

"Elizabeth..." Evan nudged her gently, intimately, in the most private of ways.

"What, Evan?" Her question was followed by the oh-so-familiar compression of her full lips.

"You've lost the battle and the war, Elizabeth. It's time to sheathe your sword." Evan ran his tongue across the edge of her lower lip.

"I haven't got one."

"Nay, lass, I'm the sword, you're the sheath. Do you submit willingly, I promise you pleasure. Do you fight me, you'll earn only pain, like before." He ran his fingers across her brow, stroking back the springy curls, to expose the vulnerable curve of her temple. He placed his next kiss there, soft and sweet. He could feel the tension in her body, like the string of a longbow, from her head to her foot.

"What do I have to do?" Elizabeth asked uneasily.

Evan drew back his head and studied her face in the dim light, cast by a lone lamp burning in their bedroom. "You don't have to do a thing. I'll show you all the sweet touches that I know. The one requirement is the generosity of your spirit. Trust me. Yield to me. I believe I can make you a contented woman with all my heart, *ma dow*. I will do my very best not to hurt you in any way. Do you believe me, Elizabeth?"

She had to think about his promise and his question a long moment before she could grant him a tentative answer. "I want to believe you, Evan."

That answer pleased him greatly. He nodded his head, satisfied. "Good. I grant you back the privilege of using your hands, with one caution. Remember what it feels like now, to be powerless against me. Do you hurt me, or try to stop me from giving the both of us pleasure, I'll bind your hands to the bedpost, and you'll no' have use of them until the sun rises on the morrow."

Elizabeth shivered. "You're threatening me."

"No. I never make threats, Elizabeth. At my size, I don't have to. Now, do you yield?"

She wiggled her fingers and then her wrists, testing his resolve, as well as his grip. She was scared of his power and his size, but she did want to believe him. "No. I've something to say first."

Evan put one knuckle under her stubborn Murray chin and lifted it. "Say your piece."

"I want to apologize for my poor manners back in London. What I did was wrong, Evan. I will never take advantage of your earnest promises to me again."

"Nicely done, my lady, and said at the appropriate time. I accept your apology, and all is forgiven."

"In that case, my lord, I yield." Elizabeth lifted her chin until her lips met his.

Evan met her more than halfway. His fingers slid behind her head, lifting her to meet the triumphant assault of his mouth on hers. Beneath him, her breasts heaved and strained, and the nether parts of her were all wiggling resistance until he slid his tongue deep inside her mouth and touched hers. He knew her greatest weakness—Elizabeth loved being kissed.

The jittery bug that was lodged inside Elizabeth's belly increased a hundredfold. She blamed the wine for the uncomfortable fluttering and queasiness that would not abate. But it kept getting worse, moment by moment, as Evan slowly and deliberately unbuttoned her gown.

She could hardly breathe. She didn't know what to do with her hands, what he wanted or expected her to do with them, so she left them where Evan had left them.

He reached the last button of her simple and cool island-cotton gown. With meticulous deliberation, Evan parted the sides of her high-waisted bodice, exposing her breasts to his touch and gaze.

His fingers felt hot and rough, callused and strong, as they passed across her sensitive skin. Something inside her jumped each time his fingers stroked over her nipples. She thought she might go out of her mind when his fingers closed on the tender flesh, tweaking each nub, toying and playing with her.

That was minor torture, compared to the exquisite agony she felt when he lowered his head and suckled each breast. She almost reached out to stop Evan from doing that. Years ago, Evan had touched her with his hands. Once, he'd put the sweetest kisses there, just before he ruptured her maidenhead. But she'd never felt such a thrill, the heat of his tongue and the texture of his teeth drawing her deeply inside his mouth.

It hurt in the most delicious of ways. And Elizabeth felt something brand-new happening inside her. The jittery bug inside her belly became a tugging, raving beast, which twisted and rolled over and clawed at the muscles of her stomach, demanding to be let out. Her hips twitched, and her legs parted.

Evan took his hand away from her other breast and caught a handful of her skirt. Heedless of the value of the cloth, he bunched the whole skirt at her waist and put his hand on the raging beast. She jumped when his fingers parted her and found the slick juices pouring out of her body.

Stars, but she didn't know what to do with her hands. They clenched and unclenched into helpless fists, and she wanted to touch his skin as he was touching her, but she didn't know if she was allowed to do that. She couldn't ask a single question, because by the time a question formed, something new and thrilling happened, like the intrusion of his finger into that secret, private place.

That, she realized, was what the craven beast in her belly wanted most of all. She wanted... it wanted... no, *she* wanted... the emptiness filled. No sooner did she admit that truth to herself than Evan withdrew his finger. The void remained idle and empty while his hand tended to some other delicate spot, a nubbin of some sort, upon which his mere touch made her want to scream.

At last she found something to do with her hands. One fist became a cork that she stuffed in her mouth to stifle her screams. But one hand was incapable of holding back her cries; it took both hands to muffle her groans and screams.

His fingers tightened their hold on the spot, straining it, teasing and playing with it, flicking hard and soft, fast and slow. Elizabeth couldn't draw a breath inside her chest. She couldn't release the air trapped behind her throat.

Her skin was slick with sweat, hot and burning from the inside out. Yet the mist glazed every exposed pore, drenching her in a cloak of mystifying heat. It surrounded them completely, enveloping them both in clouds.

Evan lifted her hands away from her mouth and kissed her. His lips felt so warm and sweet. His tongue slid inside and teased hers, darting in and out, coming back to torment and stab her. She didn't know what he wanted of her. Her arms tightened around his shoulders, her fingers stroking through the sleekness of his hair. His arms moved underneath her, pressing her breasts and the naked heat of her belly flush against his.

She felt his manhood buck against the sopping wetness between her legs, and she wanted him to fill her emptiness once and for all. But how to tell him what she wanted most of all eluded her.

She opened her legs, drawing her knees up, tightening them on Evan's hips. And the next time his tongue darted into her mouth, she caught hold of that and suckled it softly, softly, as gently as he had suckled her breast.

The wonder of what was happening made her want to crawl up against him and wrap herself completely around him. She resented the cotton bunched at her waist and cupping her upper arms, because it kept an amount of her body away from his. She slid her thighs up and down his hips, loving the texture of his coarse hair abrading her sleekness.

She ran her hands down his back and discovered he'd cast off his kilt. Her palms came into contact with the hard, rounded muscles of his buttocks, and she pulled him to her, impatient.

His hands and arms left her body, and he lifted himself up and away, breaking his mouth free from hers. "No, no, no!" Elizabeth cried out. "Come back to me! Don't go away!"

"Whisht!" Evan murmured, shushing her. He slid his hands under Elizabeth's hips and lifted her to meet him, then began the sure and certain descent into her.

Elizabeth's eyes widened with shock. Surely she could not feel anything more wonderful than she'd already experienced. She panicked a little, and he soothed her with quiet kisses and soft, whispered words.

Evan groaned with his own growing need and made his exploring touches firmer, stroking and compressing her breasts, running his hand down the length of her belly to cup her and feel her heat as he guided himself into her.

"Look," Evan told her.

Elizabeth raised her head from the cushions and looked down between their bodies. His rod was an incredible sight, the head of it just beginning to disappear into her folds. Yet there was so much more to go.

She looked up at Evan's face, fearing the coming pain. He would tear her asunder, just as he had before. There was no way her body could accommodate such a thing inside her.

"Elizabeth, bring your feet up to my hips."

"I can't!" she cried out as he sunk deeper.

"Elizabeth! Do as I tell you!"

"Oh, God!" She slapped a hand over her mouth and tried to obey him. His command went against years and years of training that insisted that a lady did not part her legs so coarsely. A lady rode sidesaddle, and always kept her knees within scant inches of each other.

Evan caught her knees and tilted them, widened them to accommodate him. Only then could he complete his downward stroke. She was as slick as oiled seawater, hot and turgid and throbbing. He had to brace himself and get leverage before he was seated to the hilt.

Elizabeth sobbed. Her womb tightened around him like a vise. Evan rested for a moment on an elbow, giving her space to breathe. He caught hold of her wrist and drew her hand away from her mouth. "Stop crying."

"I'm not," Elizabeth sobbed.

"I said, stop crying. You're not hurt. There's no blood. I haven't torn you or hurt you. Stop being foolish, and listen to your body."

"I'm trying to!"

"Then tell me, what is your body telling you to do?"

Elizabeth got quiet and listened. She wiggled her hand, which was caught in his grip. "To wipe my eyes."

He allowed her enough movement of her arm to do that, then demanded, "What else?"

Elizabeth's feet moved, and she became conscious of some discomfort with her legs that lessened the minute she thought about relaxing. She lifted the lax hand, which he still held prisoner by her wrist, and laid her palm on his cheek. "To touch you."

Evan turned his head and put a kiss in the palm of her hand. "Very good, Elizabeth. Don't tighten up on me. Let your body soften."

"How do I do that?"

"You were doing it all along, until I entered you. What made you afraid? What were you thinking?"

"That you're too big."

"I'm not. Feel me inside you. Think about me. Where does my length end? Show me."

Elizabeth swallowed, and put her other hand against her throat.

"No." Evan laughed. "Thank you for the compliment, but I am not that big. Here, give me your hand. Let's find where I am."

Evan took her hand in his and laid both underneath her ribs. He pressed her fingers into her soft skin, just above her navel. "Can you feel me there?"

Elizabeth shook her head. "No."

He pulled her hand lower, midway between her navel and the crest of soft curls crowning her sex. "Here?"

Elizabeth closed her eyes and concentrated. She let the air out of her chest and just breathed naturally. Evan pressed his fingers over hers, guiding them, teaching her where to look. "No," Elizabeth said. "It's not there. It's deeper, lower, farther back."

"Here?" Evan slipped his hand underneath her hips and lifted her ever so slightly.

"There." Elizabeth opened her eyes, surprised. "You found it. You know where you are."

"Aye, I know. It's no mystery to a man. A man knows exactly how long or how thick his rod is."

"Oh..." Elizabeth let her eyelids droop halfway. "I like the feeling of fullness."

"Do you, then?" Evan grinned. He settled down on his elbows, catching her chin. "I like the fit...the tightness, the heat, and the way you grab on to me."

"I do all of that?" Elizabeth asked as she wound her arms around his neck, drawing his chest down to hers.

Evan kissed her. "Aye, and much more." He laid his finger across her lips and said, "Whisht, now. Let me concentrate on the work at hand. There's more."

She knew that. She remembered very clearly what he meant by more...his pleasure. But he'd given her so much pleasure that she was willing to let him have his.

Evan knew exactly what she was thinking. He was not about to let her lie passively underneath him, as lifeless as a chamber pot. There were hundreds of touches she'd yet to feel. He feathered his fingers along her throat, circling the sensitive places below her ears, skittering across her lips, delving a finger into her mouth.

Slowly, tentatively, she began to do the same thing. Touching him in similar places, exploring with her finger-tips and her tongue. Tasting him as he was tasting her, the sweat, the mist, the love juices flowing from each of their bodies.

It started to build inside him, the need for release, and he deliberately pulled away, withdrawing from her heat, his rod hard and stiff and bucking, wanting back inside her so badly it hurt.

She protested like a mewling cat as he rose to his feet, dazed and almost staggering. He caught her hand, pulled her before him and stripped the crumpled gown off her body, throwing it away. He shrugged his arms out of his own sark and caught her wrists, drawing her against him, belly to belly.

The lamp in their bedroom gutted, fading into dark-ness. The barest hint of light remained when Evan led her inside. He caught the coverlet and pulled it down, then lifted Elizabeth up into the bed. He crawled onto the bed from the foot, spreading her ankles, parting her knees, bringing his face down between her thighs.

She gasped when his mouth touched her, and she stiff-ened against the intimacy of his touch. He raised his head to reassure her. "Trust me, Elizabeth. Nothing I do to you is wrong or shocking. Your body is mine. All of it. Every part of it, and I may worship it with my body as I choose."

He saw the struggle going on inside her, saw her fear that a lady didn't do such things. When he touched her again, her body softened. A delicious shudder swept down her spine and pebbled her flesh, and she cried out his name, shouted it to the heavens.

Evan moved up her body, savoring her one kiss at a time. He caught her mouth and kissed her deeply. This time, as he entered her portal, he felt different, as though he'd crossed over an important threshold. He was filled with an incredible burst of possession and power.

This was his house, his land, his woman. No power on earth could take any of it from him. This was the way God meant it to be between a man and a woman.

He had all the time in the world to make love to her, to teach her all she needed to know, to bring her to fulfillment.

Chapter Twenty-Two

"What time is it?"

"Whisht, Elizabeth. I'm trying to sleep."

"Why do you want to sleep?" Elizabeth asked as she scooted up Evan's chest and laid her head on his shoulder. She very cleverly hid the fact that she was yawning by tickling his collarbone with her tongue. "Don't you realize we have five lost years to make up for? Why didn't you tell me it would be like this—fun and pleasurable?"

"At the risk of starting another argument, Elizabeth, I believe I did tell you that, several times. You have just been too pigheaded and Murray-stubborn to admit you were wrong."

"Humph." Elizabeth bit his shoulder, a tad fiercely. "You might have given me a more convincing demonstration."

Evan silently counted to ten before he ventured to say anything more. "We won't be catching up on anything, if you don't let me get some sleep between bouts of lovemaking." In spite of his words, he found his interest . . . his passions . . . rising to meet the occasion . . . especially when Elizabeth set her even white teeth to nibbling on his earlobe.

"Well, you did promise me it wouldn't be my head hurting when I wake up later on in the morning," Elizabeth drawled huskily.

"Have I created a monster?" Evan asked as he rolled Elizabeth onto her back.

"Yes," she said without prevarication. "You most definitely have. And one other thing, sir."

"What is that?" Evan inquired as he lazily kissed Elizabeth's throat.

"I love you, Evan MacGregor. Always have, always will, now and forever."

"In that case, my dearest Lady Elizabeth, I'd like the privilege of meeting you for a ceremony honoring that pledge of fidelity, on the twenty-eighth of May. Will you marry me, again, Elizabeth?"

"Are you serious?"

"Never more so."

"Yes, I'll marry you again, Evan."

Evan smiled and kissed her thoroughly, to the sweet music of numerous songbirds warbling, heralding the coming dawn. "The wedding, my dear Mrs. MacGregor, will take place at Saint Mark's in London. The church has been booked, the banns are being published as we speak, and the reception will follow at Grosvenor Mews. By invitation only."

Elizabeth's fingers tightened on Evan's naked arms, and she pushed him up to arm's length. "You are serious."

"Yes, my lady, we're doing this the correct way. By my commanding officer's orders—bridal gown, big church, and lots of hoopla, specifically planned to make us the talk of the season for years and years to come."

"Evan, I can't do that. I can't go to London and put on a show like I'm some virgin bride at the altar. No. I won't do that to Robbie."

"This isn't about Robbie," Evan told her.

"Wait just a minute," Elizabeth said, stalling.

"Sorry, can't, this is rather urgent." Evan used the necessary force to eliminate the distance between them. It was some time later before Elizabeth remembered she'd been proposed to and asked to marry in a church.

By then, Evan was tugging his Hessians onto his feet, a sure sign that he was returning to his post.

Elizabeth sat up in bed, holding a sheet against her breasts. "Evan, did you really get a promotion to major general?"

"Why do you ask?"

"Because you just said something peculiar."

"Oh, what was that?"

"You said we were to get married in a big church, on account of your commanding officer's orders. That sounded an awful lot like you were talking about Uncle Thomas."

"Could have been." Evan stood before the cheval mirror, buttoning his jacket, examining his uniform for flaws. He reached out to pick up his saber and helmet, then turned to Elizabeth and bent over her, putting a kiss on her brow. "Didn't want to alarm you unnecessarily, *ma dow*. You'd best get up and have a bath, and, er . . . see to your appearance. You'll be having company at eight sharp . . . for breakfast."

"Who?" Elizabeth demanded.

Evan straightened and smiled broadly at her. "Why, none other than your favorite uncle, *ma dow*. The family thought it best that someone of suitable mettle come with me to Dominica and make certain you were brought into line. I really have to be off, Elizabeth. Tell Robbie I'll see him at noon."

"Evan?"

"Yes, milady?"

"Why do I have the feeling I've been had?"

"Because you have, Elizabeth. Better get used to it, my lady. I intend to have you all the rest of my days and nights, as well. I think I'm going to like living in the tropics. I'll be home for lunch, and I certainly intend to enjoy siesta."

With those words, he clapped his helmet on his head and strode out the door.

Chapter Twenty-Three

June 8, 1808
Bell's Wynd
Edinburgh, Scotland

On her way downstairs from the powder room, Elizabeth spied Robbie and a gaggle of his cousins spying on the assembly from the gallery railing. His bare knees poked between the railings of the banister. Likewise, his hands gripped the rungs, and his wee face was pressed between the uprights so that he could watch all that happened on the dance floor two levels below. His bonnet and its proud three-feather cockade sat more than a little askew on his head.

Krissy Buchanan caught another rowdy bantling by the scruff of his neck and sat the small kilted ruffian down right beside wee Robbie, hissing authoritatively over the wailing skirl of many pipes, "The next one of ye that get's off yer bum is goin' ta have the hiding of yer life, or they dinna call me the harridan of Buchanan!"

Elizabeth carefully gathered her long train in hand and knelt beside Robbie. "Psst, what are you doing here this late in the day, wee Robbie?" she asked sternly.

"*Maman!*" Her son's pretty eyes rounded with surprise to see her. "*Och*, lookit ya! Yer wearing yer wedding gown!

Whisht!'' Robbie put his finger to his mouth, signaling for the utmost secrecy as he threw one arm around his neighboring cousin. "We're spying," Robbie whispered conspiratorially. "Grampa said we could all stay up t'night ta see history made. Please dinna tell Da I'm here."

Elizabeth kissed his cheek and righted the angle of his bonnet on his head. "I won't, love. Mind you keep your feet back, and don't go losing a shoe over the railing. That'd give you away for sure."

"We're being verra careful so no one sees us." Robbie shushed his noisy cousins with a voluble "Whisht!"

Elizabeth held back her chuckles. Robbie could be seen immediately when one entered the first floor foyer. He was as bright as a cardinal bird wintering in Dominica in his striking red-and-black Rob Roy tartan and *philabeg*. But the noise the few privileged-to-attend children made would never be noticed, once the drums and the pipes began.

Elizabeth tiptoed down the rest of the steps to the mezzanine, where Aunt Nicky held court for the night, as regal as any queen. A diadem glittered from her white hair, and her black lace gown looked as crisp as could be against her papery skin.

When she came abreast of Amalia on the landing where a whole row of Atholl Highlanders made an impenetrable phalanx, Elizabeth whispered, "I'm here."

"Oh..." Amalia laid her hand on her heart and blinked back tears as she examined Elizabeth from head to toe. "You look as beautiful as you did at Saint Mark's! Aunt Nicky's going to be so proud. I think I'm going to cry."

"No, you're not!" Elizabeth whispered furiously. "Help me straighten out this blasted train."

"Whisht!" Amalia said, just as furiously, as she gathered up yards and yards of satin and tulle.

Through every opened window and along the balconies, the bells from Saint Giles chimed the hour of eight. Neil Gow's lively fiddle brought the reel to a stop, and the dance floor became a flurry of couples scattering and clearing the boards now that the first set had ended. Amalia's chest rose and fell in a heartfelt sigh. Elizabeth fussed with her sleeves, adjusting the pouf that capped her shoulders above her daring décolletage.

By the time the somber eighth bell rang from the church spire, the dance floor was empty. A small restlessness swept across the crowd, normal for the time between the sets, and animated conversation rose to a buzz and filled the air.

Several brave young swains stepped out of the pack and approached Aunt Nicky's dais, escorting eager young girls with their hair put up for the very first time. Elizabeth stretched on tiptoe to see over the Highlanders blocking the stairwell, so that she could see the girls being presented. Would Aunt Nicky give the swains a kindly nod of her head, or refuse?

"Here, now, now, now! None of that. Get back here, young lady. You're not giving any of this away," Uncle Thomas scolded as he pulled Elizabeth back behind the plaid wall. "You look splendid, my dear, though I am surprised MacGregor's allowed you to appear in public in that gown again."

Elizabeth self-consciously patted her neckline. The skimpy bodice was almost counterbalanced by massive pouf sleeves. She knew it was a daring gown for London society, and absolutely risqué for Edinburgh. Elizabeth smoothed her high-waisted skirt and turned once more to double-check the drape of yards and yard of appliquéd white satin.

At some point, she'd known exactly how many seed pearls it had taken to make the bower of ivy and the turtle-doves embossed on her train, but that fact escaped her now. "The MacGregor doesn't know I'm wearing this gown. It's my contribution to the night's surprises."

"Oh? I wish you wouldn't do that, dear." Uncle Thomas took her arm and steered her around behind the thickening wall of plaid. "It upsets the harmony of my days when MacGregor gnashes his teeth at my heels."

"Where are all those men coming from?" Elizabeth asked. Her ears picked out a new noise downstairs, like the snarl of a mountain cat being squeezed to death—that distinctive and peculiar sound every Gaelic heart recognized as a set of pipes inflating a bag with wind. After a few skirmishes, the drones evened out and the chanter reed repeated three strong notes, then burst into a full-bodied *pibroch*—a Highland piper's rendition of war music.

Elizabeth strained to see past the guards. The doors of the assembly hall burst open, and with that the pipe's triumphant music reverberated all around her.

"Oh, what a sweet racket!" Thomas Graham shouted in Elizabeth's ear. "He's come. We've got to see this. Come look."

Thomas shouted a command, and the wall of Highlanders that had completely blocked the stairway formed an honor guard flanking each step.

Elizabeth's whole body tightened, and she snatched up her skirt and ran to the nearest rail, heedless of modesty, decorum and sanity. All that mattered was the ages-old lure of the pipes, the thundering cadence of the drums and the great solemnity of meaning they lent to any gathering of the clans.

Her uncle stopped her at the banister, stepping before her so that she couldn't be seen, but one riser down, so that she could easily see the sight unfolding in the hall one floor below them.

A lone piper had breached the wide open doors of the hall, while outside on High Street, a dozen more razzed, and twice that many drums made it sound as if every man in the Highlands were tramping toward Bell's Wynd. Then into the hall marched a full regiment of kilted Highlanders forming an honor guard from the street.

Amalia gasped, pointing to the foyer. "Look, Elizabeth!"

Elizabeth's fingers tightened on the railing. Her eyes got bigger and bigger as the sea of men parted. Marching up to the very dais where Aunt Nicky stood staring at this performance in her grand hall were the chieftain's tail. Proud, resplendent in full regalia, right up to the feathered cockades on their red-white-and-blue diced caps, they were splendid, all of them. Elizabeth did not recognize a single man among them.

The pipes skirled, and the drums shook the banister under her left hand, where her fingers clutched the polished wood for support. Across the hall could be heard the harsh whisper "He's come. 'Tis the MacGregor!"

Last to enter came the chief. A lone eagle feather jutting upward from his velvet bonnet identified him and set him apart in rank from his clansmen who were sporting only cockades. In kilt and tartan and argyle socks, his brown brogues polished to a satin gloss, Evan MacGregor came to a full stop in the center of the hall, all eyes upon him. A claymore glinted in its sheath at his hip, and an ermine sporran tickled his exposed knees.

The sound of the pipes swirled to a close.

The last tap of drum spattered to a stop.

Out of the stunned audience at Aunt Nicky's side came the audible scrape of a sword being drawn from its sheath, and Elizabeth's father stepped before frail auld Nicky Murray of Mansfield and roared, in a voice that was sure to carry as far as Holyroodhouse, "State yer business, mon. Be ye friend or foe?"

All seven of the henchmen who made up Evan's tail reached for their claymores. The rasp of tempered steel grating against steel cut the air. Evan raised his hand in a salute, and the noise ceased, claymores frozen half in, half out.

"I've come in peace, entailed as ordered by one dragon known as Nicola Murray, of that ilk. To apologize to the esteemed assembly for dancing with her niece, Elizabeth Murray. Stand aside, Atholl, and let yer auld woman see that I am here."

Aunt Nicky batted an impatient hand at her nephew the duke as she stepped to the edge of her dais and raised her quizzing glass to look Evan MacGregor over from head to toe. "What do ye want, ye scoundrel?"

Evan swept his bonnet off his head and delivered the most elegant bow Elizabeth had ever seen done in her life.

"A dance with Lady Elizabeth, the youngest daughter of yon Mon of the Murrays."

"And if I refuse?" Nicky demanded, as only she could. Everyone in the hall held their breath, awaiting Evan's response to that. "What then, scamp?"

Finally Uncle Thomas stepped aside and let Elizabeth pass. She ran down the last few steps, her gown flying over the polished boards, and came to a heady halt, an arm's length away from Evan.

"Aunt Nicky—" Elizabeth's voice rang out over the crowd "—no matter what anyone says, I'll dance with Evan MacGregor."

Nicky pursed her lips. She didn't like it when anyone stole her thunder. Her eyes went from Elizabeth to Evan and back again before she gave them both her most indulgent smile. "Aye, MacGregor, ye may dance t' yer heart's content with Elizabeth."

Elizabeth hadn't waited for permission before she turned and was swept up in Evan's arms. Neil Gow put his bow to his violin, and merry music filled Bell's Wynd.

"By my soul, Elizabeth, ye tempt the patience of a God-fearing man wearing that dress again." Evan lifted Elizabeth above his head and spun her around.

"And you tempt me beyond what I can bear. I love you, Evan MacGregor. Always have and always will. Now and forever."

And Evan MacGregor knew he was the luckiest man on earth. For here he was—in the middle of Bell's Wynd—and Elizabeth was throwing her lovely arms around his neck, kissing him full on the mouth, and pressing those sweetly delicious breasts of hers flush against his chest *afore God and all of Edinburgh!*

* * * * *

Author Note

I've done it again—fallen in love with a hero because his picture inspired me to dream and scheme and imagine what this wonderful hunk, Major General Evan MacGregor MacGregor must have been like in real life. But Evan was the bold Highlander chosen to present the Honors of Scotland during George IV's legendary visit to the Highlands in 1822.

The Regency fascinates me, and, I must confess, so does the romantic fantasy of elopement. I have some firsthand experience ... garnered at the tender age of sixteen. In my case, my love and I stopped to have a cup of coffee thirty miles shy of the Mexican border. Over the steaming cups, we both looked at each other and said exactly the same thing: "I want my mama!" Thus, reason prevailed.

I have often wondered what might have happened if we hadn't stopped to get a cup of coffee.

Weddings by DeWilde

*Since the turn of the century the elegant and
fashionable DeWilde stores have helped brides
around the world turn the fantasy of their "Special
Day" into reality. But now the store and three
generations of family are torn apart by the divorce
of Grace and Jeffrey DeWilde. As family members
face new challenges and loves—and a long-secret
mystery—the lives of Grace and Jeffrey intermingle
with store employees, friends and relatives in this
fast-paced, glamorous, internationally set series. For
weddings and romance, glamour and fun-filled
entertainment, enter the world of DeWilde...*

*Twelve remarkable books, coming to you
once a month, beginning in April 1996*

Weddings by DeWilde begins with
Shattered Vows
by Jasmine Cresswell

Here's a preview!

"SPEND THE NIGHT with me, Lianne."

No softening lies, no beguiling promises, just the curt offer of a night of sex. She closed her eyes, shutting out temptation. She had never expected to feel this sort of relentless drive for sexual fulfillment, so she had no mechanisms in place for coping with it. "No." The one-word denial was all she could manage to articulate.

His grip on her arms tightened as if he might refuse to accept her answer. Shockingly, she wished for a split second that he would ignore her rejection and simply bundle her into the car and drive her straight to his flat, refusing to take no for an answer. All the pleasures of mindless sex, with none of the responsibility. For a couple of seconds he neither moved nor spoke. Then he released her, turning abruptly to open the door on the passenger side of his Jaguar. "I'll drive you home," he said, his voice hard and flat. "Get in."

The traffic was heavy, and the rain started again as an annoying drizzle that distorted depth perception made driving difficult, but Lianne didn't fool herself that the silence inside the car was caused by the driving conditions. The air around them crackled and sparked with their thwarted desire. Her body was still on fire. Why didn't Gabe say something? she thought, feeling aggrieved.

Perhaps because he was finding it as difficult as she was to think of something appropriate to say. He was thirty years old, long past the stage of needing to bed a woman just so he could record another sexual conquest in his little black book. He'd spent five months dating Julia, which suggested he was a man who valued friendship as an element in his relationships with women. Since he didn't seem to like her very much, he was probably as embarrassed as she was by the stupid, inexplicable intensity of their physical response to each other.

"Maybe we should just set aside a weekend to have wild, uninterrupted sex," she said, thinking aloud. "Maybe that way we'd get whatever it is we feel for each other out of our systems and be able to move on with the rest of our lives."

His mouth quirked into a rueful smile. "Isn't that supposed to be my line?"

"Why? Because you're the man? Are you sexist enough to believe that women don't have sexual urges? I'm just as aware of what's going on between us as you are, Gabe. Am I supposed to pretend I haven't noticed that we practically ignite whenever we touch? And that we have nothing much in common except mutual lust—and a good friend we betrayed?"

HARLEQUIN®

Don't miss these Harlequin favorites by some of our most distinguished authors!
And now, you can receive a discount by ordering two or more titles!

HT #25645	THREE GROOMS AND A WIFE by JoAnn Ross	$3.25 U.S./$3.75 CAN. ☐
HT #25648	JESSIE'S LAWMAN by Kristine Rolofson	$3.25 U.S.//$3.75 CAN. ☐
HP #11725	THE WRONG KIND OF WIFE by Roberta Leigh	$3.25 U.S./$3.75 CAN. ☐
HP #11755	TIGER EYES by Robyn Donald	$3.25 U.S./$3.75 CAN. ☐
HR #03362	THE BABY BUSINESS by Rebecca Winters	$2.99 U.S./$3.50 CAN. ☐
HR #03375	THE BABY CAPER by Emma Goldrick	$2.99 U.S./$3.50 CAN. ☐
HS #70638	THE SECRET YEARS by Margot Dalton	$3.75 U.S./$4.25 CAN. ☐
HS #70655	PEACEKEEPER by Marisa Carroll	$3.75 U.S./$4.25 CAN. ☐
HI #22280	MIDNIGHT RIDER by Laura Pender	$2.99 U.S./$3.50 CAN. ☐
HI #22235	BEAUTY VS THE BEAST by M.J. Rogers	$3.50 U.S./$3.99 CAN. ☐
HAR #16531	TEDDY BEAR HEIR by Elda Minger	$3.50 U.S./$3.99 CAN. ☐
HAR #16596	COUNTERFEIT HUSBAND by Linda Randall Wisdom	$3.50 U.S./$3.99 CAN. ☐
HH #28795	PIECES OF SKY by Marianne Willman	$3.99 U.S./$4.50 CAN. ☐
HH #28855	SWEET SURRENDER by Julie Tetel	$4.50 U.S./$4.99 CAN. ☐

(limited quantities available on certain titles)

	AMOUNT	$
DEDUCT:	**10% DISCOUNT FOR 2+ BOOKS**	$
ADD:	**POSTAGE & HANDLING**	$
	($1.00 for one book, 50¢ for each additional)	
	APPLICABLE TAXES**	$_____
	TOTAL PAYABLE	$_____
	(check or money order—please do not send cash)	

To order, complete this form and send it, along with a check or money order for the total above, payable to Harlequin Books, to: **In the U.S.:** 3010 Walden Avenue, P.O. Box 9047, Buffalo, NY 14269-9047; **In Canada:** P.O. Box 613, Fort Erie, Ontario, L2A 5X3.

Name: _____

Address: _____ City: _____

State/Prov.: _____ Zip/Postal Code: _____

**New York residents remit applicable sales taxes.
  Canadian residents remit applicable GST and provincial taxes.

HBACK-AJ3

This May, keep an eye out for
something heavenly from

by Miranda Jarrett

"Delightful...5★s"
—*Affaire de Coeur*

Available wherever Harlequin books are sold.

UNLOCK THE DOOR TO GREAT ROMANCE
AT BRIDE'S BAY RESORT

Join Harlequin's new across-the-lines series, set in an exclusive hotel on an island off the coast of South Carolina.

Seven of your favorite authors will bring you exciting stories about fascinating heroes and heroines discovering love at Bride's Bay Resort.

Look for these fabulous stories coming to a store near you beginning in January 1996.

Harlequin American Romance #613 in January
Matchmaking Baby by Cathy Gillen Thacker

Harlequin Presents #1794 in February
Indiscretions by Robyn Donald

Harlequin Intrigue #362 in March
Love and Lies by Dawn Stewardson

Harlequin Romance #3404 in April
Make Believe Engagement by Day Leclaire

Harlequin Temptation #588 in May
Stranger in the Night by Roseanne Williams

Harlequin Superromance #695 in June
Married to a Stranger by Connie Bennett

Harlequin Historicals #324 in July
Dulcie's Gift by Ruth Langan

Visit Bride's Bay Resort each month wherever Harlequin books are sold.

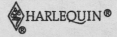

BBAYG

Bestselling authors

ELAINE COFFMAN
RUTH LANGAN
and
MARY McBRIDE

Together in one fabulous collection!

OUTLAW Brides

Available in June wherever Harlequin
books are sold.

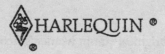

HARLEQUIN ®

LET BESTSELLING AUTHOR
ERICA SPINDLER

TEMPT YOU WITH

FORBIDDEN FRUIT

Beautiful and headstrong, Glory St. Germaine was born into one of New Orleans's finest families. But good *and* evil run through three generations of Glory's family. Her mother, Hope, and grandmother, Lily, are trapped by shame, secrets and circumstances. And Victor Santos, in love with Glory, is trapped by his own past. Can Victor and Glory find a way to put the past behind them? Or will their love remain forbidden fruit?

Available this April at your favorite retail outlet.